ONE WAY ROADS

ONE WAY ROADS

ERIK FOGE

Deeds Publishing | Atlanta

Copyright © 2018 — Erik Foge

Published by Deeds Publishing in Athens, GA
www.deedspublishing.com

Printed in The United States of America

Cover design and text layout by Mark Babcock

Library of Congress Cataloging-in-Publications data is available upon request.

ISBN 978-1-947309-26-5

Books are available in quantity for promotional or premium use. For information, email info@deedspublishing.com.

First Edition, 2018

10 9 8 7 6 5 4 3 2 1

*This book is dedicated to Jackie and my son Max,
whom I will see in heaven one day.*

"Everything I write has a precedent in truth."

—Ian Fleming

This is a work of fiction. Names, characters, government agencies, places, projects, events and incidents either are the products of the author's imagination or used in a fictitious manner. Any resemblance to actual persons, living or dead, or actual events is purely coincidental.

1. A CHANGE IN EVENTS

"The future battle on the ground will be preceded by battle in the air. This will determine which of the contestants has to suffer operational and tactical disadvantages and be forced throughout the battle into adoption compromise solution."
—Erwin Rommel

Field Marshal Erwin Rommel, Commander of Army Group B, walked under the trees with Obergruppenführer Stepp Dietrich, commanding officer of the 1st SS Panzer Corps. Dietrich glanced around, making sure they couldn't be overheard. "Is Hitler still not allowing troop movements without his approval?"

Rommel nodded and frowned, as he hated being reminded of that absurd order that had persisted since the Allied invasion of Normandy. Rommel, with his voice just below a whisper, said in a conspiratorial tone, "What if I were to tell you I am considering an unauthorized counteroffensive that will be launched within a few days?"

Sporting a grin of satisfaction, Dietrich replied, "Jawohl."

Rommel smiled inwardly, pleased with his Corps commander's response.

"Herr Field Marshal," said Dietrich, "many enemy aircraft have been seen in the last few hours; I suggest that you avoid the main road."

"It's near dusk—the darkness will hide us from allied planes." Rommel looked upward as he spoke.

"Then I would suggest you ride in a Kübelwagen[1] to be less conspicuous."

"Dietrich, you worry too much. I will be fine."

"I'm also worried about Thursday."

Rommel turned to face his Corps commander. "I believe Stauffenberg's plan will succeed; then negotiations with the Americans can proceed."

"But what if it doesn't work?"

"Failure is not an option. It has to work." Rommel referred to a plan that had been plotted by a select few members of German General Staff. If it succeeded, they planned to negotiate a separate peace treaty with the United States. They would never get that chance with the Russians because of the atrocities committed by Hitler's SS.

Rommel and Stepp Dietrich exchanged salutes, shook hands, and went their separate ways. Rommel marched straight to his personal car, a large, black, open Horch, a popular, high-performance luxury motor car of German manufacture. He took his

---

1. A light military vehicle designed by Ferdinand Porsche and built by Volkswagen during World War II for use by the German military

usual seat and placed the map on his knee, contemplating the news that the allies had broken through still another part of the ever-fragmenting western front, this time in Coutances, France.

Corporal Daniel, Rommel's driver since Africa, Captain Lang and Major Neuhaus, members of Rommel's staff, and Sergeant Hoike, whose job it was to spot enemy planes, sat quietly in the Horch, but they stared at Rommel, waiting for news of Dietrich's stance.

"I have won Dietrich over; he is with me on the counteroffensive." Rommel finally announced, grinning with delight. "It's not been a foregone conclusion." Then he ordered his driver to head back to headquarters.

They drove along the main road near Livarot, an ill-advised route littered with burned-out personnel carriers destroyed by Allied dive-bombers.

Roughly two and a half miles from Vimoutiers, Rommel tapped Daniel on the shoulder and pointed toward a sheltered road. Then he turned to Lang and Neuhaus. "The battle on the ground will be preceded by battle in the air. This will determine which of the contestants has to suffer operational and tactical disadvantages and be forced throughout the battle into adoption compromise solution."[2]

"Do you think there's a possibility that we can bring a halt to the Allied advance?" Lang asked while Rommel studied the map.

He stared into the distance and then replied, "Only if we'd acted sooner...much sooner. Now we must try to hold our ground against overwhelming odds."

---

2. Great Aviation Quotes. www.skygod.com, n.d. 1996-2011

A short while later, at 4:16 p.m., they arrived back on the main road, Route de Ste-Foy-de-Montgomery. Hoike looked up. Eight aircraft flew above in loose formation. Presuming that the enemy had not observed them, he suggested that they continue on the main road. But without warning, two Spitfires descended in attack formation. Their engines whined.

"Aircraft!" Hoike screamed, pointing skyward.

The Spitfires gained ground. Daniel slammed his foot on the accelerator. Rommel pointed to a side road, three hundred yards away, where they might be sheltered from the approaching Spitfires. But it was too late. The lead Spitfire, now only a few feet above the road and within five hundred yards of them, opened fire with a twenty-millimeter cannon; its bullets penetrated the road as they made an impact. Daniel maneuvered the car, trying to avoid being hit. Bullets made dust clouds as they whizzed by the car. A couple of them hit the car, including Daniel, as he bounced it sideways. The impact shattered Daniel's left shoulder, and splatters of blood filled the air. Though he fought to hold on, Daniel lost control of the car. It barreled down the road and jolted its passengers. Rommel's head smashed against the dashboard, and he lost consciousness. The car veered to the left and hit a tree stump. The shuddered impact threw Rommel out of the car, which continued without its most important passenger, then skidded into a ditch and stopped. Daniel and Neuhaus, unable to move, moaned in pain. Lang and Hoike, as yet uninjured, leaped from the car and raced to Rommel, dodging the twenty-millimeter rounds that danced around them. They reached Rommel unscathed, picked their commander up by the arms, and dragged him to safety.

"Is he alive?" Hoike asked. "He looks bad."

"His breathing's shallow," Lang replied. "He'll die if we don't get to a hospital soon."

"How are Daniel and Neuhaus?

"Not good. Daniel's losing blood, and Neuhaus can barely move."

Hoike leaped to his feet. "I'll find a vehicle." He ran off.

Lang lifted Rommel's injured head. Streams of blood ran down his hands and arms, as Lang uttered to himself. "Now if Stauffenberg doesn't succeed, we'll have no chance to make a separate peace treaty with the Americans."

2. THE MEETING

"One's destination is never a place, but a new way of seeing things."
              —Henry Miller

CIA Headquarters, Langley, Virginia. 21 July 2008

A musty odor from old newspapers and books consumed the damp, dark office, and the air conditioning struggled to push cold air through a rusted air vent layered with dust. A single light on the desk broke the darkness, its light dissipating over books and classified documents—draft cables and memorandums from the last years of World War II (1944—1945) and the post-war years. Behind the desk sat a medium-built man in his mid-thirties. He wore a three-piece suit and hunched over, his inquisitive blue eyes reading and analyzing sophisticated databases and computer simulations. Every few seconds he jotted down detailed notes on his hypothesis of the nation's domestic, foreign and military policies if Germany had surrendered in 1944 instead of 1945. The sound of graphite scratched the surface of the paper that echoed through the otherwise silent office. The man glanced at a computer screen as the glare reflected on his face. Bookcases filled with historical and reference books covering the European Theater of World War II, Soviet Foreign Policy, and Field Marshal Erwin Rommel lined the office walls. Behind him hung a poster of a duck sitting in a chair and staring over his shoulder at a wall that had two bullet holes by his head. The caption read, "Sitting Duck." The man turned his head away from the computer screen and glanced at the framed photograph of the love of his life. He drifted into a daydream and a grin appeared on his face. The phone rang and broke the silence. He jolted back to the present and lifted the receiver.

"This is Dr. Függer. Yes, Sir. I'm on my way."

He got up from his desk, grabbed a few folders and his notes, then placed them in his attaché case, exited his office, and locked the door behind him. The nameplate on the door read "Dr. Erik Függer, Historical Affairs Analyst." Like the other senior analysts in section thirteen, department four-six-three of the CIA, Erik networked with counterparts throughout CIA and the Intelligence Community without revealing the nature of his work. His job for the past three years had involved researching a "what if" in history. Erik had written his thesis on the likely alternative history if Field Marshal Erwin Rommel had lived rather than committing suicide by taking a cyanide capsule 14 October 1944.

Because members of Erik's family had fought with the Germans in World War II, his interest in history had begun at an early age. At thirteen he already had a personal library, a vast knowledge of the Second World War, and a tendency to correct his history teachers—a trait that lasted throughout his academic and professional career. Erik's high IQ made him seem weird to his peers, so he had few close friends, even at the university where (against his father's wishes) he majored in history with an emphasis on Russia and Europe.

While doing his undergraduate studies, Erik had done an internship as a civilian for the United States Navy and distinguished himself as a junior analyst in the underwater warfare section. He worked under Admiral Bonesteiner, who was in charge of the Sixth Fleet, for seven years as a junior analyst. After college, his internship with the Navy ended, and he became a high school history teacher. Erik thought he could make a significant difference in how people would see history, but he didn't find it rewarding. In the middle of his first year of teaching, the CIA, upon hearing good reports of his time with the Navy, recruited him initially as a Paramilitary Operations Officer, which he did for the first seven years. After he completed his training, Erik earned a Master's degree in Military History and his Ph.D. in History.

Erik waited for the elevator and mentally prepared what he was going to say. His eyes absorbed and analyzed everything, whether related to work or not. The elevator arrived, and as he stepped in and pressed the button to the office of the Director of Intelligence on level seven, a hint of perfume drifted under his nose. The elevator ascended, its motor's subtle hum consuming the cabin until it came to an abrupt stop. The doors opened, and, to Erik's surprise, his long-time friend, Jacques, walked in.

Jacques's muscular body, broad shoulders, strong arms, and thick legs made him ideal for a CIA Targeting Officer in Western Europe. His job was the planning and implementation of foreign intelligence collection by excelling in high-pressure/high-impact situations, using his skills in hand-to-hand combat and small arms weapons. Thus, a strike from him would be sure to inflict serious damage to those who opposed him. Jacques and Erik only met on rare occasions, and their reunions had a strange aura about them, as if, even though apparently by chance, there was always a reason.

Jacques' hazel eyes fixed on Erik. "Haggis!" he said in greeting, something they had done since seeing the movie *Highlander* in high school.

Erik grinned. "How are things?"

"Busy, you?"

Erik nodded. "Immersed in historical theory".

Jacques raised his eyebrows. "Hmmm. So where are you off to now?"

"Bonesteiner's office."

Jacques's eyes widened knowingly. "What did you do now? Or should I say, who did you piss off now?"

"No one that I know of yet."

Jacques gave a mischievous look and laughed. "Key word: *yet*. Like that time you made Bonesteiner spit up his drink in front of his entire staff. Remember that? Hawaii?"

"Hey, that's not my fault. He asked me about the Seawolf class submarine."

They both laughed. The elevator stopped, and a nondescript man got in.

"How is the historical theory going?" Jacques continued.

"It's complex. So where are you off to?"

"Your favorite place in the world," Jacques said sarcastically.

"Oh…great," Erik said, knowing it was France. "Let's meet and catch up before you depart; when's a good time?"

"How about lunch at thirteen hundred."

"Sounds good. What about Sunday?"

"Hmm. Last Sunday wasn't good. And I know this Sunday won't be either. So maybe two Sundays from now?"

The other passenger in the elevator frowned and asked, "What are you guys talking about?"

"August," Erik and Jacques replied at the same time.

The elevator stopped again. Erik and Jacques got out, leaving the man shaking his head. They confirmed their lunch appointment, then headed their separate ways. Erik strolled down the hallway, pondering the purpose of his meeting with the director. He remembered, in 2007. A contact told him the day would come that he would meet with high-ranking officials to discuss his historical theory on Field Marshal Rommel. Could it have something to do with the time travel project he'd heard rumors about? At the door labeled Deputy Director of Intelligence and Operations, he took a deep breath, opened the door, and entered a spacious lobby with eggshell white walls, royal blue carpet and a window behind the secretary's desk. The secretary glanced up from her typing and acknowledged his presence. She picked up the phone and told the director that Erik had arrived.

A moment later, the door of the director's office opened, and a man over six feet tall with military-style blonde hair walked out. He stared at Erik with sinister gray, shark-like eyes, then headed toward the outer door. His facial features showed no emotion, and the sharply defined muscles visible through his shirt added to his commanding presence.

Erik entered Baldric Bonesteiner's office and closed the door behind him. The office took up the complete right corner of the top floor and overlooked the tree-filled Potomac Valley. Framed artwork of naval vessels and aircraft, certificates and awards of merit, and photographs of Bonesteiner's military past—covering thirty years in the navy and nearly twenty years in the agency—covered the walls. In front of the window sat a large mahogany desk covered in neatly organized piles of folders color-coded by classification. Bookcases filled with books and scale models of military aircraft and naval vessels lined the walls, and a mahogany coffee table sat in the center of the space surrounded by four leather lounge chairs, two of which were occupied by military officers in their full dress uniforms. Each had several rows of multicolored ribbons over their left chest.

Admiral Bonesteiner—solid six foot two with gentle, yet piercing, big brown eyes—walked around his desk towards Erik with his hand extended. "How are you doing?" he asked with a grin.

"Well, I'm alive, Sir." Erik shook the hand of the man who had recruited him into the agency.

Bonesteiner nodded, then turned to the other two gentlemen, who stood. "Dr. Függer, this is Admiral Cole and Brigadier General Plackett."

Cole stood six feet tall, with a small but solid frame. "I remember you from Hawaii when you gave the briefing on the Seawolf," he said as he shook Erik's hand.

"Do you now?" Erik replied, uncertain of what Cole meant by his comment.

Cole nodded. "You were very outspoken for a Junior Analyst. Maybe times have changed since then."

"Maybe." Erik extended his hand to General Plackett, a short, stocky man whose uniform stretched tightly over well-developed muscles.

"Impressive work in the O.G.D.S.[3] Team 42," the general said as they shook hands.

"Thank you, general."

"Well, since everyone is here, let's get started." Bonesteiner motioned to everyone to take their seats.

Erik sat comfortably in a leather office chair, pulled three sets of identical folders from his attaché case, and handed them out. Bonesteiner made his way to his seat at the coffee table.

Though Cole's blue eyes appeared relaxed, they were always alert and aware of his surroundings, a skill that, among others, had helped him carve out a very successful military intelligence career culminating in his becoming the Director of ONE—the most secretive government agency specializing in black ops, both domestically and internationally. In 1947, Truman signed the National Security Act of 1947, which set up a unified military command known as the "National Military Establishment." From this, ONE was established. ONE never stood for anything. The name was purposely vague in case someone overheard it. Truman needed an agency to solve America's international threats; thus, he said, "Trust is good…Control is better." This became the agency's motto. In addition, Truman did not want any interference from congress, so the agency was placed under the black budget; therefore the agency never existed on paper; thus, they answered

---

3. O.G.D.S, Orbital Group Destination Services, a C.I.A. front that has both analysts and field operatives in hotels and other vacation locations to obtain and gather information from foreign leaders.

to no one, not even the Senate Oversight Committee or the President of the United States.

Brigadier General Plackett's brownish-black eyes showed no emotion behind his steel-framed glasses and gave a hint of the evil that had marked his military career since it began in the Green Berets. Like Cole, Plackett also worked for ONE. The Phoenix Group was a department within ONE. The Phoenix Group was similar to the CIA Special Operations Group (SOG). The assassins were responsible for carrying out covert operations that included eliminating high threat military and political targets. It was rumored they had not only killed political figures internationally but also in the United States. The assassins normally didn't wear military uniforms or carry any objects that would associate them with the United States government. However, the Phoenix Group answered to no one.

Erik began his debriefing. "Gentlemen, as we are aware, on the twenty-first of July 1944, the elaborate plot to kill Adolf Hitler failed." Erik continued by detailing the events following the failure of the plot, then broached the topic of Field Marshal Erwin Rommel. The men's eyes widened as Erik explained his theory:

"Rommel's name was disclosed by his Chief of Staff, Hans Speidel, in order to save his own life and avoid being implicated in the plot. Rommel was recovering from injuries received when a Spitfire strafed his staff car on the seventeenth of July, 1944. Members of the SS and Gestapo were arresting all members of the plot who were directly or indirectly involved, but Rommel was totally unaware of what was going on. However, MI6 had their plans, known as Operation Gaff, a six-man team of the

British Special Air Service commandos. They were to be parachuted into occupied France on the eighteenth of July, 1944, and their mission was to either kill or kidnap Rommel."

"Did the strafing of his vehicle halt that order?" Cole asked.

"Yes, Sir."

"So if MI6 had captured him, what then?"

"In my opinion, they would pressure him to make a list of all those individuals he could persuade, for example, generals and some high-ranking Nazi Party members who wanted to overthrow Hitler and sue for a separate peace treaty with the U.S. and its allies."

"Like who?"

"Speer, Stepp Dietrich, just to name a few."

"What makes you think those two individuals would, or even could, help Rommel? How could they help Rommel make a separate peace treaty with the United States?"

"Well, Admiral, there were more than those two who were going to side with Rommel if Operation Valkyrie succeeded."

"Do you happen to have the names of those individuals?"

Erik shook his head. "There were approximately eleven or twelve generals and field marshals both in the SS and Wehrmacht."

"How sure are you about that?"

"One hundred percent."

"Educated guess?"

"No, Sir. Based on my research, I believe it to be fact."

Brigadier General Plackett pulled out a document and handed it to Erik. "What do you make of this?"

Erik quickly analyzed the document. "Minus the coffee stain, this is what the provisional government would've looked like if the plot against Hitler had succeeded. However, it's missing something."

Plackett and Cole gave Erik a puzzled look, like that of a deer facing the headlights of an oncoming car. They glanced at Bonesteiner, then back at Erik.

"That is an authentic document recovered in 1944," Cole said. "How can you question its authenticity?"

"I'm sorry, Admiral, but the question mark is missing by Speer's name."

"Question mark? What in the hell are you talking about?"

Erik turned the document around to face the admiral and pointed to Speer's name. "In the real document, used by the Gestapo, it had a question mark by his name."

"How would you know that?" Plackett barked.

"I read it in a book."

Plackett shook his head in disbelief and tried not to chuckle. "A book? How do you know the book is even accurate?"

"Because it was from a firsthand account—"

"Whose firsthand account?" Plackett sneered and sat back with his arms crossed.

"Albert Speer. It was in his book, *Inside the Third Reich*," Erik elaborated, as the others listened. "Speer was the Architect of the Third Reich, who later became Minister of Armaments. Furthermore—"

Plackett squinted his eyes and pointed at Erik. "Listen here, our sources acquired that document from the U.S. Army's archives in 1944, from General Bradley's headquarters."

"Not this time, General."

Bonesteiner leans forward in his chair and placed a hand in the air. He stared directly at Erik. "Have you heard of Project Ryan?"

Erik glanced at Bonesteiner, Cole, and Plackett before answering carefully. "I believe it's when we direct our operatives to evacuate a foreign diplomat or dignitary out of their country."

Bonesteiner grinned and nodded, indicating that Erik's answer was correct. "These two gentlemen need your help with the next Project Ryan."

"Sir, I'm not a field operative anymore. I've been an analyst for nearly three years now; I just read books."

"That's correct," Cole said. "But you've had some field experience in Germany, Russia, and a few other places of conflict, and we need your expertise as an analyst to go back in time."

"True, but …" Erik frowned, unsure if he had heard correctly. "Excuse me, sir? You said 'back in time'?"

"Yes; it's called Project Pegasus, and it's when we send an individual, like you, to do research on historical events. We need you to go back to 1944."

"You need me to do *what*?"

Cole's eyes twinkled above a slight smile. "We need you to go back to 1944."

Erik's eyebrows shot up in surprise. "I didn't think that was possible."

"It is now. We've been working on it for some time."

"How long?"

"That's classified."

Erik frowned. "Okay, then, why send an analyst instead of a field operative?"

Cole smiled and nodded. "They are more able to make reliable evaluations and prudent decisions. This is especially important when unforeseen circumstances arise."

Erik nodded. "Okay, so why me?"

"We need a particular kind of analyst, one with certain qualities and expertise."

"And those are?"

"You're the foremost expert on Field Marshal Rommel and the European Theater of the Second World War. Also, you're in good physical shape, you're psychologically fit, and you have the right temperament. You can see things clearly, yet be analytical. Most of all, you can blend in, seeing as you dress in clothing from that period and know the mannerisms." Cole gestured to Erik's retro-look clothes—a double-breasted cocoa suit with blue and gray pinstripes, a crisp, bright white oxford shirt with a heavily starched collar and sleeves, and a tie that matched the colors of his suit. He even wore a pocket watch with the chain neatly hidden so that it was only exposed when he moved or sat in a certain way.

Back in his office, he had a Fedora that he had purchased in 1991. People tended to look at him oddly, or think he was Italian if he wore his black trench coat with his three-piece-suit. He didn't care what they thought. He liked the way he dressed, and his girlfriend loved it.

"So you want me to go back in time?" Erik said, trying to get used to the idea.

"Yes, we do."

"I see." Erik leaned forward. "I recall the USS *Eldridge* experiencing that."

Cole responded with a cold stare.

"The Germans started their time travel experiments in May or June, 1944," Erik continued. "It was known as Project Bell."

Cole's eyes widened. "What do you know about that?"

"The USS *Eldridge* or Project Bell?"

"Project Bell," Cole snapped,

Plackett adjusted his glasses.

"Project Bell, headed by SS Obergruppenführer Hans Kammler, had the highest security clearance, Top Secret Command Matter."

Cole glanced at the others; their expressions were unreadable. "What's that similar to?"

"It would be the same level as Top Secret Yankee White."

"Very impressive. Why did they call it Project Bell?"

"Because the heart of the machine looked like a bell."

The gentlemen's eyes grew wide at the extent of Erik's knowledge, and they listened intently, absorbing it like a sponge.

"You are very well informed, Dr. Függer. Where did you get your information? A book?" Cole said with a hint of sarcasm.

"You're thinking—I like that—but no, though I do have an extensive library."

Cole's nostrils flared slightly. "So how do you know about the USS *Eldridge*?"

"Just rumors, Admiral."

"Just rumors?" Cole paused in thought. "Well, those so-called rumors are false."

"If they're false, what really happened in Project Rainbow?"

Cole, with scolding eyes, pointed his finger at Erik. "That is classified and you do not have the clearance."

Erik rubbed his chin. "That's odd; it never happened, yet it's classified. How, then, can one deny or confirm that Project Rainbow really happened? Because it's stamped with an official seal?"

A vein throbbed in Cole's temple, and his jaw hardened in an attempt to restrain his anger. He looked as if he wished he could kill Erik. "How do you know about Project Rainbow?"

"That's classified."

Cole asked again and gave him a glance of inquiry. "I'm going to ask you one more time. Where in the hell did you get your information?"

"Admiral," Erik replied, "That information is on a need-to-know basis, and you have no need to know. I'm sure you understand."

Bonesteiner interrupted before things could get heated again. "Gentlemen, let's get to the reason we're here."

Cole stared at Erik for a moment, then began: "You'll be impersonating a major in the Wehrmacht. We need you to rescue Erwin Rommel and bring him to General Bradley's headquarters in Rennes, France."

"What branch of the Wehrmacht?" Erik asked.

"The army," Cole replied. "And that's another reason you fit this mission; you're below average height for your age group now, but five foot six was the ideal height for an army man in 1944. And, of course, there are your Germanic facial features."

Like his hawk-like nose, firm lips, and triangular jaw, Erik thought wryly. "Once there, then what?"

"You'll identify yourself as an OSS agent and inform General Bradley of Germany's intentions to surrender and broker a separate peace treaty from the Russians. We don't want the Russians to be a part of the treaty because we will have to give into Stalin. That way we can end World War Two sooner and get a foothold in Europe before the Russians do. Any questions?"

"Several."

Cole nodded and motioned to Erik to ask away.

"Number one, the distance. It won't be easy due to the French Resistance, allied air superiority, and the land war."

"We have your route planned out to avoid those things. I recommend you travel in a column that would give you some protection."

"It won't be as easy as you put it."

"There are risks in any mission; you should know that. Any other questions?"

"I'll need papers to prove I'm an OSS agent."

"Don't worry, Dr. Függer, we have all aspects covered." Cole leaned forward. "After you leave the hospital you are to go to Impasse des Ecureuils, 14250 Audrieu, France."

Erik nodded and committed the information to memory.

Cole continued. "It's a château. You'll meet one of our people there, a Colonel. He'll give you an officer's uniform and the identification you need."

"How will I recognize him or how will he recognize me?"

"He's seen your photograph, and he knows your name." Cole leaned back in his chair. "He'll be in a black SS Colonel's uniform."

Erik raised an eyebrow. "In an SS Colonel's uniform, seriously?"

"Is that a problem?"

"If I could be so bold, I would suggest either civilian or an army uniform."

"The Colonel is capable of handling any situation that comes his way," Plackett assured Erik. "You have nothing to worry about."

Erik snorted. "That's what they said on the Titanic on April 15, 1912, when it was sinking."

Cole and Plackett shared puzzled looks.

"It sank, killing all but a few survivors," Erik said to fill them in. "Have you considered that if we change history it could alter the future as we know it. 'One cannot change the past,' as Einstein said."

"Do you think we have not weighed all possibilities?" Cole said. "Our analysts and scientists have already studied this, and they've all concluded that future events will benefit the United States and NATO. Once Rommel is able to speak to Eisenhower, they can coordinate their efforts, and the Third Reich will crumble around Hitler's feet. Thus it will give the United States' armed forces a better position during the Cold War by occupying Germany, Yugoslavia, Albania and most of Czechoslovakia and Hungary."

"I doubt you've weighed *all* the possibilities, Admiral," Erik replied. "Have you thought of all the different ways it could alter the Cold War?"

"We've spent thousands of hours on investigating this, and if you do it at a certain place in time, the ripples will remain ripples. The Cold War computer simulations show that the United States and our allies will benefit."

Erik analyzed every word Cole and Plackett said. He knew that planning the infinite details of a covert operation was one of the most stressful jobs there was, especially when this would be executed in twenty-four hours. If an op was planned at the last minute, details would likely be missing or overlooked. Erik adjusted himself in his seat. "You can't be sure it'll prevent conflicts such as the Vietnam or Iraq War, and it could cause an unseen event that could radically alter the world as we know it today."

"You'll not have to worry about that. We've weighed every possible aspect."

Erik narrowed his eyes, unconvinced.

Plackett leaned forward. "Your job is to bring General Rommel to General Bradley's headquarters. Do that, and this plan will work."

"Field Marshal," Erik corrected.

"As I was saying, your job is to bring Field Marshal Rommel to General Bradley's headquarters."

"Persuading Rommel to come with me won't be easy."

Plackett shook his head. "You were able to persuade some of our enemies when you were a part of the O.G.D.S. Team Forty Two. In comparison, this should be easy."

"That wasn't as easy as you may think."

Bonesteiner addressed Plackett. "One of Dr. Függer's natural abilities is being able to persuade people and have them trust him. He's also good at knowing people's weaknesses and how to exploit them."

"Sir," Erik said, "those individuals we targeted had a hunger for information on the U.S. Military and Intelligence. They fell for fabricated information. But we're talking about Field Marshal Rommel. He has no weakness, or if he does, I haven't found it."

Bonesteiner turned to Erik. "Then how do you plan to persuade him?"

Erik shrugged. "I don't know. The only thing I can think of is convincing him that the United States will join Germany in attacking Russia."

"You're serious about that?" Cole blurted out.

"I am, Admiral. That would be one thing he'd ask for. Then he'd broker a separate peace treaty."

"That'll never happen," Plackett interjected.

"Exactly! So unless you know of another card we can play, I think we're out of options."

"Lie to him," Cole said with a conspiratorial gesture.

"Lie? What if he calls our bluff? What then?"

"I wouldn't worry about that now." Cole's lip curled slightly on one side. "We're sure you'll think of something, and we'll have things in place to aid you."

"Aid me?" Erik's voice rose. "My God, do you realize that if this isn't done carefully, with the least amount of resistance, we can royally screw things up?"

"Royally?" Cole asked.

"Yes, royally. I was trying to put it nicely."

"So you are saying things could be—"

"Fucked up, if we're not careful."

Cole nodded. "We're aware that things may not go as planned. That's why you'll have help."

"Help? We're talking about a time when the Gestapo was trying to find anyone who was involved in the plot to kill Hitler!"

"We are aware, but you needn't worry about that."

"Needn't worry?" Erik asked, looking from one to the other in disbelief. "What, are you going to try to kill Hitler?"

"Your job," Plackett restated firmly, "is to bring Field Marshal

Rommel to General Bradley's headquarters and not worry about Hitler. Clear?"

"Why, are you sending someone back to kill him?"

Plackett's eyes narrowed and his jaw hardened. "Listen very carefully," he said. "Your job is to bring Field Marshal Rommel to General Bradley's headquarters and not worry about Hitler. Clear?"

"I emphasize again," Cole said, his eyes hard, "that doing this will be a great service to the United States and NATO."

"Do I have a choice in this?" Erik asked, but his only response from Cole and Plackett were emotionless stares.

"What do you think?" Bonesteiner asked.

Erik shook his head. Clearly, the answer is no. *But what if Rommel could be saved? The world could be a better place if he lived. Would it be worth it if saving his life could prevent the Korean or Vietnam War?*

Cole interrupted Erik's thoughts. "Well?"

Erik continued pondering. *But what if it causes another unseen war or conflict?* He stared at Cole; thoughts raced through his mind.

"Will you do it?" Cole asked.

Erik leaned back in his chair and ran his fingers through his hair. "I don't know if this is a good idea. There are too many variables that could change the outcome of the Cold War."

"Have you heard of Operation Unthinkable?" Cole asked.

Erik shook his head. Cole explained that Churchill did not trust Stalin and believed he was going to keep Soviet forces in the countries he occupied. Thus Churchill and Roosevelt had met secretly and planned military operations in the Balkan Peninsula known as

Operation Unthinkable. It involved re-arming 100,000 German soldiers to join the Allies, and he also wanted the US to use the atomic bomb should the Soviets refuse to surrender. Roosevelt agreed to the operations, and they planned to begin in December, 1944.

"That's insane." Erik rubbed his eyes and shook his head. "The American public would be too weary for another war."

"I disagree because the Nazis still occupied the Balkans. We'd be liberating more countries and making them NATO allies and crippling the Russians in the years after the war. And you rescuing Rommel can make this all possible."

Erik took a deep breath. *It could save lives, stop those wars before they start…* And aside from his deeper concerns, Erik found the idea of going back to the period he had studied in detail awfully tempting—to actually live it, not just study it from afar. "I'll do it. But I have one more question."

Grins filled the room. "What is it?" Cole asked.

"When do I go, and how will I get back after I finish my mission?"

"The Colonel and you will come back to the states, go to the project location, and then both of you will return to 2008. You leave tomorrow in the afternoon between 1200 to 1500 hours. A car will be sent to your residence at 0600 hours, and you will be flown to the project area."

"Tomorrow?"

"Is there a problem?" Cole asked.

Erik nodded. "I normally have a month to prepare before I go on an op."

"There's no need for preparation. It is an easy in-and-out. We've planned this to the last detail. Everything will go smoothly."

Erik sighed. "I just hope your machine gets me to Rommel before he's transported to the other hospital."

"What do you mean?"

"Rommel is scheduled to leave the Luftwaffe hospital in Bernay at 0500 hours on the twenty-third of July. He'll be taken to the hospital at Le Vésinet, which is located just outside Paris, and there he'll be guarded even more closely."

"You'll get there before he is transported. Now, since that's covered, our conversation is over."

Erik turned to Bonesteiner. "Sir, my vacation was scheduled for next week."

"I'm aware of that, but it will have to be put off until you get back."

"Understood," Erik said in a distant voice, knowing his girlfriend would be mad about it.

"Erik, go home and prepare yourself," Bonesteiner advised.

Erik nodded and exchanged handshakes with Cole and Plackett. He pushed back his chair, got up, grabbed his belongings, and headed to the door.

Bonesteiner approached him just before he exited. "Good luck and Godspeed."

"Thank you, Sir."

Bonesteiner closed the door behind Erik and turned to Cole and Plackett. "He's the best historical analyst we have."

"I don't understand how you put up with him questioning authority all the time." Cole snapped. "He was that way when he gave the briefing on the Seawolf and when you sent him to my office."

"I agree. Can we trust him for doing Project Pegasus?" Plackett asked.

"I appreciate your frustration," Bonesteiner replied," but Erik is the most knowledgeable person for the period, and I respect a man who speaks his mind. Most of all, I know he'll succeed."

Placket frowned. "How long has he been with the agency? His clearance level?"

"Ten years. Top Secret—Sensitive Compartmented Information/ Special Intelligence."

"Damn," Cole muttered to himself, not realizing Erik's security clearance was so high. Most CIA Senior Analysts have top secret clearance, but Cole knew that Sensitive Compartmentalized Information clearance meant he was one of the few analysts that the intelligence community trusted. That meant Erik had fewer constraints on sensitive information, and the ability to do real harm if he knew ONE's real intentions for sending him back in time.

Cole opened his laptop and opened the file that contained Erik's dossier. He glanced at it, then looked up at Bonesteiner and asked, "Correct me if I'm wrong; Dr. Függer had some training at the farm?"

Bonesteiner nodded.

"The reason I'm asking is because his dossier has holes, mainly about his training." Cole met Bonesteiner's gaze. "I feel that information is relevant."

Bonesteiner crossed his arms and shook his head.

"How much training has he had there?"

"Enough."

"Do you care to share?"

Bonesteiner shook his head again and dismissed the subject with a short sideways jerk of his hand. "That's a need to know basis, and you don't need to know." He saw no reason to tell Cole that Erik had received fifty-two weeks of Paramilitary Operations Officer training which is equivalent to the Navy SEAL Buds.

"It seems he has proven himself from the beginning. Does he have any family?" Cole asked.

"No, his parents and brother were killed in a car accident five years ago."

"Well, at least no one will miss him," Plackett states. Bonesteiner glared at him, and Plackett corrected himself, "I mean, should he meet with a problem he can't handle, we wouldn't have to explain his death to the next of kin."

Bonesteiner shook his head. "Someone will miss him."

"His girlfriend will."

"And who might that be?"

"Sorry, that information is classified." Bonesteiner gave a self-satisfied smile.

Placket snorted in derision.

Cole found the information on his laptop and showed it to Placket. He had no photo, but that would be solved today. Her name was Jamie Anderson, and she worked in the records department in the Pentagon. They glanced at each other and nodded slightly without Bonesteiner noticing. "How resourceful is he?" Cole asked.

"He knew about the flaws of the Seawolf Class submarine," Bonesteiner said while staring at Cole. "You do remember that Admiral? He also knows about Plum Island, among other things."

Cole nodded with disgust. "I remember he brought up the Seawolf flaws in Hawaii, but how in the hell did he know about those things?"

"Like he said, all he does is read. If he can't find the answer, he's able to get the information he needs."

"He's that good?" Plackett asked.

"Let me put it this way: He probably already knows who you work for." Bonesteiner met the gaze of each man in turn.

"That's impossible."

"That's what he's known for doing."

"And that's why he's dangerous," Cole whispered to Plackett, nodding discreetly. He closed his laptop and gathered his things. Bonesteiner got up from his desk as the men prepared to leave, and Cole and Plackett extended their hands.

"I hope that Dr. Függer doesn't let us down," Plackett said.

"He won't. He might even surprise you."

3. RED HERRING

Immediately following the meeting, Erik went to his office to drop off the classified documents and placed them in a locked filing cabinet. As he exited, Erik grabbed a book, locked the door to his vault (office), and proceeded to the main floor. He strolled through the Original Headquarters Building lobby and noticed that two more stars had been added, and stopped by the Memorial Wall on the north side. The stars symbolized the CIA analysts and field operatives who gave their lives for the United States and government. He hoped a visit to 1944 wouldn't mean a star for him on this wall.

He continued out of the lobby and stopped at the south wall to read the agency's motto fixed in stone. "And Ye Shall Know the Truth and the Truth Shall Make You Free—John 8:32" Erik smiled, noting how much he believed exactly that, then exited through one of the three security checks, headed to his car, and drove to meet Jacques for lunch.

Erik entered the restaurant and looked for Jacques. Groups involved in animated conversations filled the various dining rooms—each themed according to a different Chinese dynastic era—while host, servers, and bussers worked as a team like a well-oiled machine. Neatly organized condiments and a small candle sat in the center of each table. Erik found Jacques' large frame seated against the rear wall of one of the rooms. He strolled over and took a seat and dropped his attaché case beneath the table. Jacques' hazel eyes focused on Erik for seconds at a time, then danced around the room, analyzing people's body language and reading their lips. A subtle bulge on the upper left side of his suit jacket concealed his sidearm.

"So how's it going?" Jacques asked.

"I'm alive," Erik said with a smile.

Jacques tilted his head forward and squinted his eyes. "I know you're alive, but how are you doing?" His eyebrows rose.

"Okay." Erik reached under the table and pulled a book from his attaché case.

"And Jamie?"

"She's doing great and still loves her job." Erik sighed deeply. "She's going to be pissed off."

Jacques gave a puzzled frown. "Why?"

"I have to go away."

His doubtful look intensified. "Another one? You're just an analyst."

"True, but I don't have a choice. I leave tomorrow." Erik held the book out to Jacques.

He stared at it but didn't take it. "Why are you giving me this?"

"Because history may change, and I need you to watch over Jamie for me until I get back."

Jacques raised his hands and shook his head. "How long will you be?"

"Just watch over her for me, okay?" Erik waited for Jacques' reassurance.

It came with a nod; then he took the book.

"I need you to pay close attention to the marked chapter," Erik said. "Especially the map of Belgium. If it changes, show it to Bonesteiner."

Jacques glanced at the book, *Battle of the Bulge: Hitler's Ardennes Offensive, 1944–1945* by Danny Parke, then back to Erik. He still frowned. "Changes? Seriously?"

Erik leaned forward. His voice lowered to a whisper. "If history changes, the records of that history will change too, right?"

"Yes, but ..."

Erik shook his head. "Don't ask," he said, sitting back again.

Jacques' eyes narrowed. "What's wrong?"

"I noticed they added two more stars to the Memorial Wall. Do you know anything about that? Who they were?"

"Not field ops."

"Analysts?"

Jacques nodded.

"Do you know their names?"

Jacques slammed his fist on the table. "No. Stop being so damned curious."

"That's my job as an analyst."

"No, it's not. Just be careful. This is not like when we were in college."

"I know. Maybe that's why they hired me."

"They probably hired you for your skills, and to watch you."

"Watch me?"

"Yes. I don't know if I ever told you this, but when I worked for Bonesteiner when we were in college I was approached by a man, most likely an operative, and he advised me to tell you to stop digging or else. Then he drove off before I could question him."

Intrigued to know more, Erik grinned. "I see, and why did he say that?"

"Maybe because they thought you were sticking your nose where it didn't belong." Jacques pointed at Erik and emphasized, "You did have a habit of doing that. You better watch your back."

"Well, nothing has happened yet."

"Yeah; yet."

The server walked up to the table and hovered, smiled, and waited for their orders. Jacques signaled Erik to go first and while Erik placed his order, he opened the book to the marked chapter and flipped through pages filled with facts, diagrams, and black and white photos. His eyes widened when he stumbled on a photograph of an SS Colonel he recognized. *It was Ahriman, whom Jacques had worked with briefly on an op. But why is Ahriman wearing SS clothing, and why is he back in World War Two? And why does Erik have a photo of the rogue field operative who kills whomever he's ordered to without mercy, without thought, and most of all without prejudice?* He glanced at Erik and understanding dawned. *Oh, shit!* Jacques quickly schooled his expression into something relaxed and placed his order. Then he stared directly at Erik with a piercing gaze. "Watch out for the red herring in black. He might be stalking you."

"Excuse me? What?"

Jacques rested his hand on the book with his finger nonchalantly pointed at the photo of Ahriman. "Make sure a red herring in black isn't stalking you."

Erik gestured with understanding to Jacques and repeated what Jacques had told him with a puzzled look.

Jacques squinted. "Listen to me, damn it!" he said, his voice deadly serious. He tapped on the photo.

Erik looked down, then up again to meet Jacques' eyes.

Jacques gave the bare hint of a nod to acknowledge the understanding he saw there. "I've known you for a long time, and I also know you have a lot of enemies, maybe on every continent, so you need to be careful."

Erik grinned. "Like the ones in college? My fan club?"

Jacques shook his head, and his words turned cold. "No. Worse. And these guys don't take numbers."

The food's arrival cut off further discussion, and over lunch they exchanged stories, laughed about old times, and joked. "So is Jamie going to be upset with you that you can't take your vacation?" Jacques asked.

Erik nodded. "What do you think? She really has wanted to see the Eiffel Tower, ever since I told her about opening day on the thirty-first of March 1889." Erik grinned and chuckled to himself, shook his head.

"What are you laughing about?"

"Well, when we go see it, she wants to wear a school girl outfit and wants me to pose as her professor. She wants me to tell her the history again, and after we go up and come down, we're planning to have a picnic on the grounds by the tower."

"Only you." Jacques shook his head and laughed.

They opened and read their fortune cookies, then exchanged their fortunes and read them with a smile and a nod. Jacques got his attention.

"Hey, are you still thinking about writing a book?" Jacques asked as they prepared to leave.

Erik nodded and picked up his attaché case.

"You know you'll never be able to as long as you work for the company."

"I'll find a way."

Jacques tilted his head and regarded his friend with a knowing smile. "The only way you'll be able to is if you start a new life."

Erik nodded again.

Jacques shrugged. "Okay, see you when you get back."

They shook hands, embraced lightly, and parted.

4. BROKEN PROMISE

"We live in a wonderful world that is full of beauty, charm and adventure. There is no end to the adventures we can have if we seek them with our eyes open."   —Jawaharlal Nehru

Pentagon, Washington D.C.

On the third sublevel of the Pentagon, in the Records Department, an attractive, well-manicured young lady in her mid-twenties sat at her neatly organized desk, her jobs arranged in a pattern according to her priorities. Jamie Anderson was an Administrative Support Assistant for the Department of Defense, in the Records Department. She spent most of her time completing administrative tasks, managing files and records, and other office procedures. Jamie's bosses found her a valuable employee because she was dependable, showed initiative, and took her responsibilities seriously.

Right now, she had little to work on, so she pulled out her cell and texted her boyfriend, Dr. Erik Függer—something she did several times a day, along with admiring the photograph of him she had on her desk. Even after dating and living together for nearly three years, Jamie was still amazed at his intelligence and delighted by his old-fashioned mannerisms and protective nature. She hoped Erik would propose to her in Paris.

An admiral walked in and approached Jamie; she adjusted her posture. "How can I help you, admiral?" she asked in a professional tone. Jamie had the ability to learn quickly, but it was Erik who had helped her recognize the ranks of the different armed forces.

"I need information on these two naval officers." The admiral handed over documentation that would allow her to access their personnel files.

Jamie nodded and turned to face the computer monitor. Within seconds she accessed the database. She typed in the names Lieutenant Commander August Christopher and Lieutenant Commander Laurence Justinian but got no results. While she tried a few other databases, the admiral glanced at her nameplate, Jamie Anderson, and at the photograph of Erik.

"Is that your boyfriend?" he asked.

Jamie nodded but kept working. A moment later she faced the admiral. "Sir, are the names spelled correctly?" As, he nodded, his eyes narrowed and he motioned her to keep trying. She tried again, frowning in concentration. How could she miss them? After she had repeated her actions, she shook her head and faced the admiral. "Sir, these officers aren't in our database. Is there anything else I can do for you?"

"No." The admiral grabbed the paper with the names on it and headed out.

Jamie frowned at him, then pushed back her sense that something wasn't quite right, and locked up the databases. She looked up at the sound of her boss walking in.

"Jamie," he said, "I know Admiral Cole can be intimidating, but don't worry; he's harmless."

Jamie grinned. "Thanks, I'm fine. It's just a little strange to be asked to look up data on someone who isn't even in the system."

Her boss chuckled. "Get out of here and have a great time in Paris. See you when you get back."

Jamie didn't know that Admiral Cole had met Brigadier General Plackett down the hallway. He confirmed that Jamie Anderson had been identified and told the Brigadier to go ahead with the plan to tie up all loose ends once Erik was back in 1944.

Kennedy Warren Apartments, Washington D.C.

Erik opened the door to his two-bedroom apartment and was greeted by music—the Pet Shop Boys singing *Always on My Mind*—and the smell of freshly burnt incense. Erik grinned. Jamie, who always attended to his needs, had prepared for his homecoming. Though he doubted he'd have any reason for an altercation with this loyal, understanding, and trusting woman, he appreciated the effort she put into keeping their relationship harmonious. Erik locked the door behind him and glanced around his white-walled condo, analyzing everything he saw and heard. He walked across the hardwood floor and enjoyed the woman's touch in his otherwise purely functional home and stopped by the first painting that he and Jamie had bought together at an auction house. The painting of late nineteenth century couples dancing in a baroque ballroom with a painted ceiling, large central chandelier, and wall panels of huge mirrors in gilded frames had, in some weird way, taken Jamie back to that time. She'd felt that she and Erik had lived and known each other in that period in history and that they'd made a serendipitous promise to find one another if they were separated. Erik hadn't believed in soulmates until he met Jamie; now he didn't doubt that they were linked in exactly that way. He strolled through the living room to the hallway leading to the bedrooms. A sweet, seductive voice called through the doorway to his library.

"Hi, professor."

Erik stopped and looked into the library. Jamie, the love of his life, sat on his desk, slender legs dangling over the edge, her petite, toned body clad in a short, blue-green plaid miniskirt that hugged her hips and defined her curves. Her fitted sheer-white top drew attention to her small, firm breasts and revealed a defined cleavage. White knee-high socks and black high heels enhanced her tan legs. The lamplight gave a shine to her long brown hair, and makeup highlighted her soft brown eyes. She seductively licked her moist red lips and opened her arms.

Erik, already aroused, grinned and walked into her arms. She wrapped her legs and arms around him like a squid positioning its prey, and a hint of sweet perfume drifted under his nose. Their lips softly touched, and their tongues slowly explored each other's mouths. Erik wrapped his arms around her, and she squeezed him closer. Their kissing increased in passion. His lips slowly released from hers, then kissed her neck and caressed her breasts and nipples. She moaned softly, then looked up at him and smiled. "I love you, babe."

"I love you, too."

Jamie combed her fingers through his hair and stared at him with love in her eyes. "What's wrong, babe?"

Erik took a deep breath. "The project's going crazy." He tilted his head down, closed his eyes, and then looked up into Jamie's eyes. "I can't go to Paris next week."

Her happiness evaporated. "No, babe! Why not?"

"The museum needs me to go somewhere and take care of some business."

"But you requested the time off. They need to get someone else!" Jamie said with an underlying tone of anger.

"I wish they could, I know I promised, and I do really want to go, but …" He stepped back.

Jamie slid off the desk. Tears filled her eyes, but she hugged him tightly. Erik hugged her just as tightly. "Erik, I love you," she said. "Can't you do anything to change their minds?"

"I know you do. And I wish there *was* something I could do." He shook his head, then wiped tears from her eyes. "I'd much rather be with you."

"Erik?" She narrowed her eyes slightly. "What do you do for the museum?"

Erik frowned and cocked his head. "You know what I do. I'm one of their historical researchers." He avoided her gaze, hoping she wouldn't see the lie in his eyes. "Why?"

"Like some of the people in the intelligence branches, all hush-hush about what they do."

"I'm working on a World War Two Project. You'd probably find the details boring. My work at the museum changes people's view of history. That makes me feel good."

"Babe, I love when you tell me about the past," Jamie said

sweetly as she stroked the line of his jaw. "But the way you don't talk about your work makes me feel you're hiding something. It reminds me of the people I work with at the Pentagon."

Erik frowned, not liking her probing. "Like who?"

"I don't know. Maybe some government agency."

Erik gave a fake laugh. "I don't think so."

"Come on, I've known you for three years, and I've never heard anything about your work."

Erik sighed. "Okay, you're right. But let me say this: I'm no James Bond." He took her hands. "I'm doing the exhibit at the museum on Field Marshal Erwin Rommel."

"We watched a documentary about him and D-day last week."

"Yes, he was the German field marshal who designed the defenses on the Normandy beaches. He also fought the British in North Africa. He was the commanding officer of the Afrika Korps."

"I think I remember Rommel's name from my grandmother who spoke about meeting a German general in France during World War Two." Erik grinned and Jamie smiled and gave him a peck on the lips. "I love it when you talk to me about things like that. Like the second time we met, remember when I was on a field trip with my college."

Erik nodded. He remembered; it was clear as yesterday. "I'll never forget it. But, Jamie, sometimes my research would bore you.."

"Never. Remember when you told me about the Tucker Forty-Eight?" Erik nodded. "Well," she continued, "if it interests you, it interests me."

Erik smiled and met her gaze—so full of love and passion—he kissed her deeply, and a wave of emotion overcame him. He pulled back and looked at her again. "I love you, Jamie."

"What was the name of your grandmother? Was she one of the nurses who took care of the German general?" Erik questioned.

"Raquel Bonheurve."

Erik grinned.

"Babe, when you go on your trip, will you promise to be careful and not do anything dangerous?"

"I will."

"Promise me."

Breathing in a sigh, he replied, "I promise. Now, what would you like to know about in history?" Before she could answer, he covered her with kisses, picked her up and carried her to the bed. They lay together, staring into each other's eyes.

"Tell me about the opening of the Eiffel Tower."

Grinning at her, and with love in his voice, he began, "Imagine us back in Paris on the thirty-first of March, 1889."

Erik finished his story, and Jamie squeezed him tight. "I love you, Erik," she mumbled into his neck; then she kissed him passionately and rubbed her hands across his back. "Will you tell me that story when we see Paris?"

"Yes, I promise."

They snuggled together, their lips embraced once more, and eventually their bodies became one.

5. SEEN AND UNSEEN

"Like all travelers, I have seen more then I remember and re-member more than I have seen." —Benjamin Disraeli

Erik handed his attaché case to the driver as he glanced back at Jamie and saw tears falling from her eyes. He ran back into her open arms. The embrace was so strong they didn't want to let go.

"I'll try to be strong," she murmured into his chest. "I just hate not knowing when you'll be back."

He gazed into her eyes and brushed a finger across her cheek, wiping her tears away. "I promise you, we will go to Paris."

Jamie sniffed, and she knew he might be away for quite a while. Erik replied, "I'll always come back to you." Hope dawned in Jamie's eyes at Erik's assurance. "Besides, our love keeps us to-gether, no matter where we are."

Jamie squeezed him tightly and kissed him with so much pas-sion that it bordered on desperation. "Have to go," he murmured, as he slowly disengaged himself.

As they parted, Jamie slipped something into his jacket pock-et. "I love you, Erik," she said in a hollow voice.

"I love you, too."

"If you don't come back, I'm going to come for you." Her tone and the suspicion in her eyes told him that she still suspected that he was more than a historical researcher at the museum.

"I know." That's pretty much impossible, Erik thought. If she knew where he was actually going, she might never let him go—and with good reason. This was his third trip without her knowing where he was going and when he would be back. He was, after all, going into a war zone. Being a Paramilitary Operations Officer, Erik knew operations were rarely the quick in and out. He hoped this one would go quickly.

Jamie turned and ran inside. Erik stepped into the car, closed the door, and looked back at the apartment. He felt as if he'd left a little of himself behind. Jamie appeared in the window, used her warm breath to fog up the window, and then wrote the numbers, one-four-three-seven. Just before the car drove off, Erik mouthed, *"I love you, Jamie"* and blew her a kiss. Then he sat back in his seat and they proceeded toward the Dulles Airport. A few minutes later they turned onto the congested highway and the driver maneuvered carefully through the traffic. Erik stuck his hand in his jacket pocket and pulled out an antique-looking black and white photograph of Jamie looking innocent and loving. He flipped it over and read:

My babe, Erik, though our paths might split us apart, my love for you will never die. Whenever you're down, think of me and I'll be smiling back at you. Stay healthy and safe until we meet again. I'll be thinking of you. Hugs and kisses. Love forever and always, Jamie.

He took a deep breath and released it slowly. Thoughts of Jamie raced through his mind, but he pushed them aside and turned his attention to his mission. From his inner suit pocket, he pulled a German Officer's ID book from World War Two. Greg, his contact in ONE, gave it to him back in 2006 and said that he would need it if he ever went back in time. Back then, Erik had thought it was highly unlikely, and Greg had been unable to confirm or deny that such a thing was even possible. And he said little else, just insisted that Erik remember the book should such an opportunity ever arise. As instructed, Erik planned to keep the book to himself. Though Greg couldn't say why, he'd given it to Erik for a reason.

As Erik neared Dulles, the main terminal slowly got larger and the details of architecture became more defined. Sounds from horns, people yelling for loved ones, taxis, and car brakes screeched and their sounds bounced off the car windows. As the car pulled into the departure zone, it slid into a parking spot, and the driver jumped out and opened the door for Erik, then retrieved his luggage and handed it to him. An armed escort, made up of two individuals, stood nearby. One of the escorts stepped forward.

"Dr. Függer?" he inquired. Erik nodded. "Follow me, please."

Erik followed the man and the rest of the escort fell in around him. The terminal was filled with people of all shapes, sizes, and states of consciousness. Each had their own agenda. The multitude of languages merged into a loud mumble. As he walked, Erik noticed a sports trivia question in a sports bar: WHAT TEAM WON THE WORLD SERIES IN OCTOBER, 1943? ANSWER: THE NEW YORK YANKEES. Erik took note of the fact, even though he cared little about sports.

Erik and his armed escorts bypassed the metal detectors and

headed down the apron. Erik followed closely behind them, and they came to a nameless gate with an intimidating emotionless gentleman standing guard in front of the entrance to the gangway. He instructed Erik what to do before allowing him to go down the gangway. There was a door at the end, and just beyond the door was a set of stairs that led to the ramp. Immediately as Erik opened the door, cold air hit him, but his jacket kept his warmth in. A jet stood ready before them. Erik saw the pilots in the cockpit busy checking gauges. A stewardess stood outside and welcomed Erik. He gave her a smile in return, and as he entered the jet, the ground crew performed their pre-departure duties. Erik took a seat by a window and heard the jet's hatch sealed behind him. He glanced around the interior of the Gulfstream V C-37A and realized that he was the only passenger, minus the pilots and stewardess.

The plane taxied onto the runway, then quickly picked up speed. The engines' hum grew louder as the jet raced down the runway. The stewardess and Erik were forced back into their seats. Then with an uplifting feeling, the jet ascended into the sky. Erik glanced out the window at a sea of blue sky above a blanket of clouds that stretched as far as he could see. The jet leveled off, and the stewardess offered him a drink. While he waited for his beverage, he closed his eyes.

With a sigh, he flipped open his attaché case, pulled out his binder filled with notes, dropped the tray in front of him, and placed the binder on it. The stewardess arrived with his drink. He took a sip, then set the cup beside the papers and started to read.

Field Marshal Erwin Rommel, at the Luftwaffe Field Hospital, room 247, in the town of Bernay located on 5 Rue Anne de Ticheille.

Erik rubbed his chin and pondered his mission.

Getting to the hospital … easy, getting to Rommel … easy, getting to speak to him … easy, but convincing him about my mission … not a chance. Getting him to General Bradley's Headquarters while trying to avoid the Gestapo, French Resistance, Allied Forces and German checkpoints … what am I thinking? You're probably not going to succeed. Then Erik recalled what his mother always said, *"Don't tell Erik that he can't do it because he'll prove you wrong."*

Erik leaned back in the chair, closed his eyes, and tried to make sense of what he was going to try to do, but thoughts of Jamie raced through his mind. Eventually, with a smile on his face, he fell into a restful sleep. The pilot woke him with the announcement that they had arrived at Denver International Airport. Within minutes, a muffled mechanical sound below him told Erik that the landing gear was being lowered. Soon after, the tires touched the runway with a high-pitched screech.

The jet finally came to a halt. The hatch was opened, and a rush of cold air raced in. Like water pouring into a sinking ship, it consumed all the warm air in the cabin. Eventually, everyone exited down the gangway. Three men wearing dark suits and sunglasses that hid their eyes but not their apathetic expressions stood at the foot of the gangway. One approached Erik with his hand extended.

"Dr. Függer, welcome to Denver. May I take your bag for you?" Erik shook hands and declined the hospitality. "This way, Sir," he said, motioning Erik to the midnight black Suburban with tinted windows. The heavy grillwork and large headlights gave the vehicle a dominating presence that said "get out of my way." Erik got in with the others, the engine turned over with a deep roar, and the driver navigated off the tarmac and through a maze of airport roads.

Erik studied the landscape—the usual hodge-podge of airport-related services—then turned to his apathetic sentry. "Where are we going?"

Turning his head to acknowledge Erik, he replied in a cold voice, "Sir, you are not authorized to know that."

The Suburban came to a halt at a metal door at the base of a soot-darkened concrete building with tinted windows. It appeared to be an abandoned warehouse. A sign in chipped silver-leaf lettering, which sat just below the roof line on a weathered white band, read ALL SOURCE INCORPORATED. The driver's window went down, and the driver gave his identification to a small ATM-like machine. With a creeping metallic sound, the door slowly opened, and the car proceeded through the door and down a gradual incline into a parking basement. The driver parked the SUV, and Erik and the sentry got out and headed for a single door in the distance. Inside a spacious lobby, a receptionist sat at her desk, flanked by two armed guards carrying high caliber weapons.

"Good afternoon, gentlemen; please identify yourselves," she said.

At machines that looked like voting booths, they placed their right hands on a scanner and looked forward and had their retinas scanned. After they were cleared, Erik and the guard were allowed to proceed to the elevator. Once in, the elevator descended hundreds of feet under the Denver International Airport. The elevator came to a halt and the doors opened. Erik and his guard walked into what Erik assumed is a D.U.M.B. (Deep Under-

ground Military Bunker). He knew there were many such places connected to others by a vast network of underground tunnels
containing high-speed trains on magnetic rails. Erik stared at everything, impressed by the work of the Corps of Engineers who
constructed such underground complexes from 1958—2008 under every major airport in the United States. This bunker, like
any other subway system in the United States, was filled with
all kinds of people, mainly uniformed military personnel, government officials, service personnel, and those not easily identified. They passed a bookstore, coffee shop, and several restaurants
and assorted stores, then walked onto a platform by the railway
tracks. People stood around them waiting for a train, but unlike
other subway stations, there were no maps of the tunnel systems.

Erik turned to his sentry. "Is this what I think it is?"

"That information is classified."

Erik snorted quietly at the predictable reply. "Do you have
the time?" The sentry glanced at his watch, but before he could
respond, Erik said, "Sorry, I forgot; that information is classified."

His guard's jaw tightened, but he said nothing, just stared
straight ahead once more.

The platform vibrated slightly, and, within a few minutes, a
sleek blue gunmetal bullet-like train appeared and stopped. Erik
took a closer look and realized it was a Maglev train, recalling he
had seen one in Germany. The train used magnetic levitation to
move without touching the ground, and it traveled along a guide-
way using magnets. The train had no windows except for the op-
erators in the front and rear, and the doors were flush to the body.
The doors opened, people exited, then others, including Erik and
his sentry, took their seats and fastened the seatbelts. A few mo-

ments later, the doors closed, the lights dimmed, and the train quickly accelerated.

The sentry turned to Erik. "Don't get too comfortable, we're almost there."

Erik stared back. "Gee thanks, I was afraid that was classified," he said sarcastically.

The train's speed reduced as swiftly as it had accelerated, and it came to a halt. Only Erik and his sentry got off the train at this stop. A group of armed guards stood on the platform and looked straight at Erik. Above them, a sign read HIDDEN MEADOW APARTMENTS. Erik shook his head in disbelief, actually knowing where he was— the headquarters of ONE, one of many elite government agencies not known to the American public.

Courtesy of his clearance level, Erik knew that Hidden Meadow Apartments, located in Colorado Springs, was a virtually self-contained facility with ONE's headquarters hidden in plain sight. At first glance, it looked like your typical apartment complex with manicured lawns and landscapes, private gated pool and hot tub, and there were a dozen apartment buildings, a leasing office, and clubhouse. All this hid antennas, microwave relay systems, and security cameras. Surrounding the complex was a ten-foot-high, chain-link fence topped with razor wire and patrolled by armed guards. Hidden Meadow Apartments concealed its real secrets hundreds of feet underground. This huge secret underworld had one and a half miles of corridors and it covered up to nine acres. The corridors spread out like spokes from a wheel from two center locations: the time machine and the command center. Also underground was a sewage-treatment plant with a 200,000 gallon-a-day capacity and two tanks holding 500,000 gallons of water that could last more than a month for the entire staff of 700. In addition, it stored computer mainframes. There were a total of twenty top secret electrical grids in the continental United States that could deflect an electromagnetic pulse (EMP) attack. ONE was on one of those electrical grids. It was known as Grid Eight. Most importantly, this location contained Project Pegasus.

At the door on the edge of the platform, the sentry swiped an ID card, did a retina scan, and then punched in his six-digit security code. The door opened. They entered to an almost exact replica of the last foyer. A receptionist sat at her desk with an inscription above her head reading TRUST IS GOOD. CONTROL IS BETTER. Two armed guards with M4As with a Close Quarter Battle Receiver stood on either side.

"Gentlemen, please identify yourselves."

After clearing the same kind of security check as they entered the D.U.M.B., the secretary ordered that they both sign in, then she gave an identification badge to Erik, and he attached it to his shirt. The phone rang and she picked it up. "Yes, Sir. They're on their way in." She turned to Erik. "They're expecting you."

"I feel so honored," Erik said with a grin.

She rewarded him with a tiny smile but quickly restrained it.

Erik and the guard proceeded through the entrance of GRID EIGHT, across a foyer, and down a bare corridor. The temperature was comfortable, Erik guessed around seventy-six degrees, but the lighting was a bit blinding, though his eyes soon adjusted. He heard footsteps in the distance and saw a man walking toward them. When they got closer, he identified the man as Admiral Cole.

"Welcome, Dr. Függer. How was your flight?"

"Uneventful."

"That's good to hear," Cole replied with a superficial smile.

The guard left them, and Erik and Cole continued down the busy corridor lined with doors. While listening to Cole, Erik analyzed every aspect of the facility. A huge amount of conduits for plumbing and electrical wiring ran over the ceiling fifteen feet above—everything needed to run the agency's installation. Erik was impressed how such an amazing structure was built. Many of the individuals passing them wore military uniforms, from all four branches, carrying documents in their attaché cases. Others were civilians. Some corridors were twenty to fifty feet high and wide enough for a small truck to drive through with room to spare. Each section was color-coded to prevent staff from getting lost.

Erik was taught at the Farm that perception is everything. He looked for spatial and/or temporal patterns. He noticed that every individual wore a lanyard with an identification tag around their neck. As with the CIA, each identification had a colored border indicating either their security or access clearance. He overheard one gentleman say to another that his department had been busy sending people back and noted that the color of their ID border was black, white and red.

"Why would you keep time travel only to your agency?" Erik asked.

"You will be doing your country a great service and will make the world a better place," Cole stated in a dismissive, mysterious, bureaucratic tone.

"Admiral Cole, I'm not half the theorist you are." Erik stopped to make his next point clear. "In my opinion about history, I believe that things only happen once and avoid changing it." Erik leaned forward. "If they have happened, then there's nothing we can do to change them— nor should we try."

"Why would we miss an opportunity like this and avoid it? Time travel is a reality and we will change history." Cole pointed to Erik. "I know you would love to change history for the better."

Erik shook his head. "I don't have your appetite for playing God with history."

"Any questions before you get ready?" Cole asked.

Erik's eyes sparkled at the opportunity to satisfy his curiosity. "Who else knows about Project Pegasus?" he asked bluntly.

"Well…myself, Brigadier General Plackett, the people who work here, Bonesteiner and yourself," Cole replied cautiously, then his voice became cold. "Why do you ask?"

"I'm just curious. No particular reason."

"Dr. Függer, your job is not to be curious. Your job is to be a historical analyst. Be ready at 1230 hours," Cole snapped. Eventually, they proceeded to a corridor that had few doors and little traffic but seemed to go on for miles. Cole stopped outside a door and held it open. "You can prepare yourself in here. Anything else, Dr. Függer?"

"Just curious about one thing."

Cole raised an eyebrow. "Hmmm, what might that be?" he asked with a wicked squint.

"Why is ONE involved with Project Pegasus?" Erik asked as he stepped into the room.

"What did you ask?" Though Cole replied in a hard tone, carefully schooled to be devoid of emotion, Erik heard a tinge of disbelief and surprise.

"Oh, it's nothing. I'll be ready at 1230 hours." Erik closed the door on Cole and locked it. Cole's footsteps faded into the distance.

Erik quickly took in the bare desk and chair. The coat rack held a German uniform, and there was a camera hidden in the ventilation—he waved to those watching on the other side. He sat at the desk, pulled Jamie's photograph from his pocket, flipped it over and read, focusing on one line, *whenever you're down, think of me and I'll be smiling back at you.* He turned it right side up and kissed the photograph before slipping it back into his pocket. Then he stood and took a look at the German uniform.

It is an officer's tunic—silver thread on the eagle on the right breast and around the collar tabs—everything appeared to be okay. In the jacket's inside pocket, he found money and official papers that identified him as a major in the German Army. He flicked through the pages, felt the texture, and looked at the stamp impression and the photograph. Erik's eyes widened. *What are they trying to do to me? Are they trying to compromise me?* He sighed. *Just as well I didn't trust them to get it right.* Erik would have to do what he was taught on the Farm, *"improvise, adapt, and overcome."*

Aware of the hidden camera, he walked to the light switch by the door, turned the knob to unlock the door, and quickly switched the more genuine identification paper in his pocket with the badly reproduced one they had given him.

Erik stepped outside and noticed a man approaching him, with the same color ID border of black, white and red, that he had seen in the hallway earlier. As Erik subtly got in the way of the man, he accidentally bumped into him, causing the man's ID to

come off, removed his own ID and swapped them as they landed on the floor.

"Excuse me, I didn't see you coming," Erik said.

The man stopped and turned to face Erik. "It's okay. I am on
break and then back to the grind. You know how it is."

Erik nodded. "Everyone needs fifteen minutes to recharge."

"I agree." The man looked at his watch. "Well, I have thirteen
minutes left." The man started to walk off.

"You dropped this." Erik handed him the guest ID badge,
keeping the other.

The man smiled, walked back and took the badge. "Thanks."

"No problem. Busy day?"

The man nodded. "Yeah, we're sending another guy back today."

"What time?"

"Around thirteen hundred."

"Fun, fun."

"Yeah. See you later."

The man continued down the corridor, and Erik headed back
the other way to an office he had passed on his way in. He smiled
at his good fortune and knew he had about five minutes to get
information sent to Jacques, who was in Langley, and get back to
the prep room to get ready. It's not easy for outsiders in a secure
facility to move around, but the border of his new ID would give
him clearance all the way to the time machine room. He needed
to send information quickly, and some role playing was needed.
Erik noticed security cameras in key areas. If they saw him, would
they escort him back to his prep room? He opened the office door
and walked up to what looked like the secretary's desk. She and

some of the other office staff looked up and stared at him. Erik took a deep breath and composed himself.

At least the secretary had soft eyes. "Can I help you?" she asked in a pleasant tone.

"Yes, can I have an overnight envelope, a pen, and a piece of paper, please?"

She reached in a desk drawer, pulled out an envelope and a piece of paper, and handed it to Erik. "There you go. Pens are over there." She pointed to a container of pens on the edge of the large desk.

"Thank you."

He grabbed a pen, found an empty chair, and quickly wrote a short note on the paper, then to a secure address on the envelope. He placed the note, the switched ID badge, and the bad reproduction identification papers in the envelope. Then he sealed it, walked to the desk, and handed it to the secretary. "Will this go out today?"

"Yes."

"Thanks." Erik left the office and headed back to the prep room. Once inside, he dressed in the uniform, filled his pockets with handy items, including a Zippo Chrome Lighter, and adjusted the ribbons on the left breast. He hung his own clothes on the rack, then wrapped the German military belt and holster containing a 9mm Luger around his waist. A solid knock came from the door. Erik opened it to another mindless-looking sentry.

"They're ready for you," the man said in a monotone voice. Erik nodded. He transferred his identification papers and the picture of Jamie from his own clothes to the jacket pocket of his uniform, then placed a major's cap on his head and walked out of the prep room. "This way," the sentry said and headed further along the corridor. Erik followed him down several hallways. Security cameras and warning signs announcing a restricted area appeared with increasing frequency. Finally, they approached a heavily armored door flanked by guards. Above the door, a security camera focused on those entering and exiting the secure area.

The sentry swiped his identification card and punched in a six-digit security code. A buzzer sounded, and they entered the heart of Project Pegasus, an enormous room, approximately three stories tall and two hundred yards long. Erik glanced around; the room reminded him of NASA's mission control room in Florida. Eight rows of adjoining, nearly identical, workstations buzzed with activity. Each had one or two computer screens, a keyboard, and an assortment of switches, buttons, and dials. Technicians and work crews were busy checking and rechecking vital systems, like mechanics working on a NASCAR racecar. Erik looked up. Twenty feet above the floor, well-armed guards in black body armor, carrying high caliber weapons, walked up and down the catwalk that covered the full length of the room. Their eyes were fully alert and watched every inch of the control room.

Erik brought his gaze down and noticed that the floor, unlike any he had seen before, was clear, like glass, with pull-back panels and, beneath that, different sized bundles of multi-colored cables branching out and twisting like the root system of an oak tree. The cables merged into several large groups as they approached the gray concrete wall at the front of the room. A single black door sat in the center of the wall. Erik presumed it was the entrance to the time machine.

Brigadier General Plackett and Admiral Cole appeared out

of nowhere from among the organized chaos and walked toward him, accompanied by a buffed individual wearing a uniform. The man had an unyielding jaw and grayish-blue, shark-like eyes that raked over Erik.

Erik picked up the last bit of Cole's conversation. "Mr. Crowley, we'll finish the briefing at 1800 hours, and, yes, on the second of October, Project Wolf Den will be executed." Crowley nodded, and the Brigadier turned to Erik. "Ready?"

"Yes, Sir," Erik replied with a smirk. "Can I have the name of the SS colonel I'm supposed to meet?"

"He doesn't go by a name. He goes by his rank—Colonel."

Erik wondered what the full story was. "Colonel?"

"Yes. Colonel," Plackett said. "He's one of my people."

"Do you have the name of the château where we're meeting?"

"Sorry, we don't. You've memorized the address?"

"Yes."

"Good. Let's get you in the machine."

"How about the French resistance?"

"You don't have to worry about them. They were taken care of by the German Army or the SS."

"Are you sure?"

"Trust us."

"Sure," Erik said, but he didn't trust them, not after the dodgy ID papers they tried to pass off on him.

They strolled toward the black door and stopped at the last row of workstations. The concrete wall towered over them.

Admiral Cole glanced at an empty seat at the console. Looking as if he had misplaced something, he turned to the man in the next seat. "Where's Gordon?"

"I don't know, Sir." He paused for a moment and continued. "Admiral Cole, I have recalculated and we have a two-minute window."

The tension grew in Cole's face, as Erik questioned. "A two-minute window?"

Cole addressed Erik. "Time travel is not as easy as you think. For the ripples in time to remain ripples, we have to send you back with the least amount of resistance." Then he turned to the technician. "Can you operate this panel? We can't wait for him."

"Yes, Sir."

Plackett asked with his hand extended, "Your ID."

"I left it back in the prep room," Erik replied.

Plackett studied him in silence and suspicion was growing as he got pulled away to get a call.

"Go through that door," Cole said, looking as if he wanted to strangle Erik, "head all the way to the back room, and try to relax. And try not to get yourself killed."

"How many people went before me?"

"Two."

Erik remembered the two stars added to the Memorial Wall. "Were they analysts by any chance?"

Cole's mouth tightened into a thin line. Though he said nothing, it was answer enough for Erik. "Do you have their names?" he asked innocently.

Cole thrusted his face right up to Erik's face. "Don't you ever stop fucking asking questions?" he growled.

"No. And since I'm volunteering for your mission, I have the right to know."

"You listen to me, you son of a bitch, I don't have to tell you a damn thing." He pulled back and smirked. "By the way, you know what they say about volunteers, don't you?"

"They're expendable."

Cole nodded, and as he turned away, his smirk widened into a grin.

"Now move," Cole said, motioning him to the door. Cole glanced at Erik. He looked relieved to get rid of him.

Erik took a last look at the room. All the technicians stared at him. He walked past them and stopped thirty feet away from the wall at a foot-wide, bright red line on the floor. DANGER: RADIATION. ONLY TRAVELERS AND AUTHORIZED PERSONNEL BEYOND THIS POINT was written on it in block-bold lettering. Erik's heart beat increased, and his palms started to sweat. *Why can't it be like the time machines in the movies? They should've consulted H.G. Wells when designing this.* Erik took his last glimpse of 2008. His audience looked at him as if he were a rat in a cage.

In the near distance, Erik heard Plackett, who was still on the phone. "What do you mean he's having trouble with his ID?" Plackett's eyes enlarged with rage. "What? Why? Was his ID badge not allowing him in secure areas?" Plackett gave Erik a cold stare, and Erik grinned back.

"Hey, Cole!" Erik yelled. Cole turned to face him, and Erik quoted from Willem De Kooning: "The past does not influence me; I influence it."

The black door slid open, revealing stark white hallway fifty feet in length. Erik walked to the end and entered a circular room. The walls, floor, and ceiling were covered in raised metal strips that formed a pattern of rectangles, and a gunmetal rectangle sat in the center of each. The walls began to emit an electronic bee-like humming. It consumed the room and grew louder by the second, assaulting Erik's eardrums. A blinding, bluish-white light appeared. Erik took a deep breath. A chill suddenly ate through his body, and he had the sensation of being pulled back. His eyes bulged and he felt as if he was falling.

"Oooooooooh Sssssshhhhhiiiiiit!" Erik screamed as he got transported back to 1944.

Plackett walked back to Cole's side, as he shook his head. "Has he always been this way?" he asked Cole as they watched the proceedings.

"Yes! Bonesteiner always protected him, but no one will be able to protect him where he's going."

Plackett smiled. "I made sure of that. Cerberus will be waiting for him."

"Your people better get the job done; there's a lot at stake," Cole said.

"They won't fail. You can be assured of that," Plackett replied with confidence, and the men exchanged grins.

"Well, I want Cerberus informed of what we just learned from Dr. Függer's briefing. He needs to know what Rommel's intentions are."

Plackett looked troubled.

"What is it?"

"He has already been sent back."

"Damn it! Is there a way we can get him that information?" Plackett shook his head. "What if he is successful in bringing Rommel to Bradley's headquarters?"

"Dr. Függer is a threat to this agency and our objectives. You gave orders to kill both him and Rommel," Cole said.

"Yes, Sir. But we'll have a problem if, by some chance, Rommel lives."

Cole shrugged. "The worst he could do is influence other generals. It's safest to have him out of the way, but what's really important is killing Hitler. Once he's dead, the Third Reich will fall, and the United States will have a better position in Europe during the Cold War. Kennedy will not be elected president, and we will have control of Southeast Asia."

"In which case," Plackett said, "we don't have to worry about sending someone back to November 1963 to solve that issue in Dallas."

"Yes. I have a meeting with the Bilderberg Group, and they might agree that it's better to deal with him in 1943 than in 1963."

"I'll start planning for that."

"Good. Now we have to send Ahriman to take care of Dr. Függer and Crowley to kill Hitler."

"Cerberus can fix that," Placket said. "We don't need Ahriman."

Cole shook his head. "I'm not taking any chances. He's much more resourceful than the other two analysts, Mulder and Knight. Just make it happen."

"Yes, Sir."

Footsteps stomped up behind them. They turned to see Gordon race in and take his seat. "Where were you?" Cole asked.

"I had trouble with my ID, Sir. I was on my break and on my way back I was not allowed in certain areas. Then I realized it wasn't mine and someone swapped my ID."

Plackett walked over to Gordon and requested his ID. "How was someone able to swap your ID?" Plackett asked as Gordon handed it to him.

Gordon explained a man bumped into him, and when he described his looks, Cole and Plackett knew by the description it was Erik.

"What's wrong?" Cole asked, seeing the panic in Plackett's eyes. Plackett placed the ID in Cole's hand, and Cole realized it was Erik's. "Oh God!"

6. THE JOURNEY BEGINS

"Two roads diverged in a wood and I—I took the one less traveled...."
—Robert Frost

Bernay, France

Erik tried to stand and stumbled forward as if he were drunk. He opened his eyes but saw only a blur. The world felt as if it had flipped upside down, but as his eyes adjusted it went back to normal, and his surroundings slowly came into focus. Flat, open grasslands reached to the horizon in all directions and gradually gave way to hills. A gray Kübelwagen drove down a country road near him.

Without warning, a P-51 Mustang roared above Erik's head, and its six machine guns unleashed their bullets of death on its target, the Kübelwagen. The P-51, like a hawk, attacked its prey, closed on the Kübelwagen which swerved from side to side, trying to escape. Bullets tore the earth apart and left a trail as they inched their way to the defenseless Kübelwagen. Dirt flew in the air. They penetrated the thin metal exterior of the Kübelwagen, accompanied by the sharp, pierced sounds of metal being twisted. The driver lost control; the Kübelwagen swerved off the road and hit a tree with a loud thud. The engine cycled one last time, then stopped. The P-51 circled around and made sure its prey was disabled, then it disappeared as fast as it came.

Erik sighed, relieved he was still alive, but apprehensive about what he might find in the car. "Oh boy," he said under his breath, then raced to the motionless Kübelwagen bent around the tree.

The smell of petrol and seared blood and flesh emanated from the metal carcass, and numerous puncture wounds riddled the sides. Erik took a deep breath and peered inside; his eyes widened in shock. The driver's chest cavity had been torn open, exposing vital organs that slowly oozed out like jelly from a jar. His lungs, no longer held by his shattered ribcage, looked like hamburger meat. His arm was severed at the elbow and the skin was torn off, revealing biceps and triceps that were slowly detaching themselves from the exposed bone. The hand of the severed limb still held the steering wheel. A corpse with the right side of its face blown off—probably impacted by a fifty-caliber shell—slumped against the seat in the back. The jawbone had detached from the fractured skull. The right eye was gone, and the left hung out of its socket, still attached by the optical nerve. Flesh and bone fragments covered the back seat. The rear passenger's chest slowly leaned forward, and to the sounds of tearing flesh and cracking bones, the head detached itself from the body and plunged to the floor, landing with a muffled thump. Brain matter rolled out of the skull in a spray of blood. Erik gulped and retreated from the Kübelwagen. Then he reached back inside, grabbed the briefcase from the back seat and ripped it open. He quickly scanned the organized documents and occasionally glanced up and looked for oncoming troops or vehicles.

He stumbled across a document that looked familiar. *Oh, my God.* He realized that it was a flow chart of the individuals in the provisional government. *Dear God, they were on their way to arrest Rommel, and this attack stopped it from happening.*

Erik looked up at the sound of vehicle engines that rumbled in the distance and saw a group of army vehicles draw closer. He slipped the document back into the briefcase, grabbed a useless paper and crumpled it while he walked to the fuel tank cap and drew the cigarette lighter from his trouser pocket. He opened the cap, lit the paper, shoved it in the gas tank, and ran. Within seconds, a large explosion of fire and a shower of metal shattered the quiet countryside.

Erik sat on the side of the road and stared at the mangled mess. The fire consumed the vehicle and spewed thick-black, choking smoke into the air. The smell of burning flesh and leather mingled with the acrid smoke. The first of many vehicles—troop carriers and a staff car—stopped with a screech a few feet from the blazing Kübelwagen, and soldiers jumped out.

One raced toward Erik, squatted down beside him, and stared into his eyes. "*Herr warden sie verletzt?* Are you okay, sir?"

Erik stared back, too shocked for emotion. He glanced at the Kübelwagen and took a deep breath. The soldier quickly and gently patted him down, examining him for injuries, then he turned his head and yelled, "*Bekommen sie einen medizinstudenten hier schnell!* Get a medic here quickly!" Erik placed his hands by his sides for support and pushed upward, trying to stand. The soldier assisted him and helped him to the closest staff car, again yelling for a medic. He tried to comfort Erik. "*Herr wird die Sanitäter kommen. Herr alles wird gut.* Sir, the medic is coming. Everything will be fine."

The soldier opened the back door, and Erik took a seat as the medic arrived and pulled out his equipment. He asked Erik routine questions while he checked his vitals. Erik reassured him he was okay, just a little shaken up from the ordeal. He closed his eyes and switched his mind to speaking German.

"Sir, we will take you to the Luftwaffe Field Hospital in Bernay, where a doctor can further check you out," the medic said.

Erik nodded. The medic closed the door, and the car headed to the hospital, leaving some of the troops behind. On the way to the hospital, the driver made small talk while Erik reevaluated the various ways he might convince Rommel to go with him. He pulled out the picture of Jamie and wondered what she was doing right now. *Try not to worry about me. I've seen things I hope you'll never see.*

They entered the congested streets of Bernay. Cars and trucks roared down the roads, and people busy with conversations and activities filled the footpaths. It appeared that everyday life continued as if there wasn't a war—apart from the huge, blood-red Nazi flags with the overbearing black swastika that hung from flagpoles and buildings.

At the hospital gate, a guard approached with his hand extended. Another stood at point with his finger on the trigger of his MP-40. The car drove up and the driver lowered his window as the guard walked up. "Papers." The driver and Erik handed over their identification. "State your business," the guard said as he scanned their documents.

The driver explained the situation. The guard handed the documents back, and he and Erik exchanged salutes. The staff car pulled up directly in front of the hospital's entrance where a stream of people flowed in and out. The driver quickly got out and opened the door for Erik. Erik assured him that he could walk on his own. They exchanged salutes and the driver headed toward the parking lot.

Erik headed to the entrance and collected his thoughts on what to say to Rommel. Inside the hospital, the outside noise became muffled. Low whispers and the sound of wooden heels against the linoleum tile floor echoed throughout the hallways and open areas. Erik made his way to the elevators and waited with several nurses, doctors, and a few visitors. He caught a glance from an attractive nurse. Her warm smile and batting eyelashes made Erik grin back and nod in acknowledgment.

The doors opened, and a flood of people exited and spread out in every direction. Erik and the others got in, and with a bump and a low-pitched metallic moan, the elevator ascended to the next floor. Once out, everyone dispersed like atoms being split in a nuclear reaction. Erik glanced at the sign on the wall that displayed room numbers and directions. A calming voice broke his concentration.

"What room are you looking for?"

Erik turned to a petite, stunning young woman, maybe in her early twenties, with soft brown eyes and long brown hair neatly put up. She wore a white nurse's dress, baby-blue pinafore apron tied in the back, and a nurse's cap.

"Room 247."

"Follow me." She proceeded down the hallway. "Who are you seeing?"

"A friend." Erik smiled. Clearly, he was in the right place, as he saw Hans Speidel and other members of Rommel's staff walking with a doctor down the hallway toward them. Erik overheard their conversation.

"Doctor, we will move him to the hospital at Le Vésinet," Speidel demanded.

"I wouldn't recommend moving him until a few more tests are completed," the doctor replied. "You know he's a very demanding patient."

"I know, doctor. He'll be checking out tomorrow."

"I don't agree with this. He needs to rest a few more days."

Speidel stopped and faced the doctor. "I am not asking you; I am telling you," he said in a stern voice. The others stopped behind them, and Erik and the nurse passed by. He slowed his pace to keep within hearing distance as long as possible.

The doctor sighed. "What time are you planning on moving the field marshal?"

"Around five in the morning."

The nurse tapped Erik on his shoulder. "Is everything okay?"

Erik nodded. "Yes, thank you."

"I hope your friend is doing well."

"I hope so, too."

She stopped before they got to the room and looked at him with a puzzled frown. "Do I know you?"

"No, I don't think we've ever met before."

"Well, my name is Raquel Bonheurve. Nice to meet you; here's your friend's room."

"Nice to meet you, Raquel. I'm Erik …" He stopped his train of thought and stared at her. "What's your name again?"

"Raquel Bonheurve. Is there anything wrong?"

Erik realized he was talking to Jamie's grandmother and hid his surprise. "No, everything's fine. Once again, thank you. Have a nice day."

"You, too. Bye."

Erik waved goodbye and collected his thoughts before he opened the door to Rommel's room and stepped inside. Sunshine poured in through a large window and warmed the room, flooding it with light. Rommel lay still in his bed with his head tilted to face Captain Lang, who sat in a chair like a guard dog. He stood abruptly the moment Erik placed a foot in the room. Both he and Rommel stared in Erik's direction, no doubt trying to make out who he was.

Lang, a medium-built man in his late forties wore a gray field uniform, stomped toward Erik, stood directly before him, and said in a strong voice, "Can I help you, Herr Major?"

"I'm here to see the field marshal."

"State your business, Sir."

"Herr Captain, I cannot discuss my business with you. You do not have the security clearance."

Lang raised his eyebrows. "Oh really. What clearance is that?"

Erik stared into Lang's cold expression, trying to think of something that would be higher than the traditional Top Secret. "How dare you question me?" He said in an authoritative manner. "This is state business, and for your information, the clearance is War Decisive. Now I demand to speak to the field marshal."

Lang's stare changed to a look of puzzlement.

"Who is it, Herr Captain?" A deep voice asked from behind Lang. Lang moved aside so Rommel could look at Erik.

"Who are you?" Rommel peered at Erik through his right eye; his left was swollen shut.

Erik stepped forward, clicked his heels and saluted. The man's brown hair—thinning on top—high cheek bones and straight aristocratic nose were unmistakably Rommel's. Even in his bathrobe, he looked like every photo Erik had ever seen of him, his chiseled features softened by the serenity in his gaze.

"Herr Field Marshal, my name is Major Függer. Sir, I have an urgent matter I need to address with you. However, I cannot state my matter in front of the captain."

Rommel glanced at Lang, who crossed his arms and locked his jaw. Lang glanced at Rommel then back at Erik. "Why is that, Herr Major?" Rommel asked.

"Herr Field Marshall, what I have to tell you is Top Secret War Decisive, and it is for your ears only, Sir."

Rommel motioned Lang over, and he leaned over so Rommel could whisper in his ear. Lang nodded while he kept his eyes on Erik. Meanwhile, Erik mentally prepared the points that he had planned to use to try to win his case with Rommel. A few minutes later, their conversation ended. Lang strolled by Erik and gave him a bitter glance before he left the room. The door closed.

"So, Herr Major," Rommel said when the door was closed, "what do you have to tell me that's so important? I'm assuming you are from Berlin?"

"Before I start, Herr Field Marshall—"

"Wait, I need you to speak up. I can't hear out of my left ear."

Erik increased his volume. "Herr Field Marshall, did you hear the news about the failed assassination attempt of Der Führer?" Rommel nodded, and Erik continued. "At this present moment, the Gestapo is arresting all those involved directly or indirectly in the plot to kill Hitler. And no, Sir, I am not from Berlin."

Rommel sat up, frowned thoughtfully, and rubbed his chin while looking at Erik with his one good eye. "Why is this important to me? I'm not involved, and I know nothing about the plot. Therefore, the Gestapo would have no business arresting me."

Erik took a deep breath. "Bormann is certain of your involvement, but Goebbels is not."

Rommel's eye narrowed. "Herr Major, how do you know of such things in Hitler's inner circle?"

"Herr Field Marshall, I have my sources."

"Herr Major, I do not believe you have any sources. What I do know is that Bormann will do anything to gain more power and influence. He is a pain in the ass every time I see Hitler, but I have one advantage—Hitler holds me in high favor."

"That is true, Herr Field Marshall, however—"

"You don't know the power I have, and my influence."

"I do, Sir, but there's another issue." Erik pulled out the sheet with the flow chart of the provisional government and handed it to Rommel.

"What is this?" Rommel glanced over the document, his expression flickered between guilt and careful neutrality.

"It's the provisional government."

Rommel peered up from the page. "Where did you obtain this?"

"As I said before, I have my sources."

"You must know some powerful people to obtain this." Rommel paused. "The Gestapo is not known for giving such information."

"I can be very persuasive."

Rommel continued looking it over. "Go on, Herr Major; tell me what else you have. Or should I ask, what else have your sources told you?"

"Your Chief of Staff, Hans Speidel, claimed you had orders to start a military plot to overthrow Hitler. He said that to save his own life."

Veins popped out from Rommel's neck, and his hands balled up in fists. "That bastard! He'll be sorry he crossed me."

"Sir, I have a chance of saving you and you not being arrested."

"How is that, Herr Major?" Rommel placed the paper on the table by his bed, next to his coffee and his book, *The Tunnel*, by Bernhard Kellermann. "How do I know you are not the Gestapo trying to make me say something?"

"I can assure you I'm not."

"These days people are testing people to save their own lives." He paused and collected his thoughts. "What makes you any different?"

"I'm trying to save your life. I gave you everything the Gestapo will use against you." Erik pointed to the sheet to get his point across.

"So you said. But you have to do better than that, Herr Major, to convince me you are not Gestapo."

"I didn't want to tell you ... but ... I work for the OSS, US Intelligence. My job here is to take you to General Bradley's Headquarters and try to end this war."

Rommel's eye widened. "American? OSS?"

"Yes, Sir."

"Why would the OSS have an interest in rescuing me?"

"We want to end this war, just like you and the others in Operation Valkyrie."

Rommel pointed at Erik. "You have no proof that I was a part of that, Herr Major," he said in a scolding tone. "I disapprove of Stauffenberg's actions."

"If that's so, why are you getting a defensive tone? I'm not here to argue whether you were or not."

Rommel's facial muscles tightened. "I can make a call right now, have you arrested by the SS as a spy, and have you killed."

Erik leaned forward. "But you won't, because you want to end this war as much as we do. So if you want to make your call, then do it." He picked up the phone receiver and extended it to Rommel. "I don't care, but Germany will be devastated if the war continues."

Rommel ordered Lang to come in. He appeared at the doorway as Erik placed the receiver down. Rommel picked it up and began to dial. "You might have a two-minute head start before the Gestapo get to my room. I suggest you leave now if you want a chance to escape."

"Herr Field Marshall, there is a chance that we can convince Eisenhower that America should help the Germans attack the Russians."

Rommel placed down the receiver and glared at Erik. "How sure are you about that?"

"I wouldn't bring it up if I wasn't sure, and you're wasting time."

Rommel turned to Lang and ordered him to leave. "Why would Eisenhower go along with my demands?"

"I can tell you this. There are members of his staff, like Patton, who do not trust the Russians."

Rommel tilted his head and considered for a moment. "You're asking me to take a huge gamble. And I'm not at all sure I should trust you. Maybe you're just telling me what I want to hear, and you're a very clever member of the RSHA[4]."

"Herr Field Marshall, are you willing to take that chance with your life?"

"Are you willing to take a chance with your life, Herr Major? Come now, you have to do better than that. Tell me something the RSHA would not know." From the tone of his voice, Erik guessed that Rommel was losing his patience.

He strolled to the window, stared out, and racked his brain to find something to convince Rommel. After a moment, he smiled, remembering what Manfred Rommel, the Field Marshal's son said in a book. He turned to Rommel. "How about Lu's birthday gift this year?"

"What about it?"

"You bought her Italian made shoes and they were too small. I also know she didn't like them."

"How in the hell do you know that?" Rommel demanded, his face flushed.

"In the OSS we know everything."

"You are with OSS? And with the Americans?" Rommel reconfirmed what he had heard earlier.

"Yes, Sir."

---

4. Reichssicherheitshauptamt (Reich Main Security Office or Reich Security Head Office)

"Lang, get in here!"

Lang threw open the door and marched straight to Rommel. "Yes, Sir."

Rommel turned to Erik. "Will you excuse us, Herr Major?"

Erik nodded. "Yes, Sir." He saluted, clicked his heels and walked out the room, wondered what Rommel would say to Lang in his absence.

"I do not trust him, Herr Field Marshal," Lang said impassively.

"Based on recent events, I'm starting to believe him."

"But, Sir, how do you know it's not a setup by the Gestapo or RSHA?"

"He brought up Lu's birthday gift."

"The shoes?"

Rommel nodded.

"How in the hell did he know that?"

"I don't know, but I know for a fact that RSHA wouldn't know about that. Secondly, he's American, and he's given us another chance to make peace with them. It could be our last."

"American? What if he was sent here to kill you?"

"If he wanted to kill me, he would've done it already and taken you as well." Rommel paused. "I'm going to take a leap of faith."

"I must object, Herr Field Marshall. Why would the Americans send someone here to rescue you? It sounds suspicious."

"Even if there is a slight chance that we can make peace with America and then convince Eisenhower to help us attack the Russians, we must take it. At this time, he's our only option."

"Herr Field Marshall, I still have to protest against this."

"I've made my decision. Now, my final order to you is to protect my family and get them to a safe location until the war is over." Rommel grabbed a blank sheet of paper and began to write a letter to his wife. "Get the major."

"Yes, Sir."

Erik paced up and down the hallway, like a father expecting a child. Sweat beaded on his skin as his tension built from not knowing what was going on inside the room. Erik rubbed his hands together to remove the moisture building up on his palms and wondered if he had done the right thing by telling Rommel who he worked for. Would Rommel really give him to the Gestapo as a spy? Two SS officers in their black uniforms walked down the corridor toward him, making the hair on the back of Erik's neck stand up. He breathed deeply to remain calm beneath their glare, but he feared Rommel had made the call. If so, he would have to find a way to escape and might never return to 2008 and to Jamie. The door swung open, breaking the tension; it was Lang.

"He wants to speak to you."

Erik walked in and heard the last bit of Rommel's telephone conversation. "I know…I will…See you soon."

Rommel stood and looked at Erik. "Major Függer, I believe you are correct. However, there is the issue of my family. Captain Lang has agreed to take them to a safe, undisclosed location until the war is over."

"Excuse me, Sir, can I be informed of that location?"

Lang glanced at Rommel and without hesitation, Rommel replied, "No, you may not."

Erik nodded. "Understood. We'll leave when you're ready, Sir."

Rommel walked to the closet, pulled out his uniform and a fresh shirt, and headed to the bathroom and closed the door behind him.

Lang walked over to Erik and fixed him with a steely gaze. "If you're not who you say you are, and you kill the field marshal, I will never forget your face, and I will hunt you down and kill you," he said in a cold, threatening voice.

"I understand your point of view, but I'm not here to kill him. I'm here to save him." Erik walked to the end table and reached for the sheet with the provisionary government flow chart. Accidentally, he knocked Rommel's coffee, and it spilled onto the sheet. Erik quickly lifted the sheet so the coffee wouldn't ruin it and was about to hand the paper to Lang when he noticed that there was no question mark by Speer's name. He recalled the coffee-stained document he saw in 2008. *Could it be?* "Did he show you this?" Erik asked Lang.

"He did." Lang shrugged complacently. "It means nothing to me."

"This proves they'll arrest and kill him."

Lang grabbed it, glanced over it, and then looked up, meeting Erik's gaze. "Time will tell if you're correct." He handed it back to Erik, who placed it in his right tunic pocket.

"Just get his family to safety."

Lang pointed at Erik. "You make sure he doesn't get killed."

Rommel interrupted their conversation. "Herr Captain." Lang turned to Rommel and stood at attention. "Good luck, my friend." Rommel extended his hand to meet Lang's. "I hope to see you in the future." He handed Lang two letters. "Give this letter to my wife, and the other to Manfred."

"Yes, Sir. I hope to see you again, Herr Field Marshall." Lang snapped a salute and clicked his heels.

Rommel returned the salute and then started packing his personal belongings.

Lang turned to Erik and saluted. "Take care, Herr Major, *Alle Gute*[5]."

"You too, Herr Captain."

Erik and Lang exchanged a nod and a handshake; then Lang walked out of the room, and Erik strolled over to the window.

"So Herr Major, are you working alone or in a team?" Rommel asked as he closed his suitcase.

Erik stared down at the parking lot. "Solo, but I'll have help." A black Mercedes Benz with an SS license plate pulled up at the entrance of the hospital. Erik glanced back at Rommel. "Sir, if we were able to get you to General Bradley's Headquarters in Rennes, do you think we could end this war sooner?"

Rommel rubbed his chin, deliberating. "I would like to hope so. Are there other individuals doing the same thing as you?"

"I really don't know, Sir." A chill raced up Erik's spine, leaving goosebumps on the back of his neck. He glanced out the window again. An SS officer with shark-like eyes and a sadistic grin now stood by the car. The SS officers who were in the hallway earlier were with him, pointing up in Erik's direction. Erik vaguely recalled seeing those cold eyes before, and he realized it was the gentleman who was exiting from Bonesteiner's office the day he gave his presentation. *What's he doing here?* Erik's eyes widened

---

5. All the best, good luck. A phrase often, no doubt, poking cheerily before comrades set off on a semi-suicidal mission

as a realization hit him. *The red herring in black!* It was the man in the photo that Jacques warned him about. The man suddenly raced into the hospital with the other SS men. Erik's heart rate increased. Turning to Rommel, he ordered, "Sir, we need to leave now."

Rommel frowned. "What's wrong, Herr Major?"

"There's no time to discuss that now," Erik replied, heading for the door.

Rommel grabbed his suitcase and followed. Once in the hallway, Erik glanced right and left, looking for another set of elevators or stairs to make their escape. He saw Raquel strolling down the hallway with a huge smile, just like Jamie.

"Where are the stairs," he called out, trying not to sound as desperate as he felt, "or a service elevator?"

She looked a little taken aback. "What's wrong with the main elevators, the ones you used last time? Why can't you use those? Wouldn't they be easier?"

"No! Where are the stairs or a service elevator? Please."

Though clearly shocked by his rudeness, she replied calmly, "The service elevator is all the way down the hallway on the right about ten meters past the nurses' station."

"Thank you, Raquel."

She smiled. "You're very welcome. Maybe I'll see you later."

Rommel and Erik, his heart pounding, raced down the hallway, navigating through people who stopped and stood rigid as they ran by. The echo of their shoes bounced off the walls and ceiling. Aware that he had no idea what was behind every corner and in every room, Erik squinted into the distance, trying to see where he was going.

Rommel stopped at the nurse's station, leaning on it to catch his breath. "Do you know where you're going?"

Erik glanced around for the elevator. "She said it was by the nurses' station."

A high-pitch bell sounded just as Erik discovered the elevator around a corner. "Come on," he called to Rommel, waving him on. The elevator doors slowly crept open, exposing an individual inside. Erik unbuttoned his holster and reached for his Luger. His hands began to sweat and he heard his heart beating in his ears. The doors finally opened. A man stepped out, raised his hands and headed for cover at the sight of Erik's Luger. Erik realized the man was a hospital orderly and released a huge sigh, knowing they were safe for the time being.

"Were you expecting someone else?" Rommel asked.

Erik nodded and motioned for Rommel to get in. Once inside, he pressed the number one button firmly, and while the elevator descended, he took a few deep breaths and tried to focus on an escape route. Once on the first floor, after checking the hallway for anything suspicious, he and Rommel exited. They walked down several hallways, then came upon the loading docks at the back of the hospital. Erik analyzed every foot of the dock, looking for a vehicle in which to escape.

"Where's your vehicle?" Rommel asked. "Do you have one?"

"Yes Sir, I do. It's in front of the hospital." At least he hoped it was. Erik and Rommel made their way to the front of the hospital, Erik checked to made sure they were not seen by the Gestapo. Once out front, Erik desperately scanned the parking lot. With relief, he recognized the soldier who'd brought him to the hospital leaning against the Kübelwagen, having a smoke.

Erik strolled toward him. "Private, I need this car."

"Excuse me, Sir?"

"I'm taking your car and the keys. Now!" Erik extended his hand.

"Keys, Sir? I don't have any keys."

"What're you talking about? You must be able to start the car somehow!"

"Sir, I use the primer and the choke," the private said, completely baffled.

Erik's anger grew. "The what?"

The private pointed to the dashboard inside the Kübelwagen. Erik leaned forward and saw the buttons to which he was referring. *You have to be kidding me! No keys! Damn it, that's right, key ignition doesn't come out until 1948.* Erik looked to the heavens. *Sorry dad, I forgot you told me.* Trying not to sound like a complete idiot, he asked, "How do you start the Kübelwagen?"

"Well Sir, you press the primer several times." The private pointed to the primer. "Next you pull the choke."

Erik motioned Rommel to get in, and while Rommel placed his belongings in the back seat, Erik walked over to the SS's black Mercedes, aimed his Luger and shot two tires flat. Then he walked back to the Kübelwagen, placed the Lugar in the holster, got in, and noticed an MP-44 in the back seat. Erik pulled out the choke and the engine cranked over. He placed his foot on the accelerator, the air-cooled engine revved up, and the car lunged forward. Erik took one last glance at the hospital and saw the man from the black Mercedes staring back at him from Rommel's room. Even from this distance, Erik felt the coldness in the man's gaze.

"Do you know where we're going?" Rommel asked.

"Audrieu, France."

Rommel's eye widened. "That's in Normandy, you are aware of that?"

"Yes, Sir, I am."

"You are aware it's not going to be easy getting there."

"Trust me, Herr Field Marshal, you have no idea how many times I've pondered the same things you're expressing." Erik pulled out the map of Northern France and handed it to Rommel. "If you have any suggestions, I'm all attention."

"It is not the Gestapo or our troops that bother me. It is the French resistance and the Steel Weather."

"Steel Weather?" Erik asked as he navigated down the streets.

"Yes, Steel Weather. You know the Allies have complete air supremacy, and they strafe all our vehicles on the roads. It would be best if we travel at night or on roads that have a lot of cover."

"I agree. I just wish I was driving my Phaeton," Erik replied without thinking.

"What is a Phaeton?"

"You know, it's Volkswagen's ..." Erik suddenly realized that he was talking about a car that didn't exist yet and hadn't even been thought of. "Ah ... new prototype."

"Ferdinand Porsche is designing a new automobile? I've not heard of this."

Erik tried to put an end to the conversation. "Well, in a way."

Rommel shot off questions like an inventor wanting to know more about his experiment. "In a way? What way? Do you know the specifications of the Phaeton?"

"It's bigger and faster than Kfz 17," Erik replied, once again not thinking about what he said, then he realized that he made it worse. He needed to do damage control and fast.

"How big and how fast does it go?" Rommel asked.

"Almost twice the size, and it can go 140 miles per hour."

"140 miles per hour! My God, Porsche has outdone itself!"

Erik mentally kicked himself and tried to correct his mistake. "I meant to say, 140 kilometers per hour. Don't worry about Phaeton. Let's focus on something else."

"I would like to continue our discussion on the Phaeton. That speed is amazing! What else do you know about it? Does Reich Marshal Speer know about it?"

"Mmm…No, I don't think he does."

Erik saw an isolated petrol station on the outskirts of town and pulled in. The old wooden structure of weathered white paint on horizontal boards had a single paned window and open door. A single early twentieth-century gas pump stood in the center of a loose gravel driveway, which crackled under the tires as they drove up. An old man peered out the window. Erik climbed out as a half dozen Sdkfz 251/1 half-tracks, a Sdkfz 7 fitted with quadruple-barreled Flakvierling 20mm anti-aircraft guns, and a Tiger I tank rolled by. The metal tracks and road wheels made a high-pitch metallic squeak each time the wheels rotated. One of the Sdkfz 251/1's half-tracks barreled in and kicked up gravel like shrapnel from a grenade. Its metallic brakes squealed as it came to a halt. Waffen SS troops, the elite of the German ground forces, poured out of the sides, like rats escaping a barn on fire, and walked around to stretch their legs. Erik overheard some of them saying *brozen*[6]

---

6. A phase commonly used in similar context to American "Brass" high ranking military officers

and *Wüstenfuchs*[7]. Several nodded at Erik, and he nodded back. An SS lieutenant approached and saluted him.

"Have you run into any Steel Weather, Herr Major?"

"Not since this morning."

"Did you get hit?"

Erik nodded.

"Thank God, we've had nothing yet. Goering needs to get the Luftwaffe to stop the Allied strafing."

"I couldn't agree with you more. Excuse me." Erik turned and strolled over to the shack.

"Herr Major?" The lieutenant called. Erik turned his head. "Which way are you headed?"

"North," Erik said.

The lieutenant grinned. "We're headed in the same direction. We'll give you cover."

Erik grinned. "Sounds good, thank you." Erik walked into the structure where the old man sat scowling on a stool behind a counter with his tanned, leather-skinned arms crossed against his chest.

"Sir, can you turn on the pump?" Erik asked. "We need some petrol."

"Haven't you Germans already taken enough from our country?" the old man asked bitterly. Anger simmered in his foggy blue eyes.

Erik felt the tension in the air, walked to the door and closed it, then turned to face the old man. "Listen. I know how you feel."

"Do you, major?" the man snapped and pointed an accusing

---

7. A nickname bestowed to Erwin Rommel aka The Desert Fox.

finger. "In my lifetime Germany has invaded my country two times." He leaned forward. "You're too young to remember The Great War and what your countrymen did."

"I know what happened. And the faster we refuel," Erik pointed in the direction of the fuel pump, "the faster we can leave."

"I hope all you Germans die," he muttered under his breath.

Erik leaned even closer, stared into the man's intense blue eyes, and whispered in English, "Good thing I'm not German. On a final note, Paris will be liberated on the twenty-fifth of August. Now, turn on the pump."

The old man stared at Erik as if he were a ghost. His fingers trembled as they flipped the switch that turned on the fuel pump's electric generator. The door swung open. Erik turned to look at the soldier coming in.

"Sir…"

"The pump is on, start refueling."

"Yes, Sir." The soldier left and closed the door.

"Are you an American spy?" the old man stuttered.

"No, just an analyst."

"Then how do you know about Paris?"

Erik grabbed a postcard off the counter. "Just say I have an insight." Then he strolled to the door.

"Major," the old man called, getting Erik's attention one last time, "if what you said is true about Paris, you'll be a hero of France."

Erik shook his head and thought he had never seen himself as a hero. "Have a good day."

Erik walked to the Kübelwagen. Men started to climb back in the half-tracks.

"Herr Major," the Lieutenant said, "you're all fueled up, and we're ready to move."

"Thank you, Herr Lieutenant." Erik climbed into the Kübelwagen, turned over the engine and drove off as the half-tracks followed; each had two men stationed by heavy machine guns. "Well at least we have some support from Steel Weather," Erik said.

"That's true." Rommel sighs. "I just hope we don't run into it."

Erik placed the postcard on the dashboard and focused on the road ahead.

"Tell me more about the Phaeton," Rommel said.

Erik rolled his eyes and wished he'd never brought it up. "Isn't there anything else you'd like to talk about?" Erik stared at the Eiffel Tower on the postcard and wondered what Jamie was doing.

7. JAMIE REMEMBERS

"Anyone can catch your eye, but it takes someone special to catch your heart."   —Author Unknown

Washington, D.C.

Jamie sat at her desk in the Records Department, staring at Erik's picture and a postcard of the Eiffel Tower. She picked up the framed black and white photograph of Erik dressed in 1940's attire, standing by a Tucker 48 and rubbed her fingers down the glass, wishing she could feel him. "I love you, babe. Be safe wherever you are," she whispered to herself.

"So Erik wasn't able to take you to Paris?" a voice said from behind her.

Jamie swung around to face her co-worker, Sarah. "No. He had to go on a business trip for the museum. It was a last-minute thing." She wiped her hand across her eyes and sat on the edge of her chair.

Sarah shook her head. "No surprise there." It was not the first time she had heard something similar from Jamie. "How can you stand it? You can do so much better than Erik."

"I won't leave him."

"Why?" Sarah asked in disbelief. "And why not date a guy around your age, someone who can spend more time with you?"

Jamie's gaze blazed with determination. "Because I love him. Obviously! I still remember the first time we met—so handsome and such a gentleman." Jamie crossed her arms.

"You were in college, right?"

Jamie shook her head. "Just before I graduated high school." She paused, remembering the day. "I wanted to date him, but he didn't. So I prayed that one day I'd meet him again, and I did when I was a senior in college."

"How much older is he?

"Thirteen years."

"That's creepy." Sarah looked as if she had a bad taste of heartburn. "He's like, almost double your age!" She pointed to Erik's photo. "He looks like someone from the 1940's. Why not date a guy from the twenty-first century?"

Jamie looked at Erik's photo, shook her head and smiled. "That's why I love him."

"Really? I don't get it."

"He treats me with respect, and he loves me for me."

Sarah shrugged. "Look, I'm just trying to be a friend. I don't like to see you hurt, and I know you can do better than Erik." She raised an eyebrow and gave a cheeky smile. "I know a couple of hot guys who'd love to meet you."

"No. I'm happy with Erik!" Jamie jabbed her finger at Sarah, emphasizing each word. "He's my soul mate, and I don't care what you or anyone else thinks. So don't ever talk bad about the man I love! Okay?"

"Fine. Whatever. Are you ready for dinner?"

"Sure." Jamie and Sarah walked out of their office on the third sub-level of the Pentagon and headed to the elevator. They bustled out of the building, got into Sarah's car, and raced to dinner in rush-hour traffic. While Sarah drove to the restaurant, Jamie told her about her second meeting with Erik three years ago, in 2005 at the National Museum of American History.

"Welcome to the National Museum of American History," the director of the museum said, "I'd like to introduce you to Dr. Függer. He'll be your guide at the museum today." He shook Erik's hand and left him with my history class of seniors from Georgetown University.

I stood in back with some of my friends while my classmates stood passively, most of them trying to stay awake. I, of course, was one of the interested ones. We walked through Transportation Hall, and he pointed out the 1898 Washington, D.C., electric streetcar and Ford Model T and talked about how technology had evolved throughout the decades. I built up my courage, raised my hand and asked how fast the Model T went. He explained that it traveled up to fifteen miles per hour at top speed, but that was pushing it because the cars shook violently at ten miles per hour and the transmission fell out at fifteen miles per hour. Most of my class laughed, but I just stood and admired him.

"Was the Model T used in Europe?" I asked quietly in my sweetest voice. He squinted, having a tough time hearing my question—which was my intention—and he asked me my name and would I please repeat my question. I moved to the front of the crowd and stared into his amazing blue eyes. As soon as our eyes met, I knew he remembered me, but he acted perfectly normal.

"My name is Jamie, and I asked if the Model T was used in Europe."

"No, they had their own cars," he replied with a perfect text-book answer.

"What kind did they use?" I asked, knowing that some in my class were rolling their eyes.

"Mercedes-Benz, to name one."

"Wow!" I shot him a wink, trying to make him fumble on his words. "Did all people drive them?" It didn't work; Erik was a true professional.

"No," he replied. "Only the very wealthy. Taxi companies used horse and buggies, as did most of the population. This was not un-common in 1889, which is when the Eiffel Tower first opened."

I smiled and he grinned back at me. The tour continued, and Erik talked about the other artifacts, but I couldn't keep my eyes off him. I loved the way he made history interesting. My friends tried to break the spell he had on me with nudges and giggles, but I was mesmerized and absorbed everything he said. The tour came to an end, and now free to walk around the museum, the rest of my class scattered. I stayed behind and approached Erik, but the museum director got to him first. I waited while they talked.

"Erik, my old friend," The director said. "Thank you very much for helping me out."

"Not a problem, Alan, really. I enjoyed doing it."

Alan started to walk off, then stopped and turned back. "Do you still report directly to Bonesteiner?"

Erik nodded.

"Tell the admiral thank you for letting you come out on short notice."

"I will."

"Good to see you again. Just like the old days. Thanks again."

Erik waved, then turned to face me. I couldn't stop smiling at him. He looked so amazing in his suit, like something out of a gangster film.

"Hi, Erik," I said before he could say one word, "I see you're still making history interesting, just like the first time we met."

"Thank you."

"You're welcome. Can I ask you a few more questions?" I twirled a strand of hair around my index finger, still smiling.

"Okay," Erik replied, cautiously.

"What's the I.C.? Is that another job you have?"

Erik looked a little taken back. "Ah … Interstate College."

"So you teach history now?"

"From time to time."

"Do you have time to tell me about the Eiffel Tower?" I asked. Erik pulled out his pocket watch, checked the time, and nodded. "That's a neat watch. Can I see it?"

He held it out to me and I stepped closer. I could feel him getting nervous. "So you want to know about the Eiffel Tower?" he asked.

"Mmhmm," I replied, with a seductive look.

"Okay. Imagine you're in Paris on the thirty-first of March, 1889—"

"No. Let's imagine we're both there together." I smiled.

"Okay then, we take a taxi, which was a carriage back then, from the hotel to the World's Fair, where the Eiffel Tower, the 'Three-hundred Metric Tower,' was officially opened." Erik made the sounds of a horse galloping on cobblestone and reached into his pocket. "Once there, I'd ask you how much of a tip you want to give." Erik looked at me and waited for me to respond.

"A good tip."

Erik nodded. "Then I'd pull out twenty-five centime coins for the fair and a ten centime coin for the tip."

"Was that good for back then?"

"Yes, for 1889."

"Please continue."

"In front of you are the flags of all the countries represented at the World's Fair. You look to your right and see a huge globe of the world. On the left, you see a Ferris wheel. We make our way to the Eiffel Tower, along walkways filled with curious, enthusiastic people. Protestors who want the tower removed mingle with the crowd, carrying petitions. Fistfights break out around the tower, and you hear rumors that the French Government thinks it'll cause riots in the streets. Near the tower, we see a line of people waiting to get tickets." Erik stopped and looked at me. I was daydreaming, imagining what it would be like if we were there together during that time period. Erik grinned and continued, saying that we finally get to the cashier, and he asks what level we want to go to.

"The very top!" I replied.

"Then we'll go to the very top. Going to the first floor will cost two francs each; for the second level, it will cost three francs each; and finally, if we go to the very top it will cost five francs each. I pay the attendant and we head to the elevators where we wait once again. Eventually, we get to the very top and look at Paris." Erik finished his story, and all I could do was smile ear to ear.

"That was exciting."

"I'm glad you liked it." Erik grinned back.

"Can I ask a personal question?"

Erik nodded.

I had to know since I hadn't seen him for two years. "Do you have a girlfriend?"

He chuckled a little. "No, I don't."

"Really? Still? Why?" I asked, a little shocked. I thought he would've had one by then, but I was excited to know he wasn't taken.

"Because I work a lot of long and often different hours, and sometimes I have to leave on business trips on short notice. That makes it hard to maintain a stable relationship."

I decided to take a chance. "I know a girl willing to put up with that. And she has been waiting for two years," I said, my heart beating faster at my boldness.

He raised an eyebrow—oh so cute. "Really? Do you now?"

"Yes, I do." I flashed him a fragile smile and invaded his personal space.

He drew back a little but didn't step away. "Who might that be?"

I didn't know if he was playing hard to get or he really couldn't pick up my hints. So I laid it all out for him. "She's standing right in front of you."

"Oh boy," he said under his breath.

"What time do you get off work?" I asked. A friend called my name, breaking the spell somewhat. I did my best to ignore it.

"Eighteen hundred."

"Huh? What's eighteen hundred?"

He shrugged. "Sorry, six o'clock."

"Great, so you can see me cheer tonight."

Erik frowned—a cute confused look. "Excuse me, Jamie? Cheer? What?"

"Yeah, you know, cheerleading?" I said, sounding like I did when I cheered.

Erik tilted his head and raised one eyebrow higher than the other. "I don't think that would be a good idea."

My heart sank, but I wasn't about to give up. "You said that last time we met." I stepped even closer. "But I think it'd be a great idea. I want you to come. I'm inviting you, and I won't take no for an answer."

"No pressure, huh? Why do you want me to see you cheer?"

"Because I think you're cute." I gave him the biggest smile and stared at him, batting my eyes, trying to make it impossible for him to say no.

"Cute. Right. I guess that made all the difference." Erik shook his head and I wished I could tell what he was thinking.

Again my friend yelled my name and got louder as she approached. I had to respond.

"Jamie, we need to go," she said as she started to pull me away. "The bus is leaving in a few minutes." I didn't move. I didn't want to go; I wanted to spend as much time as possible with Erik. "Come on." She yanked on my arm, but before I left I asked Erik, "Are you going to come to the Verizon Center?"

I could see he was thinking about it. "Yes, I'll come."

I nearly squealed with delight, and I felt my heart pounding in my chest. "Great; see you then! By the way, I'll leave you a ticket at the box office. One-Four-Three-Seven!" I waved, then allowed myself to be dragged off to the bus.

The Verizon Center was filled with screaming fans in school colors, cheering on their teams. The players on the basketball court, ignoring the crowd, focused on executing a combination of offensive and defensive maneuvers against their opponents. The rest of the cheerleading squad and I stood by the basketball hoop, just past the end line, cheering on our players and motivating our fans. I looked up and saw Erik standing at the entrance in his three-piece-suit and that amazing fedora hat. He looked around the arena, trying to find his seat. As he walked down the stairs, my eyes met his, and all I could do was smile, wave frantically, and yell his name to get his attention.

One of my fellow cheerleaders leaned toward me. "Who are you yelling at?"

"Him!" I pointed in Erik's direction just as he looked at me. Again I waved; Erik waved back, then found his seat.

"The guy in the hat?"

"Yes! Isn't he handsome? He's smart, too."

"I guess. Who is he?"

"My boyfriend."

The other girls in my squad shook their heads in disbelief and rolled their eyes, all while they continued cheering. But I didn't care what they thought. It was fun seeing Erik watch the game. He seemed to be analyzing it, like an NBA scout. I couldn't stop staring at him.

At halftime, the fans got up to stretch their legs and get refreshments. I saw Erik stroll down the stairs and I raced up to meet him and gave him a big hug.

"Hey, I'm glad you made it."

"Not a problem. Would you like to get something to drink?"

"Yes." I locked arms with Erik as if he were escorting me to my prom, and we headed up the stairs and toward the concession stand. The girls in my squad gave me bewildered looks, but I didn't care.

We exchanged small talk until interrupted by his cell phone. "Excuse me," he said and took the call.

I heard only one side of the conversation.

"Yes…I'm fine, Gary. Are things good with you? Yes, I know about Germany… I can't really talk now, though…because I'm at a basketball game …Yes, I know it's weird, but I was invited…a friend…To be honest with you, I really don't know who's playing."

I cut in. "The Bulldogs and the Bisons."

Erik mouthed *thank you*. "The Bulldogs and the Bisons apparently…I don't know the score …" Erik scanned the stadium, and his gaze settled on the scoreboard. "The Bulldogs are winning thirty-four to twenty-one. Gary, I really need to go…I'll talk to you later…Bye." Erik hung up.

"Who was that?" I asked.

"A friend."

He was vague, so I wanted to know more. "What's happening in Germany?"

"He was asking if I knew about the possible strike at Volkswagen."

I never took him for a news junkie, but I tried to get him to open up. "I drive a Passat. I never heard about the strike."

"I drive a Phaeton, and it's nothing important."

At the refreshment stand, when we reached the counter, I recognized the guy from behind the counter from one of my classes. I ordered. Erik seemed relaxed, though preoccupied.

"Who is this?" the guy asked, looking at Erik, as he handed over our drinks.

"My boyfriend," I said before Erik had a chance to introduce himself.

Erik swung towards me with a frown of confusion. I rubbed his arm to relax him.

"That's cool. I heard a lot about you from Jamie. That'll be seven dollars."

"Here you go." Erik pulled out his wallet and handed over the money. "Your boyfriend?" Erik said as soon as we stepped away, staring at me with his intense blue eyes.

I nodded. "Is that okay?" I paused, waiting for his reaction, not sure if I'd gone too far. "I didn't mean to upset you."

"You didn't; I just would've liked a little warning."

I let off a huge sigh.

People returned to their seats for the second half, and in the middle of a conversation, I suddenly saw a camera view of both of us on the Jumbotron. I yanked on Erik's sleeve and pointed to the screen. It went black, then filled with bright, bold-yellow letters, ERIK AND JAMIE FOREVER. I turned Erik's head to face me and kissed him with all the passion I'd accumulated over the two years since I'd met him. He was as helpless as a fish out of the water, but he didn't take long to respond, and his kiss stimulated me beyond words. It was everything I'd dreamed and more.

After the game, we met up outside and I asked him to go to Pizza Milano with me.

"Jamie, do you really think this is a good idea, for me to go with you?" he asked with that cute frown of his. He seemed scared, but maybe it was a lack of confidence.

"Don't worry, it'll be fine. You're with me."

"Yeah, that's what they said on the Titanic on the 15th of April."

"What?"

"Nothing." He stared at me and took a deep sigh, "Jamie, I'm older than you, a lot older. Doesn't that bother you?"

"No, it doesn't. Do you remember that I wanted to date you two years ago?"

He nodded.

"Well, I'm older now, and I really want to get to know you. I've been waiting two years for you to come into my life again, and I don't care what others think, okay?"

"Okay. I believe you. I just never thought it would happen."

"Us meeting again?"

"Yes."

"Remember when we first met I told you I believed in soul mates?"

Erik nodded again.

"Well, you're my soul mate." I grabbed his hand and squeezed tight, then we walked hand-in-hand to his car. Erik opened my door for me and closed it behind me, then walked around and slid into the driver's seat.

The moment he got in, I reached over and kissed him on the cheek. He turned his head, and I noticed him biting his lower lip, but I was just as nervous. "Where's the pizza place?" he asked.

"L Street Northwest."

He pressed a button on the ceiling and a deep commanding voice said, "This is the major."

"Yeah…uhh…this is Dr. Függer," he said, sounding a little tongue tied. I thought it funny, yet cute.

"Identification," the voice in the speaker said.

Erik flushed and almost winced.

"Your identification," the voice asked again.

"The Saint, department four-six-three," Erik replied.

I winked and blew Erik kisses to see if he would stumble on his words, while he tried to keep his composure.

"Are you on a company line?" the voice asked—a weird question for OnStar.

"No, I'm in my car. I need directions to Pizza Milano."

"Is that On-Star?" I whispered.

Erik placed a finger over his lips. The voice gave detailed directions from our location to Pizza Milano, and Erik wrote them down while I freshened up my makeup.

"There's a local speed trap on New Hampshire Avenue Northwest," the major said. "So watch your speed, Saint."

"Thank you, major."

"Major zero-out."

Erik started his car, backed up, raced out of the parking lot, and headed to the restaurant. I rested my head on his shoulder.

"My mom's car has On-Star, too."

"Uh huh," Erik said like he didn't know what I was talking about.

"You know, how you got the directions."

"Oh yeah." He never looked away from the road, acting as if being asked for identification was completely normal.

"Well, I never heard her On-Star operator ask for her identification," I probed.

"This one's for government employees."

I had a feeling that was only half the answer. "That's cool.

But why does he call himself the major and you call yourself the Saint?"

"I can't answer for him, but as for me, that's my nickname." Then Erik's tone turned defensive. "Jamie, I really don't want to talk about work, please. I'm here to spend my time with you like I promised."

I felt he was hiding something, but I could tell he was being honest with me, at least so far as not wanting to talk about work. "I'm just trying to make conversation," I said.

"I know, but I don't like talking about work when I'm off."

"Are you putting up your wall like the first time we met?"

Erik shook his head, and I stared out the window, wondering what my life would be like with him. A smile came over my face. Erik focused on the road but occasionally glanced at me. I didn't want the night to end. His cell phone suddenly went off. Erik glanced at the caller ID, turned off the ringer and tossed the phone to the floor.

"Don't you need to get that?"

He shook his head.

"Is it work?" I thought it odd, but maybe something had changed since the last time we met.

"Yes." Erik sounded disgusted.

"Alan?"

Erik shook his head and focused on the road again.

"Do you think it's something important?"

"It normally is, but not more important than me spending time with you."

That shocked me—that he thought I was more important. "Really?"

"Yes. I want to get to know you better. Oh look, there's the speed trap."

"Oh my gosh, you're right! My mom's On-Star doesn't give warnings about speed traps."

"Lucky me."

Erik pulled into a parking space on the street, which was filled with cars. People from my college were streaming into the entrance. Erik got out, strolled around the car, and opened my door for me, like a true gentleman, and we walked into the noisy restaurant holding hands. Our basketball team and my squad sat in their usual section of the restaurant and turned to stare when we walked in. The way they tilted their heads and whispered I knew they were talking about us. Erik and I found a table in the corner, then Erik excused himself and walked off, said he'd order. I could honestly say I was beginning to fall in love with him.

Keith, a guy that had wanted to date me ever since high school, walked toward me. I turned away, feeling uneasy. The big asshole thought he was God's gift to women and always had to prove something.

"Hi, Jamie."

I sighed and looked up. Keith—tall blonde, medium-built, and sloppily dressed—hovered over me with his muscular arms crossed against his chest. He scowled down at me with angry brown eyes, then pulled up a chair and sat so close to me that I could smell the alcohol on his breath. He placed his hand on my upper thigh and started to stroke. I grabbed his hand and pushed it away.

"Don't take liberties," I said tersely, then I scanned the room, looking for Erik and hoping he would show up soon.

"Who's that guy with you?" Keith asked.

"That's none of your business." I tried to sound strong, but the hairs on my neck stood up. The other basketball players were watching, and some stood up. I figured they could see the tension between Keith and me.

"Oh, I think it is my business. Who is he?" Keith plonked his paws back on my thigh and started caressing me.

"Keith, stop it!" I shoved his hands away and imbued the words with all the force I could muster, but he ignored me and put them straight back again.

Suddenly, Erik appeared behind Keith. I smiled. There was hope after all. Keith looked around and immediately jumped up and faced Erik. I gulped, noticing that Keith was taller and possibly stronger then Erik.

"Who in the hell are you?" Keith demanded. I winced at the arrogance in his voice. He paused and tilted his head, appraising Erik, "You look vaguely familiar."

I tried to reply. "He's…"

"I didn't ask you, bitch," Keith snapped. Then he poked at Erik's chest with two fingers. "Answer me, asshole." His eyes suddenly brightened. "I remember you."

"You still haven't learned," Erik replied calmly. "I warned you when I first met you. Now show her some respect."

"Fuck you." Keith kept poking Erik.

"No thanks, you're not my type, or did you forget that, too?"

The basketball team and my squad slowly inched their way toward us, the girls giggling.

"You are really beginning to piss me off," Keith growled.

"Good, then I'm doing my job," Erik replied, still cool and calm. "I'm asking you to apologize to Jamie and stop poking me."

"Oh, am I hurting you?" Keith mocked, and the other basketball players chuckled. "I don't need to apologize to you or anyone when I'm about to kick your ass." Keith continued to poke Erik.

I had the horrible feeling that Erik wouldn't stand a chance in a fight against Keith. I wished he had walked away before he got hurt, but Erik was taunting Keith as if he wanted a fight. I wanted to do something but I couldn't move, let alone think what to say.

"Since you haven't changed. I guess you just have to prove how big of an asshole you can be in front of all your peers, hmmm?"

Keith's face turned, his eyes filled with rage, and he balled up his fists, then knocked Erik's fedora off his head. The basketball players and cheerleaders laughed. Yet Erik didn't do anything. I wished he would just walk away now.

"Well, I'm the asshole in your face," Keith snapped.

Then in a flash, without batting an eyelash, Erik grabbed the two fingers Keith was poking him with and pulled them back. The expression in Keith's eyes changed from rage to horror to extreme pain. Erik forced Keith to his knees, while everyone, including myself, looked on in disbelief. Then Erik leaned forward, his eyes narrowed, showing no sign of mercy.

"Since you're a slow learner, I'm going to help you out. I'm going to teach you manners in four quick lessons. Ready to start learning?" Erik said in a sinister tone.

"Kiss my ass," Keith muttered between his gritted teeth.

"Now, that's a negative attitude," Erik mocked. He continued to pull Keith's fingers back, and Keith's face contorted into a grotesque mask. "I said, ready to learn?" Erik said coldly.

"You're going to break my fingers!" Keith whimpered in a strangled voice.

But Erik didn't stop. "I'm glad you paid attention in anatomy class," he said sarcastically, "but we're not learning anatomy. Lesson one: if a lady tells you not to touch her, you listen and stop. Do you understand?" Keith's jaw had gone rigid from fighting the pain, but Erik pulled his fingers back further. "Do you?"

Keith nodded.

"Good. Lesson two: Never! And I do mean never call Jamie a bitch or anything else. Now say you're sorry to her. Clear?"

Keith nodded again. His eyes were watering.

"I didn't hear you say it." Erik's voice became even more intimidating, and his eyes grew more intense. "Say it now!"

Keith turned his head to face me and mumbled, "I'm sorry." Then he turned back to Erik.

Erik's eyes narrowed. "You're learning fast, but we're not done yet. Two more lessons to go. Lesson three is to respect people's property. Now pick up my fedora and put it on the table."

Keith tried to get a few words out but failed.

It appeared Erik could read Keith's lips. "You're not about to disagree with me, are you?" Once again he pulled Keith's fingers back. I heard his knuckles pop. Then Erik jerked his head toward the hat and let one hand go. Keith reached out with his free hand, picked up Erik's hat, and placed it on the table.

Erik's free hand flashed out and grabbed Keith's fingers again before he could do anything else. "Now the final lesson: respect your elders. Is that one clear?"

"Fuck you," Keith growled in one last act of defiance.

Erik gritted his teeth. "No. Fuck you," he whispered, "and next time you touch her they won't be able to identify you with dental records!" Without hesitation, Erik pulled Keith's fingers back so far that they snapped. Keith's eyes widened with hor-ror and moistened with tears, as he cupped his hand and pressed his lips tight, apparently stifling a scream. Then as quickly as he'd grabbed Keith's fingers, Erik released them, and Keith rose slow-ly and, somewhat unsteadily, made for the door, his face livid. The team and squad, looking almost as horror-struck, turned and walked back to their table without a word. Erik glanced back at me, then held out his hand and pulled me close.

"Are you okay?" Erik asked in a soft tone.

I nodded, still in disbelief at what had just happened. I wrapped my arms around Erik and squeezed him tight. "Thank you, babe," I said and placed my head on his chest.

"You're very welcome."

The server brought our food and placed it on the table. Erik motioned that our order would be to go and paid the server.

While we waited for him to return with it in a take-out con-tainer, I had to ask: "Erik, where did you learn to fight?"

"On a farm."

"A farm?"

He nodded.

"Oh, so you were born on a farm?" I never would've figured Erik was a country boy.

"No, I was born in New Jersey."

Now he had me confused. "But you said you learned how to fight on a farm."

"I did. I mean I visited a farm once…in Virginia."

8. A DESCENT INTO HELL

"If you are going to go through hell, keep going."
—Winston Churchill`

"Are you serious that you regret bringing up this topic?" Rommel asked as the car bumped along a battered road.

"Absolutely," Erik said, as he nodded.

"But this car that Porsche is planning on designing sounds amazing. I'd love to know more about it."

Erik took a deep breath and sighed. "Isn't there anything else you'd like to talk about?"

"What do you have in mind?"

"What's your opinion of Adolf Hitler?"

"In the beginning, I had a great respect for the Führer for his tactical mind and his ability to adapt and survive in the political turmoil of post-war Germany. He brought a sense of national unity to Germany, whether you agreed with his methods or not." He pointed at Erik to emphasize. "He brought order from chaos."

Erik tried to get a word in but Rommel continued. "But, of course, this was not meant to last. The man's ego and extreme distrust of his fellow man, coupled with his severe overreach later in the war, revealed his weaknesses and a tendency toward instability."

Erik nodded and absorbed everything he heard. "When did you think the war was lost?"

Rommel sighed and looked suddenly gloomy. "As I watched German defenses begin to crumble."

"Stalingrad? El Alamein?"

Rommel nodded and added, "Also in the weeks that followed the Allied invasion of Normandy. It became clear to me that our situation was in peril. The sheer volume and tenacity of Allied troops, coupled with our tactical overreach on so many fronts, had left so many in doubt."

"Did this make you lose faith in Hitler?"

"It did indeed. This doubt ate away at our morale and confidence in the Führer and reduced us to a fractured people once again. The Führer increasingly withdrew inside himself and was less and less responsive to the suggestions of his general staff."

Erik adjusted himself in his seat. "In your opinion, who's a better general, Montgomery or Patton?"

Rommel rubbed his chin, pondering. "Both men are excellent leaders and fierce competitors. However, I found General Patton to be the better of these two men in combat. This is simply because his eccentricities combined with his dogged tendencies made him an almost feverishly dedicated adversary."

"Would you agree he was unpredictable?"

"No, not entirely unpredictable. He was nonetheless tireless in his pursuit of victory and personal glory."

"What are you going to do after the war if we succeed?"

"First and foremost, I'm a soldier. If I survive this conflict, I'll dedicate myself to rebuilding my country and restoring it to a place of respect in the world. Germany will decide how best I can serve this purpose. A true warrior seeks peace above conflict, and it is this very peace I seek for our people in the end. I will also spend time with my family, which they rightfully deserve."

"BEES!" a voice screamed, cutting Erik and Rommel's conversation short.

Erik looked around bewildered.

Rommel pointed to the sky. "There!" he screamed.

Erik craned his neck upward and saw the silhouettes of four aircraft. He divided his attention between watching the road while the four planes approached quickly. Erik stared with trepidation at each of the aircraft's large "chin" radiators beneath each nose and the rocket rails under each wing.

"Oh, shit!" Erik muttered as he realized they were Hawker Typhoons, ground attack dive-bombers. The faint sound of machine guns that burped in the distance tipped the balance; their escorts prepared for battle; the men ran on instinct. The crew of the quad 20mm anti-aircraft gun scrambled to take their positions and prepared the gun.

"Seven hundred meters … six hundred meters" the range finder's voice strained out the distance of the aircraft.

The vehicles came to a halt, and the panzer grenadiers catapulted over the sides of the SDKFZ 251/1's while they prepared their weapons. Two men remained in the troop compartment of the half-track and positioned themselves behind MG 42 machine guns, located on both ends of the half-tracks. They swiveled and fixed their sights as they looked down the barrels to the approaching Typhoons. Simultaneously, all the machine guns fired into the sky, hoping to hit their targets.

"Five hundred meters…four hundred meters…fire!" The quad 20mm anti-aircraft guns pumped out their shells.

THUMP! THUMP! THUMP! THUMP! THUMP! THUMP! THUMP! THUMP!

The Typhoons, with their aero engines whining, did a tail dive in a line formation with the squadron leader, who had tilted his wings sharply to port. While half turned, the other pilots dove straight into the direction of the German column as they lined up their sights and prepared to fire.

THUMP! THUMP! THUMP! THUMP! THUMP! THUMP! THUMP! THUMP!

Black puffs of smoke from exploding flak littered the sky. Erik's heart felt as if it were going to pound right out of his chest. His throat constricted, and his stomach contracted into a tight ball. The 20mm cannon shells thudded to earth, ripping the ground apart. Their dirt trails inched closer and closer.

"Watch out!" Rommel screamed.

Erik swerved, nearly missing a Sdkfz 251/1 and caused the Kübelwagen to skid violently out of control. He yanked on the wheel, trying to get control of the car while 20mm rounds danced around them. One tore off the driver-side mirror. The Kübelwagen stopped abruptly in a ditch on the side of the road. The roaring of the Typhoons' aero engines drowned out the range finder's orders. Stationed by the quad 20mm anti-aircraft gun, his face suddenly turned pale, a snarl of agony spread over it and blood misted in the air. Erik blinked, horrified to see that the man's left arm was shredded off. With his right hand, he made a futile attempt to stop the bleeding and turned to flee, but cannon shells exploded out of his chest, leaving a wake of blood and flesh in the air. His face darkened with pain. Within minutes, the once powerful quad 20mm anti-aircraft gun was silenced forever; its crew lay disfigured around the gun. Freshly spilled blood coated the gun and the bed of the half-track.

"Get out and take cover!" Erik ordered Rommel.

"What are you planning on doing?!"

"I don't know, I'll think of something!"

"You'll get yourself killed if you go out there!"

"That's what I'm trying to avoid!"

Erik and Rommel leaped out of the Kübelwagen and headed in separate directions. His chest heaved and his legs worked like pistons. Erik ran toward a disabled half-track. A sudden spurt of adrenaline coursed through his veins as he saw the Typhoons, one after another, pulling out of their deadly dive. He knew that each pilot had carefully plotted and fired his missiles in the same approximate location as the other pilots. The missiles launched and released a high-pitched whistling sound. In the near distance, eight missiles, one following another, raced toward their assigned targets in a bombardment of death. Moments later, with a flash of reddish orange flames followed by black smoke, the earth shook violently, forcing Erik backward as if an invisible hand had picked him up and thrown him.

Screams of pain and metal twisting rang in Erik's ears. The Typhoons continued their attack, tearing holes into metal and men as if they were paper. Within seconds, flames started to emerge from disabled vehicles. Small at first, they flickered and grew, and finally consumed the vehicles in fiery cocoons that released midnight-black choking smoke. Erik made a quick dash to the disabled half-track and took a deep breath, realized he was safe—for now. All Erik heard was his heart pounding in his ears and the haunting aero engines of the Typhoons burping blasts of machine gun fire. A hysterical, guttural scream came from behind him, and he smelled the nauseating odor of raw flesh being burnt.

Erik glanced over his shoulder. In the gloom he made out a man engulfed in flames, attempting to crawl out of the half-track. His face and hands were brilliant red and peppered with blossoming white blisters that grew, like balloons being inflated, until they exploded. Instantaneously, his skin turned charcoal black and began to melt off the bones, like wax from a candle. Erik recoiled in horror.

While attempting to stand, Erik saw the Tiger I stranded among the burning vehicles. The tank commander fired wildly at the Typhoons. Without warning, a loud thud followed by a thundering explosion rattled Erik's ears. He gulped for air. The turret of the tank was torn off like a cap on a bottle and landed inverted on the hull. Erik crawled forward on all fours, grabbed an MP-40 off the ground, chambered a round and glanced around to locate the Typhoons. A faint cry for help came from the tank. Erik gritted his teeth and navigated through the debris of metal and corpses as a secondary explosion went off somewhere amongst the disabled half-tracks. The radiant heat waves from the tank forced Erik back, but he fought it and carried on. He saw fingertips trying to slide the tank hatch open and reached up to help, but his fingers jerked back as if he had touched a hot stove. He grabbed the MP-40 and pounded the hatch open with the butt of the gun. A young man attempted to crawl out. He looked as though he were emerging from the pits of hell. His face was blackened from the smoke, uniform torn, and one of his arms was now nothing but raw muscle, and he had a skeleton for a hand. Erik, heart wrenched in sorrow, grabbed the man's other hand and tried to pull him out.

"Push with your legs!" Erik pleaded.

"I'm trying!" The young man whimpered.

Erik freed the man from the tank and fell down with the man on top of him. He took a deep breath and said, "You're out." Erik looked to heaven and thanked God. But the man didn't move. Erik pushed the body off him and saw, to his horror, that the man's legs had been ripped off, one at the kneecap and the other at the upper thigh. His flesh was shredded like torn jeans, and the broken bone was exposed. Erik felt sick to his stomach. He knew this sight would haunt him forever. He turned his eyes away from the gruesome sight and saw Rommel standing by the Kübelwagen. He slowly got up and staggered toward him as the Typhoons disappeared into the horizon.

"Are you okay?" Rommel asked.

"What do you think?" Erik snapped.

"There was nothing you could have done. I've seen this before."

Erik threw the MP-40 on the ground. "I hate this fucking war. Let's end it as soon as we can."

Rommel nodded, looking grim.

Glancing around, Erik saw nothing but death and destruction. Only he and Rommel remained alive. Erik took a deep sigh and thought, *looks like I've been left behind.*

9. LEFT BEHIND

"Don't be afraid of missing opportunities. Behind every fail-
ure is an opportunity someone wishes they had missed."

—Lily Tomlin

CIA Headquarters, Langley, Virginia

Jacques' anger and tension grew. He was hunched over a computer; his eyes sore from the intense focus, and pain crept up his
spine from sitting for too long. He had been trying to access Top
Secret databases that had lists of government operatives.

"Damn it!" he said forcefully, pounding his fists on the desk.
The screen continued to show Access Denied or No Matches
Found. He continued to try different passwords and databases.
The pounding of the keys sounded like a machine gun being fired.
The book Erik gave him lay beside the computer opened at the
photo of Ahriman, who was wearing a black SS Colonel uniform.
Jacques emptied the envelope Erik had sent him. It contained a
security badge from Grid 8, the papers Erik should be using as a
German officer during World War Two, and a letter that said:

ONE is up to something. The question is what.

"My God, what have you gotten yourself involved in now?" Jacques said under his breath.

A shadow fell over him and a deep voice said, "Working late, Jacques?"

Startled, Jacques jumped back in his chair and tried to cover up Erik's letter and envelope. Bonesteiner appeared from behind him. "Yes Sir," Jacques said and got to his feet.

Bonesteiner stared at Jacques and then glanced at the desk. Presumably recognizing Erik's handwriting on the envelope, he said, "So what did he have to say?"

"Excuse me, Sir?"

Bonesteiner took a seat and gave Jacques the don't-play-games-with-me look as he studied Jacques' expression and awaited his answer.

Jacques took his seat, built up his courage and made a bold statement: "Erik believes he was set up, Sir."

"That's a rash statement. What made him think that? Or should I say, what made you think that or ..." Bonesteiner said with emphasis... "both of you think that?"

Jacques handed over the papers and the letter to Bonesteiner, who placed his glasses on his nose and started to read. He chuckled to himself and shook his head in amazement, then asked for the book and looked at the marked page. An envelope dropped out. Bonesteiner flipped it over and saw it was addressed to him.

Jacques leaned over to look. "What is it?"

"He is really something, isn't he?" Bonesteiner stared at Jacques' puzzled face and opened the envelope. "He had to meet some people in my office yesterday. I told them he might know who they were working for, and he did. That resourceful son of a bitch!" He tossed the German officer's documentation on the desk. "These papers would've gotten him in a world of trouble. They're bad forgeries and Erik knew that." Bonesteiner drew the paper from the envelope and studied the marked page carefully. "When did you get this?" He held up the book.

"The day before he left." Jacques paused for a moment. "Erik advised me to pay close attention to the map of Belgium. But I'm not a historian so I wouldn't know what to look for."

Bonesteiner looked at the map. After a moment, a look of realization came over his face. "According to this, Bastogne was occupied by German forces during the Battle of the Bulge, but that didn't happen. At least, not until now." His face twisted in disgust and he pounded his fist on the desk.

"What?" Jacques asked.

"This book has changed." Bonesteiner collected his thoughts. "History has changed …" He flipped through the book. "And not for the better."

"They? Who? What?"

Bonesteiner raised a finger. "They said Ahriman was going to assist Erik. But I think Ahriman had other orders." Bonesteiner stared directly at Jacques. "Are you trying to find Ahriman in the databases?" Jacques nodded. "You won't find him. He works for the Phoenix Group."

"What's the Phoenix Group?"

"In short, they're assassins."

Jacques grimaced and nodded slowly.

Bonesteiner continued. "The chief aspect of the Phoenix Group is to collect intelligence and information on those individuals who the United States government sees as a threat to national security. Then, without getting approval from the Senate Oversight Committee or the President, they infiltrate and capture, using terrorism-like methods, torture and/or assassinate their target."

"What's their jurisdiction?"

"Both domestic and international."

"Did they send Ahriman to kill Erik?"

"It appears that way. They're going to send him back in time."

"Back in time?" Jacques' frown deepened.

Bonesteiner nodded.

"So you're saying Erik is back in time? When?"

Bonesteiner continued to nod. "1944."

"1944? I didn't know it existed or that we had the technology for it."

"People thought that about the Manhattan Project and Project Rainbow, too." Bonesteiner removed his glasses and rubbed his eyes. "It's been in operation since 1943."

Jacques shook his head in amazement. "But why would they want Erik out of the picture? He's just an analyst."

"True, but for some reason, they consider him a threat. The reason is still unclear to me." He adjusted his glasses. "I found it interesting that Admiral Cole had an interest in Erik's historical theory." Bonesteiner pondered for a moment. "Maybe he had an interest in Erik even before."

"Has he set him up to fail?"

"It does seem possible." Bonesteiner took a deep, long sigh. "But he stacked the deck against him, hoping he would fail on his own accord. Looks like they sent Ahriman, and maybe another one, just to make sure."

"Why would they want him dead?"

"He's very resourceful and has a habit of finding out things people don't want anyone to know. On top of that, he questions authority too much. Those two things make him a threat. ONE and the Phoenix Group don't like individuals like that."

"Who's ONE?"

"That's a topic for another discussion."

Jacques paused for a moment, then decided to let that one go—for now. "Okay, what can we do to help Erik? We can't let ONE or the Phoenix Group kill one of our own."

Bonesteiner nodded but said nothing, just sat there and looked grim.

"So what? There's nothing we can do? He's on his own, right?" Jacques came to a realization. "If they send Ahriman to kill Erik, he won't have a chance."

Bonesteiner turned to Jacques. "You don't know what Erik did for the first five years when he joined the agency do you?" Jacques shook his head. "He was a Paramilitary Operations Officer." Bonesteiner looked closely at the ID from Grid Eight. "How he was able to get this, I don't know, but Plackett and Cole know nothing of his training or what Erik is capable of."

"How can you be so sure?"

Bonesteiner held up the envelope addressed to him. "Because once Cole sees this, he'll realize he underestimated Erik."

"But we can't just leave him."

"You're right. We don't leave any of ours behind." Bonesteiner got up and looked at the ID to Grid Eight again. "Maybe there is something we can do. Let's talk in the car. But first I need to pick up a *2008 Edition of World War Two for Morons*."

10. UNWELCOMED GUESTS

"When you travel, remember that a foreign country is not designed to make you comfortable. It is designed to make its own people comfortable."

—Clifton Fadiman

Audrieu, France

Trees with branches shaped like Neptune's forks lined both sides of the driveway. The smell of their paradise-green leaves reminded Erik of freshly-pressed laundry. The sun's warmth gave way to dusk as they drove through the ornamental gate, and the gray walls and sloped roof of the château appeared smooth in the waning light. Erik noticed that a low stone wall surrounded the château. He knew he might be walking into an ambush and looked for places where attackers would hide. He didn't doubt they would kill him on sight. His palms became clammy, and he clasped and unclasped the steering wheel.

"Is your contact here?" Rommel asked as he scrutinized Erik's face.

Erik shrugged and again glanced at his surroundings. "He should be."

Several disturbing clicks of guns being loaded were audible as Erik focused on the sound of the low hum of the car.

"Maybe he's running late," Erik added, little above a whisper.

Suddenly, voices thick with insinuation yelled, "*Arretez la voiture*! Stop the car!" And again, over and over. "*Maintenant*! Now!"

Two dozen well-armed members of the French Resistance climbed over the walls, their eyes smoldering and faces red from shouting. They swarmed the Kübelwagen like piranhas attacking their prey. Erik stopped the car. Rommel's lips curled with disgust. He turned to Erik; his good eye simmered with a mixture of incredulity and betrayal.

"*Mettez vos mains*! Put your hands up!" The loading of rounds into the barrels of MP-40s reinforced the order, and members of the French Resistance inched forward slowly. "*Faites la maintenant ou mourir*! Do it now or die!" Erik and Rommel placed their hands up. "*Sortez de la voiture maintenant*! Get out of the car now!"

Erik cautiously reached for the door handle, opened the door, and slowly inched out. Rommel followed his lead and made no sudden movements. Erik stared at the numerous rifles and sub-machine gun barrels pointed in his direction and slowly lifted his hand and interlocked his fingers with his other hand on top of his head. He recalled the first lesson had learned on the farm—*never get caught*—and concluded that he probably now faced one of the following, or all three: severely beaten, tortured, and possibly killed. He knew that the French Resistance didn't keep German soldiers, much less officers, alive.

Standing tall, Erik stared into the blazing, murderous eyes of the men near him. Their faces were swollen with resentment. Two burly men, one with a sack, maneuvered deftly around those with guns. One thrust his fist into Erik's gut, knocked his breath from his lungs, and Erik fell to his knees. The sack was positioned over his head, enveloping him in darkness. Erik's fingers were squeezed like a wet sponge and forced up while someone removed his Luger from his holster. Then they dragged him off like a tired dog on a leash. He heard Rommel being taken in a different direction. Someone would be waiting to interrogate them, and he didn't doubt that they'd do anything to make them talk. Erik knew one thing for certain: his captors had no idea of the man they had in their possession or that he knew history and what was going to happen. He planned to use that to his advantage.

The warm summer air slowly transitioned into a damp, humid atmosphere. The musty odor of rotten hay and animal feces breached the sack and filled Erik's nostrils. He figured from the smell that he was in a horse stable. He prepared himself for the worst, took a deep breath and slowly exhaled. Then he cleared his head and recalled his knowledge of the French Resistance. CIA training taught him to deal with being interrogated. He felt slightly disoriented from the attack and might very well have to get used to sleep deprivation and isolation. Getting over the hurdle of questions is not so much the problem, but the uncertainty of not knowing how long he had until they put a gun to his head and pulled the trigger was definitely problematic. Erik was pushed and forced to sit on a hard chair. His hands were pulled behind his back, and the coarse rope was wrapped around his wrists and pulled tight, which caused a sharp pain in his wrists.

"Quel est votre nom?" A deep, calm voice asked in a demanding tone.

"I don't speak French," Erik replied in English.

Erik smelled cigarette smoke and heard the owner of the voice suck in a long breath, presumably taking a drag from his cigarette. "What's your name?"

"Erik Függer."

The voice drew closer. "I want you to be aware of the severity of the situation you are in."

Erik felt and smelled his interrogator's breath, which reeked of an acid mix of cigarettes and coffee. The sound of hay cracked underneath the man's feet that told Erik that the interrogator walked to his other side. "It's important that if you want to leave here unharmed, much less alive, you have to be completely honest with me."

Erik nodded. "I understand." He heard the interrogator walking away, followed by the scrape of a chair and the sound of a body settling on a seat. Suddenly, the sack was removed, and Erik sucked in a welcomed breath. His eyes slowly adjusted to the dimly lit, airless room and confirmed his assessment of his whereabouts. The clear-span construction stable had a gable roof and stalls with hinged doors, but no horses. A stocky man sat in front of Erik. The light from a single kerosene lantern exposed his bullish bloodshot eyes. Behind the interrogator stood two solid individuals with muscular arms, holding MP-40s. On the wall behind them, there was a battered map of Northern France with military tactical symbols indicating size and type of unit. Small pins with flags—apparently red for German and blue for allied—extended from the symbols. Beside the map was a flow chart of the German leadership in France with both names and photographs; some had a red X marked on them. Erik recognized most of the officers on the chart. Out of the corner of his eye, he saw two solidly built figures that hovered behind him. He looked forward and into the eyes of the interrogator.

The interrogator raised one eyebrow in a questioning slant, and, exhaling smoke, observed, "You speak very good English for a German officer."

Erik nodded.

"Are you working for the Nazis?" The interrogator leaned forward. "Or are you a spy?" He leaned back again.

"I'm a field operative with the OSS."

He folded his arms across his chest and gawked. "I see," he said with a you-don't-really-expect-me-to-believe-that tone. "What are you doing in this part of France? We're normally aware of any operations." The interrogator leaned forward, his aristocratic face emerging from the darkness. He had a round chin and shrewd-looking eyes and studied Erik's features with a bewildered expression. "Strange, that in this case, we're not," he replied in a biting tone. "You care to explain yourself?" He squared off his shoulders, took a drag of his cigarette and waited for Erik's answer.

"My mission is to take Field Marshal Rommel to General Bradley's headquarters in Rennes."

"The American General Omar Bradley?" The interrogator scoffed as if the idea were preposterous.

Erik nodded again.

"Now that is a lofty goal," he said with a condescending grin, then gave a mocking chuckle.

Erik stared at him impassively.

The interrogator got up, strolled by Erik and blew smoke in his face. "I was not aware the field marshal was located in this area of France." His tone turned serious and he squinted his eyes. "Why would he trust you?"

Erik, having insight into the interrogator's body language, replied with a sardonic grin, "In the OSS we have ways of persuading people to see our point of view."

The interrogator rubbed his chin, and a grin of rapport appeared.

Erik's eyes narrowed. He sat sphinxlike and refused to let the interrogator intimidate him. "Are you afraid? We in the OSS had this encounter with you planned before our meeting with General Bradley." The interrogator opened his mouth to try to get a word out, but Erik continued before the man could draw a breath. "Reach into my right tunic pocket and pull out the paper."

The interrogator motioned for someone behind Erik to retrieve the paper. With his elbow against Erik's neck, the man pulled out the paper and placed it on the table. The interrogator quickly unfolded it and studied it. "What's the significance of this?"

"Those are the individuals who were to be a part of the provisional government if Hitler died."

"You mean the failed attempt to kill him?"

"Exactly. Since the plot failed, I'm to get Rommel to General Bradley's headquarters so we can end this war."

The interrogator's gaze bounced back and forth from the paper to Erik.

"If you don't release Field Marshal Rommel and me, you and

you alone will be responsible for the failure of the Allied campaign of occupied France."

The interrogator pointed an accusatory finger at Erik. "I hope you are who you say you are." Then he leaned forward with his hand on the table. "We will have to confirm it." He got up, strolled away from the table, then looked at Erik out of the corner of his eye, and asked, "What is France's favorite composition?"

"Beethoven's Fifth Symphony," Erik said without hesitation, knowing that the first three notes of the symphony were similar to the Morse Code for V, V for victory and that BBC radio played it on June fifth, 1944 so the French resistance would know the invasion was coming.

The interrogator tossed the paper on the table and motioned to the man behind Erik. Erik's hands were untied. "Coffee?" The interrogator asked, his voice suddenly pleasant as he gave his cigarette a final draw, then killed it on the table.

"Thank you."

"While you are here," the interrogator said, "you will be escorted everywhere you go."

"Do you mind if I get my map out of the Kübelwagen so we can plan my journey to Rennes?" Erik said. "I don't think I need an escort for that."

The interrogator nodded. "Agreed. The car is right out that door," he made his next point clear, by squinting his eyes with his arms crossed. "If you try anything or leave, I assure you, you and Rommel will die."

One of the men entered the room with a tray covered in steaming mugs. He served the coffee and motioned Erik to get his map.

Coffee in hand, Erik walked out of the stables and strolled toward the gravel driveway. If he was being escorted, his tail was staying well out of sight. As his eyes adjusted to the brightness, he contemplated what Jamie was doing at this very moment and wondered if she was thinking of him. The smell of sweet wildflowers drifted under his nose. He glanced up; boundless puffy white clouds floated in the sky, and birds chirped gaily in a nearby tree.

Suddenly, a chill ran up Erik's spine, just like it had back in the hospital when the man in the black SS colonel's uniform had turned up. He faced front and found himself staring into a 9mm Luger pointed directly at him by the same sinister-looking individual. The Colonel peered contemptuously at Erik with cold blue-grayish, shark-like eyes. A lump appeared in Erik's throat, and he approached with caution. The man studied Erik, apparently taking a quick inventory. Erik noticed his gaze register the coffee in Erik's right hand. No doubt, he noted it as Erik's dominant hand.

Erik stopped. "Are you the one who's supposed to help me get to General Bradley's Headquarters?"

"Isn't that obvious?" the Colonel replied venomously.

"With that Luger pointed at me, I have my doubts." Erik analyzed the situation, and he felt the Colonel's eyes examining him carefully. He guessed that since the Colonel held the Luger with his right hand, he was right handed also. Erik knew nothing about his opponent, except that, by the man's physical appearance, he could inflict serious damage. Slowly, Erik closed the distance between them, tightening his grip on his coffee mug handle. "You are aware the French resistance is in the château right now," Erik said.

The Colonel shrugged slightly as if the news was of no consequence.

"They almost killed me," Erik continued, "and they are especially not going to like you, much less trust you, since you're wearing an SS uniform."

His eyes sharpened. "The resistance is of little concern. As for you, Dr. Függer," the Colonel continued with an edge of impatience in his voice, "this will be over quickly, and I'll leave as quickly as I came in."

"So you know my name, and you were at the hospital?"

The Colonel nodded impassively.

"What's yours?"

The man said nothing, his expression blank.

Erik jerked the mug that tossed the scalding coffee into the Colonel's face, at the same time he side-stepped to the left, out of the path of the Luger. The man squinted and shielded his face with his left hand, while squeezing off a round, barely missing Erik. Moving swiftly, Erik turned his back to the Colonel's front while he used his left hand to grab the side of the gun to control the barrel. Then he used his right hand to control the Colonel's right arm into an arm-bar-position causing extreme hyperextension, which caused him to drop the Luger. Erik immediately kicked it away. Seizing the opportunity, Erik continued his attack and smashed his left forearm into the Colonel's neck. The Colonel cringed from the force of the impact.

Reacting as trained, the Colonel exhaled sharply to control his pain, then without warning, he executed a solid hook to Erik's right rib cage, knocking the wind out of him, causing several ribs to crack. Erik, in a brief state of disorientation, released the Colonel's right hand, and they both stepped back, putting distance between them. The Colonel shook his head and took a deep breath through his nose. His eyes turned even colder, and the men squared off in a fighting stance.

"You'll be sorry you did that, bookworm," he said, his mouth crimped in annoyance.

Erik took a deep breath, and a sharp pain lanced through him from his cracked ribs, but he didn't let it show. "Don't you care about the peace treaty?" he demanded and tried to make sense of the man's motives. "Do you understand the opportunity we have here if we take Rommel to Bradley's headquarters?"

The Colonel gave a blank stare. "I have my orders, just like you." An evil smirk came over his face. "But I came prepared. In a manner of speaking, soon the trouble of this war will be left behind you."

"Are you interested in ending this war?" Erik studied the Colonel's posture and dropped into a crouched position, while slowly moving to his left in preparation for the next attack.

"You surprise me; you still don't have a clue." The Colonel shook his head in disbelief. "Peace is no concern of mine. I'm simply following my orders."

With a sinking feeling, Erik realized that the Colonel was an assassin and could be with the Phoenix Group and this would be a fight to the death. So he took a gamble and replied. "You're with Phoenix Group, part of ONE."

The Colonel grinned and nodded. "I was born in the flames of hell and baptized in human blood. I'm the nightmare the devil dreams about."

Aimed to confuse Erik, the assassin jerked his head to fake a change in direction, then closed the distance between them and threw a combination of punches at Erik's face. Erik blocked with his hands. The assassin performed a swiping push kick that caused Erik to fold and stumble back. An explosion of pain hit his right knee, and a snarl of agony spread over his face. He grinded his teeth against the pain.

The assassin advanced and threw a punch toward Erik's face, but he blocked it. In the corner of his eye, Erik saw the assassin's oncoming attack and did a low squat to avoid the Colonel's right hook. Erik's mind was focused on his next attack. He knew exactly what he had to do, and how to do it, and he was glad that the moment of his attack had come. Before the assassin could re-position himself, Erik countered with all his strength, and threw a solid jab to the assassin's bladder. A spasm and a look of confusion crossed the assassin's pale face and it caused him to buckle over. Next, Erik launched an explosive uppercut to the assassin's chin as he leaped up. Clearly, he never believed Erik was capable of getting the better of him. He backed up, giving Erik enough time to get to his feet. Again, they distanced themselves from each other and squared off in a fighting stance.

"You're competent for an analyst, unlike the other two before you. I believe their names were Knight and Mulder," the assassin said coldly.

"I try," Erik said boldly. "But I thought you'd be better."

The assassin launched a Blitzkrieg attack, quickly throwing a fist as a decoy while delivering a front-snap-kick, which caused Erik's left patella to dislocate upward. A sickening wave of pain rushed through Erik; he cried out in pain and fell to the ground with tears in his eyes. The assassin strolled over, pulled out his SS dagger, and prepared to complete his mission. He looked at Erik as one would a cockroach needing to be stepped on. "Are you going to give up now?"

Erik shook his head.

"You're only prolonging the inevitable," the assassin said. "There's no need for you to suffer. Like your girlfriend, you can enjoy a swift death."

The assassin's words hit Erik like a punch to his gut. His anger built to rage, and his nails dug into his palms. "You bastard!" He shouted. "Why? She had nothing to do with this!"

"You can ask her yourself in the afterlife. Are you ready to meet your woman now, analyst?"

Erik reached into his pocket, grasped the Cross pen Jamie had given him, and slowly pulled it out, while waiting for the assassin to come closer. Then, when in striking distance, Erik screamed in hatred and stabbed the assassin's left Achilles tendon, which caused the man's eyes to bulge from their sockets. He cried out from the pain and dropped his dagger. The assassin's veins in his neck stood out in livid ridges as he picked up Erik and threw him against the Kübelwagen. Erik lost his breath for a second, and the assassin fell back, pulled out the pen, and went to retrieve the dagger.

Erik scanned his surroundings, evaluated what he could use to defend himself, and noticed the MP-44 in the back of the Kübelwagen. The assassin picked up the dagger. While he kept one eye on his foe, Erik reached in the backseat, grabbed the MP-44, and got it in firing position. The assassin prepared to throw the dagger. Then he saw that Erik had already chambered a round in the gun and looked down the sights at him. The Colonel's face was deathly pale, and perspiration was dripping off his chin and he looked intently into Erik's cold, blue, murderous eyes. He suddenly understood and waited, almost fearfully, for the terrible punishment that he was about to receive.

"Surprise, you son of a bitch!" Erik squeezed the trigger, released rounds into the assassin's body, and turned it into Swiss cheese. When the firing stopped, the assassin's body lay on the ground; blood trickled out of the open wounds and slowly penetrated the soil. Erik took shallow breaths because of his cracked ribs, and, in extreme pain, leaned against the Kübelwagen for support. Members of the French Resistance came running from all directions.

"What the hell have you done?" asked the interrogator, as he stared at the assassin's lifeless body and then back at Erik. "You've sealed our fates!"

Erik quickly defused the situation. "You have nothing to worry about."

"You killed an SS colonel!"

"Because he was after me! Not you! Lastly, he was an American like me."

The interrogator walked up to Erik, his eyes red. "How are you so sure?"

"Because if he wanted all of us dead, he would've called for reinforcements, and they'd already be here."

"You walk a thin line," the interrogator whispered. His eyes narrowed. "I don't trust you, but you have me in an awkward position."

Erik nodded, his eyes strained from his injuries. "Neither do the individuals who sent me here," Erik replied, thinking of Cole and Plackett.

"I can see why. You leave in the morning and never come back here."

Erik nodded.

"Are you injured?" He motioned two men forward.

"My left knee is dislocated, right knee bruised and several ribs cracked on the right side."

"I'll make sure you're taken care of, but you leave tomorrow at first light."

11. SECRETS REVEALED

"Secrets are made to be found out with time."
—Charles Sanford

Washington, D.C.

Jamie rollerbladed in perfect form, gliding like a figure skater on the ice, while she listened to her IPOD. A song came on that reminded her of the day she had taught Erik how to rollerblade. The memory brought a smile, and she wondered what he was doing at this very minute; maybe convincing someone how important history is. She hoped she would get a call or text message from him, but she would have loved to hold him in her arms and kiss him. A glance at her watch told her that she had to get back and get ready for dinner. She rolled out of the park just as a silver Audi A6 pulled up to the curb; the passenger's tinted window slid down and she heard a familiar voice.

"Jamie, we need to talk," Jacques said as he opened the door.

"Hi, Jacques; what's wrong?"

He sighed deeply. "It's about Erik." He motioned her to get in. Once she was seated, he drove toward their residence.

Jamie's palms started to sweat. Jacques' behavior had made her uneasy. "Is anything wrong with Erik?"

He glanced in the rearview mirror, then gave her a blank stare.

"Is he okay?" she said, as a lump formed in her throat.

Jacques squared off his shoulders and said in a tight voice, "Just be quiet and listen to me."

Jamie nodded. Her heart was sinking fast.

"I think he is…"

"What?" She shook her head, not wanting to hear. "No, he can't be. Is he dead?" Her eyes began to water.

"No, he's not…dead…Let me finish! This isn't easy to explain. And it's not something I should even be telling you, but …" He turned to face Jamie, and he saw her pale reflection in the polarized lenses of his aviators. "I believe the people who sent him on his business trip want him dead."

"The museum?"

He shook his head.

"Alan?"

Again he shook his head.

"Then who? Why do they, whoever they are, want him dead?"

"I don't know why, but once we get to your place you need to pack lightly and bring a few personal things."

"Why? Jacques, where is he?" she demanded. "Why do I need to pack?" She stuck her hands on her hips and jutted out her chin.

He shook his head and looked as if he didn't expect her to believe him. "The real question is what year is he in?"

"What year he's in?" Jamie said in confusion. She shot Jacques a look of annoyance. "Okay, you can stop with the games now."

Jacques removed his aviators and looked at her with narrowed eyes. "Jamie, this is going to be hard for you to understand, but Erik is in France—in 1944. And I'm not playing games. It's the truth. That's where he is, and when he is."

Jamie gasped. Jacques' voice left her in no doubt that he was dead serious. Her mouth opened but she couldn't find words to express and the mixture of shock, disbelief, and anxiety that was crashing through her in waves.

"I don't know how or why." Jacques continued. "All I know is that he's in trouble and we need *your* help to help *him*."

"Me?" Jamie squeaked.

Jacques nodded. "And there's another thing."

Jamie stared out the front window and tried to process the information. *1944?* Her stomach fluttered and she gripped one hand in the other.

Jacques took a deep breath and exhaled slowly. Jamie glanced at his face. Jacques looked as though he were forcing himself to speak. "Erik doesn't work for the museum; he works for the CIA."

Jamie's eyes bugged out. "What? He lied to me? I can't believe this. Any of it!"

"Jamie, let me explain…"

Jamie folded her arms defensively across her chest. "There's nothing to explain. I thought he was different, but apparently, he's just like every other guy out there—a liar."

Jacques pointed an accusing finger at her. "Damn it, Jamie," he snapped, "don't assume what you don't know! One …" Jacques held up one finger. "He did it to protect you." He held up a second finger. "Two: I don't know if you know this, but he has a lot of enemies." He held up a third finger. "Those enemies, if they knew what he really did, would kill him." He held up the fourth finger. "I also know he loves you very much, and he doesn't want to see you get hurt."

Jamie pursed her lips, but Jacques made his point well. "Enemies?"

Jacques nodded.

"Like who?"

"President Putin of Russia and King Abdullah of Saudi Arabia, just to name a few."

Jamie's jaw dropped. *Powerful enemies!*

Jacques pulled into the Kennedy Warren parking garage. "And I'm sure there are others in this great world of ours." He parked the car and stared at her. "He even has enemies within Washington and in the intelligence community."

"Why? Why does he have so many enemies?"

Jacques shrugged. "You'll need to ask him. If he's willing to share with you, but I wouldn't be surprised if he doesn't. Don't forget who his employer is, though. That should explain a lot."

Jamie sighed. "How long have you known Erik?"

A grin lightened Jacques' face. "High school." He slipped on his aviators. "He was a weird character then and still is, but I love him like a brother because of it. He's my best friend and I'm going to miss him."

"So is he all alone in 1944?"

"I'm afraid so, but from what I was told, he's used to that because of what he did with the agency when he joined."

"What did he do?"

Jacques shook his head.

"Tell me."

"I can't. I wasn't supposed to tell you any of this." He handed Jamie a small sheet of paper. "When you see him, give him this."

"I'm going to *see* him?" Jamie's voice raised.

"Don't you want to?"

"Of course, but … 1944?" Her mind reeled. Not only had Erik traveled back in time, it seemed as if she were going, too. She pinched herself, just to make sure. It hurt. "How do I get there?"

"Safely, if I can manage it." Jacques got out of the car and scanned the surroundings, looking for anything out of place, while Jamie got out and rollerbladed to the elevator.

Jacques walked by her car and suddenly sprinted to the door, closing it behind him. He joined her in the elevator and cursed beneath his breath. "I can't believe they'd do that," he muttered.

"Do what? What's the matter?" she asked.

He exhaled forcefully. "Is there another way out of here?"

"A back door into the lane. Why?"

"That's the way, we're leaving."

"Why?"

He turned to look at her. "There's a bomb in your car."

Jamie's jaw dropped. "Oh my God." The terrible reality of the nature of Erik's employment struck her like a slap, and her heart rate soared.

The elevator stopped. Jamie glided to the apartment door and unlocked it.

"Let me go first," Jacques said and motioned her to stand back.

Jamie stepped inside, sat on the chair by the door and yanked off her roller blades while he did a quick search of the apartment. After Jacques checked all the rooms, he came back and locked the door. She stared at him with wide eyes, aware that her life suddenly resembled a spy movie.

He crouched on one knee before her and looked directly into her eyes. "Listen to me very carefully, Jamie. Do not leave the apartment or even open the door for anyone, and I mean anyone."

She nodded, biting her lip.

"As I said before," he added, "pack a few personal things, and I'll be back soon." He stood and gave her a smile that she figured was supposed to look reassuring. It failed. "Do you have prior engagements?"

Jamie glanced at her watch. "I'm meeting Sarah, a friend from work, for dinner in forty minutes."

He shook his head. "Don't even call, text her, or reply to any of her messages. Understood?"

Jamie nodded. "What are you going to do?"

"Shift my car into the alley and make a telephone call."

"What about the bomb?"

"I figure it's set to go off after you start your car. I need to get you away from here as soon as possible."

Jamie nodded. "Will Erik be okay?"

"Yeah, he'll be just fine. I only hope he doesn't piss anyone off."

"Does he really do that?"

Jacques snorted. "Let me put it this way—you either like him or you hate his guts. There's no gray when it comes to Erik."

Jamie shook her head. "This is a lot to take in." She wrung her hands on her lap.

"Don't worry. You can do it." Jacques patted her shoulder. "I'll be back in half an hour, keep the door locked, and don't answer it for anyone."

"Sure. I can do that." Jamie said.

"See you soon." Jacques left, closing the door with Jamie locking the door behind him.

Jamie glanced around the living room and wondered how Erik could be so good at hiding who he worked for. At least now she knew why he never talked about his work.

She raced into the bedroom and opened the closet and looked for a suitable overnight bag—not the one with wheels; for sure they didn't have them back then. She found an old leather suitcase that Erik had picked up from a trash and treasure sale and threw in some basic necessities and enough underwear for a couple of days. She also slipped out of her jeans and into a retro dress that Erik liked. She thought it was from the 1940s, and the tweed jacket with the nipped-in waist that she shrugged on over the top completed the style. A pair of classic black flats finished the outfit, and she switched her wallet and the things in her purse to an old leather one her grandmother owned. She left her credit cards and anything else they wouldn't have had in 1944 and hoped that Jacques had sorted out details like money. Then she clicked the suitcase closed and looked at the clock. It told her that she had packed in ten minutes.

"You go, girl," she murmured and resisted the temptation to start thinking about what she had packed. She had better things to do than second guess the contents of the suitcase.

She strolled to Erik's office and took a closer look at the photographs on the wall. She had never paid them any attention before. Her eyes widened with surprise, and her face glazed in disbelief. How did she not notice these before? There were pictures of Erik inside the National Museum of American History, standing by the evilest men of the world—King Abdullah of Saudi Arabia, Gurbanguly Berdymuhammedov of Turkmenistan, and Vladimir Putin. Other photos displayed him with leaders such as President Horst Köhler of Germany and Prime Minister Gordon Brown of England. She walked around the office like a kid in a candy store and sat behind his desk and wondered how Erik was able to get so close to those people and what he could've been doing in those countries.

Jamie's feet felt something odd beneath the desk. She glanced down and noticed that a square had been cut in the carpet. She squatted down and lifted the patch of carpet and revealed a hidden safe buried in the floor. She glanced around, trying to figure out where Erik would hide the key. She looked up, down, over things and even under things, but found nothing.

With a sigh, she sat again and searched his desk for hiding spots. The framed photograph of her caught her attention but dismantling it revealed nothing. Jamie drummed her fingers on the desk and absently ran her finger over the computer tower. Without meaning to, she pushed the CD eject button, and the CD tray slid out. A crafty grin came over her face at the sight of the key that rested on the tray. She snatched it up, got down on her hands and knees and tried it in the safe. It fit, and with a turn of her wrist, the door opened. She reached in and pulled out Erik's Heckler & Koch MK 23, two spare magazines, and finally his CIA ID.

"Wow. It really is true." She placed the articles from the safe on Erik's desk, then walked to the closet door and tried to open it. No luck; it was locked. She turned around, pulled the pistol out of the holster, and smashed the doorknob with the grip. Slowly the lock in the doorknob released, and the door crept open.

"Double wow!" Jamie exclaimed, as she stared in disbelief at the military uniforms that filled the closet. She flicked through them and realized that they were from different countries—Russia, Germany, and even one from the US Navy. Frames poked out from the shelf above the uniforms, and one-by-one Jamie pulled them out.

"Triple wow!" She shook her head in amazement at the medals they contained. The first was a HOSTILE ACTION SERVICE MEDAL; next was an INTELLIGENCE COMMENDATION MEDAL, and finally a DISTINGUISHED INTELLIGENCE MEDAL. Each had the signature of the Director of the Central Intelligence Agency and the President of the United States.

Jamie went to the computer, signed in and googled CIA MEDALS. She found the information and read:

HOSTILE ACTION SERVICE MEDAL: For direct exposure to a specific life-threatening incident in the foreign field, or in the U.S., where the employee was in close proximity to death or injury, but survived and sustained no injuries. The incident must have occurred during work-related activities or events, which were targeted by armed forces or persons unfriendly to the U.S. Government[8].

INTELLIGENCE COMMENDATION MEDAL: For the performance of especially commendable service or for an act

---

8. Central Intelligence Agency. https://www.cia.gov/library/publications/additional-publications/the-work-of-a-nation/items-of-interest/medals-of-the-cia.html, n.d. December 2011

or achievement significantly above normal duties which resulted in an important contribution to the mission of the Agency[9].

DISTINGUISHED INTELLIGENCE MEDAL: For performance of outstanding services or for achievement of a distinctly exceptional nature in a duty or responsibility, the results of which constitute a major contribution to the mission of the Agency[10].

Tears filled Jamie's eyes. She loved him so much that her heart ached, and she couldn't wait to see him, even if she had to go back to 1944 to do it. Erik's fedora sat on his chest of drawers; she plonked it on her head and discovered that Erik's cell phone was sitting underneath it. Unable to stem her curiosity, Jamie powered it up and tried to guess the code to access his numbers. She tried his birthday—failed. Her birthday—failed. Their anniversary—failed. She racked her brain, trying to come up with a four-digit combination. His lucky number—failed. Then she smiled, remembered, and pressed one-four-three-seven. She was in.

Erik had missed several text messages in different languages and several calls. Jamie scrolled down his stored numbers. She gasped and her eyes widened. They're like something out of a movie. DIA, 703-695-0071, DMA, 703-545-6700, NSA, 240-295-2270, NATIONAL SECURITY COUNCIL 202-395-

---

9. Central Intelligence Agency. https://www.cia.gov/library/publications/additional-publications/the-work-of-a-nation/items-of-interest/medals-of-the-cia.html, n.d. December 2011
10. Central Intelligence Agency. https://www.cia.gov/library/publications/additional-publications/the-work-of-a-nation/items-of-interest/medals-of-the-cia.html, n.d. December 2011

3000, and other numbers. A knock made her jump. She dashed to the door, looked through the peephole, and saw Jacques.

Jamie opened the door. "I'm nearly ready."

Jacques saw Erik's cell phone and held out a hand. "I'll take that."

She dropped it into his hand.

"You look the part," he said. "We have a uniform for you, but what you're wearing can go in your suitcase if it'll fit."

"It will."

Jacques smiled as if he were proud of her; then he glanced at his watch. "Damn! That took longer than I expected. Come on, it's time to go."

Jamie raced back into the bedroom, grabbed her suitcase and shoulder bag and returned to the door. Her heart was already pounding as they hurried down the stairs. She led him out the back and found his car parked in the alley. They hopped in, and Jacques drove off.

At the end of the lane, they heard the thump of an explosion coming from the forecourt of the apartment building.

Jamie gulped. "Was that…my car?"

"I'd say so." Jacques turned quickly onto the main road and navigated through traffic toward the Pentagon while Jamie took deep breaths and concentrated on stopping her hands from shaking. She tried not to think too much about the bomb meant for her or about what was to come. She trusted that Jacques had it all worked out. She just wanted to help Erik, and she would do whatever it took.

The burr of Jacques' cell phone broke the silence of the room. He answered it, then hung up.

"Who was that?" Jamie asked.

Jacques glanced at her. "A friend."

"Did you know he was awarded three medals?" She asked.

Jacques rolled his eyes and mumbled some incoherent words to himself. "Did you enjoy going through his things?"

"I was curious."

He gave her a measured look, then shook his head.

"Do you know what he did to get them?" Jamie asked.

"No Jamie, I don't. He didn't share with me."

"I thought he would since you're his best friend."

"Jamie, I'm sure you're familiar with the word 'classified.'"

Eventually, they passed through the security gate at the Pentagon and Jacques parked the car. Then they proceeded to the main entrance of the Pentagon and waited.

"I don't understand why we're here," Jamie said, and she searched his face.

"All in due time."

Jamie grimaced and perched on the edge of a concrete planter box at the foot of the steps below the impressive portico. She looked into the clouded sky and wondered what Erik was seeing when he looked up in France in 1944. A shaft of sunlight breached through at that moment, and she smiled and took it as a sign that they would be together soon.

Jacques paced back and forth. He glanced at his watch and peered down Pentagon Access Road. A few minutes later a car with its high beams on quickly approached. Jamie saw Jacques place his hand on his gun. Her muscles tensed, ready to run. He squinted to read the front license plate—G18 1971S—then relaxed. Jamie breathed again; it must be a friend. The midnight black Town Car came to a halt under the canopy. The rear right passenger door flew open and a man in a military uniform stepped out. "We don't have much time."

Jacques nodded.

The man extended his hand to Jamie. "Hello, Jamie. I'm Admiral Bonesteiner, Erik's boss."

"How long has he worked for you?" she asked. "And what does he do for the CIA?"

Bonesteiner's eyebrows raised at her bluntness. "Ten years, but that's not important now. What's important is that you type up these files with the old typewriter in your office." Bonesteiner handed her two dossiers.

She glanced inside one of them and discovered blank files from 1942 and two black and white photographs, one a passport photo of a gentleman and one of Erik.

"That man's mission is to stop Erik," Bonesteiner said. "Your mission is to stop him from completing that mission. Make him look like a spy and you'll have a good chance."

Jamie nodded and swallowed. Her hands went clammy, and her stomach felt queasy, but she was determined to do whatever she had to. Getting overwhelmed wouldn't help anyone—least of all her. "There's no typewriter down there, only computers."

"Trust me, Jamie, you'll find it, and you need to work fast." He handed her a book—*the 2008 Edition of World War Two for Morons*. "Give this to Erik as soon as you see him. I can't stress how important this is."

"In the car," Bonesteiner said, "there's a duffle bag containing $100 bills from the 1930's and 40's. This will help you with your financial matters. Now go." He jerked his head toward the entrance and Jamie headed off.

Jacques turned to Bonesteiner. "Do you think this will work?"

"Yes, I do," he replied with the utmost confidence.

"Sir, you are aware that it is virtually impossible to get into Grid Eight unless you are a part of ONE or the Phoenix Group." Jacques paused. "Also, how are you going to avoid running into Cole and Plackett?"

"Nothing is impossible. You just have to know how to do it," Bonesteiner replied with a peremptory gesture. His cell phone rang and he answered it.

"But, Sir …"

Bonesteiner raised his pointing finger, indicating that Jacques should hold his thought. "When did they leave?" He asked into the phone, then looked at his watch and grinned. "Have you heard from Alan?" Bonesteiner nodded and listened with an expression of contentment. "So are we all set when she arrives? Good."

Jacques tried to follow the conversation but drew a blank.

Bonesteiner continued. "Okay, Greg, we'll be there in four hours."

"Greg?" Jacques whispered.

Bonesteiner stared at Jacques with a conspiratorial grin.

12. UNKNOWN FUTURE

"I know not what the future holds, but I know who holds the future."

—Homer

Audrieu, France

The door swung open and struck the wall with a thud. Erik looked up from the narrow bed and blinked. The interrogator and two armed escorts stood in the doorway.

"Time for you to go," the interrogator said with a dismissive gesture.

Erik nodded and mustered all his strength to get up. Pain scattered throughout his body and it was not all from physical wounds. He'd spent the night trying to come to terms with the assassin's claim that Jamie was dead, and he'd failed. In the depths of his despair, he would have been glad of his physical injuries because they distracted him from the much harder to handle emotional pain. The prospect of life without Jamie would be no prospect at all. Only his training and the fact that he had a job to do kept him going.

Erik breathed shallowly in deference to his cracked ribs and made his way through the château toward the Kübelwagen.

"Sleep well?" The interrogator asked.

"No."

"I'm sorry we couldn't offer you more medical attention, but we're short of medical supplies. We put additional petrol in your automobile."

"Thank you for everything you did."

"No problem."

Once they reached the car, the interrogator unfolded a map on the hood. "I have drawn out the route," he traced it with his finger, "that you can take to General Bradley's headquarters."

Erik nodded in appreciation and folded the map. Rommel arrived, accompanied by two armed members of the Résistance. One jerked his head toward the car to indicate that the German Field Marshal should get in, but they didn't open the door for him. Rommel climbed into the Kübelwagen without saying a word, as he glared at Erik.

"Your vehicle is marked so the Résistance will know not to ambush you," the interrogator said.

"Thanks."

"You will still need to be alert for American and British fighter planes."

"Do you have locations for safe houses on the map?" Erik asked.

The interrogator shook his head.

"Can I have my Luger back?"

The interrogator pulled it out of his holster and gave it to Erik.

Erik extended his hand; the interrogator was a little hesitant at first, but then he extended his. "Once again, thank you for everything. What's your name, since you know mine?"

"Valensky."

They shook hands, and while they said a few departing words, a man placed a basket of bread, cheese, fruit, and a few canteens of water in the back seat of the staff car.

Erik hobbled to the driver's side and opened the door. "Ready, Herr Field Marshal?" he asked as he slid in and adjusted his leg so it wouldn't cause as much pain during the trip.

Rommel said nothing, just stared out the passenger side window.

The alternator choked as the engine tried to turn over, then the air-cooled engine sputtered into life and Erik drove off. "How are you feeling, Sir?" He asked as they left the Résistance behind.

Rommel sighed. "Better now, since they are not in our presence."

"I understand, and I know you are not pleased…"

"You're damn right." He turned to Erik, eyes blazed. "How in the hell did you persuade him not to kill us and, much less, let us go? Did you tell him you were OSS or whoever you belong to?"

"Yes."

Rommel's eyes narrowed in suspicion.

"I was not informed that the Resistance was there," Erik explained.

The field marshal snorted. "How would your intelligence service not know that? And who was that SS officer you killed?"

"I think it was planned, and he was after me."

Rommel regarded Erik with cold speculation. "Your government wants you killed?"

Erik shrugged as if to say maybe, maybe not, and kept on driving.

Rommel gawked in disbelief. "I didn't think the American government would do something like that."

"Well, they do."

"Why?"

"I don't know. I'm sure they have their reasons."

"You're trying to help them? Aren't you?"

"Yes, I am, damn it!" Erik smashed his fist against the steering wheel. "I volunteered."

"So you were willing to risk your life to try to end the war."

Erik nodded.

"That's very noble of you."

Erik drove on in silence, trying to sort everything out. He recalled the conversation he had had with Jacques in the restaurant.

Rommel cupped Erik's shoulder. That broke his concentration. "You okay?"

Erik nodded and focused on the weather-beaten road. The dreary, uninviting grassland stretched to the horizon. Silhouettes of abandoned tanks, from a previous battle, appeared like islands in the vast ocean of open fields.

"Do you have any family?" Rommel asked.

"No, my parents and my brother were killed five years ago. Now the same agency that wants me dead killed my girlfriend." Erik thought to himself, *I was going to marry her*. Erik's eyes moistened and a pain not associated with physical injuries pierced his chest.

"My condolences."

"I hope she knew how much I loved her," Erik said as he looked up to the clouds and blinked to clear his eyes.

"I'm sure she did."

"I'll never know now." Erik grabbed the postcard of the Eiffel Tower and tossed it out the window. "It doesn't matter anyway; she's dead." He pulled Jamie's photograph from his coat pocket and placed it on the dashboard in place of the postcard.

"Was that your girlfriend?"

Erik nodded, his face felt tight with sorrow. He suddenly pulled over, parked the Kübelwagen under a tree and turned the engine off.

"What is it?" Rommel asked.

Erik pointed to the sky. The silhouettes of several aircraft roamed above them.

"Ah," Rommel said with a nod of approval.

Erik turned and grabbed the basket. "How much do you know about the Miracle Weapons?" he asked as they started to eat.

Rommel's eyebrows raised. "What do you know about those?"

"Not much, just rumors mostly."

Rommel frowned. "What rumors did you hear?"

Erik finished a mouthful of bread while he carefully considered how to tackle the question. "I've heard there's a new panzer in the developmental stages."

Rommel grinned in rapport and motioned Erik to continue.

"They said the armor is thicker and has a bigger gun than the Tiger I. Thus it will be able to go up against any allied tank."

"What else do you know?"

"How about SS Obergruppenführer Hans Kammler who's in

charge of Peenemunde East and West?" He tried to suppress his knowledge but an incriminating grin overcame Erik's face.

Rommel steepled his fingers and assumed a judicial expression. "How do you know about that, Herr Major? There are only a handful of individuals in the Reich who know about that."

"I read a report on it." Erik tried to keep a blank expression to hide that he knew the truth. The Peenemunde Research Complex was the equivalent of a combination of Silicon Valley and Area 51, with approximately 40,000 staff members and 6,000 institutes all guarded and protected by elite SS units. Peenemunde East, the Wehrmacht's testing facility, dealt with such things as A-4 rockets and derivatives, new types of artillery, nuclear research, and space travel. Peenemunde West, the Luftwaffe's testing facility, dealt with designing revolutionary new aircraft, unconventional propulsion systems, new weapon technologies, and rocket powered long-range aircraft. They planned to create "Miracle Weapons" that would be used against the allies and win the war for Germany. "So, have you met Obergruppenführer Hans Kammler?" Erik asked.

Rommel nodded. "I met Obergruppenführer Hans Kammler earlier this year to discuss a highly classified project."

Erik smiled.

"He told me it would change the outcome of the war," Rommel continued.

"Project Bell?"

Rommel said nothing.

"Was that it, Herr Field Marshal?" Erik probed.

Rommel's answer was a blank stare.

"Was it about time travel?"

"Herr Reich Minister Speer would know more about that than I would."

"So, it's true." Erik paused. "Did they get it to work?"

"Why do you think Operation Barbarossa was so successful?" Rommel said. "The first time we tried, not involving time travel, we failed, but the reason it failed the second time was because the individual sent back was killed."

"I need to know who we can rely on to have Germany do a separate peace treaty with my government," Erik said bluntly. "Anyone in Hitler's inner circle?"

"Herr Reich Minister Speer."

"Would you trust him?"

"I would."

"Is there anyone else you'd trust in Hitler's inner circle or the general staff?"

"There are a few. However, we cannot rely on the Reserve Army."

"That's because they are under Himmler now since the plot failed."

"That is correct." Rommel's eyes filled with dark portents. "For being in the OSS you are very well informed. Is your intelligence service that good?"

"For the most part, we are very good at what we do. Germany happens to be my expertise." Erik placed the basket in the back seat, placed the Luger in his holster, cranked over the engine and proceeded down the road. They traveled a good distance. Then Erik left the road and drove down a track to an abandoned barn.

"So, you are a spy?"

Erik gave a demure grin. "No, I'm just an analyst." As Erik

neared the barn, he slowed the vehicle to a crawl and maneuvered the car so he could back it into the structure.

"An analyst?"

Erik nodded.

"So, have you been to Germany?"

"Several times, even Berlin."

Rommel got out and assisted Erik in backing in the Kübelwagen. Erik did a textbook perfect parking job and Rommel closed the doors to the barn. "You still have any family in the Reich?" he asked as he joined Erik.

"No, they left after the war and moved to the United States," Erik replied through the open window.

Rommel helped Erik out of the car. "Did you have any family that fought in the Weltkrieg?"[11]

Erik climbed out, struggling with the pain. He nodded, and Rommel grinned.

"What do you suggest we do for the rest of the day, Herr Major?"

"Sir, I suggest we have a full day's rest. That way we can travel at night or early morning."

Erik reached for Jamie's photograph and placed it back in his pocket. Then he placed his belongings in the corner and leaned the MP-44 against a wooden wall of the barn. It was early evening, the shafts of light pierced the roughhewn wood, making it dim inside. A gentle breeze embraced the rustic structure, and the earthy smell of compost consumed the atmosphere like the fog in San Francisco Bay.

---

11. What the Germans call World War One.

"Would you like some more to eat?" Rommel asked as he pulled out the picnic basket.

Erik nodded and hobbled over to the field marshal. He took a deep breath and made an awkward attempt to sit down. Rommel helped ease him to the ground.

"Thank you, Herr Field Marshal."

"What are you thinking about, Herr Major?"

Erik shook his head and bit into an apple.

"Erik, I know it must be hard for you, losing the woman you love." Erik nodded and blinked to keep tears from filling his eyes. His simmered anger helped to keep them in check, but he mustn't let his fury jeopardize his mission—or his own safety. "How long had you known each other?"

"Five years. She met me when she was a month away from graduating secondary school. Then we met two years later when she was in university."

Rommel nodded knowingly. "You are older than her?"

"Thirteen years. I was already working with the OSS when she met me."

"Did she know what you did?" Rommel asked between sips of water. "Or should I ask, were you allowed to tell her what you did?"

Erik shook his head. "I'm going to miss her."

Erik and Rommel talked on about each other's personal lives and about the war. Erik questioned Rommel like a reporter and absorbed every answer. All this time, Erik had thought he knew Rommel, but now he learned about the man behind the uniform and spotlight of Nazi propaganda.

For his part, Rommel was amazed at Erik's knowledge of the

Nazis and the Wehrmacht. Over the next couple of hours, the two previous strangers built the basis of a strong friendship. Then Rommel assisted Erik back to his corner in the barn, and Rommel headed back to his spot. He grabbed a lantern and a wooden bucket, lit the lantern and inverted the bucket, and used it for a desk. Erik eased himself onto the floor in the corner and adjusted the MP-44 against the wall. He stared at Rommel and pondered what he might be writing. Seconds turned to minutes, minutes turned into hours, and Erik fell into a deep sleep.

Erik wakened and found Rommel asleep. His forehead throbbed as if someone had struck it with a hammer. It could be stress, sinuses, both, or any combination of things, but the real problem lay beyond his sunken bloodshot eyes, in his psyche—a place very few people knew or were exposed to. He pulled out the photograph of Jamie and stared at it long and hard. Erik habitually buried his problems behind sarcasm and denial. Being a part of an O.G.D.S. Team, he was used to being alone and knew he had no support. He had spent nearly ten years infiltrating different countries' governments and military installations, all in the name of national security. But, this time it was different. They had killed his girlfriend, and they wanted him dead.

The knowledge gnawed in the back of his mind, and he tried to find a reasonable explanation. Maybe they had tried this before, but he overlooked the signs. Berlin? Boone's death? He always did the right thing and was always in control of every situation. He could handle the unnerving thought that he would be stuck in 1944, but not without Jamie. She was the only thing that kept him human. Now she was dead, and there was only one way he would be able to see her.

His eyes swelled and tears ran down his face. With Rommel asleep, he no longer tried to stem them, and a sense of hopelessness overcame him. He pulled out the Luger, removed the magazine, and reloaded it, then stared at the Luger and the photo, eyes bloodshot with pain. All he could do was think about the times he and Jamie had together, her loving brown eyes, her silky smooth skin and the smell of her perfume. Erik pointed the Luger toward his head and squeezed the grip. His palms grew clammy. He stared into the black nine-millimeter barrel and took a deep breath. With his right thumb, he released the safety, placed it on the trigger, and put the muzzle firmly to his forehead. He tried to gather the courage to pull the trigger, but a soft sweet voice drew his attention. He looked up and saw no one, so he placed the muzzle, again, to his head. Once more he heard the voice and recognized it—*Jamie.*

"Erik, babe, don't give up."

His gaze danced around the barn, not knowing if she were somehow there or if the voice were a figment of his imagination. "Why not? With you gone, I have nothing to live for."

"Yes, you do."

Erik wiped the tears from his face. "Even if I do finish my mission, I'll never get to see you."

"Babe, I'll always be with you. I'll never leave your side."

"But I need you now more than ever," Erik pleaded. No answer. "Jamie? Jamie!" No answer. Erik slammed the grip against his forehead in frustration, then placed the gun down with a sigh. Whether she was here or not, he knew Jamie wouldn't want him to kill himself. Luckily, Rommel was still asleep; Erik didn't want anyone to witness his pain.

He managed to lie on his back, though his ribs and knees flared up in pain as he tried to get comfortable. He propped Jamie's photo against some hay, then tilted his head and tried to get some sleep.

A sudden noise jolted Erik awake, eyes fully alert. As he struggled through the pain from his cracked ribs, he sat awkwardly and glanced toward Rommel. The field marshal was already up and stared in his direction. Artillery fire sounds were in the distance. Erik grabbed the Luger, placed it in the holster, and picked up Jamie's photo. He rubbed his swollen, bloodshot eyes to get the sleep out, then pushed against the wall and mustered all his strength to stand. He failed, fell back, and winced at the pain. Rommel came to his aid. Erik balled up his fists, his knuckles turned white, and with determination and Rommel's help, he made it to his feet.

"Morning, Erik, how are your ribs and knee?"

"They hurt, Sir." Erik tossed his hands up in a show of disgust, then he thanked Rommel for his assistance. Erik took several deep breaths to focus and built up momentum. He hobbled to the Kübelwagen and maneuvered himself into the driver's seat. He pulled out his identification papers, opened them, and was about to put Jamie's photo in when he saw a small piece of paper—his fortune from the time he and Jacques had had lunch. It read:

You are bound to travel on one way roads.

Erik shook his head in disbelief. It seemed that his fortune had come true. Rommel opened the door to the Kübelwagen and joined him inside.

Rommel turned to Erik and handed him a folded piece of paper. "This is a list of individuals who are in Hitler's inner circle and general staff we can rely on to help us." Erik took the paper and placed it in the lower right pocket of his tunic while Rommel waited. "This one is for you," he said when Erik looked up again. He handed him another note. "Do not open it unless we don't succeed. Understood?" Erik nodded and tucked the paper in a different pocket. "Now let's get going."

The Kübelwagen drove through a damp, cool morning; its headlights slashed through the darkness, and small arms and artillery fire could be heard in the distance.

"Sir, did you sleep well?" Erik asked while he concentrated on the road.

Rommel stretched in his seat. "Yes, thank you. Did you?"

Erik shook his head.

"Hopefully, when we get to Bradley's headquarters they will give you better medical attention."

"I'm hoping that, too."

Erik turned on a flashlight and peered down. "Looking at the map, it appears we'll get there in just under an hour, around 0700 or 0730." He looked up and around; the artillery seemed closer than before. "That is if everything goes well. But that doesn't mean anything. Who knows what's ahead of us? We're stuck between the lines."

"We're taking a big gamble," Rommel said.

"I will agree with you on that" Erik replied. "Tell me, is there anyone you don't trust on the Allied side?"

"The politicians. They look for personal gain, not the interest of the people of Germany or Germany itself. Politicians have been that way in every war in history, and I expect it will be the same in the future."

"What do you plan to tell Eisenhower?" Erik asked.

"We must not repeat what the Allies did at the end of The Great War. Also, I would advise him that the Russians are a threat to Europe and possibly America."

"I agree. Let's hope we see eye-to-eye and not give a wrong answer."

13. WRONG ANSWER

"Yes, the past can hurt but the way I see it you can either run from it or learn from it."　　　　　　　—Author Unknown

Erik secured a pole with a white flag attached to the Kübelwagen and got back in the car.

"You have my letter and the other document?" Rommel asked.

Erik nodded. Both men were deeply suspicious, but not of each other. Rommel was suspicious of the Americans and their terms for peace and Germany's future in the post-war years. Erik was suspicious of what else Cole and Plackett had planned. It was not over yet.

"Ready, Herr Field Marshal?"

"I am."

Erik drove slowly down the road to the château that housed General Bradley's headquarters while Rommel adjusted his uniform and made himself more presentable. In the distance, Erik saw a guard post with three soldiers who were talking and smoking. As he closed the distance, the soldiers' eyes and relaxed bodies became alerted, like sharks that sensed blood and movement in the water. Erik turned off the headlights and slowed the Kübelwagen to a crawl. The soldiers lifted their guns and squinted down the barrels, their trigger fingers ready to fire.

Once within yelling distance, a soldier barked out orders: "Stop your vehicle! Do it now!" They cocked their guns and fired warning shots in the air. "This is your last warning! Stop your vehicle or die!" Erik stopped the Kübelwagen. He and Rommel raised their hands.

Rommel turned to Erik. "I don't believe they're expecting us." Erik nodded. "It might help if you tell them you're American."

"Might is the key word," Erik said. "Being in a German uniform might work against me."

The soldiers quickly surrounded the car, their eyes fixed upon Erik and Rommel. "Keep your hands up, you Nazis!"

Erik studied his surroundings. Two soldiers stood on each side of the Kübelwagen, and one stood on point.

"Get out of the vehicle now!" the soldier on point yelled.

Erik and Rommel slowly exited the Kübelwagen.

The two soldiers grabbed Erik and Rommel and threw them to the ground, like trash being tossed into a dumpster. Erik landed on his bad knee. Pain shot from it to every part of his body. The soldiers patted him down and took his Luger.

"Who are you?" The soldier at point barked out the question.

Erik glanced up at him. "Erik Függer, I'm with the OSS."

"You speak good English for being a Nazi!"

"I am not a Nazi," Erik protested. "I'm an OSS operative, with Field Marshal Rommel."

The soldier behind Erik grabbed him by his hair and yanked his head up so he could see his face. "Speak when you are spoken to, you Nazi!"

The soldier on point continued his questioning. "What are you doing here!?"

"We are here to see and speak to General Bradley."

"General Bradley?"

"Yes."

The soldier leaned back, looking suspicious, and folded his arms across his chest. "How in the hell do you know the general is here?" He squatted, pulled out his pistol, and rubbed it against Erik's temple.

"As I said before, I'm Erik Függer; I'm with the OSS."

"Why do you want to see the general?"

Erik noticed that the soldier had his finger on the trigger. "I can't discuss that matter in front of an enlisted man."

The soldier hovered over Erik, planted his foot in the middle of his back, and placed the barrel to his head. "If you want to live, you Nazi, you will tell me the real reason for you being here!"

In training, Erik had been taught that there are several different kinds of interrogations. Being captured in the field can be one of the easier ones to deal with because you can tell a story. Storytelling will keep you alive until you find a way to escape, and it keeps your captor listening so they ask fewer questions. Then again, sometimes it's not that easy, not with a captor who's willing to kill you if you give them a reason.

"We're here to talk to General Bradley about a peace treaty. Now get the officer on duty on the phone and tell him we're here," Erik demanded.

"Listen here, you Nazi," the squatted soldier replied with a disgusted tone. He cocked the gun and pressed the barrel into Erik's temple, "Don't tell me how to do my job."

Erik stared into his eyes without a flinch and said nothing. The soldier got up and started to search the Kübelwagen. During his search, he retrieved the MP 44 and the few clips. Then he strolled back to the staff car, placed the weapon in the back seat, and picked up the radio. Erik tried to focus on the conversation.

"Command, this is gate one." A few seconds went by and the soldier tried again. "Command, this is gate one."

A static voice came over the radio: "Go ahead, gate one. This is Captain Cerberus."

"Sir, this is Sergeant Court. I have two Nazi officers wanting to speak to the general."

"Is that right, Sergeant? Who are they?"

"Field Marshal Rommel and Erik Függer. He claims to be an OSS agent. They are talking about some peace treaty."

"Are they alone?"

"It appears they are, Sir. I don't see or hear anything."

"Stay alert; it could be a decoy. I'll send someone out for them and to secure the perimeter."

"Yes, Sir."

"Sergeant, make the one claiming to be an OSS agent feel comfortable if you know what I mean."

"Yes, Sir, I do." Court grinned, squinted his eyes and rubbed his hands together. "Stand that Nazi up." He cracked his knuckles and loosened his neck muscles by rotating his head and rolled his shoulders. Erik stood, took shallow breaths, and prepared for what was coming next. The soldier slowly walked toward Erik and sized him up.

"Put your hands up, you Nazi."

Erik placed his hands above his head and stared directly into Court's menacing eyes. Then Erik swiftly found himself on the receiving end of a combination of well-placed punches to his gut that knocked the wind from him. Erik cringed in pain, and the soldier laughed. In the near distance, the humming sound of motors and squeaking tracks slowly grew louder. Eventually, several M3 half-tracks and jeeps appeared. Vehicles filled with armed men passed on by and then headed down the road in different directions to secure and protect the flanks. One jeep stopped and the crew got out. The soldiers showed their displeasure of Germans by their looks and verbal complaints. Then they approached Erik.

"Pick that Nazi up," a soldier barked. Next, he stared at Rommel. "Put that one in the Jeep."

Then he turned and focused on Erik. He whipped out his pistol and pointed it at Erik's head. Erik, with his hands on his head, felt his eyes on him, but he stood like a blank slate and looked straight ahead.

"Most people flinch when they have a gun pointed at them," the soldier said in a taunting voice, "but it appears you do not. Why is that?" Erik leaned his head forward, so the barrel of the pistol touched his forehead. "Can you speak English, you Nazi?" Erik nodded. "Yes or no!" The soldier howled with a veiny throat.

"Yes."

"I heard you claim to be in the OSS. By the looks of you, you do not look like you can knock off the wings of a fly." Spit hit Erik in the face, but he ignored it. "Get in the jeep."

The soldier behind Erik gave him a shove and cocked his submachine gun. Erik saw Rommel in the front seat and, with his bad knee, struggled to get in the back. The jeep moved off and slowly approached the château. Erik casually glanced at his surroundings. At least the trip was over. But he would never, ever get back to 2008, and he would spend his life without Jamie.

"What are you staring at, you Nazi?" the soldier barked.

Erik glanced at him and shook his head. A lone soldier with a Thompson submachine gun stood at the entrance of the château, his eyes transfixed on the jeep. Oddly, the waiting soldier stared intently at Erik.

Rommel tilted his head and whispered to Erik, "Remember what I told you."

Erik nodded.

The soldier smacked the back of Rommel's head. "Shut up, you Nazi!"

The lone soldier, by the château, moved his hands as if he prepared to fire his weapon.

"Soldier …" Erik said as he stared at the lone soldier.

The soldier shook his head casually. A malevolent grin appeared on his face. He slowly walked down the steps and raised the submachine gun. A chill raced up Erik's spine.

"Soldier behind you!" Erik exclaimed as the lone soldier aimed his weapon.

A spray of bullets flew across the jeep; they impaled everything in their path. Blood and flesh danced in the air. The jeep took a hard right and slowly came to a halt, the driver dead. Erik's eyes widened in horror. The soldier beside him was hunched over with blood pouring out of multiple exit wounds.

The lone soldier pulled out his empty magazine and loaded

another while he moved closer to the jeep. Erik shook Rommel's shoulder, but he didn't respond. Erik glanced up and saw the soldier raising his weapon. His cold gray eyes stared directly at Erik above a satanic grin. The soldier fired. Erik rolled over the side of the jeep and landed on his injured knee. A lightning bolt of pain surged through his body. Glass shattered as bullets flew, and the air rang with the dull sound of bullets that penetrated metal.

Erik leaned against the rear tire and gathered the strength to talk. "I'm an OSS agent. I'm on your side!"

The Thomson Submachine Gun stopped. Erik took a few deep breaths and tried to stand, but the soldier saw Erik trying to stick his head up and fired again. Erik ducked and crawled to the front of the jeep. He heard Rommel's last words.

"Don't let this change the future of the war."

Erik leaned against the front tire and hoped that others heard what was going on and would come out. *I spent my life working for the agency and sold my soul under an oath, and I'm still in the dark.* He grabbed the front bumper of the jeep with his left hand and slowly tried to get up. He heard heavy breathing and looked up. The soldier hovered over him with a Thomson Submachine Gun at point blank range. Jamie's face flashed into Erik's mind. "I love you, Jamie," he whispered.

Erik stared at the soldier and the soldier stared back. "You were never to get this far, Dr. Függer." Then he pulled the trigger and … nothing.

Erik's eyes widened. He realized this was another operative from the Phoenix Group, mainly because the soldier knew his name and knew he was coming. The soldier tried to fire again, and again nothing happened. He turned the gun around, held it like a baseball bat and swung it and struck Erik across his right temple. Erik reeled backward and felt the early stages of a blackout coming on. He used all his strength, scrambled his way out, and gripped the bumper bar with his fingers. Without warning, the butt of the gun smashed down onto Erik's fingers. The sound of cracked broken bones filled Erik's ears and pain exploded through his body.

"Time to die," the operative said.

"Fuck you." Erik glanced up. "If you had the guts, you'd put a gun to my head and finish your mission."

The operative pulled out his pistol, pointed it at Erik's head and grinned. "You'll be remembered by a star, like the other two analysts before you."

"Come on, do it! I've nothing to lose, you son of a bitch!"

Cerberus pulled the hammer back.

A loud, high-pitched scream stopped the moment. "Stop! Stop! He's one of ours! Stop!"

The operative looked over his shoulder. A large group of enlisted men ran toward him.

"Drop your weapon, soldier, and step away from the prisoner!" General Bradley ordered.

The operative stared at Erik, and he stared back while machine guns were being cocked and footsteps raced closer. Erik mustered his strength and shoved the operative hard. He discharged his weapon, barely missing Erik.

"Drop your weapon!" a soldier barked.

With a dozen Thomson Submachine Guns pointed directly at him, the operative realized he was too late, that he had failed at his mission to kill Erik. Now he had to come up with another plan to get Erik killed. Erik was helped to his feet and pushed in the direction of General Bradley and his staff.

"Bring that prisoner over," Bradley demanded. While Bradley waited, a female officer handed him two military dossiers. "Lieutenant, I don't have time to read these."

She insisted they were important because they dealt with the two gentlemen headed in his direction. Bradley took a deep sigh, quickly read, and then glanced at the photographs. He looked at Erik and the operative, then back at the photos and back up at them.

Erik stared at the lieutenant. He couldn't believe his eyes. He didn't dare to hope that he saw what he thought he saw.

Bradley turned to her. "Lieutenant, where did you get this information?"

"I'm with the OSS. I'm under the command of the gentleman wearing the German uniform." She even sounded like Jamie.

"And the other?"

"Cerberus is a German agent."

Bradley stepped forward and stared at Cerberus. "Captain, you have some explaining to do."

"Sir, this German officer," he looked to his right, "is claiming that he and Field Marshal Rommel were here to do a separate peace treaty with Germany. In reality, he was going to assassinate you."

Bradley looked at Erik. "What's your story?"

"I'm Erik Függer, an OSS operative. My mission was to bring Field Marshal Rommel to your headquarters. From there we were to start the process of a separate peace treaty from the Russians," Erik said while he looked at the operative, Cerberus. "However, we were ambushed by your captain, killing two of your men and Field Marshal Rommel…"

"Your men?" Cerberus interrupted rudely. "They're *your* men who were going to help you kill the general. Good thing I outsmarted you English speaking Germans."

Cerberus and Erik volleyed back and forth, each one giving his version of the truth, explaining what had just happened and accusing one another. Bradley, like a judge in a courtroom, listened to both sides of the story.

Erik and Jamie's eyes met. She smiled and gave him a little nod, and assured him that it really was her. Erik realized that she had traveled back in time. Bonesteiner and Greg, his contact in ONE, must have done it without Cole knowing. She stared at him with glistening eyes, and Erik realized what she saw: his battered face, his left hand dripped in blood, fingers mangled, and left knee injured. She clicked her heels subtly like Dorothy in *The Wizard of Oz*, glanced at Cerberus, and looked at the dossiers Bradley held. Erik quickly put two and two together: Jamie set up Cerberus as a German agent. He grinned discretely and knew he had to set a trap for Cerberus.

Erik shot out a question and hoped to catch Cerberus off guard. "So captain, how did you get this information?"

"That's top secret."

"Oh, really?" Erik asked mockingly. "Are you in the OSS?"

"No. I mean," Cerberus sheepishly shrugged his shoulders, "I'm a part of Army Intelligence."

"If that's so, where's your uniform shoulder patch?"

Bradley took off his glasses and studied the files again.

Cerberus tried to salvage his credibility and tried to take some of the heat out of the conversation. "Sir, how can we trust him? He's wearing the uniform of the enemy. He has no proof for what he's saying and who he is."

"General Bradley, my proof is in my right tunic pocket."

Erik raised his hands and Bradley motioned a soldier to retrieve the documents. The documents were handed to Bradley. He unfolded them, quickly glanced over them, and then stared at Erik. "What am I looking at?"

"The document with the names is what the provisional government would have looked like if the plot for Hitler had succeeded. However…"

Cerberus butted in. "However, the plot failed, and that document is useless because everyone will be killed by the SS or Gestapo."

"Captain, I'm aware the plot has failed." Bradley looked at Erik. "Continue."

"That might be true, but not everyone on the document has been killed."

"General," Cerberus protested, "how can you believe anything he's saying? He's going on a leap of faith. The Germans don't want peace."

"If that was the case, why did Rommel make this trip?" Erik barked, as Bradley looked at the second sheet of paper. "Secondly, he made another list of those we can use as allies to overthrow Hitler and his inner circle."

"What other list are you talking about?" Cerberus gasped, his eyes enlarged.

"I'm surprised at you, captain;" Erik said, "for being a part of Army Intelligence, your knowledge is limited, and you're not very informed about certain things."

"My superiors do not always inform me about everything!"

"Oh really, captain? Did they forget to give you that intel? What else did military intelligence forget to do or tell you?"

Cerberus turned red, and the veins on his neck started to pop out. Erik stared calmly at him. But Bradley lost his patience.

"Both of you, shut up!" Bradley glanced at the personal files again, then looked directly at each of them in turn. "So gentlemen…you both tell me there is a Nazi spy among us. Interesting." Bradley placed his glasses back on. "So tell me this…who won the last World Series?"

Cerberus chuckled as if he couldn't believe Bradley was asking such an easy question. Jamie, knowing that Erik knew nothing about sports, looked horrified. She closed her eyes, and her lips moved as if in prayer.

Erik, however, replied without hesitation. "The New York Yankees."

Cerberus let out a huge laugh. "You can't be serious; you Nazi spies need to pay more attention to America's pastime."

Erik turned to Cerberus. "Then you, with your great wisdom, please correct me."

"Love to. It was the Philadelphia Phillies."

Bradley motioned, and two of the soldiers behind Cerberus grabbed his hands and forced them behind him, while another pointed a gun in his face, and a third handcuffed his hands. Cerberus started to struggle, and panic slowly stretched across his face.

Erik faced Cerberus and, with a mischievous grin, mouthed, "Oops, wrong answer." The Philadelphia Phillies won the World Series in 2008, not 1943.

"You son of a bitch!" Cerberus yelled.

"It's Dr. Erik Függer to you, or should I say *The Saint*," Erik whispered so only Cerberus could hear.

Bradley walked up to Erik and placed his hand on his shoulder. "Son, you look like the worst has gotten the better of you." Erik nodded, and with a smile, Bradley continued, "I'll have my personal physician look you over and patch you up." Then Bradley looked at Jamie, who beamed with relief. "Good thing the Lieutenant gave me these dossiers." He held them up. "I would never have known there'd be a Nazi spy in my headquarters."

"The lieutenant is my aide, and she's very good at what she does," Erik said while Cerberus was carried away, still struggling and insisting upon his innocence.

"General, I need those dossiers back," Erik said as Bradley handed them back to Jamie. "What are you going to do with the captain?"

"He'll be sent to a prison where he'll await trial for treason."

"With all due respect, Sir, my orders are to kill him."

"Oh. Well, I can't question the authority of the OSS, but you don't look like you're in any condition to do that, so I'll carry out that order for you, Sir."

"Very good, general."

General Bradley snapped Erik a salute, then he turned around and gave two separate orders. "Kill that Nazi spy and get my personal physician out here now!"

Members of his staff dashed off in separate directions.

Jamie rushed toward Erik with open arms. With no strength left, Erik fell to the ground. Jamie kneeled and cradled his body close to hers. Erik felt something in his pocket. He reached in and pulled out the letter from Rommel. Jamie helped him open it, and he read it aloud:

> *Erik,*
>
> *These past several days have been interesting, to say the least. I am hopeful that the meeting with General Bradley will be successful and that our two countries will make a peace because I know it will not be possible with Russia. However, I am being skeptical. I do not believe this meeting with General Bradley will be successful and so the war will continue. However, if it is, I know that your government will not allow us to see each other or let me write this letter, and I will have to obey their concessions and conditions. If the peace treaty does not work between our nations, it is because of the politicians with their tender mercies of injustice. Nevertheless, this is nothing to grieve over because you know the truth; we were trying to end this war. You gave me something I never expected to find from an American officer, your gift of trust. I will never forget that. If the war continues, then do your best to end it with less bloodshed. Do your best, and do it well.*
>
> *I will remain as ever your friend, Field Marshal Erwin Rommel.*

Erik swallowed back the lump that formed in his throat. "It's okay, babe, I'm here. I'm not going anywhere." He looked up at Jamie. She smiled down at him and combed her fingers through his blood-soaked hair. Tears of joy ran down her face.

"How did you know where I was?" Erik asked as he stared into her beautiful brown eyes.

Jamie reached into a pocket and pulled out a fortune from a fortune cookie. She opened it up and showed it to Erik: *Your gift is to bring friends together*. Erik realized it was Jacques' fortune from the restaurant. Jamie turned the paper over, and Erik read the message written in Jacques' handwriting.

Good luck in your new life.

Erik grinned and looked into Jamie's eyes. "Now I can take you to the Eiffel Tower like I promised."

A huge smile came across Jamie's face and she held him tighter as if she never wanted to let him go.

14. SURPRISES

"That I exist is a perpetual surprise which is life."

—Rabindranath Tagore

CIA Headquarters, Langley, Virginia

Bonesteiner stood in front of the Memorial Wall and watched a man placing a star symbolizing Erik's death; like the others, his name would be marked as unknown in the Honor Book. Footsteps in the distance grew louder and approached him from behind.

Cole joined him. "I see they told you about Dr. Függer's death. Looks like history will remain the same."

Bonesteiner glared at him. "Don't assume anything, Cole."

"Well, you were wrong about him being one of your best."

Before Bonesteiner could reply, Cole's cell phone went off. Bonesteiner saw Plackett's name on the caller ID before Cole excused himself and walked away. Bonesteiner edged a little closer and eavesdropped.

"What the hell are you talking about?" Cole said into the

phone while he glared at Bonesteiner. "They should have been back hours ago. I'm on my way; have Mr. Crowley with you."

"Lost some operatives?" Bonesteiner asked as he suppressed a grin. If the two assassins didn't come back, they'd probably failed to kill Erik. No doubt Cole had figured that out, too.

"Not at liberty to comment."

Cole turned and left but turned back when Bonesteiner spoke: "I thought you'd like to look at this." Bonesteiner handed him two photocopies of a page from the book Erik gave Jacques. The first was a black and white photograph of Ahriman in an SS Colonel uniform, and the second was a 1944 map of Belgium, during the Battle of the Bulge.

"What is it?"

"Something you might take a closer look at."

"Photocopies from a history book?" Cole chuckled.

"Look closer."

Cole looked at the photocopies and his eyes widened in shock. "Where did you get these?" Cole muttered under his breath.

"He did tell you he had an extensive library."

"So he did."

Bonesteiner's words turned cold. "He is much more resource-ful than Knight and Mulder, the other two you set up to fail and had killed. However, whatever you and Plackett have planned for World War Two, I hope to God he fucks it up."

"We shall see." Cole started to walk off.

"Cole!" Bonesteiner got his attention one last time. "I don't know if you are familiar with William Shakespeare's play, *The Merchant of Venice*." Cole shrugged his shoulders. "Since you've crossed paths with Erik, I think you'll find this quote from Act

III relevant: 'If you prick us, do we not bleed? If you tickle us, do we not laugh? If you poison us, do we not die? And if you wrong us, shall we not revenge?'"

Cole's expression hardened. The side of his mouth twitched, and his eyes narrowed. He sneered, then turned on his heel and stalked off.

15. LOOKING OVER SHOULDERS

*"Why is it that people like us choose to serve for nickels a day
in a profession that makes us constantly look over our shoulder to see who's watching us?"*
    —Philip Allen from the movie *The Good Shepherd*

Saint-Jacques-de-la-Lande, France. 23 August 1944

Five grueling and painful weeks of physical therapy later, Erik
was still in a military hospital under the name Joe Turner. Jamie laid her tired head on Erik's chest and gently held his right
hand. He was proud of her; not only because she had come back
to help him and did an excellent job of playing the role of a lieutenant—and probably saved his life—but also because of how
well and quickly she adjusted to life in France in 1944. She found
a place to stay, bought a car, and had been working on improv-
ing her French. She even jogged every day—in case, she said, she
had to run away from someone—and never blanched when Erik
taught her to handle a gun—as much as one can in a hospital
room. France was nearly liberated, and Erik had assured Jamie

that things would get better after the twenty-fifth of the month when the last German garrison would surrender the capital.

Erik lay restlessly in his hospital bed; his eyes fixed on every detail of the room and stared often to the door since he didn't know who from 1944 or 2008 would come through. He was intensely aware that the longer he stayed in the hospital, the more likely it would be that it was someone he didn't want to see.

From time to time, Erik tilted his head to kiss Jamie's soft, silky-brown hair. He thought how lucky he was to have a girlfriend so loving and supportive that she was willing to leave everything and everyone she knew to be with him in 1944. Erik knew the history and the mannerisms of the people in 1944, but he was uncertain of his personal future and haunted by his past. He felt he constantly needed to look over his shoulder, and maybe would have to for the rest of his life. The door slowly creaked open and drew Erik's immediate attention. His muscles tensed, but relaxed when the doctor walked in with Erik's chart. Jamie lifted her head and sat up.

"Good morning, Joe," The doctor said as he read over the documentation in Erik's chart. "How are you doing?"

"I'm alive, doc."

The doctor flashed a knowing grin as he asked Erik to sit on the side of the bed and started his routine checkup on Erik's vitals and injuries. "Your eye is completely healed." He gently touched Erik's ribcage. "How does that feel?"

"The pain's still there, but not as sharp as before."

The doctor nodded, then cupped his hands over Erik's left patella and signaled him to slowly bend his knee, testing the flexibility. Erik took a deep breath, winced, and flexed his knee as far as he could. Jamie held his hand for moral support.

"Can you go any further?"

Erik shook his head, wrinkles etched in his forehead.

The doctor repeated the request several times and measured how much it had healed. "You're very fortunate that you can still walk, but I don't think you'll ever have the full potential and movement of your knee again."

Erik nodded.

"Doctor," Jamie asked, "is there anything you can do to restore his knee?"

"I wish we could. Maybe in the future, we can. I am, like my colleagues, astonished at how quickly Joe has recovered from his injuries."

Erik tapped Jamie's hand and shook his head discreetly to remind her they were in 1944, not 2008, and not to ask too many questions. Then the doctor ordered Erik to squeeze his hand as hard as he could, which he did with some discomfort. The doctor shook his head in disbelief at how rapidly the healing had taken place. He made some documentation in Erik's chart and finalized his examination.

"Any questions?"

"When can I be discharged?"

The doctor pondered before he replied, "I'd have to say, with the progress you've made and if it continues, you'll be discharged and can go back to work in another two weeks."

"That's great!" Jamie said cheerfully, her smile filling the room. Erik just nodded.

"Anything else?"

"No."

"Well. Have a good day."

The doctor exited and closed the door behind him. Erik whipped his head around to face Jamie. "Get my clothes. We're leaving." He stood up, grabbed his clothes as Jamie handed them to him, and started getting dressed.

"But babe, what about what the doctor said?"

Erik looked directly in Jamie's soft brown eyes. "I appreciate that you want me to be fully recovered, but trust me, I know what I'm doing."

"But you're under an assumed name. No one can find out."

Erik tilted his head as if to say, "Do you really believe that?"

"By the way," she continued, "why did you pick the name, Joe Turner?"

He patted her hand and replied, "No one will find out … hmmm. Now that's wishful thinking." He put on his shirt. "I got the name Joe Turner from the movie *Three Days Of The Condor*. He was on the run, like me, or should I say, like us." He raised his finger. "You're correct. I'm under an assumed name. That might delay the Phoenix Group from finding me, but there's a new player in the game now."

"Who?"

"The OSS, the Office of Strategic Services."

Jamie raised an eyebrow in a silent request for further explanation.

"The predecessor of the Central Intelligence Agency. They will be looking for me, and if they do find me, they will detain and question me. If that happens, things can get ugly."

"What would they do?"

"They will try to get information from me." Jamie tried to get a word out, but Erik held up a finger, telling her to wait. "The problem is the methods they'll use to get the information." Jamie gulped. "They'll place me in a seat for starters, then they'll ask a question and if I don't give an answer or the answer they want, they'll hit me. Third, if all else fails, they'll break fingers or toes, and then finally…" Erik saw the pure shock in her eyes. "Yes, you guessed it. They'll kill me." As he put on his shoes, he said with a grin, "So we have nothing to worry about because we're not at that stage yet. You ready to go?"

She nodded.

"Okay, go find me a doctor's lab coat, a stethoscope, and my chart."

Jamie gave him a grin and left the room while Erik got rid of anything that could identify him or be used to track him. He even wiped surfaces to make sure he didn't leave fingerprints behind. He reached under the pillow as the door suddenly swung open. Erik whipped the Luger from beneath the pillow, released the safety, and aimed at the individual who was coming in.

Jamie stepped inside, closed the door behind her, and stared wide-eyed at the gun pointing at her.

"Sorry," Erik said, as he lowered the gun. "It could have been anyone."

Jamie swallowed. "You weren't joking were you?"

"No, I wasn't." He approached her a little like one would a frightened child and reassured her that everything would be okay.

"Erik, I can't imagine—"

He filled her last thought. "What it was like when I worked with the agency?"

She nodded.

Erik knew there was no possible way she would be able to

comprehend, so he used a quote he remembered that William Parrish had said in the movie *Meet Joe Black*. "Multiply it by infinity and take it to the depth of forever, and you will still have barely a glimpse of what I'm talking about."

"Yeah. I get that." Her hands trembled, and Jamie gave Erik the items he requested. He slipped on the coat, then opened the door, and next he glanced around and analyzed his surroundings. The medical staff and doctors were preoccupied. "Come on." He gestured to Jamie, and she followed him out.

They quickly strolled to the elevators. Erik pressed the button repeatedly while he tapped his foot and glanced over his shoulder. His fists were starting to ball up from the tension when the door suddenly drew open. They leaped in just as he overheard his doctor asking the nurse where his chart was, and the nurse stated that the patient, Joe Turner, was missing. The elevator doors closed, and Erik and Jamie shared a cunning grin. They descended to the first floor and headed to the car Jamie had for them.

In the foyer, Erik saw two distinguished-looking gentlemen in dark gray, three-piece suits; one wore Club Master Eyeglasses. Erik thought to himself, *the OSS has arrived and it is none other than Edward Wilson*. He eavesdropped on their conversation as he walked by.

"That's the problem. We don't even have a photograph of him and know vaguely what he looks like. All we have is his name, Joe Turner, and a sketch."

Just as Erik placed one foot out of the hospital, someone grabbed his shoulder. He whipped into combat mode and used his peripheral vision to see who was behind him: Edward Wilson. Jamie's eyes widened, and she hurried off toward the parking lot.

"Excuse me, doctor, can you tell me on what level the recovery floor is?" Edward Wilson asked.

"That would be level two," Erik replied straight-faced. "Have a good day."

"Thank you, doctor." Edward walked away, and Erik stepped outside, delighted with his performance.

Jamie pulled up the car and opened the door. Erik slid in. "Who were those guys in suits?" Jamie asked as she drove quickly away.

"OSS."

16. PROMISE KEPT

"For you see, each day I love you more. Today more than yes-terday and less than tomorrow."   —Rosemonde Gerard

Paris, France. September 1944.

Jamie stepped out of the bedroom. Her radiance was blinding, and the only thing Erik could do was to stand there mesmerized. She wore a brilliant form-fitting, ruby-red evening dress that enhanced every curve. Her makeup was stunning, from the eyeshadow that made her lustful brown eyes glisten in the light to her astonishing red lips. She sauntered toward him, left him speechless, unable to utter a single syllable.

"Hi, professor." She did a slight bow and stared seductively at him. "I'm ready, but guess what?"

Oh dear God, if it isn't enough that she looks amazing, I have to play guessing games. Still tongue-tied, Erik motioned as if to say, "What?"

She whispered that she was wearing a white lacy garter belt with nude stockings. He tried to remain calm but failed and gulped. All he could do was think, *God, I wish there was room service and that we didn't have to go out.* He extended his arm; she hooked hers in his, and they headed out on their way to the Eiffel Tower.

Though the war in Europe continued, Paris had been liberated from the Germans, so it was once again a happy place to be. Jamie and Erik joined in the recent celebrations with great excitement—he'd never thought he'd actually participate in something he'd read about in history books.

They walked arm in arm down Rue Bonaparte. Dusk was falling, the sun's warmth slowly faded under a steel gray sky, and the sound of traffic bounced off the buildings around them. The small café at Quai Malaquais was full of people with warm smiles, enjoying tiny cups of coffee and eating pastries, while cars, trucks, buses, bicycles, and countless people, including Allied soldiers, streamed by on the sidewalks. When the traffic light turned red, Erik and Jamie crossed quickly. The light posts in the tree-lined street were still dark, however. Erik knew the lights wouldn't come back on until after the war was over in 1945.

Erik attempted to wave down a taxi while trying to recall the word for *taxi* in French. Jamie smiled and told him. Oddly, it's the same word. He used his best French accent to yell "Taxi!" but he failed to be understood and thought to himself that Paris hadn't changed at all since he was here last—many years in the future. They continued walking and took in the raised lettering on storefronts and dim-white lighted doorways and windows. Despite the hustle and bustle, people were relaxing in this warm evening.

In the distance, Erik heard a deep, thick, French accent repeatedly yelling, "Major!" He paid it little attention and he and

Jamie continued walking and looking for a taxi. A moment later, a well-dressed man in a three-piece suit approached him. Erik prepared himself for the worst, but the man opened his arms and gave a warm smile.

"Major, it's so good to see you again." The old man's blue eyes were filled with delight. "How have you been?"

"Do I know you?" Erik asked, thinking that the man could have memory loss or a case of mistaken identity.

"You do, indeed." The man grabbed Erik's hand and squeezed it firmly, then looked at Jamie and said, "He's a great man, a saint."

She smiled and pulled Erik closer to her. Erik thought the man's mind was completely lost, and he just smiled back. "Where have I met you? It has slipped my mind."

The man shook his head in disbelief and poked Erik's chest, but his eyes remained friendly. He explained to Erik and Jamie that he had met Erik at a petrol station on the outskirts of Bernay. Erik, now realizing who he was, nodded and grinned, while Jamie listened with wide eyes.

Erik looked the man in the eye. "I don't know your name."

"D'Artagnan Astor, at your service, major," He replied.

"I'm Er…"

D'Artagnan cuts Erik off. "Major, I know who you are and what you did, and I and the people of France thank you."

Baffled, Erik asked, "What did I do?"

"You liberated Paris."

"Excuse me?" He shook his head, trying to make sense of what he had just heard. "I did what?"

"You liberated Paris." D'Artagnan turned to Jamie. "Is he always this modest?" Jamie nodded and D'Artagnan looked back at Erik. "Major, since you liberated Paris, how can I help you?"

Erik motioned to Jamie that he needed to speak with D'Artagnan alone. She smiled, mouthed *okay* and stepped away. Erik beckoned to D'Artagnan to follow him, and once they were a good distance away from Jamie, Erik turned to D'Artagnan. "How did I liberate Paris?"

"You knew the date, and my son told me you were with the OSS and your mission was to liberate France with Rommel." Erik tried to get a word in, but D'Artagnan continued. "Eisenhower must think highly of you to carry out such an operation." D'Artagnan looked around and then whispered. "What else do you have planned for the Nazis to fail?"

"Who is your son…?"

D'Artagnan gave a dismissive gesture and waited for an answer.

Erik sighed. "Yes, the Nazis are going to lose this war, but it won't be anytime soon. It will happen, though."

"What can the French people do to help?"

Erik smiled. "I'll need to think it over, but if I need your help I'll let you know. Wait, yes, there is something." Erik pointed to Jamie, who smiled back at him. "You see that lovely lady?"

D'Artagnan nodded.

"I'm going to propose to her."

D'Artagnan butted in. "I know the perfect place…" Raising his hand in the air, he whispered, "The Eiffel Tower." Erik smiled in agreement. "Then I will take you to Le Jules Verne to end the evening perfectly."

"But I don't have a reservation."

"Nonsense, I know the owner, and it won't be a problem since I'll be bringing the individual who liberated Paris from the Nazis."

Erik grinned. "Sounds great. Let's go."

Erik strolled over to Jamie with his hand extended.

"What's happening?" she asked.

"It's a surprise." He took her hand.

Jamie grinned with delight, and her eyes shined with expectation.

"D'Artagnan will be driving us."

D'Artagnan led the way to his car, which was parked nearby, and opened the back door for them. Jamie and Erik climbed in, and D'Artagnan closed the door and made his way to the driver's side. He got in and proceeded down Quai Malaquais and gave them a guided tour. When they reached the Pont Royal Bridge, D'Artagnan pointed across the river to the École du Louvre and explained that it was an educational institution dedicated to archaeology, art history, anthropology, and epigraphy. Jamie whispered to Erik that he could teach history there, but only if he were able to speak French.

At the Pont de la Concorde Bridge, D'Artagnan told them that if they looked to their left they would see a building with stone columns and raised bold letters that read ASSEMBLÉE NATIONALE. They looked across the bridge and also saw the Luxor Obelisk. Jamie asked what it was, and Erik told her that it was nearly 3,300 years old and marked the entrance to the Luxor Temple in Ancient Egypt. He deliberately said it loudly so D'Artagnan could hear him and correct him if he was wrong. D'Artagnan nodded and added that it had arrived in Paris in December 1833. King Louis-Philippe had it placed in the center of Place de la Concorde three years later.

The traffic grew heavier as they proceeded deeper into the heart of Paris, but that didn't stop D'Artagnan from pointing out historical locations like the Paroisse Saint-Paul Saint-Louis Cathedral . Then D'Artagnan made a slight left and pointed to the Eiffel Tower in the near distance. Erik tapped Jamie's arm and pointed as well. She looked ahead, and her eyes enlarged with excitement; then she hugged him tightly and kissed him so thoroughly that Erik felt all her passion and desire.

The silhouette of the Eiffel Tower's metal structure, rose higher in the sky as they drove closer, and the streets became more alive. Jamie took in everything around her and her eyes filled with joy. At the base of the Eiffel Tower, the streetlamps glowed around the square where countless people waited to go up. It had become a popular outing since the city's liberation because no one had been allowed up during the German occupation. D'Artagnan swung the car around in front of the tower and stopped. He got out and opened the door for Erik and Jamie, but two members of Sûreté Nationale approached him and ordered him to move the car immediately. D'Artagnan spoke to the police officers and pointed toward Erik.

"Babe, what's he saying to them?" Jamie asked.

Erik just shrugged.

D'Artagnan and more members of Sûreté Nationale approached the car. Was this a trap? How could he have been so easily fooled? Erik looked to see if the keys were in the ignition. *They're not! Shit!* Then he remembered, same as the Kübelwagen, there was a primer and a choke. *I wish I had my VW Phaeton.* He looked around, analyzed the situation, and prepared himself to do whatever it took to escape with Jamie by his side. It was almost dark now. They could stick to the shadows. *Great way to propose to her,* Erik thought, *fleeing from Sûreté Nationale, being shot at and popping the question…how romantic.*

D'Artagnan opened the door and Erik leaped to his feet, but to his surprise, the members of Sûreté Nationale smiled and extended their hands. He shook each hand in turn, and they repeated, one after another. "Thank you, major."

Dear God, in 2008 I'm hated by half the French government, and they would've loved to see me dead. But here, just because I told one person when Paris was going to be liberated, I'm a national hero. Jacques would never believe this, nor anyone at the agency. Erik looked back and extended his hand to help Jamie out of the car, and then the members of the Sûreté Nationale, with D'Artagnan in front, escorted them to the stairs while everyone stared, pointed, and whispered.

"Does everyone really think you liberated Paris?" Jamie whispered.

Erik grinned. "Apparently."

D'Artagnan motioned.

Erik and Jamie came to the front of the line where more people greeted them, shook Erik's hand, and thanked them. Eventually, they got to the stairs with D'Artagnan and began their ascent up the Eiffel Tower. D'Artagnan looked over his shoulder with a smile. "How are you doing, major?"

Erik grinned back. "To be honest with you, I really don't know."

"You have nothing to worry about; you'll have a wonderful evening."

"How much do I owe you for your troubles?"

"Troubles?" D'Artagnan raised his eyebrows, but his eyes were bright and warm. "You owe me nothing. It's the people of France who owe you."

Wow, that's the first time a French person actually said that to me. Erik thought.

D'Artagnan looked at Jamie while he pointed at Erik. "He's a good man; you shouldn't let him get away."

Her smile glowed. "That's why I love him, D'Artagnan, and I won't."

They got to the second level, where Le Jules Verne was located. D'Artagnan turned around to face Erik. "Major, I would like to inform you the top floor is not reachable at this present time. However, if you want to propose to her, go around the corner." He waved goodbye, and Erik nodded and grinned.

Erik escorted Jamie as they walked around the corner and explained they couldn't get past the third level of the Eiffel Tower because the elevator cables were cut to prevent Hitler from going up in 1940. They headed to the edge and held each other. Jamie laid her head against Erik's shoulder, and they stared over the city of silhouetted buildings against the blanket of night.

The streets of Paris were defined by lights on vehicles. Soft white lights that normally illuminated the windows were covered by boards at night, blending into the dark buildings. Erik took a deep breath and drew a ring box from his right pocket. He opened it, pulled out the engagement ring and stepped back, gently disengaging her arm. Then, he looked into her eyes and asked, "Jamie, will you spend the rest of your life with me?"

Jamie looked at the sparkling marquise diamond engagement

ring in Erik's hand and gasped. Her eyes moistened with happiness. "Yes, I will," she whispered and nodded vigorously.

Erik's heart leaped with joy. He gently raised her left hand and slipped the ring on her finger. Jamie threw her arms around him and kissed him passionately while he held her close and rubbed her back.

This is the greatest day of my life. Nothing will ever be able to match it, Erik thought.

Their lips separated and he felt the warmth of her breath. Then he wiped the tears from her face. She stared at her engagement ring as if she were mesmerized. Erik took her hand, led her back to the restaurant, and they were again greeted by D'Artagnan who was waiting for them.

Erik smiled and nodded to D'Artagnan, indicating that Jamie had accepted his proposal. D'Artagnan grinned and hugged them both and offered his congratulations. A thundering roar of applause consumed the second level. People walked up to Erik, thanked and congratulated him, and D'Artagnan escorted them to the entrance of Le Jules Verne, where they were greeted with open doors and smiles. The owner of Le Jules Verne, Aramis, a short, heavyset man with an overbearing belly, a handlebar mustache, and wide-set, sparrow-brown eyes, made his way toward Erik and Jamie and gave them a warm welcome.

The Le Jules Verne décor was reminiscent of an airship from the early twentieth century. Floor-to-ceiling windows overlooked the vast city of Paris, and recessed lighting honeycombed the metal ceiling, casting a soft light over the dining area. The deep ruby-red carpet gave the room a warm, comfy feeling, and ornate plates, cutlery, and glasses glistened on tables covered in chocolate linen tablecloths. Black metal-framed chairs with maroon and chocolate fabric completed the picture.

Aramis discreetly congratulated Erik and Jamie on their engagement and showed them to their window table for two—the best in the establishment. Paris lay below them in a sparkling grandeur from the moonlight, extended from an assortment of buildings that extended all the way to La Tour Montparnasse. The moon, low on the horizon, peeked between the clouds and rose above the Seine River, which twisted and curved under its bridges.

Jamie reached for Erik's hand and stared at him with love in her eyes. Erik smiled. After all the hardships they'd had, she seemed to love him more than ever.

"Have you been to Paris before?" she asked.

"Yes."

"When you were here, did you do this or were you with the…?"

Erik gently grabbed her hand and leaned forward, nearly touching her lips. "I was here on business."

She mouthed, "*CIA?*"

He nodded. "I was never in this restaurant, or for that matter, never took a girlfriend to Paris. You're the first."

"Were you going to bring me here and propose in the same way?"

He nodded and kissed her gently.

Their first dish looked like a piece of artwork, light and elegant. It was gratin moelleux de macaroni truffé, jus de veau perlé, a truffle macaroni gratin served on a rich, pearly veal juice. Black truffles filled the tubular pasta which was presented as a crown, topped with a shaving of parmesan cheese.

"It tastes heavenly," Jamie said after a bite.

Later Aramis returned and asked how they were enjoying their meals. Both Erik and Jamie nodded. Then Erik excused himself and asked Aramis to join him for a short walk.

When he was far enough away where Jamie couldn't hear, he said, "I'd like to thank you and your staff for the amazing hospitality."

"You are very welcome, major. We're delighted to have honored guests such as you and your fiancé. After all, you liberated Paris."

Erik shook his head in disbelief from hearing this all night. "I did not liberate Paris. The US Army did."

"Come now, major, I know you had a part of it." Aramis became a little defensive, but his eyes remained friendly. "D'Artagnan said you even knew the date Paris was going to be liberated. You must be a spy." Aramis raised his eyebrows in curiosity, as he leaned forward in a half whisper, "Major, I won't tell anyone. Your secret is safe with me."

"I'm not a spy, I'm an analyst. I just read books."

Aramis doubled over with laughter, then placed his arm around Erik and looked him in the eye. "You are funny, major. D'Artagnan didn't tell me you had a sense of humor."

"How much do I owe you?" Erik asked.

Aramis's expression became stern. "Nothing major. You're a hero of the French people; everything is on me."

"Thank you." Erik grinned and made his way back to his table, as he thought *If only Aramis really knew.*

Jamie stared at Erik as if she asked what that was all about. He shook his head, telling her it was nothing.

Their mouth-watering dessert arrived on a plate with a lit candle and accompanied by all the staff, including Aramis, who wished them a happy engagement on behalf of Le Jules Verne and the people of France. Jamie and Erik made a wish and blew out the candle while they admired the cursive chocolate Des Moments Heureux Ensemble (Happy Times Together) writing on the white plate.

When completely satisfied, they walked hand-in-hand to the exit, everyone in Le Jules Verne stood up and applauded. Jamie whispered in Erik's ear that he should smile and be happy. Erik raised his hand to thank everyone, and Jamie smiled and waved gracefully. They strolled to the elevator, climbed in, and descended to the ground where D'Artagnan was waiting for them.

"How was it, major?"

"I know I can speak for both of us; it was wonderful. Thank you, D'Artagnan."

"You are very welcome, major. Where to now?"

Erik glanced at Jamie. She mouthed *home.*

At Erik's instructions, D'Artagnan drove off, and as they approached the hotel entrance, he glanced into the back seat and said, "Major, if you need anything let me know."

Erik smiled. "I will."

D'Artagnan opened the door for them again, then closed it behind them. After they said their goodbyes, he got back in the car, leaned out the window and said, "Oh, major, my son said hi and congratulations."

Puzzled, Erik frowned. "Who is your son?"

"You met him the same day you met me." Before Erik could ask for something more specific, D'Artagnan drove off.

Back in their hotel room, Jamie stripped down to her white lace bra, panties, garter belt, stockings, and red ruby heels while Erik watched with delight.

She winked and gave a suggestive smile and said, "Hi, professor."

Erik thought to himself, *Oh boy, this is going to be a long night…* and it was.

17. JUST THE BEGINING

"There will come a time when you believe everything is fin-
ished. Yet that will be the beginning."   —Louis L'Amour

Jamie was in the shower, relaxing after a long, delightful afternoon playing tourist, while Erik lay in bed pondering what restaurant they would go to for dinner. He checked the duffel bag to make sure they still had plenty of money and sent a silent thank you to Bonesteiner for sending it with Jamie. A file Erik hadn't seen before lay against the side of the bag; he pulled it out and discovered a post-it note from Bonesteiner on the outside:

Erik, I found this. Use it to your advantage and watch your back.

Erik opened it and read. It was a dossier from 1944, and, he noted it with interest, it was about him.

OFFICE OF STRATEGIC SERVICES
FILE NUMBER: OSS1-JLCF-TS46-357

NAME: Erik Függer
ALIAS: Joe Turner

DATE OF BIRTH: unknown

HAIR COLOR: Dark Brown

EYE COLOR: Blue

HEIGHT: 5 feet 6 inches

WEIGHT: 180 lbs

DISTINGUISHING MARKS/FEATURES: small scar above left knee

PLACED OF BIRTH: unknown

KNOWN PHOBIA(S): unknown

AVERSION(S): unknown

ALLERGY(IES): Penicillin and Sulfur

RESIDENCE: unknown

CONTACT NUMBERS: unknown

FATHER: unknown

MOTHER: unknown

SIBLING(S): unknown

KNOWN RELATIONSHIP(S): Jamie Anderson

CURRENT POSITION: unknown

WEAPON(S): small firearms

LANGUAGE(S): English (native), German

HOBBY(IES): History

LIKE(S): unknown

DISLIKE(S): unknown

POLITICAL AFFILIATION(S): unknown

RELIGIOUS AFFILIATION(S): unknown

EDUCATION: unknown

AUGUST 1, 1944: At 1600 went to Château d'Apigné, General Omar Bradley's headquarters. Spoke to General Bradley about an individual claiming to be an OSS agent named Erik Függer.

He said he gave the rank as Major. General Bradley advised me on 23 July 1944 that there was small arms fire outside the Château, killing two GIs and German Field Marshal Erwin Rommel. A female lieutenant gave General Bradley two dossiers: 1- Erik Függer, claiming he was an OSS agent and 2- Captain Cerberus, who was a German agent. Files are now misplaced, lost or taken. Függer was treated by General Bradley's physician and taken to Clinique Mutualiste de la Sagesse. General Bradley's physician stated that Függer had the following injuries: left kneecap dislocated, three fingers were broken on the left hand, and five ribs cracked on right side. Went to Clinique Mutualiste de la Sagesse and he was not there.

AUGUST 2, 1944: Went to several hospitals in the area and there was no trace of him.

AUGUST 7, 1944: Continued search. All leads were coming up negative.

AUGUST 15, 1944: Results were back from OSS database, no agent named Erik Függer. Also, there were no German agents named Cerberus. I am beginning to wonder what country or what agency they worked for. Still looking for Függer, no leads or luck yet.

AUGUST 23, 1944: Got lead that Függer was using the name Joe Turner and was located in Clinique du Moulin-Bruz in Saint-Jacques-de-la-Lande. We got there too late; he left on his own accord. The good news is that I interviewed the doctor who was taking care of him and got a good description of him (see drawing in file). Also, found that he has a girlfriend named Jamie Anderson. Ran her name in the database search, came up negative.

AUGUST 30, 1944: He disappeared, checking surrounding areas.

SEPTEMBER 4, 1944: Függer went to General Bradley's headquarters, the reason was unclear. I heard he and Field Marshal Montgomery got into an argument over Operation Market Garden. Függer said he believed that Germany was not defeated, and they would launch another offensive in the west (did not say where), and they were coming out with new weapons. Later that day, we got a lead he was staying in the L'Hôtel, 13 Rue des Beaux-Arts, 75006, in room 310, Paris, France. Got in fire-fight, my one partner was seriously injured: one was shot in the knee. The other was killed: right elbow had compound fracture, Body of sternum was shattered and neck was broken. I had never seen such a thing before. As for myself, my head was grazed by a bullet, destroying my glasses.

SEPTEMBER 7, 1944: No trace of him again.

SEPTEMBER 21, 1944: Still nothing. Függer had either changed his identity or died. Case closed.

TO BE UPDATED AS NECESSARY

Erik exhaled forcefully.

Jamie, wearing just a towel, gave him a bear hug from behind and kissed him on the cheek. She looked over his shoulder and asked, "What are you looking at, babe?"

"A dossier." He turned to her with a raised eyebrow.

"Oh babe, I'm sorry; Admiral Bonesteiner told me to give that to you."

"Try not to forget these things." Erik gently tapped the folder on her head. "Have you looked inside this?"

Jamie shook her head. "Who or what is it on?"

"Me."

Her eyes lit up. "So I can see what you did in the CIA?"

"Mmm, no." He poked her between her breasts and tugged the towel. "You, including me, will never be able to see my dossier with the agency." He loosened the towel a little. "It is in a very secure location, unlike this towel."

"Where would your file be kept?"

Erik gave her a look as if to say *why are you asking me this now?*

"Babe, I'm just asking. So do you know?"

He nodded.

"So can you tell me?"

"Langley."

"CIA Headquarters?"

Erik nodded again.

"I bet it's very hard to get into that room," Jamie said.

"Really, you think so?"

"Erik don't be sarcastic, I'm curious." Jamie looked over his shoulder and began to read; her expression grew puzzled. "The dates are all 1944."

"It is about me, from 1944."

"But you weren't around then." Her eyes widened as the realization dawned on her. "Oh my gosh, we're in 1944. This is because you were sent back in time."

"Bingo."

She peered again at the document, then recoiled. "I'm in there, too." She clutched the towel tightly around her. "Babe, I'm scared."

Erik hugged her, then looked into her eyes and said, "I'll never let anything happen to you. I made you that promise and I intend to keep it." He rubbed her cheek, then kissed her deeply until she melted in his arms. "Every time we go out," he said and paused for a breath, "we'll be low key and keep to ourselves. We'll always leave and come back together. According to this, we have nineteen days until we'll be in the clear." *Unless things change. Which they can*, Erik thought.

"Can we just disappear?" Jamie asked.

Erik shook his head. "If we change anything, we'll change the timeline, and that could make things worse. No, we'll just play it cool and not alter history."

"Oh, there's something else, too." Jamie dug into the duffle bag and pulled out a book. "Another thing Admiral Bonesteiner told me to give to you. Sorry I didn't remember sooner. I'll make us some tea."

She handed him the 2008 edition of *World War Two for Morons*.

18. ON THE EDGE OF THE WORLD

"The world is very different now. For man holds in his mortal hands the power to abolish all forms of human poverty and all forms of human life."   —John F. Kennedy

While Jamie made tea, Erik flipped casually through the pages of the 2008 edition of *World War Two for Morons*. On page 276 he discovered a section on how, in 2008, the European Theater of War World Two was changed when ONE sent someone back in time to 1944. Erik's blood surged and he slammed his right fist into his left palm. He had to force himself to calm down before reading:

After the failed attempt to kill Hitler in July 1944, another assassination attempt was undertaken in October in Berlin, inside the Führer's Bunker. The attempt succeeded and Hitler was assassinated.

On October 2, 1944, at 12:55 p.m. while the advancing American and British armies neared the German border in the west, and Russian armies continued their attacks in the east, Hitler was in his bunker when shots were heard in the Reich's Chancellery.

From eyewitness accounts, the assassin, in an SS officer uniform, approached the entrance of the bunker, presented his identification, then single-handedly killed the guards. He then shot the other guards in the area and proceeded down the stairs to the bunker. Hitler's SS bodyguards were not able to stop the assassin.

Hitler was in a meeting with a high-ranking SS officer. They were leaning over a table studying maps and diagrams, and discussing how Germany would change the tides of war with their new Miracle Weapons, such as the V-2 rocket, when the assassin barged in, shooting and killing Hitler. The high-ranking SS officer, Lieutenant General Hans Kammler, survived the assassination with minor injuries and gave this account.

No one knew whether the assassin was sent by the Allies or a member of an inner faction of the Reich. But Hitler's death didn't end the war as the Allies had hoped; it caused turmoil and chaos within the hierarchy of the Third Reich. The result of Hitler's assassination was a more organized and stronger Third Reich.

Erik shook his head. He should lay low and try to survive, but Bonesteiner was telling Erik he needed to find a way to resolve the problem. He continued reading and learned that immediately after Hitler's death, a power struggle within the Reich occurred. Goebbels, Himmler, and Goering each set up their alliances to cut-throat the others and gain control of the party. The end result was that Goebbels became Führer of the Reich and Goering was murdered. In addition, Goebbels listened to Admiral Karl Dönitz and the OKW (German High Command) and increased production of U-boats, new jets, and tanks. Goebbels gave total freedom to the German Staff to plan their attack in the west, giving Germany more time to develop new weapons.

Goebbels, along with other generals and high-ranking Nazis, knew they couldn't win the war in Europe with America and Russia's mass production of weapons, so they planned psychological victory with Project "Prufstand XII" which targeted New York and Washington D.C.

Dönitz, Kammler, and Speer began work in late 1944 at Peenemunde on developing a U-boat that was able to carry V-2 rockets with atomic warheads. Since the size of V-2 rockets (length forty-five feet, eleven inches) rendered them too large to be placed in a U-boat hull, the conning tower of a Type XXI U-boat was modified to house three V-2 rockets. Once in launching position, the V-2 would be fueled, its guidance system set, and the rocket would be launched and head toward its target. With all these new Miracle Weapons, Goebbels was positive he could force England and the United States into a separate peace treaty and then he could focus on Russia.

Jamie brought the tea, took hers onto the balcony and left Erik to his book. He ignored the steaming cup on the table before him. Erik shook his head in disbelief at what he read. He stood and walked around to release some of his frustration. The information in the book was clear what will happen and even if Erik tried to present this to Bradley to make an attempt to change history, they would want solid proof. He would try, but an opportunity needed to present itself. Erik sighed and continued reading.

The new history still had the Germans launching their offensive in the Ardennes, as they had done in 1940. The only major difference was that the offensive was to start in late November, and the heavily overcast weather would ground the Allies' overwhelmingly superior air forces. Within eight weeks, at night, the Germans were able to assemble thirty Divisions. Then on 27 November 1944, the Germans launched their offensive known as Watch over the Rhine, or better known as The Battle of the Bulge. The German goal was to retake Antwerp and set up the launch pads for the V-2 rockets that would carry the atomic warheads. Within eight days, the German offensive was a complete success and on the fifth of December, the Allied forces surrendered at Antwerp. The Battle of the Bulge was over. The question the Allied commanders had was, "What's next?"

Erik continued reading about Germany's nuclear program from its developmental stages to testing of the A-4, A-10 and V-2 rockets from a U-boat. Its first successful test was in early December of 1944. This new class of U-boat was the XXIN, modeled after the XXI class U-boat. It housed three V-2 rockets within the modified conning tower. What made it a deadly weapon, and one of a kind, was the Anechoic tiles on the outer hull. They were about four millimeters in thickness and made from a material called Oppanol, a synthetic rubber with sonar absorbing properties. Erik rubbed his forehead, amazed and concerned. He took a deep breath and continued to read.

The new rockets, which were going be used on England and Russia, were known as the A-4 and A-10. What made the rockets even more deadly was that the Germans used a Binary Computer known as Z-3 (Konrad Zuse built the first Binary computer in 1938, called Z-1). Z-3 was to be used to program the V-2, A-4 and A-10 rockets for their new targets: New York City, Chicago, Washington D.C., London, Southampton, Leningrad, and Moscow. On March 15, 1945, roughly around nine o'clock eastern standard time, the Germans launched the rockets to their assigned targets. The U-boat launched its rockets, and in Europe rockets launched from Antwerp and Peenemünde. Moments later, bright lights flashed above each city from a blast radius of approximately five miles, and a mushroom cloud rose above the ruins and death. The book states the official estimated death totals:

New York City: 176,000—260,000
Chicago: 90,000—166,000
Washington D.C.: 60,000—80,000
London: 100,000—160,000
Southampton: 90,000—130,000
Leningrad: 150,000—210,000
Moscow: 200,000—286,000

Goebbels and the German High Command thought these attacks would make the Allies sue for peace. The Germans were correct in their assessment that the targets were of great importance and caused a great psychological effect in each country. However, they were wrong in their idea that it would make the Allied powers sue for peace; it made the war continue for another seven months.

Germany never got what they were hoping for—peace with the Allies. From the ashes and ruins, the Allies united again. The public wanted revenge and no mercy for Germany for what they did. From March fourth to fifteenth, Prime Minister Winston Churchill, President Franklin D. Roosevelt, and General Secretary Joseph Stalin met again at the Yalta Conference. Both America and Britain had plans for ending the war more quickly in Europe, and the Russians planned to attack Japan even before Germany was defeated.

On April 12, 1945, Roosevelt died, and President Harry S. Truman took office. In his speech to the American people he said, "Carry the battle to them. Don't let them bring it to you. Put them on the defensive and don't ever apologize for anything.[12]" The same day Truman was briefed on the effects of the atomic bomb, and said, "America was not built on fear. America was built on courage, on imagination and unbeatable determination to do the job at hand.[13]"

Next came the planning to end the war in Europe, known as Operation New World. Truman was briefed on carrying this attack against Germany. The United States Army Air Corps (USAAC) built a base in Newfoundland, where in 1945 three of the new B-36 Peacemaker bombers were stationed. The USAAC considered the B-36 an intercontinental bomber because they could fly from Newfoundland to Berlin round trip.

In this alternate history, on July 3, 1945, at 6:00 p.m., air crews started preparing the three B-36 Peacemakers for their historic flights. The names of the three B-36 Peacemakers were the Niña, the Pinta, and the Santa Maria. It took approximately six hours to prepare the bombers, each of them carrying two atomic bombs. At approximately 12 noon, the bombers took off on their historic mission to end the war in Europe. It took them a little over twelve hours to reach their targets in Germany: the Niña to

---

12. Democraticunderground.com 2001—2011
13. www.theheroesclub.org 2011

Cologne and Frankfurt; the Pinta to Bremerhaven and Hamburg, and the Santa Maria to Berlin.

American jet fighters from the Red Tail Squadrons (the 100th, 301st, and the 302nd), also known as the Tuskegee Airmen, were stationed at Mildenhall Royal Air Force Base. The Red Tail Squadrons were given the great honor of protecting the bombers. Three days after the atomic bombs were dropped on Germany, Truman addressed the American public over the radio and told them that Germany had surrendered.

The book quotes his speech:

Three days ago, three American bombers dropped six atomic bombs on five strategic cities in Germany; one of those cities was Berlin. Each bomb had more power than 20,000 tons of T.N.T., which is the largest bomb ever yet used in the history of warfare. The Germans began the war with the invasion of Poland in 1939. They attacked us with their atomic rockets on March 15, 1945. They have been repaid many times over. With each of these bombs, we have now added a new and revolutionary increase in destruction to supplement the growing power of our armed forces, which the world now knows. We are currently developing these bombs and producing even more powerful ones. The force from which the sun draws its power has been loosed against Germany because they brought war to Europe and The United States of America."

On August 6, 1945, the Enola Gay, a B-29 Superfortress, dropped an Atomic Bomb on Nagasaki. Three days later, on August 9, 1945, Boxcar, another B-29 Superfortress, dropped an

Atomic Bomb on Hiroshima. Then on August 14, 1945 Japan surrendered to the United States, thus ending World War Two.

"Dammit!" Erik jumped up and hurled the book across the room, barely missing Jamie on her way in from the balcony. Jamie stopped and stared at him, wide-eyed and speechless. He took a deep breath and said calmly, as if nothing had happened, "Thanks for bringing me tea." Then he walked over and picked up the book.

"What's the matter?" Jamie asked as she sat tentatively on the bed.

Erik just shook his head in disbelief. It was all too much. Jamie motioned to him to come sit by her, but he shook his head, pursed his lips and flipped through the pages of the revised history, thought about the other effects Hitler's assassination would have had on history, effects not mentioned in the book. Erik, normally calm and analytical, found himself angry and reduced to cursing over the results of ONE's intervention in history. He closed his eyes, took a few breaths, then turned and smiled at Jamie.

"Babe," Jamie asked cautiously, "would you like a pastry with that tea?" She picked one from the plate and handed it to him.

"Absolutely." He realized that he'd been so engrossed in his book that he hadn't noticed the pastries which had arrived with the tea.

Erik took a seat by her, placed the plate on his lap and took a huge bite of the pastry. He savored the bite of freshly made pastry, custard and fresh apple, then took a sip of his rapidly cooling tea. Jamie said nothing; she just sat and waited for him.

"Jamie," he said when he'd licked the last dollop of custard from his fingers, "do you still like when I tell you about history?"

She nodded.

Erik took a moment to collect his thoughts and figured out how to express what he had to say. But there's no nice way, so he put it bluntly. He assured her that he was not mad at her. She had her doubts, but after some explaining, she believed him. He summed up what he had read with all its gruesome detail.

She shivered as he read the death toll from the atomic bombs, and tears trickled down her cheeks. She choked and asked, "Is that because we went back in time?"

"No, it was because ONE was trying to play God and end the war in Europe sooner, but it backfired."

"Who's ONE?"

Erik took a deep breath. "Not who but what!" He paused to collect his thoughts. "ONE is an elite dark agency that could do anything and get away with it."

"Are they what conspiracy theorists' talk about?"

"I guess."

"And how do you know about them?"

"I was exposed to their world briefly." He gave a dismissive gesture. "But that's not the issue at hand though." Erik raised the book. "Killing Hitler and how it changed World War Two is the issue."

"Is this," she pointed to the book, "what we're going to have to live through?"

"If Hitler is assassinated, yes."

"Is there anything you can do to stop that from happening?"

Erik shrugged and gave her a maybe-or-maybe-not look. "I could try to help the Allies win Operation Market Garden." Then he contemplated the unthinkable. "Or save Hitler's life."

"Do you think you'll be able to do either one?"

Erik shook his head. "To be honest, I don't think so."

Jamie placed her soft little hand on his and raised her big brown eyes to meet his gaze. "Babe, won't you try?"

Erik nodded reluctantly. *What else could I do?* "But I'll be a man against the world and time."

The odds were stacked against him. He had no support team, he was operating out of a hotel room in 1944 and planning an op which would take weeks or even months. When Erik was with the agency, he had direct access to the information in federal databases; now he only had the 2008 Edition of *World War Two for Morons*. With that in mind, Erik reread what little information was in the book. He knew he would spend hours upon hours planning and brainstorming. But mostly, Erik would need lots and lots of luck.

19. MAN AGAINST THE WORLD AND TIME

"I've always made a total effort, even when the odds seemed entirely against me. I never quit trying; I never felt that I didn't have a chance to win." —Arnold Palmer

Rennes, France

Erik stood at the foot of the steps of General Omar Bradley's headquarters. He wore suitable attire for his identity as an OSS major—a green U.S. Army service tunic, a beige shirt, tie, trousers, and an overseas side cap with a golden oak leaf. Jamie stood at his side in an officer uniform consisting of an olive drab jacket and a pink-beige blouse and skirt. She also wore a tie and an overseas cap with a sterling silver bar that identified her as a U.S. Army First Lieutenant. Erik gathered his thoughts in preparation for trying to convince the Allies to prepare themselves for the German offensive through the Ardennes Forest. If he could be persuasive enough, it would change the outcome of Operation Market Garden.

He felt Jamie's soft touch on his shoulder. "I'm sure you'll do great. They'll listen to you," she said in a warm sweet voice.

Erik shrugged and looked up at the château. "I'm not so sure. If they believe me, then the war and the history books will be changed. If they don't believe me, it'll be up to me to stop Hitler from being killed." He took a step up, but Jamie, with a deeply inquisitive face, held him back. He looked back at her.

"Erik, I saw your military uniforms from different countries. When you wore them, is this the sort of thing you did?"

He shook his head.

"Can you tell me what you did?"

Again he shook his head. He wasn't allowed to talk about it. "Let's go."

They walked up the stairs to the château in which General Omar Bradley had his headquarters. Erik focused, as he did when he was overseas doing an op, to get into character. He was trained to use whatever resources were available, and General Bradley was the resource. The downside of coming was that Erik knew he could give a play-by-play of what was going to happen, something he must not do. All he could do was drop "what ifs" and give hypothetical situations. Erik was also trained in predicting human behavior, but maybe his predictions would work out or maybe not. He just knew he had to try.

At the top of the stairs, the MPs at the entrance snapped to attention, saluted and opened the doors. Once inside, Erik made a quick analysis of the room and individuals in it—military personnel, each attending to their assigned duties.

"Can I help you, major?" Erik turned to the voice. A sergeant sat behind a desk.

"I'm here to see General Bradley."

"Sir, do you have an appointment with the general?"

"No." Erik leaned forward, "It's a matter of national security." Erik pointed to the phone. "Call him and tell him Major Erik Függer is here. He'll know who I am."

"Sir, he's very busy, but I can see if he's able to meet you today."

"Listen, sergeant, I'm with the OSS. I'll see him now." Erik squinted at the man and lowered his voice. "Do I make myself clear?"

The sergeant nodded and picked up the receiver.

A door opened and a commanding voice drifted through the foyer. "Major?"

Erik turned to the voice. General Bradley walked toward him with a warm smile and his hand extended. They shook hands and saluted. "You're looking well," Bradley said. "How have you been?"

"Thank you, Sir. I'm well."

Bradley looked over Erik's shoulder and smiled at Jamie. "I see the lieutenant is with you."

Erik glanced at Jamie, then back at Bradley. "Yes."

Bradley motioned them to walk with him. "What are you up to these days?"

"Trying to find a way to defeat Germany, just like everyone else."

Bradley cupped his hand on Erik's shoulder and nodded. "Speaking of that, maybe you should accompany me to my office."

"Why is that, Sir?"

Bradley looked around, then leaned close to Erik and spoke in a half whisper, "Montgomery has a plan that could defeat Germany."

"Is that so?" Erik found it hard to keep his distaste for the man off his face.

Bradley nodded and grinned. "Apparently you, like many others, don't care for him, but do me a favor and just listen to him. Give your feedback; speak your mind. I'm sure he'll listen to you."

Erik smirked. "Do I have your permission to do just that, Sir?"

Bradley nodded. Erik smiled and thought if things were to get ugly, he had an exit strategy.

Bradley's office was obvious because two armed sentries stood at the entrance. Bradley ushered them inside and closed the door. The huge office had standard government-issue desk, chairs, and bookcases, all brought over from the US. On the left side sat an oversized wooden table used to discuss military strategies. Montgomery, some members of his staff, and a few members of Bradley's staff stood around it, studying a map of Europe that showed both Allied and German troop locations.

Montgomery turned around. "Brad, it's so good to see you again." He approached Bradley with a huge grin.

"You too, Monty; how are things with you?"

"Could not be better." Montgomery turned his focus on Erik and Jamie. "Who did you bring with you?"

Bradley turned to Erik. "This is…I'm sorry, I forgot your name." Erik excused him and introduced himself and Jamie. "He's with the OSS; the lieutenant is his aide."

Erik and Montgomery exchanged salutes and handshakes, and then he exchanged salutes with Jamie. "So you are with American Intelligence?"

"Yes Sir." Erik looked over his shoulder. "And Lieutenant Anderson is my aide."

"Dashing to have an attractive young lady as an aide," Montgomery said, and laughter filled the room.

Erik turned to Jamie to make sure she was okay, and she nodded, though her smile looked forced.

"Let us get down to business," Montgomery announced as he walked to the table in the center of the room. He turned to Bradley. "I don't believe the major and the lieutenant have clearance to be present for what we'll be discussing."

"I assure you…" Bradley began.

Erik butted in. "I can assure you that as members of the OSS, not only do we have the proper clearance for this briefing, but we also have the authority to be here."

Montgomery grinned. "I'm sure the little lady doesn't want to hear this anyway. She can be excused." He motioned her away.

"She stays, Field Marshal. What I see and hear, she will, too," Erik declared. "Is that understood?"

"Is that so?" Montgomery's brows furrowed with suspicion. "Under whose authority?"

"The President of the United States."

Bradley stepped into the conversation. "Major Függer was able to find a spy in my headquarters."

Montgomery stared at Erik, then back at Bradley.

Bradley continued, "He has coordinated the French Resistance to help our troops in regaining control of occupied France. Monty, in my opinion, Major Függer should be and needs to be at this meeting. He could give his feedback."

Erik stepped forward, paused for a moment, stared at Montgomery, and then, looked slowly around the room and into everyone's eyes and spoke with a tone of authority. "I am Major Függer with the OSS, and Lieutenant Anderson is also. My presence cannot be mentioned outside these doors due to security reasons. Any breach of this will result in severe disciplinary action and court martial. Do I make myself clear, gentlemen?"

Everyone in the room said, "Yes sir." pretty much at the same time.

Erik turned to Montgomery. "You have the floor, Field Marshal."

Montgomery pressed his lips together, then apparently accepted that Erik was telling the truth. He nodded. "Thank you, Major Függer."

He walked to the table and opened a huge, black leather portfolio case. Bradley, Erik, and Jamie followed him and squeezed themselves into an available space. Montgomery pulled a map of the Low Countries from the portfolio case and began his briefing.

"Gentlemen, this is Operation Market Garden. General Eisenhower agrees with me that my plan when it succeeds ..." His right hand made an embracing gesture over the map. "It will end the war in less than one hundred days." A smile appeared on Montgomery's face. "With that said, it will bring our boys home before Christmas." Nods and grins filled the room, but Erik gave Montgomery a cold stare.

Jamie, who knew little about the war, listened with a placid expression while she looked at Erik for nonverbal clues.

"What's the plan?" Bradley asked.

Montgomery rubbed his chin and gave a crafty grin. "The plan is very simple; we are going to drop 35,000 paratroopers behind enemy lines in occupied Holland." He stabbed a finger at the map and everyone in the room drew near to the table and examined it closer. "Compared to Operation Overlord, this will be the largest airborne assault ever mounted." Montgomery chuckled with delight. "To put it quite honestly, gentlemen, this has never been attempted before."

"Where is all this going to take place?" A member of Bradley's staff asked.

Montgomery stared at him, then met everyone's eyes in turn. He pulled out a pointer. "The ground forces, Thirty Corps commanded by General Horrocks, with their 20,000 vehicles are located here." He tapped the end of the pointer on Leopoldville, Belgium. "They'll do a single thrust up this road." He dragged the end of his pointer across the map and stopped at each key place. "They link up with our airborne forces, which will lay a carpet over Holland. The airborne forces, with total surprise, will seize and secure the bridges and hold them until the ground forces link up with them." The men around the table examined the map closely.

"Who is going to be assigned to what bridges?" Bradley asked. He rubbed his chin, adjusted his glasses, and glanced at Erik.

"I'm coming to that. General Taylor's One-hundred-and-first Airborne will be assigned to the Son and Eindhoven Bridges, General Gavin's Eighty-second Airborne will seize the Grave and Nijmegen Bridges, and finally General Urquhart's First Airborne will get the prize, Arnhem Bridge. From there, we can pour into Germany's industrial center, the Ruhr, and then Hitler's Reich will collapse. Any questions?"

Bradley studied the map at different angles, motioned Erik to come closer, and directed a question to Montgomery, "How many miles did you say Thirty Corps has to travel?"

"Sixty-three."

"How long will it take for them to reach Arnhem?"

Montgomery replied briskly with a theatrical gesture. "Two days. Worse case, if we're delayed due to weather, four days tops."

Bradley turned to Erik and said in a half-whisper, "Do you think it can be done?"

Erik, stood with his arms crossed against his chest, and subtlety shook his head.

Montgomery glanced sharply at him. "Is there anything wrong, major?"

"Two days from Leopoldville to Arnhem?" Erik asked.

Montgomery nodded.

"Isn't that a bit rash, considering the Germans might know that the bridges are important to our advance?"

Lieutenant-General Browning cut in. "Our intelligence, including SHAEF's intelligence reports, states that these are not elite troops at all. Jerry lost them in Normandy. These troops are made up of old men and boys."

"You absolutely believe that?" Erik stepped back from the table and stared at Browning. Next, he glanced at the map. "What about the reports from the Dutch Underground?"

"Yes, I do," Browning said. "The reports from the Dutch Underground are not reliable." He pointed at Erik with an accusing finger and glanced around the table. "Christ, Major General Kennedy in the British War Office, as well as myself, Montgomery, and others believe that if we have the same amount of success as we have had since August, we'll be in Berlin late December or early January. You should have faith in Montgomery and his reports. They've served us well."

"Being in the OSS," Montgomery gave a cursory glance at Erik, "I'm surprised you're not informed that children are to be seen, not heard."

"And the field marshal forgets that one day the child will replace the parent." Erik smashed his pointing finger at Arnhem. "If Thirty Corps doesn't get to Arnhem in four days," Erik made a circular gesture, "the Germans will have fortified the area around General Urquhart's troops, and then we'll have a disaster on our hands." Erik strolled toward Montgomery. "If I were you, I would send in additional troops to make sure the Arnhem Bridge will be held and secured for Thirty Corps." Erik paused to make his last point very clear. "Maybe you are going a bridge too far."

Montgomery approached Erik and pushed his face close to Erik's. "Major, I can assure you General Urquhart's First Airborne is quite capable of holding their own."

Erik mocked, "I forgot, you and MI6 know all."

"That's correct, major."

Bradley positioned himself by Jamie, leaned in and whispered in her ear, "I hope the major knows who he's talking to and knows what he's doing."

Jamie turned and replied in a half whisper, "He does; he knows the German Army very well and what they're capable of doing."

Erik took charge of the conversation: "Like in May 1938, when General Oster and Beck warned the British government that Hitler was going to start a war." He held up one finger. "And urged resistance toward him." He held up another finger. "They also asked you to help them overthrow Hitler." He raised a third finger. "Your government was extremely doubtful that the German opposition could overthrow the Nazi regime. Thus, they ignored those messages." Erik tapped his foot while he waited for an answer.

"What else do you know, major?" Montgomery asked, his expression sour.

"That Rommel thought Patton was a better general, among other things, Sir."

Montgomery tilted his head, his right eyebrow raised. "How do you know that?"

"I knew him personally."

Montgomery rubbed his chin. "What else do you know?"

"Oh, do you really want to know?"

Bradley stepped between them. "Gentlemen, Germany is our enemy, not each other." Montgomery glared at him. "Monty, I have to agree with the major that you should put additional troops in Arnhem."

"Who would you recommend, major?"

"Why not the First Polish Parachute Brigade?"

"Are they under the command of General Sosabowski?" Montgomery asked, looking at Browning. Browning nodded and Montgomery stared back impassively. "Since we're working together, I will modify my plans to incorporate the First Polish Parachute Brigade. Anything else, major?"

"I recommend you fly them at the same time you fly General Urquhart's First Airborne."

Montgomery shook his head. "Major, leave that up to me. I don't need your help or opinions on field operations."

"If the plan succeeds…" Erik replied with dramatic, false sincerity.

"*When* it succeeds, major." Montgomery gave Erik a look of disdain.

"Of course, if the plan succeeds, we can pour into the Ruhr?"

Montgomery nodded but maintained his glare.

"Would you say Antwerp will be your next goal?"

"Explain yourself, major."

"Operation Crossbow," Erik stated and offered nothing more.

Montgomery and Browning stared at each other as if a trapdoor had opened in the floor beneath them. Montgomery raised one eyebrow in a questioning slant and gave a keep-your-mouth-shut-look toward Erik. "Finished, major?"

Erik tilted his head as if to say maybe or maybe not.

Dripping with spite, Montgomery added defensively, "Major, this is neither the place nor the time."

"It may not be the place nor the time, but Antwerp is just as important to us as it is to the Germans. If we take it, they will launch an offensive," Erik said.

"With what? Germany is defeated! They're fighting with old men and boys!"

"Oh dear God, Monty, you actually believe that bullshit?" Bradley tried to voice his opinion, but Erik shot him down with an open palm gesture. Bradley looked at Jamie as if to say Erik needed to watch what he was saying, but Erik continued:

"The Germans have a new tank out, the Tiger Two. It'll destroy any tank we put against it."

Montgomery reached over and with a forefinger stirred his intelligence reports and pulled one out. Then he leaned toward Erik, tapped a hooked forefinger on his report and spoke clearly with an undertone of anger and resentment. "Major, this report states that they are not capable and do not have the resources to build a new tank."

"You can count on two things that will happen by the end of this year," Erik replied, "one, the Germans will launch another offensive in the west, and they will have marginal success. And two," Erik looked the length of the table where the map laid and glanced back at Montgomery, "Operation Market Garden will fail."

"How dare you mock me and my plan?" Montgomery shot back with a sour look on his face. "Now major, I should ask you, do you, actually believe your bullshit?" Montgomery waited to see if Erik had any more comments.

Erik's face heated and his jaw tightened. "Yes, I do! If anything, they will launch their last offensive in the Ardennes forest!"

"How can you consider yourself an intelligence officer of the OSS since you do not know the facts about the German Army?"

"I know more than you will ever know. Now I must ask this—how can you consider yourself an effective general when you failed to take Caen with the initial landings on June sixth?"

Silence fell upon the room. Montgomery gave Erik a mad, dismissive gesture and pointed to the door. "Get out! Leave the room now, major!" Then he turned to Bradley. "I will not take this badgering from a pathetic major who knows nothing about Germany and has never been in combat."

Erik got in Montgomery's face. "Listen here you, bloody bastard, I've seen more death face-to-face in combat then you ever will."

Bradley separated them both, like a referee in a boxing match, and then motioned Erik to excuse himself politely. Erik snapped a salute to Montgomery and did an about-face. Bradley excused himself, so did Jamie, and they caught up with Erik.

"Major, what was that all about?" Bradley asked. "You were way out of line. You could be court martialed for your actions."

"I don't care."

"You should because I won't be able to go to your defense."

"I'm not asking you to." Erik leaned in so only Bradley could hear. "The Germans are making more advanced weapons, and the British know that. This grand plan, Operation Market Garden, will fail, but Montgomery will not listen to anyone but himself." Erik looked around and then continued, "You need to go to Eisenhower and advise him this is a bad plan."

"I can't."

Erik leaned back; his eyes widened, unable to hide his surprise at Bradley's statement. "Why in the hell not? Eisenhower will listen to you."

Bradley shook his head and removed his glasses. "Monty can be difficult. I know your feelings are shared and expressed by a lot of the generals."

"You avoided my question…I'd like an answer."

"You wouldn't understand."

"Try me." Erik waited, then began to understand. "Political reasons?"

Bradley gave a subtle nod.

"Things never change."

"Major…"

"Call me Erik."

Bradley motioned Erik to walk with him and Jamie followed

behind. "Erik, how do you know Operation Market Garden will fail?"

"Just call it a gut feeling."

Bradley glanced at Jamie. "Your aide said you know a lot about the German Army." Erik nodded.

"What are you going to do now?"

"Sir, I really don't know."

"I could use a man with your knowledge and expertise on my staff. All I have to do is make a few calls."

"Thank you, but I have to decline."

"Why?"

"I prefer working alone."

"Do you really think you can make a difference all by yourself?"

Erik smirked and nodded.

Bradley cocked his head and appraised Erik with a knowing smile. "Major, will I see you again?"

"I don't know…now I want you to be straight with me." Erik pointed at Bradley to make his point clear. "How do you know about me and the French Resistance?"

"We have a contact in Audrieu, France, and he mentioned your name."

"He who?"

"He goes by the name Hawk."

"The Hawk?" Erik tilted his head forward, as Bradley nodded his head. "What is his real name and why do they call him the Hawk?"

Bradley looked around and said in a half-whisper, "Valensky and because of his eyes."

Erik smirked and snapped a salute. Bradley returned one, and they shook hands and parted ways. Jamie caught up with Erik at the sergeant's desk. "Sergeant."

The sergeant gave his undivided attention. "Yes, Sir?"

"Where are the NCO's quarters?"

"Head out these doors and take an immediate left. It's the stone structure about twenty yards away."

Erik nodded as he absorbed the information and took mental notes. "Thank you, Sergeant. As you were."

"Yes, Sir."

Erik and Jamie walked down the stairs and headed in the direction of the NCO's quarters. He bit his lower lip while he thought about what had just happened and about the other possibilities that he could pursue to prevent the Germans from launching their rockets armed with atomic warheads, like saving Hitler's life.

"Wow, babe, Montgomery and you really didn't see eye-to-eye," Jamie said. Erik glared at her for a second then nodded. "He really doesn't like you."

"Thanks for the recap," Erik said. "He's a pompous ass and will get what he deserves."

"Jacques told me that people either like you or hate you."

Erik arched his brow and tilted his head slightly as if he considered the possibility.

"Is what you did back there the reason why?"

"One of many reasons."

Jamie grabbed his arm and turned him around. "Will Operation Market Garden really fail?" Erik looked at her as if she should already know the answer. "Erik, please tell me. I want to know."

"Most definitely, and unfortunately a lot of British and Polish paratroopers will die in Arnhem." His stomach suddenly surged, and his hands balled up into fists. "Damn it. Damn it. Damn it." If he hadn't antagonized Montgomery quite so much, the outcome might have been different. Now he'd be responsible for a lot of Polish paratroopers' deaths.

Jamie grabbed his shoulders and looked into his eyes. "What is it?"

Erik shook his head in disgust. "It's nothing. Forget it."

Jamie shrugged. He was glad she knew him well enough not to push the issue. Erik turned around and barged through the door of the NCO's barracks. Men recognized he was an officer, snapped to attention and saluted. Erik returned the salute and gave the order, "As you were." He approached an individual who was busy reading a Life magazine.

The individual snapped a salute and Erik did one in return. "Can I help you, Sir?"

"Where are Sergeant Court's belongings?"

The soldier glanced down the row of bunks and pointed. "Over there, Sir."

As Erik walked off, all eyes focused on Jamie, who followed him in. Erik glanced over Court's area and saw the MP-44 that was taken from the Kübelwagen he drove. Erik grabbed it and the extra magazines. At that moment, he heard a loud, outspoken voice.

"Nice legs! When did they allow women in here? Though it's not like I'm complaining."

Erik glanced up and recognized Court, the sergeant who punched him in the gut when he first came to see General Bradley. He stood quickly.

"Hey lieutenant, are you here for business or pleasure." Court eyed Jamie from head-to-toe. "I hope it's for pleasure because I'm up for it if you get my meaning." He laughed, and Jamie looked to Erik for help.

"Hey, Court, some major is in your things," someone said.

"What in the hell?" Court and Erik's eyes met like two gun-slingers in a western film. "That's my gun!" Court stormed to his bunk. Erik simply motioned Court to come get it.

Erik studied his opponent, looking for an angle to attack. Court pointed his finger at Erik and left his abdomen exposed. Erik placed his right foot forward, and at the same time slammed the butt of the gun into Court's gut. Court gasped and peered up. Erik again slammed the butt of the gun into his belly which caused him to fall to his knees. Jamie and the others stood motionless.

"Before I introduce myself, you do know how to salute an officer?" Erik forced Court around to face Jamie and then jerked him back around to face him. "Did you forget?"

Court shook his head, his expression confused.

Erik shouldered the MP-44 and pulled out his pistol. "Remember me?" Though he appeared calm, something unmistakably ominous festered inside Erik. "Let me give you some clues," he said evenly.

Jamie stepped forward with her mouth open as if unable to find words. Erik shook his head and gave a look that told her not to interfere. Then he forced Court's head back and placed the gun to his head. Erik's brow wrinkled in vexation and he said bluntly, "You speak good English for a Nazi."

Court's eyes enlarged in horror. "I … I was just doing my job."

Erik gave a sadistic grin with a gleam of satisfaction in his eyes. "So was I." Then Erik swung the grip to the back of Court's head and knocked him unconscious. He released his body which fell to the floor.

Jamie stared at him white-faced. Erik met her gaze without emotion and jerked his head toward the door. She followed him out. They climbed into the car, and Jamie reached for his hand.

"Erik, can I ask you something?"

"You can ask, but it doesn't mean I'm going to answer."

Jamie nodded sheepishly. "What happened back there?"

Erik squinted at her, shrugged as if to say it wasn't worth acknowledging and started the car.

"Why won't you tell me?"

"Because he's an asshole, and I only did to him what he did to me."

Erik drove off.

Jamie sighed and quickly changed the subject. "You did well back there."

Erik glanced at her as if to say, what are we talking about now?

"You know the meeting with all the generals."

Erik rolled his eyes. "I should've done better."

"I'm proud of you."

He grinned and gently tapped her hand. "You did well, too."

"Thanks, babe. Could you go to Eisenhower and warn him that Operation Market Garden will fail?"

Erik shook his head. "Even if I tried, it'd be almost impossible to see him, and he'd ask me too many questions. I remember reading something he said, 'It is not the big decisions that weigh heavy…it's the details, the small ones.'"[14]

"Bonesteiner said you were the best. I can see why he said that."

Erik remained quiet. His thoughts raced, but there was nothing he could do. Then he remembered the First Polish Parachute Brigade and smashed his fist against the steering wheel.

Jamie tried to comfort him by rubbing his arm. "Babe, if you want to talk about it, I'm here for you. It might be good if you vent versus keeping it bottled up."

Erik shook his head and tried to clear his thoughts, but a flashback hit him from his time in Iraq: three of his friends were killed when an al Qaeda RPG hit their Humvee. Then, like now, there was not anything he could do except watch and blame himself for their deaths because he made a small mistake. His hands trembled.

"Are you okay, babe?" She stared into his eyes. "What are you thinking about?"

"I'm fine." He took a deep breath to still the violent shakes that overcame him. He felt her eyes on him and fought to contain his emotions but failed. He pulled the car over.

"Babe? Talk to me." Jamie tilted her head.

His eyes began to water. Then Erik told the story of when he was in Iraq in 2002. The memory was so vibrant that he could remember every word spoken.

It was a long day. I was impersonating a member of the

---

14. Harmon, Robert, dir. Ike: Countdown to D-Day. A&E Television Networks (US), 2004. TV Film

Bundesnachrichtendienst, BND, (Germany's Federal Intelligence Service) in order to interrogate a member of al Qaeda, who was in the hands of the German Army. The member of al Qaeda had sensitive information that the Russian Navy was going to make an attempt to sell a few of their nuclear submarines and other weapons of mass destruction. But I got nothing out of him. After that, I hooked up with my military contacts, who were on routine patrol. The air was dry and hot, like an oven, though the temperature was slowly becoming bearable. Tensions were high, eyes alert, and all were trying to keep in good spirits and humor. Parker, who was manning a .50-calibre machine gun in the Humvee's turret, was going to see his girlfriend, a nurse in Germany. Jim, whose tour was ending in a few days, was behind the wheel. Ray, a Navy SEAL who was called out of retirement, mainly because he worked in Intelligence, was in the front passenger seat, and I was in the back seat. Everyone was eager to get back to base.

"Hey, Függer, when do you head out?" Ray asked, looking over his shoulder.

"0700," I replied.

"Must be nice, Sir," Jim said.

"You'll be joining me soon."

"Not soon enough, Sir." Jim looked in the rearview mirror. "It has been a pleasure knowing you."

"Hey guys, first round's on me," Parker yelled from the top side.

I pointed to a side street and said, "I think this is a shortcut to the base."

Ray chuckled and shook his head. "You've been here only four days and you think you know this shithole of a place." Jim turned onto the side street, and Ray stared at me and said, "For being a squirrel, you're not bad."

As we approached a bridge, a group of Iraqi men scattered. They looked suspicious, as if they were planning something. Some ran to the left, behind some burned out vehicles, and some scurried down an embankment under the bridge. Ray said there was something wrong with the situation and ordered Parker to keep alert and man the .50-calibre. But it was too late. We heard the whistling sound of a rocket-propelled grenade that came our way. Everyone braced themselves, and Jim slammed his foot on the accelerator.

Parker yelled in terror, "RPG!"

As soon as he said it, the RPG slammed into the left side of the Humvee, and screams of pain exploded in my ears. The blast ripped off the left side of Jim's face, exposing burnt muscle and parts of his skull. Parker was killed instantly from the blast. Ray yelled at me to get out, and members of al Qaeda reloaded their weapons. He jumped out, aimed his M4 carbine, fired and killed several individuals. I crawled out while rounds of AK-47s penetrated the skin of the Humvee, and high-pitched pinging rattled my ears.

"Incoming!" Ray yelled as a wire-guided rocket whizzed toward us. Part of the bridge exploded, kicking up asphalt and dirt. I crawled back to the Humvee and grabbed the radio receiver.

"Company X-Ray, this is Victor Six!"

"Victor Six, this is Company X-Ray. Go ahead," came the reply.

"Company X-Ray, Victor Six wants to report we are taking heavy fire on both forward flanks! Requesting a QRF![15]"

---

15. Quick Reaction Force

I smashed the button on the dashboard and yelled into the receiver, "Sending Victor Six's current grid Via Blue Force Tracker! Prepare to receive! Out!"

Then I crawled behind a bridge pillar, squatted down and prepared to fire. I saw members of al Qaeda approaching on my right flank, and I opened fire. After the first rounds all I heard was a constant low-pitched ringing in my ears, and with each round fired, a dull sharp pain punched my eardrums. Ray and I emptied magazine after magazine, but al Qaeda started to outflank us and inched closer and closer.

"Where in the fuck is our QRF!'" Ray screamed.

"They should be coming," I said between rounds, "and they've got our location via Blue Force Tracker!"

"Another RPG round went off, and Ray shielded himself behind a bridge pillar. He took a quick glance and then repositioned himself to get a better aim. That was his last move. When I looked again, I saw Ray's lifeless body slumped over. I burned with rage and cursed like you've never heard.

"Then I heard low muffled engines and the dull thumping sounds of an M242 Bushmaster chain-fed auto-cannon. The al Qaeda scattered like roaches when a light comes on. I heard orders barked amongst the gunfire as members of the US Army set up defensive positions and slowly advanced across the bridge. Then a large explosion rocked the ground from missiles being launched from an Apache Helicopter. The thirty-millimeter automatic Boeing M230 chain gun mopped up what was left from the missiles. The day was over for me, but I lost three of my best friends.

"It was my fault they died because I gave the wrong directions."

Jamie, looking pale and blinking back tears, wrapped her arms around him. "It's not your fault." Erik tried to break away from her hug, but she squeezed tighter. "It's okay, let it go."

"I miss them. And the ache in my heart didn't go away."

"I know you do." Jamie rubbed his back and placed his head on her chest. "I am sorry, babe. I know it's hard for you."

Erik began to sob. He hated it, but he couldn't help it.

"Babe, I love you so much. I'm so proud of you."

"I've lost so many friends. I'm tired of it." He sniffed and buried his face in her chest.

"I know." She patted his back.

But Erik knew she would never understand. Not this and not all the other experiences he had faced that he continued to hide. Only those who've been in such a situation would have had any possible idea of the terror and the lasting trauma. Erik sighed. Sometimes surviving sucked. It's the second time he had broken down since Jamie had known him, and she seemed happy that he did so. He had to admit that it felt good to let it out. To tell someone.

Jamie lifted his head, rubbed his cheek and smiled. "Can I ask a personal question?"

He nodded, though his gut knotted up a little.

"What's it like when you kill someone?"

Erik took a deep breath, wiped his eyes and began to drive again. Jamie waited patiently for his answer.

He finally said, "That's a tough one to answer." He glanced at her, then shook his head. "It's not like in the movies. They get it all wrong. Being a soldier or working for the agency is a messy job when you have to go into a combat situation. You go in knowing that you'll have to kill or be killed, but that's only the first step." Erik pondered a little more before he continued, "And if you're lucky, you get out with your ass in one piece, but the battle continues psychologically speaking." He took a deep sigh. "Killing a fellow human being is not as easy as killing an animal. You'll be haunted by that dead man's image for the rest of your life."

"Do you have those?"

Erik nodded.

Finally, they arrived at the hotel. Erik parked the car, and they headed to their room where they got out of their uniforms and back into civilian clothes. Once dressed, they headed down to a local café and sat outside. Erik was still troubled. Every time he remembered, he relived it. He wished he could forget. And then there was his failure today.

Jamie rubbed her finger over the creases in his brow. "It's okay, babe. Really."

Erik shook his head. "No matter what I did to try to help the Allies, it was pointless. No matter how hard I tried to make them listen, they wouldn't."

"You tried your best to warn them. That's all you could have done."

"Tried? What I did was sign the death warrants for the Polish Independent Parachute Brigade at Arnhem. Me and my big mouth. Damn it!" Erik threw a napkin to the ground and stood up.

Jamie stared at him with a worried look in her eyes.

"Sorry …" he said. "Would you like some wine?"

She nodded.

"Be right back."

Jamie watched him head off to get the wine. She had never seen him like this before and would hate to see him if he really lost his temper. At least she felt she could help by supporting him and encouraging him to talk about the terrible things he had seen. She wondered how many more such stories he had that she might never hear, then glanced at her diamond ring again. It gave her great pleasure that she was engaged to the man she loved, and she felt in perfect harmony with the accordion music that played in the background. Suddenly, shadows covered Jamie. She stared up and saw a grinning soldier hovering over her. He looked her over from head to toe.

"Hey Frank, look at this dish," he called over his shoulder, and another soldier strolled over as the first one asked, "Do you think she speaks English?"

"It doesn't matter for what I'm going to do to her." They both chuckled and rubbed their chins while they discussed things they'd do to her.

Jamie stood, but the soldiers positioned themselves one behind her and the other to her left side. She scanned around, looking for Erik. Other customers looked her way. "I can speak English," she said, as she glared at both of them. She felt as if a spider was crawling up her back. "And my husband will be back soon. He won't be happy about what you've been talking about." She saw Erik heading in her direction, and a wave of relief washed over her.

The soldier behind her played with her hair. "Well, you might have to tell him you found someone else." They both laughed. Jamie tried to leave, but he held her shoulders. "Oh no, you're not going anywhere."

"If you know what's good for you," Jamie said as she turned and stared him in the eye, "you'll go elsewhere before my husband gets here."

"Ha!" the soldier said, still grinning. "I think we can handle him."

"Be smart and think again," Erik said as he placed his two glasses of wine on the table.

The soldiers turned to face him. "Hey, you brought us some wine. Thanks," the first one said.

Erik's eyes darkened and took on a ferocious intensity. He glanced at a knife on the table. The soldier on the left picked up a glass and threw it on the floor. Jamie breathed heavily, fearing what Erik would do. "Hey guys, this is my husband, Erik," she said trying to defuse the situation.

The one behind Jamie pulled her back and chuckled. "Hey, Erik, you speak English?"

The soldier on the left shoved Erik. "Yeah, Erik, do you speak English?"

Erik calmly looked to his left. "Would you prefer a different language, or should I ask, are you able to comprehend another?"

Jamie swallowed. Erik appeared calm and cool, but she knew he was boiling inside.

The soldier shoved again. "Frank, he thinks he's a wise guy."

Frank focused his attention on Erik. "You think you're a wise guy? Why don't you scram and get me and Richard some more wine. We'll give her back after we're done with her."

"Seriously, guys," Jamie said in a rush, "you really don't want to mess with him. He's had a really bad day." They all ignored her. Even Erik. *Men are so stupid sometimes*, Jamie thought.

"Let her go, Dick," Erik demanded with emphasis on the last word.

Richard snarled and his eyes narrowed. "What did you call me?"

Erik stepped forward, and Jamie's stomach fluttered with anxiety. She remembered when they first met, how Erik took two jerks, who were trying to assault her, on with little to no effort.

"I called you Dick, which is very appropriate considering your behavior."

"Hey, Frank, I wonder where his uniform is." Richard tried a different way to antagonize Erik. "Where's your uniform, Erik? Or are you too much of a pussy to wear one?"

Jamie shook her head in disbelief. The soldiers clearly wanted a fight, but she was pretty sure they were going to get more than they bargained for. Well, she did try to warn them.

Erik took a step closer, glanced at the knife, and stared at the soldiers with complete apathy. His left knee lifted slowly. Jamie's heart beat faster. She feared what was about to happen, and rightly so because, at that moment, Erik launched a blitzkrieg attack.

He pushed Jamie out of the way, and before she knew what was happening, one of the soldiers was on the ground, screaming and clutching his kneecap. Erik grabbed the knife off the table and kneed Richard in the groin. Richard's eyes bugged out from the pain, and he began to slide down, but Erik grabbed his neck and thrust him against the window and held the knife to his throat.

"She's right," Erik said in an acid tone. "I'm having a *really* bad day." He pondered for a second. "Make that a bad year. But that's not the issue. What you need to know is that I'm going to kill you now. Would you like to know how I'm going to do it?" Erik's eyes narrowed and his hands squeezed harder on Richard's neck. "I'm going to slit your throat from ear-to-ear and then pull out your tongue."

"Erik, no! Don't do it! He's not worth it!" Jamie wanted to touch his arm, to hold him back, but she was scared he would react badly.

Erik just stared at Jamie. She pleaded with her eyes.

Frank moaned in pain. "You broke my knee, you bastard!"

Erik stared down at Frank and looked back at Richard, who was turning purple, and thrust his knee several more times into his groin. Then he released Richard, who curled up in a fetal position on the ground. Erik turned to Frank. A malevolent grin appeared on his face.

"Hey, man. I'm sorry. Okay," Frank said. "You've made your point. No more, okay."

Before Jamie could say she agreed, Erik raised his left foot and stomped on the GI's left ankle, which caused a muffled cracking sound. Frank screamed in pain. Members of the Sûreté Nationale came running toward Erik with their pistols drawn.

"*Officier, il essaiyait de me protéger!* Officer he was trying to protect me!" Jamie said. Fortunately for Erik, Jamie speaks, reads, and understands French fluently. She suddenly realized that the rest of the customers outside the café had either got up and left or were standing ready to flee and stared at her fiancé as if he were a monster on the loose.

The officers pushed her out of the way and started giving orders: "*Tu arrêtes! Mettez vos mains en l'air!* You stop! Put your hands up!"

One of them aimed his pistol at Erik. Erik raised his hands to shoulder level, while he stared into the police officer's eyes. Then he grabbed the officer's wrist with his hand, grabbed the barrel with his other hand and turned it on the officer. Jamie heard a sickening cracking sound. The police officer's eyes enlarged and his face grimaced in pain. Jamie gasped, figuring that Erik had broken the man's finger. But Erik didn't stop there; he finished his attack by kicking the officer in the groin. Jamie winced. The man fell to the ground and writhed in pain, unable to get up.

"Erik, stop!" Jamie said. "Please!" She couldn't imagine that assaulting a police officer was going to help anything, but Erik simply motioned to the other officers to bring it on. He even stepped forward to meet them.

Then seemingly out of nowhere, a man with bullish, bloodshot eyes stopped the police and persuaded them to lower their weapons.

He stared at Erik, then approached. Jamie moved tentatively to Erik's side. She wanted to stroke his arm to help him calm down, but she feared it might have the wrong effect, so she hoped her proximity would be enough to bring him back to his senses.

"You need to leave now," the man said in an acid mix of cigarettes and coffee breath. "I'll be at your place in one hour. Now go."

"I'm not finished, Valensky."

"You're drawing unnecessary attention to yourself." Valensky motioned to Jamie to get Erik out of there. "Leave now! Don't argue with me, just go!"

Erik turned and strode from the café, not looking behind.

Jamie ran after him. He was barreling along the street with

his head down. "Erik, stop! Please, Erik!" She said breathlessly as she caught up to him.

He stopped and turned to face her, rage was still in his eyes. She placed her arms around him, hoping it would cool him off, but he stood rigid in her embrace. She pulled back and looked in his eyes. "Babe, what happened back there?" He said nothing. Jamie frowned. Was this the man she fell in love with? Could she trust someone who was like a grenade that could explode at any time? Erik walked on, but not as fast as before. "When did you become that crazy person I don't know?" Jamie asked as she walked beside him. "They didn't deserve that." Again he met her question with silence; though she noted that he was taking deep breaths in an effort to calm down. That, she figured, was progress. "Talk to me, babe."

He stopped and turned to her. "I don't care if they deserved it or not. I did what was necessary." Erik's voice took on a frigid, hostile tone.

A chill ran through her body. She tried to speak but couldn't find words that would safely express her horror at his attitude. She didn't want to enrage him.

Erik pointed in the direction of the incident. "I wouldn't care if they died." He turned to Jamie, his face grim. "I don't care anymore."

"What? You don't care anymore?"

"I don't care if Montgomery, his staff, and the rest of the Allied generals don't want to listen to me. That's fine. Let them get what they deserve. This isn't my war anyway. To hell with them. Let history play out and see where the dice lands."

"How can you say that, when you know what will happen?"

Erik shrugged as if he really didn't care.

"But Erik, you're the only one who can possibly stop it."

"What makes you think I can stop it?"

Jamie touched his arm and softened her voice. "Because I have faith in you."

Erik snorted and shook his head. "Faith?"

She nodded and even managed a small smile.

"You're very naïve if you believe that." He pointed to his chest. "When I was with the agency we didn't hope we could do an op based on fucking faith. We had to find a way to get it accomplished. If not, people would die!" Erik tossed his hands up. "There is not a chance in hell I can prevent what is going to happen. Jamie, we are in the middle of World War Two. I know what will happen, at least what I think could happen or how history should happen or what it used to be. Or will be. Or what the hell ever. Oh, goddamn it, I can drive myself crazy trying to think about this stuff."

Something inside Jamie snapped. She would not lose the man she loved, nor sit by and watch him destroy himself. "Lose the attitude," she demanded in a firm voice, "or I don't know if I can ever trust you. How can I love you like I did before when this is how you behave?" She pointed back at the police officers who were now tending to the guy Erik had attacked.

"What?" Erik's eyebrows raised and he placed his hands on his hips.

"Back there is not the man I know and fell in love with. I know they didn't listen to you." Erik opened his mouth to speak, but she didn't give him a chance. "Erik Függer, listen to me, damn it!"

He sighed and motioned her to continue.

"As I was saying, I know they didn't listen to you, but that doesn't mean you have to hate yourself for it and go attacking anyone that annoys you. I'll stand by you no matter what happens or what we'll go through, but I need you not to make things harder than they have to be."

He glanced away, then took a deep breath and turned back. "You said I'm not the man you fell in love with?"

She nodded.

"Well, you don't know the things I've seen and experienced that made me who I am today."

"Then tell me."

"I can't, now or ever."

"Did you hide those things from me?"

"Yes, because I didn't want you to see my other side. I can never share with you anything about the agency or what I did." Erik slumped onto a bench on the sidewalk. "I believed that if you found out who I really was, you'd reject me out of fear. I was convinced that you would never see that side of me and I would never have to tell you. However, I was hoping that day would never come … but it has and I don't know how to explain it."

Jamie sat next to him and gave him a hug. At least he softened a little this time.

"Jamie," Erik said, as he pulled back and looked into her eyes. "Why did you fall in love with me?"

She tilted her head and smiled. "Because you're honest, caring, sweet, and you loved me for me. I fell in love with you because, deep down, I knew you were the one I was meant to be with." She kissed him lightly on the lips. "Babe, I'll always be here by your side. I'm not going to leave you. I don't know what you did with the agency and I don't want to know. But I do know that whatever you did, you did it to make the world a better and safer place. This is why I have faith in you that you can put things back how they should be." They stared into each other's eyes. She saw the love return to his gaze and whispered, "If you say that we need to run, I'll run with you. If you say that we need to hide, I'll hide with you, because I love you forever and that will never change."

Erik drew her into an embrace and kissed her as if they were never going to see each other again. She responded in kind and melted into him, relieved that the Erik she knew and loved was back.

Eventually, they strolled back to their hotel room. Once inside, they cuddled in bed and she rubbed his back.

Erik's last thought before he drifted off to sleep was how wonderful her back rubs were. A knock on the door awakened him with a start, alert in a moment, as he drew his pistol and headed for the door. He signaled Jamie to open it and pointed the pistol at the middle of the opening.

"Hello," a deep, French-accented voice said.

Erik revealed himself, and even though he recognized Valensky, he kept the pistol pointed at his head.

"May I come in?" Valensky asked.

Erik grabbed him by his shirt, pulled him in and threw him in a chair. "How did you find me?"

"You forget who I work for? Don't you trust me?"

"I don't know, should I?" Erik aimed the pistol, as he started to squeeze the trigger. Behind him, Jamie cleared her throat.

"Yes," Valensky replied, "and killing me won't help you. It'll make it worse."

Erik nodded. It wouldn't be good for his relationship with Jamie either. "Shut the door and go into the bedroom," he told her and was heartened when she obeyed without question.

"If I wanted you dead I would've already done it." Valensky's voice took on an urgent tone. "And you don't have much time."

"What are you talking about?" Erik lowered the pistol and removed his finger from the trigger.

"I came here to warn you. Members of your OSS were asking me awkward questions."

"Go on."

"To be honest, they'd never heard of you." Valensky tilted his head, raised an eyebrow and gave Erik a don't-lie-to-me look. "Who do you really work for?"

"All I can tell you is that the knowledge I possess can drastically change the outcome of this war."

"How do I know you're telling the truth?"

"Have you heard of Operation Market Garden?"

Valensky nodded.

"It will fail, and the British paratroopers, including the Polish paratroopers, will be massacred at Arnhem."

"How do you know such things?"

Erik replied with a blank expression.

Valensky pressed his lips together and paused for a moment as if considering whether to push the matter or not. "Did you at least warn Bradley or Eisenhower?

"They didn't listen, and if I'm correct about Operation Market Garden, will you trust me?"

Valensky nodded again.

"So what did you tell the OSS?"

"I denied everything." Valensky sighed and peered into Erik's eyes. "Don't you think if I wanted to turn you in, I would've already done it?"

"Maybe you're setting me up."

"You have about ten minutes to make up your mind if you want to trust me. My car is parked in the side alley. I'll see you there." He got up, opened the door and walked out without a backward glance.

Erik headed to the bedroom.

"Who was that?" Jamie asked.

"A member of the French Resistance."

"Do you trust him?"

"More than I trust the OSS." He motioned to her belongings on the dressing table. "Pack your things; we're leaving."

"Again?"

"Yes, again." Erik clapped his hands to express the urgency. "And pack light." He threw the duffel bag with the money in it on the bed. "Put your things in there, and just grab two shirts for me, two pairs of boxers, two pairs of socks and one pair of pants." She nodded and he noticed her trembling. He walked to her, turned her around and gazed into her eyes. "Everything will be okay."

She nodded and swallowed, then started packing.

He walked to the bed and pulled the MP-44 and spare magazines out from beneath it. Jamie turned with a question in her eyes and watched white-faced as he slammed a magazine in, chambered a round, and switched the safety off. He did the same to the pistol. Whatever she wanted to ask remained unspoken.

"Can you carry that?" Erik pointed to the duffle bag. She lifted it with little struggle. "Good."

Erik glanced out the window to see if anything was out of the ordinary, then glanced at Jamie. She was ready to go with the duffle bag over her shoulder. He shouldered the MP-44, held the pistol in his right hand, and they both exited the hotel room. The hotel hallways were empty, almost abandoned.

Erik heard faint talking and footsteps that came from around the corner behind him. They were speaking English, so he was ready to use the pistol. He took deep breaths—he could smell his own sweat—and prepared for whatever would happen next. Erik didn't have to look because the individuals' voices were crystal clear and he estimated about twenty feet away. They headed toward the staircase. A door creaked and pistols cocked.

"Freeze!" A voice demanded.

Erik swung around, raised his pistol and aimed. Jamie ducked behind him—smart girl. He recognized Edward Wilson and another individual. They raised their guns and fired. Jamie screamed. "Get down," He hissed, at the same time he ducked himself as bullets flew by. Erik tried to aim, but Edward reloaded, lifted his gun and fired again. Erik still headed toward the stairs as Jamie crouched low behind him, Erik squeezed off five rounds, which penetrated the walls and sent splinters flying. A round found Erik's left arm. Gun smoke and plaster dust polluted the hallway, which irritated Erik's eyes so badly he had to blink. He re-evaluated his situation, holstered his pistol and reached for the MP-44.

Erik locked eyes with his targets; their eyes widened at the sight of his MP-44. It fired with a deafening roar that punched bullets into the wall like exclamation points. Erik quickly reloaded and fired, hitting the unknown individual in the kneecap and knocking Edward's gun out of his hand. They both ran into the hotel room for cover.

"Run!" Erik said. Jamie jumped to her feet, placed the bag on her shoulder, and dashed down the stairs.

At the bottom, another OSS agent stepped out in front of them. He fired his gun at Erik. Erik ducked and the bullet thudded into the wall behind him. The agent, once in the distance, grabbed Jamie and threw her violently against the wall. With a smug look, he aimed for Erik, who was still a little way up the staircase, but Erik dropped his MP-44, leaped from the stairs and tackled the agent and knocked him to the ground. They wrestled, then got to their feet, while Jamie watched, wide-eyed and frozen with shock.

Erik was in a low stance and his eyes bulged with adrenaline. He stared at his opponent, studying his body movements, at the same time the agent placed a set of brass knuckles on each hand. Erik shook his head and knew the agent's attack the second he launched it. The agent did a switch-hitter, which is a boxer technique. Erik deflected the first punch thrown. The agent launched a powerful straight punch thrown with his rear hand. This time Erik stepped back, blocked it with his right hand, and with his left forearm made slams into the agent's right elbow, something Erik knew would cause a compound fracture. The agent's agonized expression confirmed his prognosis. Immediately following that, Erik reversed the agent's direction and spun his back against the wall. Erik balled up his fists and smashed the man's temples, forcing him to the floor. While the agent was dazed,

Erik grabbed his shoulders and forced his chest into his knee. That caused the body of the sternum to be shattered. To end his attack, Erik placed his left hand in the back of the agent's head and the right hand on his chin and then quickly turned his head like a bottle cap.

Jamie's eyes were filled with horror and she trembled uncontrollably. Erik glanced at Jamie. She had tears trickling down her face.

"We need to go now!" Erik stated as she nodded unconvincingly. "Come on, Jamie, we don't have much time."

He gave her a little smile and helped her to her feet. They grabbed their belongings, continued running, and dashed out the side door. Valensky stood by a nearby car and motioned them to hurry. They raced over and threw themselves into the car. The engine was already running, and Valensky accelerated away. Jamie placed her hand on Erik's shoulder. He turned to find her still crying and trembling. He gathered her into his arms and focused on how he was going to save Hitler. The odds were against him, and he would be on his own, but he knew he wouldn't be able to live through what was to come with a clear conscience if he didn't at least try to stop it.

Valensky turned to Erik. "Now, do you trust me?"

20. TRUSTING AND BELIEVING

"You must trust and believe in people or life becomes impossible."
—Anton Chekhov

Audrieu, France

After they passed the checkpoint, Valensky pulled up to the château where members of the French Resistance welcomed him with open arms, though their eyes turned cold when they saw Erik. Individuals made their displeasure known through a mix of looks, hand gestures, and verbal complaints. A man stood almost out of sight, stared at Erik with scolding eyes, and made no effort to conceal his interest; he disappeared as soon as Erik made visual contact.

A medium-built man with broad shoulders and large hands approached Valensky. He whispered something in French while he squinted at Erik with cold, gray eyes. Valensky motioned that everything was okay, and the man helped Jamie with the duffle bag and escorted her to their living quarters. She looked behind and Erik gestured that he would be along shortly and everything would be okay.

"He doesn't trust you. He thinks you're a German spy," Valensky said as he and Erik followed Jamie. "Even though you helped liberate Paris, some still don't trust you, and they'll test you."

Erik nodded. The French Resistance was very good at intelligence work, so he would have to twist the facts to his advantage. Events would prove him right in time, and trust would be built—maybe—but right now he had to make them believe.

"Is your fiancé okay?" Valensky asked.

Erik nodded again.

"You're bleeding." Valensky pointed to Erik's left arm. "Once you're settled, we'll get the doctor to tend to that."

Jamie looked back; her eyes were full of fear and uncertainty. Erik tried to comfort her by grinning, but it didn't work. At the heavily guarded main entrance of the château, Erik glanced up at the enormous stone walls discolored from centuries of rain, wind, and sun. Individuals with inquisitive eyes stared down from windows equipped with weathered wooden shutters and secured by iron bars. They passed between the guards and headed down a hallway, their footsteps echoing on the worn stone floor. Erik noticed that through the invention of electricity they had made slight improvements in lighting, although there was still no central heating or cooling. The aroma of seasoned chicken and vegetables wafted from a kitchen in the distance, and Valensky explained they ran a sufficient operation with their own vegetable gardens, cows for meat and milk, chickens for eggs and for consumption, and lastly, they were well-armed.

They walked down hallway after hallway, and Erik made mental notes of anything of interest. He passed a closed door and thought he heard what could be a radio room. Eventually, they stopped and

Valensky opened the door to Erik and Jamie's quarters. Though not a comfy hotel room, it had everything one needed: a great bed with a heavy oak frame and sheets and pillows overlaid with a quilted wool blanket; a wooden cedar chest for garments at the foot of the bed, and a chair and small wooden table, with a candle. After they placed their belongings down, Valensky motioned for Erik to come with him. Jamie sat on the bed motionless.

"Is she all right?" Valensky asked.

"She saw some things." Valensky was intrigued to know more. "She saw things that I never wanted her to see."

Valensky nodded and changed the topic. "By the way, where did you learn to fight like that?"

"On a farm."

Valensky nodded and then made a head gesture towards Jamie. "I can have someone speak to her if that would help?"

"Thanks."

"I'll be back in five minutes so we can get that wound attended to."

Erik walked toward Jamie and tried to think of things he could say to comfort her. He realized that not only had she never seen this side of him but also she was in a different time—wartime, and decades before she was born. Would she still love him for who he was, now that she knew what he really was? Even for Erik, it was hard to take in everything. They were strangers in a strange time, with no friends, no home, and nowhere that felt safe. They lived day-by-day, not knowing where the future would take them. He placed his hand on her shoulder, and she looked at him with tears in her sunken eyes. She mumbled something and pointed to his wound.

"It's okay."

"Babe." She touched his imbrued sleeve. "Babe, you have been—"

A knock came from the bedroom door. Erik turned to face it. "Come in."

The door opened and revealed Valensky and a voluptuous lady who wore a conservative blouse and skirt, her brown hair fitted neatly into a bun. She walked toward Jamie with a warm smile that made dimples beneath her high cheekbones, but her deep-set chocolate-brown eyes were cold from seeing the horrors of war. Her hands—though probably soft once—were rough, and her short fingers terminated in the dirt under her nails. Erik moved to leave, but Jamie squeezed his hand tightly and shook her head. He turned around, squatted before her and looked into her eyes with all the love he could muster. "I'll be back in ten minutes." She shook her head. "When I come back, I won't leave your side, okay?" She sighed and started to cry. Then she dropped his hand. He gave her a parting smile, then got up and headed to the door.

Valensky escorted Erik to the medical center, made small talk about the war and Jamie as they walked. The doctor waited for him, his medical devices and bandages organized. When he saw Erik, the doctor grimaced and in a snotty French accent said, in what little English he knew, "It's you again. What has happened to you now?"

"Augustin, knock it off," Valensky snapped.

Erik climbed onto the medical table and removed his shirt, revealing rivers of dried blood on his arm. The smell of rubbing alcohol filled Erik's nostrils, and then a sharp burning feeling exploded from the bullet wound. To get his mind off what Augustin was doing (using forceps to try to remove the bullet), Erik started a conversation with Valensky.

"Can I ask how you found me, especially since I'm under a different name?" Erik asked as he grinded his teeth and tried to ignore the pain.

"I have my sources."

"And who might they be?" Erik asked and raised his eyebrows.

"Are you expecting me to reveal who they are?" Valensky chuckled and shook his head in disbelief.

Erik also chuckled, then got serious. "Yes, and you will tell me."

Valensky's eyes narrowed and turned cold. "You have the nerve to ask me that after I saved your ass? You American bastard!"

"Listen to me, you could have a German agent here right now."

The doctor stopped working and stepped back and watched Valensky's reaction.

"What in the hell are you talking about? How can you say that?" Valensky spat on the floor. "If you continue to talk like that, the others here will think you should go. I'm asking you not to jeopardize our relationship."

"Of course not," Erik replied in a quieter tone.

Valensky crossed his arms and motioned the doctor to continue.

"However," Erik continued, "don't you think it's odd that out of nowhere an SS officer was here and no other Germans showed up? That means you have someone here who's playing on all sides: American, German, and you. I believe they knew I was coming. So if you want, kick me out, and risk having everyone here compromised, or even killed."

"Has anyone told you that you are a real pain in the ass?"

Erik smiled. "All the time."

"You better be happy that my father believed you. That's why I let you live the last time."

Erik tilted his head in confusion and replied, "Your father?"

Valensky nodded slightly.

"Who?"

"You met him at the petrol station. He was the one who drove you and your fiancé to the Eiffel Tower, and to dinner. Remember him now?"

Augustin interrupted, as he gave a shoo gesture. "You're all done. You can go now."

"Thanks, Augustin." Erik got to his feet and turned his attention back to Valensky. "Yes. He told everyone that I liberated Paris," Erik said as he placed his shirt on.

"Well, it's true. Who knew that one man," Valensky pointed at Erik, "could make a difference?"

They walked back down the hall, and a few yards on, Erik asked, "Are you afraid that Augustin might tell everyone what we were talking about?"

Valensky shook his head. "He can't understand English that well. Your secret is safe."

A little distance before him, a skinny man with a narrow, sunken face and who wore frayed clothing reclined against a wall with an MP-40 over his shoulder. He approached Valensky with a stern expression and handed him a document. They walked on, and after he read it, Valensky continued the conversation. "So, what's the plan to find this traitor?"

"I don't know yet; give me time to think of one. Also, I'm working on something else."

"Need help?"

"No, but I'll let you know. I need all intelligence on German forces from here to Berlin."

Valensky stopped outside their quarters. "Will do. It seems like you always work alone," he said.

Erik nodded.

"Sounds good." Valensky started to walk off, then he remembered something and turned to Erik. "Oh, dinner will be at six o'clock. I hope you like chicken."

"I do, thank you."

Erik opened the door and the lady left. Jamie was on the bed balled up and trembling, her hands hugging her legs. She stared at Erik with fear in her eyes, and her cheeks were wet with tears. He gave what he hoped was a reassuring smile, he slowly approached her, then sat beside her and wrapped his arms around her. He rubbed his fingers through her thick hair and placed her head on his shoulder.

"Scared?" he asked softly.

She nodded.

"Jamie." She didn't look at him. "Jamie..." She glanced up at him then back down, her face blank—shock, Erik assumed. "Jamie, please listen to me." He held her closer. "I know you're scared about the things that happened earlier and the things you saw me do." Erik paused as he tried to come up with the right words to say without frightening her more. "Do you remember when you asked me where I learned how to fight and I said on a farm?"

Jamie stared at him then nodded.

"The farm is the CIA training facility, and that's where I learned to do the things you saw me do." He took a deep breath.

"This is who I really am. This is what I do for the agency." Erik turned her head so their eyes would meet. "You'll need to accept who I am and what's happening to us, even if you don't want to. I know it frightens you. I know it is difficult for you to comprehend. I didn't want you to see that side of me, but since you have, I'm asking you to trust me and not be afraid."

Jamie's eyes were full of tears. "I don't want to lose you, babe!" She wrapped her arms around him and squeezed him tight.

He kissed her head. "You won't lose me, princess, I promise you."

"But those men were shooting at you and trying to kill you and you… killed… that man."

"I know I did."

"Besides Iraq, have people tried to kill you?" Erik nodded, and she squeezed tighter. "I can't live without you. You're my soul mate."

"Yes, I am. And you're not going to have to live without me. I have a habit of staying alive."

A grin came over her face.

"Now try to get some sleep before we eat. You've had a long day."

He lifted her chin, kissed her, and rubbed her back to comfort her, then helped her lie down and covered her with the blanket. She stared at him with a warm, satisfied smile, then closed her eyes. He got up slowly, careful not to disturb her, and walked to the door.

"Don't leave me."

He turned. "I have to do something." He looked into her soft brown eyes. "I'll be back, I promise."

"Please?" She asked softly, reaching out to him.

He saw that she was still scared and realized that it would take some time for her to overcome that. He strolled back to the bed and lay beside her. She smiled and laid her arm over his chest.

"Babe, can you teach me something else in history?"

He pondered what he should talk about to relax her, and most of all, get her mind off what had happened recently. He told her to close her eyes and think of a simpler time, the Victorian Era, the year 1880. He explained that dating at that time was much different than it is today, that most people, since they had no TV or radio, saw parades, plays, operas, and even concerts that might last up to four or five hours, with no breaks. He made a joke about that and she laughed. It was hard for some single people to find a date, he told her. They would usually go with a chaperone, or if they were from money, a lead servant whose role was to make sure no mischief took place.

During social events, the young ladies stood on one side of the room and the gentlemen on the other side. Then the young ladies moved in a clockwise oval, holding a handkerchief that had their initials on it, while the gentlemen walked counter-clockwise and the chaperones watched from the sides. Eye contact was most important, and a little nod indicated interest, but girls couldn't look directly back if a gentleman caught her eye. If, after time, a girl found a gentleman she was interested in, she would drop her handkerchief in front of him. Then one of two things could happen. He would either pick it up, which meant he was interested, or he'd leave it. Erik explained that another gentleman couldn't pick it up, but the young lady could pick it back up and then drop it for another whom she had an interest in. Once a mutual interest was established, they would walk in the park, not holding hands, with their chaperones behind them. They would talk, very much like dates today, and get to know each other. And that's how it would go until they would break it off or get engaged.

Erik turned to her and saw that she had fallen asleep. He breathed a sigh of relief and stared at the ceiling. Almost immediately his mind began to work. He wondered who the assassin could be and how he was going save Hitler. If Erik couldn't stop it from happening, Hitler would be assassinated in October, and the world would take a path that was far worse than the one that led to Erik and Jamie's 2008. The twenty-first century they knew would become an alternate reality, replaced with something they might not recognize—should they ever make it back.

Erik closed his eyes and mentally role-played how the assassin would carry off his assignment.

The Führer Bunker is behind the Reich Chancellery. The elite soldiers of the SS would fill the courtyard in their black tunics with cuff title in silver and white embroidery spelling ADOLF HITLER. They'd watch with cold eagle eyes, ready to protect and give their lives for their Führer. The assassin, in an SS officer's uniform, would analyze every aspect of the courtyard as he approached the entrance to the Führer Bunker. The guards at the entrance would stand alert and motionless with their fingers on the triggers of their MP-44s. A sentry would step forward with his hand outstretched and ask for the assassin's papers. He'd examine the ID papers without emotion, then since it was a highly restricted area and only a few were allowed in the bunker, he would say, "You're not authorized to enter. I must ask you to leave the premises immediately."

Without hesitation, the assassin would do a lightning thrust left-heel stomp to the sentry on his left, causing his kneecap, fibula, shinbone and thighbone to shatter like pieces of china hitting a tile floor. Without looking to the sentry on his right, he would thrust his elbow into his trachea, cervical lordosis, and cervical vertebrae. Then as the SS guards in the courtyard started to take aim, he'd pull out his Luger, fix his sights on each guard, in turn, aim and fire a single deadly shot into each of them. Next, he'd squat to pick up the MP-44 from the dead guard; then he'd stand, and to save ammo, he'd stomp on the injured sentry's neck, killing him instantly. Finally, the assassin would continue with his objective and proceed down the staircase to the bunker.

Naturally, some of the guards from inside the bunker would come up the stairs to provide backup. The assassin, acting naturally, would raise his MP-44 and spray bullets down the staircase, killing those guards before continuing to descend into the bunker. Once inside, the assassin, who would be proficient in German, would listen to orders being given and the stomping of footsteps that raced down the hallway. He'd draw their fire, then unleash his attack when he heard them reloading. Hitler's bodyguards would try to take cover in doorways, and the assassin would quickly reload as he inched his way down the corridor and maneuvered around the guards by going into different rooms. The assassin, using his martial arts, Krav Maga, and stealth techniques, would be able to sneak up undetected and attack his victims, killing them one-by-one. The first wave of Hitler's bodyguards would fail, and the assassin would continue with caution to the staircase that led to the second level of the bunker.

To see if there'd be any guards, the assassin would act like one of them and ask for back up. There'd be only a handful left, but there could still be some below. He'd advise the guards that the assassin was down the hallway in one of the rooms, and as the remaining guards inched their way down the hallway, he'd maneuver behind the last guard.

Erik imagined the scene so clearly that he could see the guard's eyes widen with fear when he realized that the assassin was behind him.

Before the guard could turn around and warn the others, the assassin's hands would reach out, grab his head on both sides and twist like a bottle top, breaking his neck. Using him as a body shield, the assassin would then raise his Luger and kill the other guards. Next, he'd descend down the stairs and down the hallway of the second bunker. He'd kick open the door to the map room, where Hitler was, and would aim and kill the last of the bodyguards.

Hitler would demand. "Who are you?"

Then the assassin would complete his objective. He'd kill Hitler with the last rounds in his Luger.

Erik thought of all the individuals who were close to Hitler who would most likely believe him and help to save Hitler's life. He thought of those in Hitler's inner circle. Then one-by-one, he analyzed the pros and cons of each. The best choice was Albert Speer because he was the easiest to find, and Hitler considered him as a friend. The hardest part would be convincing Speer that there would be another attempt to assassinate Hitler. Erik took a deep breath, tried to relax, and eventually fell sleep.

A soft knock woke him. Erik approached the door with caution, his Luger in hand. He opened the door just enough to see who it was. It was Valensky. Erik stepped out.

"I've been thinking about who the traitor could be, and I can't think of anyone," Valensky said. "But assuming there is such a person, I suggest you wear a disguise so he or she will not recognize you. After all, they could be looking for you."

"That's true. I should wear a bandage around my neck so it looks like I have a wound and can't speak."

"Good idea. I'll get one." Valensky went to fetch the bandage and Erik returned to his room, prepared to wake Jamie and get ready for dinner.

He sat on the edge of the bed and gently touched her. "Jamie," he whispered.

After several tries, her eyes opened. She rubbed them, then saw Erik, and with a smile, sat up, kissed him, and held him tight.

"Time for dinner," he said.

"Okay." Jamie got up, walked to the basin, and washed her face. She then applied makeup and did her hair, all in ten minutes, which impressed Erik. A knock came from the door and Erik answered it. Valensky came in and greeted Jamie.

"*Bonjour, mademoiselle.*"

"*Bonjour.*"

Valensky gave the disguise items to Erik and while he got ready, Jamie and Valensky talked. Erik wrapped the bandage around his neck, and then placed a Kangol Tropic Ventair cap on his head and spectacles with thick lenses on his nose. Jamie chuckled and pointed at Erik. He just grinned back; he knew he looked silly, but it had to be done.

Erik said to Jamie. "There could be a spy, which is why I'm in disguise."

She grinned. "Okay. And if they shoot at you? What should I do then?

"Duck; get under cover, and I'll handle the rest." Erik saw Jamie's blank expression. He neared her and said in a continued half whisper, "I was trained to kill people ... and I'm very good at that."

They walked to the great hall where dinner was to be served. At the entrance, Erik felt inquisitive eyes that scrutinized him and Jamie. Valensky led them to their seats and sat by Erik. A young lady approached them and asked if they preferred white or dark meat. Then she disappeared and returned within a couple of minutes with their food and water. Erik smirked at Jamie when she sampled the water. Without chlorine or other chemicals to purify it, the water tasted different.

In the corner of his left eye, Erik saw some men come toward them. They smiled at Jamie and sat on either side of her. Erik stared impassively at them and continued to eat. One eyed Jamie and asked her a question. When she replied, he looked at her oddly, and Erik guessed that he noticed her American accent. Though he didn't understand much French, he figured out that she had told him her father was an American diplomat and her mother was from Paris. The men seemed satisfied by her explanation but still looked at Erik skeptically.

"*Êtes-vous un espion allemand?* Are you a German spy?" One asked in an arrogant French accent. He had an incredulous grin, and his nostrils contracted reflexively.

Erik said nothing and just stared at them blankly. He could not be tricked into actions or words that would incriminate him.

Valensky pointed out that Erik couldn't speak, and the men gave up and walked away.

While eating, Erik scanned the room, trying to find anyone who didn't belong. It was not easy; Erik was at a disadvantage.

He had no idea when the operative he sought was sent back. He knew the individual was from the future, another field operative from ONE, and the operative knew what Erik looked like, but Erik didn't know what the operative looked like.

This should be downtime, a time to recharge his batteries, but he wouldn't be able to because he had to come up with a plan to save Hitler. On top of that, he never knew what was waiting around the next corner. He felt someone's presence and glanced around. The man who stood almost out of sight when they pulled up to the château earlier stared at him again, this time from a corner of the room. Erik got up and headed toward the man, but he disappeared. With a sigh of frustration, Erik returned to his seat.

"Babe, what is it?" Jamie asked in a half whisper. Valensky leaned in, listening.

"That guy has been watching me ever since I got here." Erik turned to Valensky. "Did you see that man staring at me?"

Valensky shook his head.

Erik wiped his hands and mouth and got up from the table.

"Where are you off to?" Valensky asked.

"Going outside to get some fresh air and think about things."

Valensky nodded and Erik left and Jamie followed. Outside, the air was crisp and the cover of night was beginning to set in. Some guards lounged nearby, the ends of their cigarettes glowing orange, then fading away. Erik sat on the ground and Jamie joined him. He stared into the distance, momentarily free of thoughts.

"Babe, what are you thinking about?" Jamie asked.

"Stuff."

"Do you think someone is watching you?"

"I don't think, I know for sure they are, but I haven't gotten a good look yet." He paused. "But I'm pretty sure they know what I look like."

"Who could they be?"

"I don't know, but I'm not going to wait around to find out."

"You think they're from the future?"

"Yes." Erik rubbed his chin. "Something doesn't feel right."

"Have you been in situations like this before?"

He winced at her question. "I can't deny nor confirm that."

Jamie glanced at him, disappointment on her face.

"No matter what year it is, I'm sworn to secrecy," he explained.

"Can you tell me what you had to do to get the CIA medals?"

Erik regarded her in a new light, surprised and impressed that she had found out about them. He shook his head. "I can't go into details."

She held his hand and placed her head on his shoulder, and they looked up at the evening sky that sparkled above the ancient building. Erik lay down, pulled Jamie with him, and they continued to stare at the stars and constellations. Jamie rested her head on his chest and tapped her finger in time with his heartbeat, then she glanced up at his face and she asked him what he was thinking about.

He said nothing for a moment, then: "I'm wondering if someone's looking for me somewhere in some other place. Also, I remembered that my grandmother on my father's side told him a story about the FBI coming to their apartment one time because her husband was German. The agents went through their things because they suspected he was a Nazi supporter, which was totally false."

"What would someone have to do to get on the CIA Memorial Wall," Jamie changed the topic.

Erik raised his eyebrows at the unexpected question. "You have to be a very good analyst or field operative and have to die in the line of duty. If I die here, they'll add a star for me, but my name won't be listed in the CIA Book of Honor."

"Why?"

"This mission is highly classified so my name and the names of the two that died back here before me, can't be mentioned now, maybe never."

Jamie's eyes widened. "There were two others sent back before you?"

Erik nodded.

"What happened to them?"

"I only know they died."

"And now they want you dead, too."

"Sure does appear that way."

Jamie sat up. "It doesn't make sense."

"It doesn't have to make sense to us. They have their reasons. I know I was a thorn in their side because of some things I worked on and my methods of getting information. My best guess would be that they hoped I'd die while doing their mission. Also, they wouldn't want anyone to know about time travel and their interfering in the past, so I'm a loose end they want to tie up, just to make sure. I also suspect that someone pulling the strings just hates me." Erik thought of Cole. "I don't like him either." He grinned. "And I shall take great delight in fucking up his plans."

Jamie smiled. "So what about the next couple of weeks. What are you planning?"

Erik sat up. "We hide from the OSS. I find the operative and plan my trip to Berlin."

Jamie placed an arm around his shoulder. "Easy?"

He chuckled. "Yeah, no sweat," he said, wishing it to be true. "Come on, let's go to bed." He stood and reached for her hand.

During the next couple of days, Erik and Valensky analyzed everyone's behavior and actions. They wondered who could possibly know about Erik's previous visit, and Erik was still not able to find the individual who had stared at him ever since he arrived.

They brainstormed different possibilities. Then Valensky turned to Erik, looked as if a light bulb had gone on over his head. "I recall that the SS officer was the only one who showed up last time you were here."

Erik nodded and motioned him to finish his thought.

"He must have been contacted by radio." Valensky pounded his fist against his forehead for not realizing that sooner. "There's a two-way radio here but there are always two-to-three people in the radio room, so it'd be impossible."

Erik said one of Bonesteiner's quotes he lived by: "Nothing is impossible, you just got to know how to do it."

"Come." Valensky led Erik to the radio operator's workroom and tapped a secret knock. The door opened and they entered a space a little bigger than Erik's quarters, but still cramped, with every space utilized. The two-way radio utilized most of the room. The operator sat with a headset on. The other individual's job was to relay messages to the appropriate parties, Valensky being one of them. Their weapons were in arms' distance in case there was a situation. To break the monotony, they had a record player. They found no evidence there of spy activity.

Next, they went to the living quarters of those who helped protect the château. Valensky ordered the mattresses to be flipped so they could see under the bunks. Erik hoped to find a transmitter or other radio parts, but after a thirty-minute search, Valensky stared at Erik, shook his head, and motioned they should give up.

As they walked to the door, Valensky cupped Erik's shoulder. "It was worth a shot. You can't say we didn't try."

"There has to be something we've overlooked," Erik said, racking his brain.

Valensky shrugged.

"What would a two-way radio need to operate?" Erik asked a moment later.

"Headphones, transmitter, receiver, frequency range, IF-frequency, antenna, approximately thirteen meters, and ground wire approximately three meters long on Paxolin card. It also would need to be portable—light enough that one man could carry it."

Erik nodded thoughtfully. "Where's your radio from?"

"What do you mean?"

"Where was it made?"

"It's British, manufactured by the Marconi Company; they do make a smaller version."

Erik raised an eyebrow. "What size?"

"I don't know." Valensky made some hand gestures as if doing measurements. "But it'd fit in a suitcase or a record player."

Their eyes met as if they were thinking the same thing. "Record player," they said in unison.

On the way back to the radio room, Erik still couldn't believe that ONE had sent three operatives to make sure he didn't return. He wondered if they were the same team that killed the other two analysts. Again, Valensky did the secret taps, and again they entered, leaving the door open. Valensky pointed to the record player and asked to whom it belonged, while Erik checked the rest of the room. One of the men replied that it belonged to the new guy, Karawan. Valensky motioned to get him.

Erik pulled out his Luger and advised that he would do the talking with Karawan. Just then, Jamie walked by and saw Erik with his pistol drawn. Valensky motioned her to stay where she was and grabbed an MP-40 and slid the bolt. Then a fairly stocky man with crescent-gray eyes appeared at the doorway. Valensky ordered him to come in. Erik turned around.

"*Est-ce le vôtre?* Is this yours?" Valensky asked as he pointed at the record player.

The man nodded.

"*Où avez-vous obtenu?* Where did you get it?"

Erik held up his hand and stepped forward, "*Verstehst du mich?* Do you understand me?" he asked in German. The man just looked baffled. Erik asked again and studied his behavior, then repeated in English, "Do you understand me?"

Karawan tilted his head and leaned forward a little. "*Excusez-moi? Qu'est-ce?* Excuse me? What?" He tried to form a sentence in English. "Excuzie me. I do not speak good Englash."

"I see." Erik rubbed his chin while scrutinizing Karawan. Then he grabbed a record. "What's your name?"

"Excuzie me?"

Erik stared at him coldly. "Your name!"

The individual appeared to have understood. "Karawan."

"Karawan, do you like Benny Goodman?" Erik dropped the record, shattered it into several pieces. Karawan did nothing and remained calm as Erik picked up a Duke Ellington album and showed it to him. "How about him? No?" He dropped it, too.

Valensky and the others stared at Erik, wondering what he was doing. Jamie tried to approach Erik, but Valensky raised his hand to stop her. Erik breathed a deep sigh of frustration and anger grew in his voice. "So you don't understand English very well?" Erik nodded his head several times. "Hmmm?"

"*Oui.*"

"*Oui?* Yes?"

Karawan nodded.

"That's pretty impressive since you don't speak English very well. Let me see if some visual aids will help you." Erik removed his thick glasses and Kangol Tropic Ventair. Karawan's mouth jerked in shock and his eyes enlarged.

Erik realized that Karawan was another operative from ONE. Karawan had just realized that the previous assassin failed to kill Erik. Karawan reached for his pistol. Simultaneously, Erik raised his pistol and focused on his target. Jamie maneuvered around Valensky and shoved Karawan hard, which made him lose his balance and aim. Erik fired off three rounds into Karawan's chest. Karawan fell to the floor, and a puddle of blood started to form. Everyone stared in shock.

Valensky approached Erik. "What made you so certain?"

Erik touched the record player and pushed it to the ground. As it broke, Erik stated, "This part we guessed correctly." Valensky nodded as the others shook their heads in disbelief. "Do you like music?" Erik pointed at Valensky, who nodded. "What would you do if I broke your records?"

"I'd be in a rage and try to stop you."

"Exactly and Karawan—"

Valensky stole Erik's last words, "Didn't get upset."

Erik nodded.

"It seemed you already knew that."

Erik shrugged as if to say maybe or maybe not. He knew that he would have been upset if their records were smashed. He gave Valensky a nod and walked out with Jamie close behind. She reached for his hand. He extended his hand as he turned to her and thanked her for what she had done. She smiled.

"Who was that guy?"

"He was an operative from ONE from our time. His name was Karawan, which actually means an evil eye—very apt."

Footsteps echoed through the stone hallway behind them. Erik glanced over his shoulder. It was Valensky.

He extended his hand. "Good job back there …"

Erik nodded in appreciation.

"Even though I don't know who you work for." Valensky leaned forward, hinted that he'd like that information. "Will you ever tell me?"

"No."

He shrugged. "So, what's next?"

"Berlin."

Erik spent the next two weeks analyzing, reading, researching, and trying to think of how to save Hitler's life and how to convince Albert Speer to help him.

In the same cold room in which he was interrogated, Erik studied the reports from the French Resistance, including one on the failure of Operation Market Garden. A battered map of Northern France with military tactical symbols indicating sizes and types of units lay on the table. He walked to the table and unfolded a map of Central Europe over the top. The door swung open, which brought in a brisk wind. Erik closed it firmly, then rubbed his eyes and refocused on the map, trying to work out the best route to get to Berlin easily and without confrontation.

He walked around the table, took a seat, and shook his head to remove the drowsiness, went over his notes and flipped through intelligence briefings. Suddenly, he balled his hands into fists and pounded the table in frustration. Then he jumped up, pushed the chair back, and yelled in rage, and flipped the table, causing papers to go everywhere. Still frustrated, he walked to a wall and pounded his head against it, but quickly turned when he felt a presence behind him.

Jamie stood at the door with food and water. She gave him a supportive smile, and her eyes showed she understood. He was used to having CIA resources, but now he was on his own. She fixed the table, placed the tray on it, and headed toward him. Erik rubbed his fingers through his hair, and he felt hopeless. He needed more than Jamie's support.

"When I was with the agency we were taught to fight and taught to win," he told her. "We all worked together as a team, and we had unlimited resources to get the job done." He fell to the ground, held his head in his hands then looked up into her eyes. "But I can't win this one."

She knelt beside him and hugged him tightly while she rubbed his back and kissed his head. "I found this in the history book." She pulled back and handed him a color photograph. "Who are those people?"

He smirked and pointed at Alan. "You know Alan." She nodded and smiled, and he moved his finger left-to-right to identify everyone. "This is Paul, my section chief at Langley." He paused his finger on each individual. "This is Gary, he was a hacker; this is John, he did operation and simulation support; next is Carly, who made disguises and fabricated identifications." With a smug look, he added, "And that's me when I first joined the agency."

"Was that the team you worked with?"

Erik nodded.

"When was that?"

"1999 to 2005."

"What was your position?"

"I was a Paramilitary Operations Officer."

"But you can't tell me what you did?"

"You know I can't."

She sat back on her heels, tilted her head, and observed him. "Do you think you'll be able to save Hitler's life?"

"No."

"Think positive."

Erik snorted. "I'm being realistic." He closed his eyes and shook his head.

"What are you thinking about?"

He said nothing.

"Please share with me."

"One time I was called into Bonesteiner's office for my evaluation, and he read something that Alan wrote in my evaluation after I did my first op." Erik closed his eyes and recalled the words: "Erik has an amazing curiosity that scares me acutely. He never stops asking questions until he fully understands and sees all angles. He's strong mentally and has hope that he can make this a better world. Because of that amazing trait and inspiration, he has awakened me to keep going, and reminded me that what I'm doing with him must be done."

Jamie smiled at him. "Babe, Alan believed in you then, and I believe in you now."

He grinned back at her, laid his head on her shoulder and closed his eyes.

But could he believe in himself?

21. ON HIS OWN

*"All the knowledge I possess about history makes everyone
think I am odd and different, but with what is in my heart,
I can make a difference, even though I feel I am on my own."*
— Erik Foge

Audrieu, France. 2200 hours

Erik stood in front of a mirror in a German major's tunic. He adjusted everything: shoulder boards, ribbons, collar tabs, belt, and everything else. Like so many times before, Erik stared at his reflection in a poorly lit bathroom. There was no question what had to be done, and there was no turning back, just as it was when he was a part of an O.G.D.S. Team. In his mind, Erik calculated his assessment of his abilities and his odds for a successful mission. Normally, he would go over the objectives of the mission from start to finish, but not this time. Once he reached Berlin he would do that, but not before. Jamie's perfume drifted behind him. He turned. She looked him over like a drill sergeant during a uniform inspection. She tried to contain her tears, stepped forward, adjusted his lapel, and brushed something off his shoulder.

"Thank you."

They exited the bathroom and headed to the bed. Erik reached underneath it, grabbed the MP-44 and extra magazines and placed them on the bed, then he pulled the magazine from the MP-44, checked that it was full, then slammed it back in and slid the bolt back to load a bullet into the chamber. He reached for the Luger, did the same to it, and then placed it in his holster. Finally, he shouldered the MP-44 and turned to face his fiancé.

Tears trickled down her face. Erik strolled over to her, slowly lifted her head and kissed her gently. Then he wiped her tears away, stared into her eyes, and saw the same look she gave him every time he had to go away. "I promise I'll be back," he said, as he had every other time. This time, though, she knew exactly what he was going to do. And she knew there was a chance Erik wouldn't ever be coming back.

"How are you so sure?" Jamie said as she sobbed.

"When I was away all those times before, when we were dating, your love drove me to succeed so I could come back to you."

She sniffed and wiped her wrist across her eyes. "Well, this time you need to come back for both of us."

A frown stretched over Erik's face. "Both?" he whispered.

Jamie nodded with a fragile smile.

"You're pregnant?"

A smile blossomed and enveloped her face. She nodded again.

Erik paused, trying to come up with the right words to say.

"One-four-three-seven," she said.

Jamie's been saying this ever since he has known her, but Erik still had no clue what it meant. He frowned and once again tried to work it out.

Jamie kissed him and then explained: "I love you forever."

He reached for her hand. She squeezed it tightly and they walked out of their room and exited the château into a night full of chirping insects. Valensky, with his arms crossed, waited outside, leaning on a Kübelwagen. He strolled over to Erik and helped him by placing the MP-44 in the front passenger seat and gave him a map with an outline of the route he would take to Berlin. Valensky pulled Erik to the side, leaving Jamie at the door.

"Are you sure you won't be needing my help?"

Erik cupped Valensky's shoulder. "Yes." They hugged in friendship. "You're helping me by letting Jamie stay with you until I come back."

Valensky acknowledged Erik's gratitude with a nod. "Can I tell you something?"

"Of course," Erik said.

"I've met a few OSS agents during the war, but the knowledge you possess surpasses any of them. If you are going to work with them after the war, you'd be a great asset."

Erik shook his head.

"No? They say one man can make a big difference." Valensky peered at Erik, but he kept his expression neutral. "You're the most unique individual I've ever met."

"Really?" Erik quirked an eyebrow.

"Yes." A knowing grin came across Valensky's face. "Be honest with me, how did you know when Paris was going to be liberated and that Operation Market Garden was going to fail?"

"A lucky guess?" Erik replied with a shrug.

Valensky's eyes narrowed but remained friendly as he said in disbelief, "No. You're a time traveler, aren't you? That's how you know all this."

Erik gave Valensky's arm a friendly punch. "You know my secret."

They both chuckled.

"Wouldn't it be neat if time travel really were possible and we could change history," Valensky said.

Erik shrugged.

"If you could go back in time, would you make it where the Germans lose the air war over Great Britain?"

"Keep dreaming; never going to happen." Erik patted Valensky's shoulder and got into the Kübelwagen.

"Do you think Germany will start another war?" Valensky asked through the window.

Erik snickered and shook his head. "No."

"What makes you so sure?"

"The allied powers wouldn't want to give Germany an opportunity to re-arm as they did in the 1930s. I think it might be a different world after this war is over." Valensky gestured for Erik to explain himself. He continued, "Allies will become enemies and enemies will become allies. For example, do you remember the Napoleonic Wars?"

"Of course."

"During that time, England and Prussia were allies against France, and nearly one hundred years later the Great War started, but that time France and England were allies against Germany."

"You have an interesting way of explaining history."

Erik explained. "The most important lesson is that history has three views: My view, your view, and the truth."

"I never saw history in that way before, but I have to agree with you." Valensky glanced at his watch. "It is time for you to go. Take care, my friend. Good luck."

"Thanks."

Valensky stepped back and Jamie walked toward the car, sobbing. Erik hopped out and raced toward her. They embraced tightly; she grabbed his hand, pulled his fingers away from his palm, placed something in his hand, and closed it.

"This will give you the courage to continue and bring you luck," she whispered.

They embraced again, and Erik rubbed her back to comfort her. He whispered in her ear that he loved her so much, then stared into her sobbing eyes, and they kissed deeply, knowing it could be for the last time.

"I have to go," Erik said, as he pulled away.

Jamie nodded and they strolled to the Kübelwagen. Erik got in and cranked over the air-cooled motor. The car chugged into life. He looked through the window to Jamie with Valensky by her side, and said, "One-four-three-seven." She repeated the numbers back to him, and a smile wiped away her tears. Erik waved and drove into the night.

The Kübelwagen's headlights pierced the endless darkness and flashed on the trees that lined the road, their branches already naked. Erik glanced to the right and left, but saw nothing but open land beyond. Even though he was well rested, he was alone, and so he thought of random things to keep himself awake and focused.

After driving for some time, several burned out vehicles with flames still flickering inside came into view, and he remembered the Allied air attack. Adrenaline pumped to every part of his body as he recalled the horror of seeing both man and machine torn into pieces, leaving nothing behind except mutilated bodies and blackened and twisted metal. Erik breathed deeply to calm his pounding heart and slowed down so he could look at his map with his flashlight. Distant lights told him he was drawing nearer to the town of Roeschwoog.

Will it be occupied by American, British, or German troops? If Germans, worst case, they will stop me and ask for my papers. If American or British, I'll become a POW and might never see Jamie again. The best option is if it's not occupied by anyone. Oh shit! I forgot about the French Resistance.

Erik slowed as he neared some buildings, and after a quick glance around, gave a huge sigh of relief at the sight of the familiar vehicles of the Wehrmacht: Opel Blitzs, Kübelwagens, and a few half-tracks. Military activity became thicker in the heart of Roeschwoog, with armored patrols, spotlights, eighty-eight-millimeter anti-aircraft batteries and twenty-millimeter Flak 38, Flakvierlings. Erik was amazed that the town hadn't been touched by Allied bombers. If it weren't for the presence of the Germans, it would appear that the war was not happening.

No one stopped him, and on the other side of Roeschwoog, darkness engulfed him again. Erik rubbed his eyes. According to the map, the next town was Roppenheim. The good thing was that from here to Berlin, every city would be occupied by the Germans; but he still had one small problem—actually, two big problems—the United States Army Air Force bombed by day and the Royal Air Force bombed by night, which had made most of the roads unusable, and he had to negotiate checkpoints.

Closer to Roppenheim, he noticed brake lights up ahead. His first checkpoint. He came to a halt, got his papers out just in case, and took an opportunity to stretch in his seat and rest for a few moments while the vehicles slowly inched their way up to the checkpoint. Erik remembered what Jamie gave him before he left. He pulled it from his pocket and discovered that it was a locket with a picture of him and Jamie inside. Her thoughtfulness placed a smile on his face.

Within a couple of minutes, he was at the checkpoint. Two armed guards checked identity papers while a half dozen more, their eyes alert, had their hands ready on their weapons. They walked on both sides of the vehicles closest to the checkpoint. A young guard with bloodshot eyes and slumped shoulders extended his hand and asked for Erik's papers. He glanced at the papers and then at Erik and asked where he was coming from and where he was headed. Erik gave him his prepared story, and after a few seconds, the young soldier snapped to attention and saluted, eyes straight ahead.

"You may pass, Sir," he said. "I advise you to stay here for the night because we've had reports of Allied attacks. Reaching Berlin, much less Hamburg, will be almost impossible due to the Autobahn being bombed."

Erik thanked him for the tip, then asked where a good place was to get a room and something to eat. The young soldier suggested the HOSTELLERIE LA BOHEME and pointed down the road. Erik nodded in appreciation, and the guard waved for the next vehicle to move forward.

Troops walked around the town, and panzers were scattered about, like chess pieces on a board. Their crews were relaxing and smoking. Erik drove on until, at the corner of Rue Principale and Rue du Neuhaeusel, he came across a two-story building that was once a house with a faded picket fence and was now being used as a hotel. Erik parked the Kübelwagen, grabbed his few belongings, and shouldered his MP-44. He walked to the front entrance of the faded-white building but found the door was locked. He knocked and waited. No answer. He pounded harder on the door. The hallway light came on, and a man rubbed his weary eyes and peered through the narrow window beside the door. He pointed to his wrist and waved Erik away, but Erik held up a large amount of money. The man stared at it, then rubbed this eyes and stared again. He nodded his head, then slowly unlocked the door.

"Can I help you?"

Erik lifted the handful of cash. "I need a room."

"Fine."

Once inside, Erik handed him more than enough to pay for the room. The man took it and motioned Erik upstairs, then disappeared into a small office and reappeared with a key.

"The room's upstairs," he mumbled and handed Erik the key. "Second on the right. Bathroom's the third on the left."

Half way up the wooden stairs creaked, and the light from below switched off. The hallway on the second floor had just enough light so that Erik could find his room. He opened the door, flicked on the light and discovered a well-lit, spacious double room with a comfortable-looking bed. With eyelids that grew heavy, he walked to the bed and placed down his belongings.

In the distance, he heard several high-pitched muffled sounds, one after another, and each one louder than the one before. Then, suddenly, hellish explosions erupted throughout the town of Roppenheim. Erik heard the whine of salvos that land-ed nearby. The hotel vibrated beneath his feet, and windows shat-tered. He grabbed his belongings and the MP-44 and darted out of the hotel.

The night was lit up, like flashes from dozens of cameras, from a constant bombardment from Sherman tanks. The town was in chaos; the streets were filled with men and vehicles. Erik hopped in the Kübelwagen and drove, trying to escape the insanity. Walls of buildings erupted and exploded into stone rubble. Flames and black choking smoke billowed from them, followed by showers of shrapnel. Dozens of German soldiers yelled and screamed as they scrambled for cover. Panzers rumbled down the streets with troops that advanced in a zig zag pattern behind them.

Erik barreled down Rue Principale past infantrymen pull-ing their wounded off the streets behind heaps of rubble and half walls. The burping sound of MG 34 machine guns and gunfire echoed around the town. At the t-intersection of Rue Princi-pale and Rue des Près, several Sdkfz 251's passed Erik. They were filled with panzer grenadiers whose uniforms were spattered with blood and dust. Further down Rue Principale, Erik slowed and glanced down Rue des Roses.

Several ominous silhouettes drove his way, accompanied by the dreaded sound of clacking and wheezing. Sherman tanks! Their turrets swung around, muzzles leveled at their targets, and numerous thunderclap muzzle bursts hurled their shells in Er-ik's and the panzer grenadiers' direction, punching holes into the sides of the Sdkfz 251's and turning them into fireballs. Then suddenly several of the Shermans exploded, which turned them into deadly pits of fire, tossing debris into the night sky.

Tigers!—sixty-seven tons of pure fighting machine with massive hulls, sloping sides and five inches of frontal armor, moved forward by ten steel road wheels. They carried dual MG 34 machine guns, one in the hull and another on the turret beside the feared eighty-eight-millimeter gun. The Shermans and Tigers maneuvered, trying to get better angles to attack, like old naval galleons of the 16th to 18th centuries.

Erik pushed the Kübelwagen to the limit. Its engine whined, but he navigated around the rubble, and eventually the distant explosions slowly faded behind him. Erik suffered from a lack of sleep and tried to stay focused on a road that was consumed by the night. Sometime later, a loud pop came from the front of the car. He smashed the steering wheel with his fists and knew it could only be one thing—a flat tire. Sure enough, when he pulled over and stumbled out, he found out he was correct.

"Seriously!" He screamed and kicked the car. "If you don't want me to do this," he looked up as if he was talking to God, "just tell me, and I'll give up!" Erik waited for an answer that would never come. "Why are you giving me all these challenges?" he shouted. "For once, can you make it easy for me?" With a sigh, he walked to the hood and checked the spare tire. It was flat. "Really! You know I'm trying to make things as they were, so why in the hell are you doing this?"

Erik unloaded unnecessary gear, slipped the MP-44 over his shoulder, and started walking down the road. The moon slowly breached the clouds and transformed the dark pasture on both sides of the road to a soothing pale ivory. Only loose gravel under Erik's boots, chirping seasonal insects, and rattling leaves broke the stillness of the night.

In the distance, tracer rounds from anti-aircraft guns lit up the horizon, and solid beams of searchlights danced in the sky. Erik knew, even though he couldn't hear them, that British heavy bombers, maybe Lancasters, were showering bombs on a German city. German night fighters would be in the sky too, circling like sharks, doing hit and run attacks against the bombers. He stopped for a moment and stared, transfixed by the amazing sight, the magnitude of destruction being caused, and the knowledge that thousands of people would be killed tonight.

He walked on, but over time, his feet began to ache and his knee started to swell. He took the last sip of water from his canteen and tossed it away. The pain in his legs crept up like poison in his blood stream. If he stopped it wouldn't make it better, and he wouldn't lie down and sleep. His eyelids grew even heavier, and he stumbled, nearly falling. Erik made a deep sigh. He continued walking, not knowing how much longer he would be able to go on. Eventually, Erik collapsed like a card house with a base card removed. Mentally and physically exhausted, he lay on the side of the road as if he were paralyzed. He couldn't move his legs, and even his arms felt as if they were being held down so they couldn't help him to his feet. He had only the strength to clench his fists in frustration and tilted his head to see the orange glow lighting the sky from the numerous fires that plagued the city. The raid might be over, but the nightmare continued. Erik closed his eyes and fell into a deep sleep.

A sudden bump in the road awakened him. He shook his head, rubbed his eyes, and slowly got to his feet, trying to keep his balance. He realized he was in a Sdkfz 251 half-track, but he didn't know where or how he got there.

"Morning, Herr Major," a soldier said.

Erik blinked at the man. "How did I get here?"

"We found you on the side of a road and brought you along, Sir."

The buildings around them, he saw with some shock, were pretty much intact, even with the bomb raids. "How far is the Reich Chancellery?" He asked one of the soldiers.

The soldier stared back at him and replied awkwardly, "Sir, we are not in Berlin."

Erik cleared his throat. He frowned. "Where are we?"

"Wolgast, Sir."

Erik sank into his seat and realized that it was early evening on the first of October 1944, and tomorrow was the day Hitler got killed. If that happened, Germany would be the first one to use the atomic bomb, and history would be altered forever. He hoped he could find transportation back to Berlin tonight.

In the near distance, he saw a heavily guarded outpost with dozens of Waffen SS troops, Sdkfz 234/1 armored cars, with their turrets pointed down the road, two Flakpanzer IV Wirbelwinds, with their crews fully alert, and the overt presence of King Tiger tanks, their lethal eighty-eight-millimeter guns ready to unleash their shells of death. The half-track neared the checkpoint and rocked back and forth as it came to a stop. Erik heard a guard asking for identification papers from the driver. Then the back doors of the half-track opened. The guards scanned the passengers with intimidating stares and asked for their papers. Some guards nodded when they recognized their friends but remained professional.

An old SS sergeant who had menacing blue eyes and wore

steel-framed glasses came from behind, made his way between the guards, and stared directly at Erik with a look of cold speculation. Erik felt as if a spider had crawled on his back. The SS sergeant extended his hand. "Your papers now," he said sharply.

Erik pulled out his papers and handed them over. The SS sergeant ripped them from his hand, glanced over them, and in a voice dripping with spite said, "Get out of the vehicle now." Erik, heart rate raised, climbed out and stood in front of the SS sergeant. "State your business," the sergeant said with a scorched look.

"Herr Sergeant, I was on my way to Berlin and my column was hit, and I was—"

"Well, Herr Major, you are not in Berlin, are you?"

"No, I am not." *This is worse than the French Resistance; there'll be no escaping this.*

"Are you getting smart with me? Well?"

Erik said nothing.

"You're not even SS," The sergeant stated as if he had a bitter taste in his mouth.

"No, Herr Sergeant. I stated due to the bombing raids, I was diverted here."

"That's not my problem, Herr Major." He pointed at Erik with an accusing finger. "Continue and I will have you detained. Understood?"

A low-pitch horn broke the tension. Erik glanced to his left at a black convertible Mercedes with an SS plate. The SS officers inside were getting impatient. Erik had just thought things couldn't get worse when the passenger door flew open and a tall, blonde-haired, blue-eyed SS Lieutenant approached. *Great, the ideal candidate for the master race.*

The SS Lieutenant extended his hand for Erik's papers and

with a heavy, formal German accent asked, "What seems to be the problem, Herr Sergeant?"

"Herr Lieutenant, the major does not have the authority to be here."

The Lieutenant stared at Erik with chilly blue eyes. "What's your name, Herr Major?"

"Erik Függer."

The sergeant blurted out, "I will be happy to detain him and have him questioned by the Gestapo." The Lieutenant nodded in agreement, and the sergeant headed to the guard shack and ordered the guards to detain Erik. Then suddenly the lieutenant ordered the sergeant to halt and turned to Erik.

"What did you say your last name was?"

Oh, shit! Has the Gestapo been looking for me ever since Rommel and I escaped the hospital? "Függer," Erik replied calmly.

"By any chance do you have a brother?" Erik nodded. There was a chance this lieutenant had mistaken him for someone who had the same name. Függer was a pretty common surname. But he decided to see where the conversation was leading. "Where are you from?"

Erik took a gamble and remembered where is grandfather was from. "Bremerhaven."

The Lieutenant pointed at Erik as if it helped him to get his point across. "His name is Walter, right?"

Erik knew the answer was wrong but that was the name of his great uncle who served in the Waffen SS. So he nodded. "He's my younger brother."

The Lieutenant's eyes brightened; he smiled and extended his hand.

Erik shook the Lieutenant's hand and said a small prayer to God for helping him when he needed it the most. But he needed one more miracle…transportation to Berlin.

"Walter was a great friend. We served together in Russia." He looked over Erik's shoulder and ordered the sergeant to stand down and return Erik's papers. "By the way, my name is Heinz Zeuner." He gestured for Erik to accompany him to his car. They took a seat and proceeded into the base. Heinz turned to face Erik. "What are you doing here?"

"I was on my way to Berlin but was diverted here due to the Allied bombings. However, I don't know where *here* is."

Heinz gave a devious laugh. "You are on a base that does not exist." He paused to catch his thoughts.

Great; I'm in Area 51. Erik thought.

"You are at *Peenemünde*," Heinz said and flashed a superior grin. "Why do you need to go to Berlin?"

"I'm meeting Herr Reich Minister Speer tomorrow, but I have no means of transportation."

"I'll speak to my C.O. and see if you can get a lift with us; we are scheduled to leave in an hour. We are going to his office now, so just relax."

"Thanks, Heinz."

Erik leaned back in his seat and glanced out the window. They passed several damaged buildings and some that were no more than rubble. Heinz saw him staring and explained.

"On the twenty-fifth of August, American B-17s bombed the base. The attack caused minor damage to Test Stand VII, destroyed several aircraft and killed nearly thirty people. Some were scientists and technical staff. But launchings were able to resume within six weeks."

The base was busy with all kinds of vehicles transporting men and equipment. Among the buildings and trees, Erik saw all forms of anti-aircraft batteries from eighty-eight millimeters to Flak 38's, their crews fully alert, looking for enemy aircraft. Erik looked to see if he could spot something he hadn't read about in published knowledge or the classified documents on Peenemünde. They veered off the main road and pulled into a small parking lot located in front of a four-story brick building. Erik and the others got out of the car, walked to the entrance, got a Hitler salute, and entered.

Inside, a vast room greeted them. Despite ceiling lights, it was dim, and scuff marks from foot traffic had dulled the deep-brown tile floor. Behind the oak reception desk in the center of the room, individuals stood answering phones, passing hand-written messages, and conversing with those who approached the desk. The place was a hive of highly focused activity. People wore different ranks of SS uniforms or business dress or white lab coats for the technical staff. As Erik and Heinz walked past the front desk, a clerk got Heinz's attention by raising the phone receiver. Heinz raised a finger toward Erik, which indicated that he should wait.

"This is Lieutenant Zeuner…thank you, Herr Sergeant." The clerk replaced the receiver and looked expectantly at Heinz.

"Call the pilots and tell them to prepare the Obergruppen-führer's plane for takeoff," Heinz told the clerk, then motioned for Erik to follow him up the stairs. "We're going to meet my commanding officer. He's headed to Berlin this evening."

"Herr Lieutenant, is my plane ready?" A deep commanding voice declared. The Obergruppenführer walked down the stairs and past them.

"Yes, Herr Obergruppenführer. Sir, there's a matter I would like to speak to you about." Heinz turned and followed the Obergruppenführer, and Erik followed behind. Heinz explained Erik's situation and told him that Erik's brother had saved his life.

The Obergruppenführer stopped and turned to face Erik. The man's icy blue eyes penetrated his soul. "Herr Major, what is your business in Berlin?"

"It is a matter of state business. I am to meet with Herr Reich Minister Speer."

"I see. Was your brother in the Waffen SS? In Russia? He saved Lieutenant Zeuner's life?"

"Yes, Herr Obergruppenführer."

"What made you not join the SS?"

"My height, Sir."

A condescending grin came across the Obergruppenführer's face; with a mocked tone he replied, "Yes, I see that. Well, we cannot all be perfect." He paused in thought. "I don't normally fly with people I don't know. However, since your brother was in the SS and he saved Lieutenant Zeuner's life, I will give you a lift to Berlin."

"Thank you, Herr Obergruppenführer." Miracle two.

He sharply did an about face and continued on. Heinz walked alongside Erik, and Erik thanked him for his help. Outside, a polished midnight black 1940 Mercedes-Benz 770 Tourenwagen convertible with two square flag pennants pulled up in front. The flags were diagonally divided into four fields with black top and bottoms and white left and right fields. Superimposed at the center of each pennant was a silver SS eagle with a wreath and swastika.

The driver leaped out and made his way around the car. "Heil Hitler." He gave the salute, then opened the back door and closed it once the Obergruppenführer and Heinz were seated. He then did the same with the passenger seat for Erik.

The car lunged forward toward the airfield and forced everyone back in their seats. Erik absorbed everything he saw. None of it was in any book or government file that he had seen, or possibly his security clearance wasn't high enough. As they drove along the road that ran parallel to the hangers and what appeared to be several launch pads, Erik turned around, pointed in the direction of the launch pads and asked for clarification.

"That will make us win this war," the Obergruppenführer replied in a heartless tone and with a devilish grin.

As Erik continued to look, he was greeted by a scene of such horror that for several minutes he sat speechless, his eyes dazzled by the terror of the Nazis' weapon of mass destruction: the A-10 rocket, also known as the Amerika Rocket. Each projectile rested on a blunt cone of steel that rose from the ground with their tips of three severely back-swept delta fins. A lightning bolt of chills raced up Erik's spine; he felt pure evil emanating from this man. He nodded and turned around, realizing who the man in the back seat actually was: Obergruppenführer Hans Kammler. Hans Kammler was the man in charge of Hitler's most secret projects: Miracle Weapons and Project Bell, specifically projects such as the jet engines, rockets (V1 and V2), and Intercontinental Weapons (Amerika Rocket). Erik remembered that at one time Kammler had over fourteen million people that worked for him, mostly building underground factories. Erik shivered. If he didn't stop Hitler's death, Kammler's dreams would become realities.

The car came to a halt at the airfield checkpoint, which was well protected by two Sdkfz 232 armored cars and a half dozen SS troops. One guard peered into the car; the others stayed alert. Once the guard realized who it was, he snapped to attention and did the Nazi salute. The gate was raised and the car passed through. They drove slowly alongside a massive hangar with ground crews. Technical staff and pilots hovered around and worked on what appeared to be experimental aircraft. Amazed, Erik corrected himself: experimental *jet* aircraft. Though he had seen these jets—Focke-Wulf FW J. P.011-47 and Messerschmitt, ME P.1101/99—in books and government files, he couldn't believe they were in front of his eyes.

Erik thought out loud, "That's just impossible."

He glanced back at Kammler, who had a disturbing grin and replied, "Nothing is impossible. It just costs a lot of money." Then he told Erik that the pilots of the Jagdgeschwader Schlageter 26—better known as the "The Abbeville Boys" or "The Abbeville Kids" to both the British and Americans who flew against them—would once again have air superiority.

Erik squinted into the hanger and noticed that the fuselage of the Messerschmitt ME P.1101/99 was an all metal construction and contained the fuel tanks and most of the armament. The wings were swept back at forty-five degrees—almost like the United States F-117A Nighthawk stealth fighter aircraft—and it had four turbojets buried in the thickened wing roots fed by an air intake in the leading edge of the wing. The main landing gear looked like it could be retracted inward into the fuselage, and the front gear appeared to be able to retract backward beneath the cockpit. A two-man crew could sit side-by-side in the cockpit in the extreme nose of the aircraft. A long barrel, which looked like a seventy-five-millimeter Pak 40 cannon, sat in the nose along with five MK 112 fifty-five-millimeter machine cannons. This aircraft would create havoc against the B-17's. But Erik was going to do his best to make sure that would never happen.

They continued slowly past the hangar that gave Erik plenty of time to feast his eyes on the jets. He felt Kammler's pride in his weapons and suspected that he was enjoying Erik's obvious amazement. He saw that the Focke-Wulf FW J. P.011-47 was an all metal twin-jet fighter. Its wings were mounted mid-fuselage and swept back thirty degrees. One turbojet was located underneath the cockpit in the forward fuselage and one was mounted under each wing—three in all. It was similar to, or a bad knock off of, the Soviet fighters Lavochkin La-200 and MIG I-320. Unlike those aircraft, though, this had space in the cockpit for a crew of three. Erik assumed that the pilot and navigator would have sat side-by-side with the radio operator directly behind them, facing the rear. The armament in the forward fuselage nose looked like four MK 108 thirty-millimeter cannons. The P-51 wouldn't have a chance if they went head to head in combat.

A deafening high-pitched whine suddenly penetrated Erik's ears. He covered his ears with his hands and glanced around to locate the source of the noise. Heinz tapped on Erik's shoulder and pointed to the runway. Erik looked, and his eyes widened at the sight of a large winged aircraft that came in for a landing.

"What is it?" He asked Heinz, raising his voice to be heard over the noise.

"A jet bomber."

The bomber landed with a bounce, and it was soon clear to Erik from the swept-back wings with vertical fins and the two turbojets under each that it was an Arado AR E.560/4, designed as a fast, medium-range tactical bomber. The crew of two sat in the cockpit in the fuselage nose where two fixed, forward-firing MG 151 twenty-millimeter cannons were mounted. The aft fuselage held two fixed rear-firing cannons of the same kind, and one that Erik knew was fired and moved by remote control via a periscope in the cockpit. He didn't know the bomb load capacity, but clearly, it was an effective weapon.

The whining died, but a thundering roar from large aero engines took its place.

"To your right," Kammler said.

Erik's jaw dropped when he realized what was in front of him, a Junkers, Ju 390.

Kammler chuckled at his reaction, and Erik closed his mouth. He recalled that the Ju 390 was a part of the failed Amerika Bomber Project. The wings, mounted mid-fuselage, had an enormous wingspan—a hundred and sixty-five feet, Erik recalled—and each wing had three massive radial engines. The plane sat on four immense sets of dual wheels with huge axle suspensions that would retract into the wings, and there was a wheel near the end of the fuselage. Erik remembered that the intimidating looking aircraft was large enough to carry an eight-man crew: pilot, co-pilot, navigator, radio operator, and four machine gunners strategically located throughout the aircraft.

One after another, the engine's propellers stuttered into life, followed by a huge belch of thick black smoke from the exhaust pipe. Erik shook his head in amazement, but not just for the reason Kammler thought. For Erik, it was as if he had climbed into one of his history books.

The Mercedes-Benz pulled alongside the aircraft and members of the aircrew raced to the doors closest to the plane. They opened them, and everyone got out and exchanged Nazi salutes. An SS sergeant approached Heinz, they exchanged salutes, and the sergeant reported that the aircraft was clear for takeoff and that Kammler's meeting with Hitler was confirmed. Heinz turned his head slightly to Kammler and nodded, symbolizing that everything was set, and then he motioned Erik to the hatch where they were to enter. Erik walked to the plane and glanced up at the pilot and co-pilot perched high in the cockpit. They were busy going over their checklists and inspections prior to departure.

Once on the gangway, Erik felt the steady vibration that engulfed the aircraft. Inside the narrow Ju 390, he found a seat on one side of the aisle, and Heinz took a place in the matched row of single seats on the other side. Within minutes, everyone was seated and the aircraft taxied to the runway and took off. The noise from the massive engines resonated through the airframe, and the floor quivered under Erik's feet. Out the window, he saw three Messerschmitt ME 262s that flew in to escort them. He looked across the moss-green interior and saw more joining them on the other side.

Heinz leaned over toward Erik. "How are you holding up?"

"I'm fine," Erik replied.

Heinz asked if he had a family and Erik said he did. They exchanged photographs, and Heinz noticed with a silly grin and raised eyebrows, that Jamie looked younger than Erik. Erik rolled his eyes and said that she was, by thirteen years. Heinz congratulated him as if he'd won a contest and asked how he got her. They then shared the stories of how they met their wives.

Erik glanced over his shoulder and saw Kammler buried in his documents. His snake-like eyes slowly raised off the page, and he gave Erik a Cheshire cat grin.

Erik suppressed a shiver. *Can this guy be any more evil?*

Before long, the co-pilot made his way to the back of the aircraft where Erik and the rest sat and said they would be landing in twenty minutes.

Erik stretched in his seat and again considered how to persuade Albert Speer to help him. He knew that during this time since Operation Valkyrie failed, everyone in Germany was questioning each other. The Gestapo even watched ordinary citizens, and if anyone showed a defeatist attitude, they were detained and questioned. Erik would also need to find transportation to Speer's office by the Reich Chancellery.

The tires screeched from hitting the runway at Tempelhof, which indicated that they had finally arrived in Berlin. The huge aircraft taxied toward the main terminal, where various military aircraft stood ready to be launched at a moment's notice. Within minutes, the thunderous aero engines sputtered to a halt. The rear tail gunner got up, opened the rear hatch, jumped out and placed the stairs by the hatch so everyone could get out.

SS bodyguards with emotionless faces and a two-toned 1940 Mercedes-Benz G-4 Tourenwagen convertible greeted them. Erik turned to Heinz as Kammler walked on by and thanked him once again. They said their goodbyes, and Heinz and Kammler left Erik standing on the tarmac.

"Sir, someone left this behind," A voice said from behind him. Erik turned. The pilot handed him a thick file.

"Thank you." Erik took the folder as a lone Kübelwagen pulled up. He glanced at the outside of the folder and grinned. The label read, "Die Glocke" (The Bell). *What a score!* He held the complete file on Project Bell, a top secret Nazi project! All he knew was that it was either a scientific technological device, a secret weapon, or a Wunderwaffe (wonder weapon). Then Erik turned to the pilot and instructed him not to mention this to Kammler or anyone. The pilot and Erik exchanged salutes and went on their way. While walking to the Kübelwagen, he glanced through the many drawings, diagrams, and documentation.

"Hello, Herr Major. It's good to see you again," the driver said when Erik drew near.

Erik looked up at a familiar face. He paused, tried to place the man, and then asked, "Are you the private that drove me to the hospital?"

"Yes, Sir."

"Why are you at Tempelhof? And I see you got promoted to time lance-corporal."

The young man smiled and nodded, and Erik congratulated him.

"I was going to pick up my commanding officer," the time lance-corporal explained, "but I just heard it was possible he was shot down." He frowned. "The last time I saw you, you shot at the SS vehicle's tires. They were angry."

Erik chuckled, imagining their reactions. Then he leaned forward. "Since your commanding officer isn't going to arrive, could you give me a lift to Herr Reich Minister Speer's address: No. 53 Pariser Platz,"

"Yes Sir," the time lance-corporal said and gestured Erik into the car.

During the drive, Erik told the time lance-corporal that they could be informal and he could call him Erik. He learned that the young man's name was Walter Kohl and that he was assigned to an anti-aircraft battery in the city, near his parent's house where he lived.

Berlin was a mess. Block after block of buildings that had once stood with pride had been turned into rubble; it was an ominous sight. The residents' faces were etched with fear, and they regularly cast worried looks up to the sky. Among the ruins, the blood-red Nazi flag fluttered, and the words of one of the Nazis' most-repeated political slogans were painted in white bold letters: Ein Volk, Ein Reich, Ein Führer (One People, One Nation, One Leader).

Erik was amazed and impressed that even though they knew that Germany was defeated, the German people still had their pride. The trees on Lichtenrader Street had lost most of their colorful fall leaves, mainly because of the Allied bombings. On Mahlower Street, repairmen appeared to be fixing busted underground pipes, which seemed completely absurd since the same thing would happen once the Allies bombed Berlin again. Running parallel to Columbiadamm, on the right-hand side, was a large open grassy area surrounded by trees. Through the branches, Erik saw several camouflaged eighty-eight-millimeter anti-aircraft batteries surrounded by sandbags that gave some protection from shrapnel for the crew.

Walter drove deeper into the city and made a slight right to Platz der Luftbrücke and a right turn on Merhringdamm/B96.

They passed more half-demolished buildings and piles of rub-ble. It appeared that the Allied bomb raids touched every part of Berlin. Finally, they turned onto Voßstraße and Walter parked the car. He pointed to the building where Speer's office was—which was within walking distance of the Reich Chancellery—and asked Erik if he should wait for him. Erik said yes, then he darted across the street and entered the building.

Inside, Erik glanced at the list of names and office numbers and located the right name—Reich Minister Speer, room 215. Erik prayed that Speer was here and not in a meeting with Hitler. He dashed up the concrete stairs, avoiding individuals on their way down, and finally came to room 215. He paused to catch his breath, then walked in. A petite, plain woman with round black-framed glasses and hair in a bun, sat behind a desk. Her dark eyes glanced up and she straightened her posture as Erik approached.

Erik removed his cap. "I'm here to see the Reich Minister."

"Herr Major, do you have an appointment?" She glanced at an appointment book that was filled with names and times.

"No. But I only need five minutes of the Reich Minister's time."

"I'm sorry, Herr Major, but unless you have an appointment, Herr Reich Minister Speer cannot see you." She flipped through the filled appointment pages, shook her head, and then looked up. "His schedule is completely booked. If you leave your name and number I'll give it to him and see if he can meet you outside of office hours or fit you in his schedule."

Erik leaned over the desk. "My business with Speer is of the utmost urgency. It cannot wait. When he knows my business, he will want to see me."

"What's your business?"

"I can't tell you, except to say that I'm here to stop something terrible from happening to the Führer, and if you don't let me see him, you'll soon understand and wish you had."

She observed him for a moment, then, apparently satisfied that he was genuine, motioned him to take a seat. She picked up the phone and spoke in a half whisper while she nodded and looked in Erik's direction. She placed the receiver down but said nothing. Erik sat, looked down and closed his eyes. He feared the worst but hoped for the best.

Erik lifted his head at the sound of a door being opened. Albert Speer, the thirty-nine-year-old Minister of Armaments and Munitions walked in and glared at Erik. His bluish-grey eyes matched the color of an overcast sky. He wore a brown Nazi tunic with no insignia, a bare swastika armband, and an NSDAP Golden Party Badge on his left breast pocket. Erik stood at attention.

"You have five minutes," Speer said, then he turned around and went in his office.

Erik followed and mouthed a thank you to his secretary.

"How can I help you, Herr Major?" Speer asked as he stuffed his attaché case.

"What I'm about to share will be a shock, Herr Reich Minister."

Speer paid little attention and motioned Erik to get to the point as he continued grabbing documents off his desk.

"There is going to be another attempt to kill the Führer."

Speer stopped and glanced at him. "What did you say?" he asked coldly.

"Herr Reich Minister, there is going to be another attempt to kill the Führer."

Speer glared at Erik and replied firmly. "What did you say your name was?"

"Major Erik Függer."

Speer stopped, crossed his arms, and scrutinized Erik. "Herr Major, that's a rash thing to say," he said in a scolding tone. "How are you sure about this?" He pointed at Erik to get his point across. "What proof do you have?"

"I don't have any actual proof, but," he tried to salvage some credibility, "I have a very strong suspicion that there is going be an attempt on his life tomorrow around noon."

Speer gave him an incredulous look. "I can't believe I'm hearing this. You want me to believe there's an attempt on the Führer's life, but you have no proof?"

"Yes, I do. Herr Reich Minister Speer, I know what I am saying is mad—"

"Mad? No, it's either pure speculation or a figment of your imagination." Speer approached Erik. "Who are these assassins you claim are going kill the Führer?" He raised his eyebrow.

"I believe it will be members of the SS in the Adolf Hitler Division."

Speer shook his head in disbelief. "Just like in Operation Valkyrie?" he queried with restrained laughter.

Erik nodded.

"Herr Major, do you realize how crazy that sounds?" Speer looked over his shoulder. "Do you realize how close I am to Hitler?" He glanced at his phone. "With one call to the Gestapo or SS, I can make you disappear." He pointed to the photograph of Hitler on the wall. "You remember you took an oath."

"I do and so did you, and I'm trying to do the right thing by informing you, Herr Speer. If anyone would listen I would expect it to be you."

"Well, you thought wrong. Good day, Herr Major. You know where the door is."

"My God, Speer, we're talking about the Führer's life. He's going to be killed. And you're not willing to do anything to stop it?"

"How can I go to him if you have no proof?" Speer said in a commanding voice, "Explain yourself, Herr Major!"

Erik's heart raced. "Say I am just making this up," he tossed up his hands, "and he does get killed, and it makes Germany worse. Then what would you do, Herr Reich Minister?"

"I would do my duty as Minister for Armaments and as a German. I would expect you to do the same, major."

"I recall you met Herr Field Marshal Milch earlier this year, and you wanted to resign from the ministry and spend time with your wife and children. What about their future, or the future of Germany and future generations?"

"Things have changed, Herr Major." Speer closed his attaché case and started to walk to the door. He motioned for Erik to leave. "Your time is up, major."

In a last-ditch attempt, Erik recalled something that would happen the next day, the second of October 1944. "Aachen will be attacked by the American First and Thirtieth Infantry Divisions. They will start with aerial and artillery bombardments."

Speer turned sharply and stared at Erik with scolding eyes. "Get out, Herr Major! Now! I do not need to hear your delusional stories. I must say you really have an interesting imagination."

"Time will tell if my imagination becomes a reality," Erik said as he walked by Speer. Then, before he exited the office, he turned back. "Field Marshal Model will be sending a report to Army High Command requesting, if not begging, for reinforcements. Little to his knowledge, Hitler will replace him with Rundstedt and give that so famous order 'hold at all costs.'" Without waiting for a reaction, Erik strode through the door and out of the building.

He returned to the car and got in, not knowing what to do next. The fact was, he had failed. Walter asked where he should drive him, and Erik shrugged. His options ran through his head: one, let the new history play out with Hitler being killed; two, try to save Hitler, or three, head back to Jamie and live out his natural life. *What could I have done differently?* Erik sighed; it was in God's hands now. Right now all he wanted to do was get a good night's sleep.

"How did your meeting go?" Walter asked.

"It didn't."

"Oh, I'm sorry…Do you have a place to stay for the night?"

Erik shook his head.

"You can stay at my parents' house."

"Thank you, Walter, but I can't impose on them like that."

"Herr Major, it's perfectly okay."

Erik looked at Walter's earnest face and finally agreed.

Walter started up the car and headed down the street. As they drove off, Speer ran out of the building and caught and wrote down the license plate.

Night crept over the city, and people slowly filtered off the streets. They drove past people who boarded up their windows so light wouldn't seep through, and when they parked, Erik noticed that the street trolleys had stopped running and no street lamps were on, to make it harder for the British to find their targets. Walter's family lived in a three-story apartment building. The buildings around it showed minor damage, but amazingly it had remained intact.

They entered the small apartment and heard sounds from the kitchen as if someone was making dinner. The living room had a couch with a coffee table in front of it, and Erik noticed a small radio and phonograph with an extensive record collection sat on the sideboard. A hallway presumably led to the bedrooms, and through an open door, he saw a dining room with a small wooden table set for four people.

As Erik stood in the living room, he heard running footsteps that came down the hallway. A young teen wearing glasses appeared, followed by a small-framed man in his mid to late fifties. The older man had gray hair and blue eyes and wore a captain's uniform. Their eyebrows raised at Erik's appearance in their living room but quickly relaxed. The captain snapped out a Heil Hitler and did the Nazi salute. Erik returned it. Then the captain stepped toward Erik and offered his hand.

"Good evening, Herr Major," he said and shook Erik's hand. "I am Captain Hans Kohl." He looked to Walter. "I see you have met my oldest son."

Erik nodded and introduced himself as Major Erik Függer.

Hans placed his arm around his other son. "This is my youngest, Helmut."

Charged with energy and a big smile, Helmut extended his hand to introduce himself, and then he snapped a salute. "Hi,

Herr Major. I am Helmut Kohl, reporting for duty." Smiles and laughter filled the house.

Erik snapped to attention and saluted back. "What's your report, Herr Corporal?" He asked, playing along.

Helmut rolled his eyes upward, thought of something to say, and then with his eyes widened, he replied, "Sir, we shot down three American bombers."

"Great job, Herr Corporal; keep our city safe."

Helmut saluted, then his father rubbed his head affectionately and instructed him to set another place at the table. "Cäcilie," He called into the kitchen, "we have a guest."

"My wife, Cäcilie," he said when a dark-haired, middle-aged woman poked her head out the kitchen door. He introduced her to Erik, and she smiled and said good evening, then returned to the kitchen. Hans motioned for Erik to have a seat in the living room. "If I had known we were going to have company, I would've straightened my house. I apologize."

Erik flashed a warm grin. "It's perfectly okay." He removed his cap and sat on the couch.

Hans took a seat opposite. "What do you do in the Wehrmacht?"

"I am in Sicherheitsdienst."

Hans glanced over his uniform. "I thought all members of the Sicherheitsdienst were in the SS?"

Without pausing, Erik replied, "I was a member of Abwehr until it was dissolved; then I was placed in the Sicherheitsdienst[16]."

---

16. German Military Intelligence

Hans leaned forward and whispered, "Herr Major, is it true what they have said about the Russians? Please do not report me to the Gestapo; I do not have a defeatist attitude. I'm just worried about my family. I hope you understand."

Erik nodded and confirmed the atrocities in detail while Hans' eyes filled with horror. "You and your family should leave Berlin as soon as you can and head west because that part of Germany will be captured by the Americans and British, but Berlin will fall into the hands of the Russians."

"I have family in Ludwigshafe," Hans said. "Tell me, do you think Germany will lose the war?"

"I do, and in my opinion, if Germany loses it's not going to be pretty. Germany could be divided up in the same way that Poland was in 1939." Both men felt Helmut approach and looked up.

"Herr Major, you really think Germany is going to be divided up if we lose?" The boy asked.

"Helmut, listen to me." Erik stood and looked straight into his eyes. "I really don't know what's going to happen, but either way, if Germany loses the allies will not treat Germany kindly, knowing very well that Germany started two world wars."

The young man protested, and his hands clenched into fists. "The Führer said Germany was forced into war and then Germany was blamed for the first war. History is dumb."

"Yes, Germany was blamed for the First World War. Why do you say history is dumb?"

"If I was ruling Germany I would smash France and England." His face grew bright red from anger. His father gestured for him to control his emotion, but Erik motioned to him that it was okay.

"Take a seat," Erik told Helmut and they sat together on the couch. "So you think history is dumb and you would crush your enemies?"

Young Helmut nodded, stern-faced.

Erik recalled *Winds of Change,* an episode of *The Adventures of Young Indiana Jones.* "In 1919, a British historian ..." Helmut rolled his eyes upward and Erik grabbed his arms firmly to make him listen. "He said this when he knew the English and the French wanted to crush Germany after the war. Just as you feel about the French and English. He said this..." Erik quoted Arnold Toynbee. "'You cannot just wipe your enemy out. Years ago, Rome could wipe Carthage out. But now the world has changed. Everything is connected. What has happened will happen again. For better or worse. History now moves in a spiral. These men are trying to force Germany down. But it cannot be done without terrible tragedy. Push Germany down and you'll pay a price. And one day it will once more rise to the top. But these individuals who are behaving like men with no memories. Those that forget the lessons of history are doomed to repeat it.'"

Helmut pondered for a moment in deep thought. "It's hard to forgive our enemies. That's why I want to get in politics."

"I know it's hard. Trust me, I do. I'm not saying you let your enemies be your friends, but you have to respect them, and also admit when you are wrong. I will give you two important history lessons. First off, who are the good guys in this war?"

"That is easy, Germany is."

"Now who are the bad guys?"

"America, England, and Russia."

"I can see why you said that. Most Germans, like you, both

young and old, feel the same way you do, and there's nothing wrong with that. But the truth is there are no good or bad guys in war."

Hans injected. "Erik, how can you say that, especially as an intelligence officer?"

"Before I was an intelligence officer, I was a history teacher. You have to understand each government, including our own, believes they are doing the right thing. Therefore, there are no good or bad guys in any war. That even means wars from the past, present, and future." Erik paused to let his words sink in. "Now for the final lesson about history, my young friend. History has three views: my view, your view, and the truth." Helmut, Hans, and Walter, who listened in, frowned in puzzlement. "Let me explain the three views," Erik continued. "Say you are America and your father is England. Let us use the American Revolutionary War from 1775 to 1780 as an example. From your view, you called it The War of Independence. Now, from the view of Great Britain, your father's view, it was called The Rebellion or The Colonial Rebellion. But the truth is that it was another war that had two political viewpoints. Once again, though, both sides thought they were right."

"Dinner is ready," Cäcilie called out and everyone headed to the table.

Hans said, "You are very insightful. I never saw history from that perspective before."

Erik grinned, pleased that he had changed another person's view on history.

"Father," Helmut stated, "when I get to the university I want to major in History and Political studies."

Erik suddenly realized who Helmut was. Helmut Kohl would be chancellor of Germany when it was reunited in 1989. Erik turned to him and smiled. "I think you will make a great politician one day."

Everyone sat at the table, and Cäcilie stood in front of the pile of plates and served corned beef hash, the same thing Erik's mother used to make. He smiled with delight and thanked her as he accepted his plate. Within a short period of time, everyone was eating.

Walter looked around the table; his eyes sparkled with delight. "I have great news, father, and mother. I have been assigned to an anti-aircraft that is protecting a power mast."

Walter's family grinned, and his father patted him on the shoulder. Erik forced himself to smile, knowing that Walter would be killed when a bomber crash landed into a power mast. He ate in silence until Cäcilie asked if he had a family. He nodded and said his wife was pregnant with their first child. Hans raised his glass, everyone followed, and they toasted to Erik and Walter's news.

After dinner, Erik helped take the dishes to the kitchen and then headed outside, where he sat on the stoop and stared at the stars. He pulled out Jamie's photograph and the one with them together in 1944 and thought of the happy times they had spent together in Paris. A grin appeared on his face. He looked up at the pale moon and said to himself, "Jamie, I know we are looking at the same night sky; but this time I failed." He heard the door open, and as footsteps walked up behind him, he used his peripheral vision to see that it was Helmut. Erik motioned for him to take a seat.

"Herr Major, how long have you been in the Wehrmacht?" Helmut asked as he sat beside him.

"Ten years."

"Are you a Nazi?"

Erik shook his head. "No. Are you?"

A fragile smile crossed Helmut's face. "No, Sir. I would like to be a soldier like my brother and father so I can serve my country."

"One does not have to wear a uniform to serve one's country. Words can be just as powerful as bullets if they're used correctly."

Helmut tilted his head and asked, "You think so?"

"I know so, from personal experience."

Helmut grinned as if he was taking mental notes. "You are very smart. I want to be smart like you when I get older."

"Then remember what I told you about history."

"The three points of view?"

"Exactly."

"Your wife is pretty?"

"Yes, she is. And I don't know how I got so lucky." Erik handed over the few photographs he had of Jamie and him together.

"Why do you say that?"

"Because of my career. Who I am. Also, the things she saw that I did."

"I don't know you that well, but I think you'd be a great husband," Helmut said as he handed the photographs back.

Erik glanced at them and then turned the new photograph of Jamie over. He discovered that she had written words of inspiration for him:

My babe Erik, when you're on your own and you feel the world is against you, remember that I always believe in you. When we say goodbye think of me, think of me fondly until we're in each other's arms again. Hugs and kisses.

Love forever and always, Jamie

"What are you doing tomorrow?" Helmut asked.

"I'm going to try to save the world."

"That sounds like a tough job. How do you plan on doing that?"

"I don't know, but I'm sure going to try."

"I can help you."

Erik looked into the boy's eyes. "You can help by staying home."

Helmut pouted. "I promise I won't get in the way."

Then he motioned Helmut to stay, as he went inside and grabbed the folder titled Die Glocke. Erik's eyes focused on Helmut, and he stated firmly, "I need you to hold on to this until I get back. Put it in a place only you know about and don't tell anyone." Erik waited for Helmut's reassurance. "Do it now and be quick about it and come back." A few minutes later Helmut returned.

"Did anyone see you?"

"No sir."

"Good."

"What else can I do to help?"

"I need to do something by myself."

Helmut rested his chin on his hands. "Everyone thinks I can't do anything."

Erik thought of something Helmut would say in the future. "A politician once said, 'I have been underestimated for decades. I have done very well that way.'"

"Who said that?"

"I forgot. Why don't you write it down and use it if you get into politics?"

Helmut pulled a small notepad and pencil from his shirt pocket and started to write the phrase down. He looked up, "Can you repeat that?"

"Yes." Erik smiled when he noticed that Helmut had written down what he said word for word.

The door opened and Walter stepped out. "Father thinks it's best to come in now."

Once inside, Cäcilie helped Erik and made up a bed on the couch, then the family retired to their rooms. Slowly the voices got quiet and the lights went out. Erik laid in the dark with thoughts that raced through his head. Before long he had a pounding headache.

He thought about how hard it was to look at Walter, knowing he would be dead soon and that he could not even warn him or his parents. At the same time, he knew that his chances of meeting Albert Speer again and convincing him to help him were slim to none. So, what? Let the alternate history play out and do nothing? Then he remembered what his Control Officer Alan told him: *Work hard. Never compromise your integrity or honor.*

It sounded easy, but it wasn't. In 2005 when he was doing research on Project Rainbow, a project that Erik believed was unethical, he felt it was not right to dishonor the memories of the people involved and he said so, but his actions got him into quarrels with his superior. They told him never to make it personal. But Erik found that hard. He knew of several projects that had killed hundreds of people, and the truth was never told to their families or the media. He knew the truth about these projects, but he couldn't tell anyone. He had to look the other way because he was under oath. He wasn't afraid, and he wouldn't lie, but he would have to keep all the secrets he knew until he died. As he fell asleep, Erik wondered if he would be able to correct history or if he would have to adapt to an alternate history.

22. CHASING AFTER A SHADOW

"There are many powers in the world, for good or for evil. Some are greater than I am. Against some I have not yet been measured. But my time is coming."   —J.R.R. Tolkien

Berlin, Germany

A solid knock came from the door of the Kohl residence. Erik stood in the bathroom with the door closed and listened closely. The door opened and he heard a familiar voice. Albert Speer. *How did he find me?* Erik's thoughts ran wild with speculation, as he quickly slipped on his tunic and buckled his belt, with the gun in its holster. A soft knock came to the bathroom door.

"Excuse me, Herr Major, someone to see you," Helmut said.

Erik opened the door a crack. "Is he alone?" He asked in a half whisper.

Helmut nodded.

"What does he look like?"

"Tall, bluish gray eyes and black hair."

"Is he in a uniform?"

Helmut nodded.

"What color?"

"Brown."

"Did he give his name?"

Helmut shook his head.

"Check outside and see if there's anyone else, especially SS or Gestapo, and be quick about it."

Helmut opened his mouth as if to ask why, but Erik stopped him before he could speak. "Do as you're told. Now go." He snapped.

The boy disappeared. Cäcilie called for Helmut and the front door slammed shut, then opened and closed. Erik pulled out his Luger. Moments later, Helmut, out-of-breath, reported that there was no one outside. Erik left the bathroom and saw Albert Speer waiting patiently in the living room at the end of the hallway. He walked cautiously down the hall with his pistol at his side.

Speer looked at Erik's drawn weapon. "Morning, Herr Major," He said calmly. "We need to talk." Speer looked around the apartment. "Is there somewhere we can talk in private?"

"I thought our matters were concluded yesterday, Herr Speer."

Cäcilie came from the kitchen, saw Erik's weapon in his hand and gasped. She turned and disappeared back into the kitchen.

Speer continued. "I don't care what you think. I came here at great risk."

Erik lifted his Lugar and motioned for Speer to turn around and exit out the door. Erik's senses were on high alert. He had no idea what Speer had planned for him and was prepared to take any action necessary to ensure his survival. They stood in the hall-way, and as soon as Erik closed the door behind them, Speer began. "The information you told me yesterday was accurate."

"What information was that?" Erik tried to read the man but couldn't get a fix. Had Speer changed his mind? After his treatment the previous day, he found that hard to believe. It was more likely that he planned to turn Erik over to the Gestapo.

"Herr Major, I do not have time for games. You know what I'm talking about."

"Last time we spoke I had delusional stories and an interesting imagination." Erik stepped back and raised the Luger to Speer's chest. Speer's eyes enlarged, and beads of sweat formed on his forehead.

"The information you told me yesterday was accurate." Speer stared at the pistol, then into Erik's unblinking eyes. "You were correct on how the Americans launched their attack against Aachen."

Erik relaxed a little and motioned Speer to continue.

"The Americans did start their attack with the First and Thirtieth Infantry Divisions in an aerial and artillery bombardment."

Erik shrugged as if he didn't care.

"While I was meeting with Hitler early this morning, Field Marshal Model sent a report to Army High Command requesting reinforcements. Hitler exploded, stating that Model was incompetent. He then replaced him with Rundstedt and gave the order 'hold at all costs.'" Speer took a step forward.

Erik stopped him by raising the Lugar to his head.

"How did you know that information?" Speer asked in a quarter of a whisper.

"What does it matter? Why are you here? How did you find me?"

"I wrote down your Kübelwagen license plate as you were leaving." Speer pointed at Erik. "If what you said about the Führer is true, it could lead this war in a much different path."

Erik nodded, his finger still on the trigger.

"But we can stop this assassination, provided your information is correct. Is it?"

"It is. Do you trust me, Herr Reich Minister?"

Speer looked at Erik's gun. "I don't think we trust each other."

Erik smirked and lowered the gun.

"However, we will need to trust each other to stop the assassination. I can get us access to the Reich Chancellery, and, since I'm not a soldier, you can kill the individuals who want him dead."

Out of the corner of his eye, Erik saw young Helmut, who peeked out the slightly open door. Erik turned to face him, and the boy, realizing he had been discovered, pleaded, "I can help, Herr Major. I'll not get in the way. I promise."

"You would be a great help. But what I need you to do is stay home," Erik said.

"I want to be a soldier like you."

"You will be someday, but not today."

Helmut hung his head.

"Remember what I taught you and keep that information I gave you until I get back." Erik lifted the boy's head and looked into his eyes. "One day you will make Germany great."

Speer, with tense eyes, looked at his watch and then at Erik. "Herr Major, it's 10:50 am; we need to go now!"

Erik nodded. He knew the truth about the attack on Aachen was the ultimate bargaining chip, but like in poker, he could only play such a chip once. Erik had taken a huge risk when he played it. Thank God it had paid off. He holstered his gun, and, after a hasty farewell to Helmut, he ran after Speer.

They raced to Speer's car and hopped in. Speer quickly primed and choked the car, and it lunged forward.

"Do you have your papers?" Speer asked as he weaved around bomb craters.

Erik patted his pockets and found nothing. A rush of panic washed over him, followed by a sigh of relief when he found them in his upper right pocket. He pulled them out, removed the photographs and stuck them back in the pocket.

"How will the assassins enter the chancellery?"

Erik shook his head. "I don't know. What I do know is that Hitler and a high-ranking SS officer will be killed in the bunker."

"Do you know what the assassin looks like?"

Erik shook his head again. Doing an op when Erik knew he was racing against time was bad, but it was even worse when someone was talking to him while he ran scenarios in his head to solve the problem.

"How in the hell are you going to stop him without knowing what he looks like?" Speer tilted his head to face Erik.

"You have to trust me; I know what I'm doing."

"You're mad! Not only that but—"

"Albert!"

Speer applied the brakes, but it was too late. The car thumped into a two-foot pothole and jolted its occupants. Erik stared in shock as dozens of cracks spread across the windshield like a spider web. He recovered quickly, climbed out, and examined the damage. The axle was one mangled mess. It groaned like a wounded beast, shuddered once, and then, as Erik and Speer watched, it fell slowly onto its side.

Erik looked up and down the avenue, but all he saw was bombed out buildings and rubble littering the road—not a single car in sight. "Where in the hell are the cars!" Erik looked again. "Trucks or any kind vehicle!"

"There aren't any; only high party members and the army are allowed on the roads."

Erik pointed to himself. "You call me mad?" He exclaimed. "How in the hell are we going to get to the chancellery?"

"Are you a good runner?"

Erik grimaced in disbelief.

"If you want me to believe you, which I'm starting not to, then we stop arguing and start running!"

"How far are we from the chancellery?!"

"Two miles," Speer said and started running.

Erik pushed aside his disbelief and raced after him, and the further they ran, the more apparent it became that they had no option but to keep running. There was simply no means of transportation to be found, and the minutes in which to save Hitler's life were quickly running out.

"You know I could use a little help here!" Erik said as he looked up.

"Turn left here; it's a shortcut to the chancellery," Albert said.

Erik looked up to the clouds again and yelled, "Thanks, but I was hoping for a car!"

"Who are you talking to?"

"God. What time do you have?"

"Eleven-nineteen."

As they kept running, their jackboot heels clattered on the stone paved blocks. Speer started to wheeze long before Erik, but he kept running, which impressed Erik with his dedication. Eventually, a building that flew the blood-red Nazi flag on the roof appeared in the near distance.

"That's the chancellery," Speer said breathlessly. "We should be nearing the rear entrance where the top officials park their cars. It's a shortcut to the bunker."

Erik checked his watch. It was 11:35 a.m. An SS honor guard of the Adolf Hitler Division stopped them and requested their papers. They panted; Erik and Speer handed them over. Erik's mouth felt dry, and his knees were in pain, but he'd rather be running toward his goal than waiting here. He was so near now. He actually had a chance. A slim one, but it was something—until the clock outran him.

The guards looked them over, and one asked them to state their business. Speer informed them that they were here to see the Führer and that it was an urgent matter of state security. The guard shook his head and stated that all heads of government must have an appointment to enter, and if not, they must use the front entrance.

"The Führer's life is in jeopardy," Erik said urgently. "You must allow us to pass."

"Sorry, Sir," The guard said calmly, "you cannot."

Another guard tried to use the phone and Erik noticed that it had trouble. It appeared that the phone was dead. The line had been cut.

"Then give us a car so we can drive to the front," Erik said.

Albert joined in pleading with the guard, but again the guard refused to help. Erik's temperature rose with his anger and frustration, but, focused on a plan of attack, he stared calmly at the guard. Then suddenly, with a malevolent grin, he thrust his right knee into the guard's groin and smashed his fists into the man's temples. The guard from the shack dashed out, tried to aim his MP-40, but Erik retrieved the rifle from the other guard and used it like a baseball bat and smashed the butt against his head.

Albert just stared.

"Get in that car," Erik said and motioned to the nearest car, "and get it running." Other guards started appearing and aimed their weapons. He kept his gun on the guards and moved toward the car. As Erik dashed inside, Speer slammed the accelerator to the floor.

"What time is it?" Erik asked as they jolted along the road.

"11:45."

At the front entrance, they leaped out of the car, and Erik, with Speer, who wheezed behind him, climbed the wide concrete stairs that led to the Reich Chancellery with its four towering columns and enormous doors. Several SS bodyguards patrolled the perimeter of the battle-worn chancellery with its smoke-blackened walls and broken or blown-in windows. Above the doors sat an impressive carved stone German eagle with its wings outstretched and its massive claws holding a wreath of oak leaves that contained the dreaded and feared swastika. This was created in the early years of the Third Reich to inspire fear and intimidate all who visited. On top of the chancellery, several huge Nazi flags fluttered in the breeze, their black swastikas dancing in the wind over a dying Berlin.

Erik and Speer charged through the doors into a vast courtyard with barren walls and round columns aligned and balanced in perfect symmetry. Erik dashed through the courtyard toward the two bronze statues at the far end that symbolized Army and Party. More SS guards guarded the doorway, but they quickly did the Nazi salute and opened the doors to let Erik and Speer pass. Just beyond the courtyard were the gallery, rotunda, and the marble mosaic hallway, which, Erik recalled, was twice as long as the

Hallway of Mirrors in the Versailles. Erik stopped and peered over his shoulder to get directions from Speer. Speer pointed to the two SS guards stationed in front of a doorway some distance away. High ranking officers of four branches, Wehrmacht, Kriegsmarine, Luftwaffe, and SS, strolled up and down the hallway. Erik paused, trying to catch his breath.

"What's wrong?" Speer asked.

"It didn't look as big in the photographs."

"Everyone says that."

"Wonderful."

Erik pushed off again, followed by Speer, and they continued running down the hallway. Officers glanced at them, and the guards at the entrance drew and prepared to fire their weapons. One ordered them to halt. Erik stopped and Speer leaped in front of him. The guards recognized the Reich Minister, clicked their heels, did the Nazi salute, and opened the doors. Speer motioned to the guards that Erik was with him. They stepped inside a large, unornamented room with battleship gray walls, and the doors closed behind them. Three of Hitler's four young secretaries, including Martin Bormann, his Personal Secretary, were busy at their neatly organized desks, while the fourth was filing, and high ranking officers from all three branches of the Wehrmacht and the SS lined the walls and waited to see Hitler. Erik strolled across the office and approached Bormann, a short, thickset, and moderately fat man.

Erik hovered over the desk and demanded, "Where in the Führerbunker is the Führer?"

Bormann stood and assumed an ox-like posture. "Excuse me; why do you need to know, and what is your name?" He asked arrogantly.

"Major Függer." Erik took a few deep breaths. "I said, where is the Führer?"

Bormann looked behind Erik to Speer. "What do you want, Speer?"

"The major and I need to see the Führer. It's urgent."

"Damn it, where is he?" Erik said sharply.

Bormann snapped his head around. "He is not here." He eyed up Erik. "And who in the hell are you to order me around?"

Erik felt his patience waning fast. "Where is the Führer?!"

Bormann leaned over his desk to Erik. "Did you hear me? He is not here. Now leave or I can have you escorted out, major."

Erik slammed his fists on the desk. "Damn it, where is he? He's going to be killed! Do you understand me?"

Bormann raised his eyebrows, and everyone else in the office turned to Erik with expressions of surprise and horror.

"Do not ever raise your voice at me again," Bormann snapped back in a deep voice, "or it will be your last words."

Multiple gunshots rang out from the courtyard where the Führerbunker was located. Everyone in the office stood and looked around, not knowing what to do. But Erik was trained and conditioned to respond immediately when an operation went bad. He knew that every minute that went by was another minute the assassin got closer to the Führer. He also knew that the odds were against him, but he knew what he was fighting for.

"We're wasting time!" Erik exploded.

Bormann picked up his phone. Erik glanced at his Luger, then at Speer and back at his Luger. Speer nodded discreetly as Bormann said, "Herr Captain, this is Bormann—"

Erik pulled out his Luger, spun around and pointed it directly at Bormann's head. Speer locked the doors and all the secretaries gasped. Bormann's eyes widened in shock, and sweat ran down his face.

"I'll ask you one more time before I kill you."

Bormann gulped.

"Where is the Führer?"

"I am not a forgetting man."

Erik forced the barrel against Bormann's forehead. "You can stick to your guns, but mine is loaded." He started to squeeze the trigger.

Bormann's breathing became heavy. "He's in the map room."

Erik grabbed the phone out of Bormann's hand and threw it across the room.

"This way." Speer ran to a set of doors and pushed them open. Erik followed, and they closed and locked them and propped a chair against the door handles. On his way out, Erik heard Bormann screaming orders to the guards to get the doors opened. Outside, Speer stood paralyzed and stared at the bodies of the Führerbegleitkommando (Hitler's Honour Bodyguards) that littered the ground.

Erik raced past Speer to the entrance of the Führerbunker and noticed that the guards had been killed by a martial arts technique. The sounds of a firefight floated up from below. He turned to Speer. "Come on, Albert! We don't have much time!"

Speer snapped out of his dream-like state and joined Erik. Bullets whizzed by. Erik looked up and saw Bormann screaming orders as members of the FBK fired their MP-44s. Erik and Speer sprinted down the stairs and darted between the bodies.

Erik suspected that the trail of death had just begun. The smell of raw sewage met them at the entrance of the forward bunker, and voices from the courtyard drifted down the stairs. Erik peered down the hallway and saw a shadow behind a guard and lifted his Luger to take aim, but he was too late. The guard slumped to the ground, and the figure disappeared down the next set of stairs. Erik and Speer hurried down the hallway, pockmarked with bullet holes and littered with bodies streaming with blood.

"How is this possible?" Speer asked. His face was chalky in color, and he stared at the carnage with a mixture of horror and disbelief. "The FBK are the elite of the SS."

"The FBK are amateurs compared to this assassin."

"Assassin? You're saying that one person did this?"

Erik nodded, and they scurried down the second set of stairs that lead to the Führerbunker. At the bottom, they proceeded toward the map room as two gunshots echoed off the concrete hallway from inside the map room. Erik's heart stuttered and feared the worst. A sickening wave of terror welled up from his stomach. He was too late. Hitler was dead.

A nauseating spurt of adrenaline coursed through his veins, and he bolted down the hallway to the map room, which seemed to take forever. Speer tried to keep up. Erik charged through the door and saw the dead FBK guard. Hitler and Kammler were still alive, and the assassin had his back toward him.

Erik's voice exploded. "Mein Führer!"

"It's you," Crowley said in a shocked and disgusted tone, his top lip twisted into a sneer.

Erik nodded. "Trust is good; Control is better." Then Erik proceeded to empty his magazine into Crowley's body.

Hitler and Kammler sighed in relief, but the worry in their eyes didn't disappear until Speer entered the room. Erik hunched over and took several deep breaths, his hands on his knees, while Lieutenant Zeuner clutched a bullet wound in his shoulder and struggled to get off the floor.

Suddenly Bormann, with a Luger in his hand, and the rest of the FBK guards barged into the map room. He pushed Speer out of the way, and the guards, armed with MP-44s, surrounded Erik, seized his Luger, and pointed the barrels of their MP-44s in his direction. Bormann pushed his way through the guards, lifted his Luger, pointed it to Erik's head, and began to squeeze the trigger. Simultaneously, Hitler screamed Bormann's name, and Speer pushed the barrel of the Luger away from Erik's head. A round flew by Erik's eyes, and the shot reverberated in his ear drums.

"Bormann!" Hitler exploded. Bormann glanced at Hitler, who screamed again. "Bormann! What are you doing? Answer me, Bormann! Now, Bormann!"

Bormann stumbled on his words. "Mein Führer, he was trying to kill you. I was trying to—"

Hitler stopped him as he walked around the desk. "You were trying nothing! Nothing!" Bormann tried to defend his position, but Hitler raised his right hand, which trembled, and continued in his rage. "Bormann, get out! Did you hear me? Get out!" Bormann exited with a disgusted look on his face. "Oh," Hitler called after him, "and get this mess cleaned up." He gestured at the guard's body, then turned to Speer. His expression calmed. "Speer, did we have a meeting?"

Speer grinned and shook his head. "No, mein Führer. I'm with the major."

Hitler looked confused. "Oh well, you can stay." He turned to Kammler. "This officer saved my life. I wish I had more officers like him. He is a true National Socialist." He pointed to Erik and beckoned him forward. Kammler nodded and Erik stepped forward. Hitler tried to stand straight, but his haggard frame and hunched shoulders prevented him from doing so. He squinted at Erik with his pale-blue opaque eyes, and with his left hand, which trembled violently, Hitler tapped Erik's left shoulder and whispered, "Thank you. Thank you, Herr Major."

"You are very welcome, mein Führer," Erik replied while he analyzed the blueprints and drawings scattered on the desk.

Kammler walked around the desk and blocked his vision. "Is there something you need, Herr Major?" He asked in an authoritarian tone.

"No, Sir."

Hitler turned to Kammler. "I believe the major should see what we're working on. The Miracle Weapons that will turn the war in Germany's favor."

"Mein Führer, I have to protest. These documents are highly sensitive." Hitler's expression turned cold; Kammler picked up on Hitler's vibe and immediately clicked his heels and nodded. He made a space so Erik could stand closer to the desk, and while Hitler and Speer talked, Kammler stared at Erik as if trying to place him. "Herr Major, have we met?"

Hitler and Speer looked in Erik's direction, then went back to their conversation. "Yes, Sir, you gave me a lift to Berlin."

"That is right. It's a small world." From the bottom pile of papers, he pulled out three drawings of new panzers from the Entwicklung Program. "These new panzers will be able to stop any allied panzer on the battlefield."

"How about the Russian heavy tanks, like the Joseph Stalin tanks?" Erik asked.

"Most definitely."

Erik picked up the drawings and recognized the E-50 Panther III armed with an eighty-eight-millimeter gun, the E-75 armed with a one-hundred-and-five-millimeter gun, and finally the E-100, the super heavy tank armed with a one-hundred-and-twenty-eight-millimeter gun. Erik turned to Kammler. "Most impressive. When would these be in production?"

"They already are. If things go as planned, they'll be in action by March or April of next year and we can push the Americans and English back to the beaches." He handed Erik three more drawings. "These U-boats will be more advanced than anything the allies can put forth."

Again Erik recognized two of the three U-boats. One was the XXIB with six torpedo doors on each side, and the XXIC with nine on each side. Both U-boats were ahead of their time due to technological advances in design, depth capabilities, propeller construction, and submerging speed.

"Are these—" Erik began.

"Production will begin next year."

"Diesel powered?"

Kammler grinned. "No. How primitive." Erik waited patiently, and Kammler added, "We're working on a new propulsion system, first using fusion and then nuclear. It'll make sure that our U-boats stay out to sea longer."

Impressed, Erik looked at the last U-boat drawing, which he didn't recognize. "What can this one do?"

"This is the XXIN. It'll be able to launch our rockets against any city that is currently out of range."

"Conventional rockets?"

"No. These rockets will be able to destroy a city in a single blast. We are only months away from a successful test. The V-2 rocket will launch from the U-boat."

"What kind of warhead will it have?" Erik asked, knowing the answer was atomic. "Has that been tested?"

"We have already done a successful test with the atomic weapon, and the XXIN should be ready by early next year if everything goes as planned."

"Can I ask what you mean by 'if everything goes as planned?'" Erik asked.

Kammler shook his head.

"I'm guessing you have weapons for the Luftwaffe."

"We do indeed, jet fighters and jet bombers. They'll dominate the air and shoot down every Allied aircraft."

Erik remembered the aircraft he saw at the Peenemünde Research Complex. "Like the ones in the hangers, and the one that was landing?"

"Herr Major, I would like to remind you that I cannot confirm or deny what you saw."

"Herr Major," Hitler whispered and motioned Erik to come closer.

"Yes, mein Führer?"

"Walk with me."

Erik thanked Kammler and they shook hands. Then Erik and Hitler left, and Speer followed. Outside the door, members of the FBK surrounded them with their weapons drawn and ready to be fired. "Speer has told me good things about you, Herr Major," Hitler said as they strolled down the hallway where medical personnel were already clearing the corpses.

"Thank you, mein Führer. Speer is a good man also. I would listen to him."

"I do. He's going to rebuild Berlin." He lowered his voice. "Have you seen the models on the table?" Erik shook his head, and Hitler's eyes brightened. "It is in my office. Speer is my architect. He's going to make buildings that last a thousand years." Erik nodded and grinned. "So," Hitler continued, "do you work under Himmler?"

"No, mein Führer."

"Gestapo? RSHA?"

"No, mein Führer."

Hitler looked both surprised and puzzled. "Then who?" He waited, clearly eager to know who Erik worked for.

Erik knew he was taking a big gamble, but he also knew that Hitler would forget due to his unstable mental condition. "I work for the CIA, mein Führer."

"Who? I never heard of them."

"Central Intelligence Agency."

Hitler shrugged and continued walking.

"We are a fairly new agency, mein Führer." Erik quoted an ad he had seen in a newspaper once. "Our business is knowing the world's business."

"I see. Your agency sounds very important. We need more people like you, Herr Major."

They exited the forward bunker and approached Hitler's office. Erik glanced around the courtyard and saw that the bodies of the FBK guards had been removed and replacements had arrived.

"Are you a dog person?" Hitler asked.

"Yes, mein Führer." Erik saw an orderly who held the leash of Blondie, Hitler's German Shepherd.

"Blondie is smarter than most of my generals, and she is a good judge of character."

The orderly handed Hitler the leash. Blondie panted and wagged her tail. "She likes you." Hitler smiled, gave the leash back to the orderly, and looked at Erik. "If she didn't like you, I would have you shot."

Hitler ordered Erik, Speer, Zeuner, Kammler, a few members of his staff, and his Generals into his office.

Erik stood by Speer. "What's going on?"

Speer shrugged. "I wouldn't worry. He likes you."

"That's good because he said he'd have me shot if Blondie didn't like me."

"That's him trying to be funny."

"Killer punch line." Erik and Speer chuckled while Hitler's office filled up with people. "I guess it's a good thing he likes me."

Speer nodded. "Indeed. It helped me get where I am today. Otherwise, certain members of his inner circle would try to get rid of me. It helps that he thinks I'm still his architect."

"I know. He told me you are rebuilding Berlin."

Speer shook his head. "That'll never happen now, but maybe when the war is over." Speer nudged Erik. "Let me show you something."

He escorted Erik to an oversized table with a miniaturized city on it. Erik gasped in stunned silence when he realized that he was looking at the model of Germania in all its astonishing detail, both large and small.

Albert explained that Hitler hoped to win total victory by 1945, and as Hitler's architect, he was to implement the plan to construct the Welthauptstadt Germania. Erik glanced over the model as Speer explained some of the highlights, which Erik had read about in books: Berlin was to be reorganized around the five kilometers long Prachtstrasse, or Street of Magnificence, also known as the Avenue of Victory, which would be lined with trees and anti-aircraft batteries that symbolized strength. The colossal Germania Triumph Arch, also known as Hitler Triumph Arch, would be located at the South Axis. Speer explained that it would be twice as tall as and four times wider than the Arc de Triomphe in Paris.

He then pointed out The Volkshalle or People's Hall, also called Große Halle or Great Hall, the focal point for the North Axis and the center of the new capital which would tower over all the buildings. Erik asked how it would compare to the dome of St. Peter's Basilica, and Speer said it would be sixteen times larger. Erik nodded, suitably impressed, and told Speer that Berlin would've been a beautiful city if it hadn't been for the war. Speer nodded in agreement, then said they should take their place because everyone was getting ready for a presentation.

Hitler, from behind his desk, pulled a case out of his drawer, and Bormann gave Erik a frigid stare.

"Ignore him," Speer whispered.

Erik nodded and then saw a man with a camera slip into the room. *Oh shit*. Erik thought.

Hitler ordered the room to attention. Simultaneously, everyone snapped to attention and clicked their heels.

"Major Függer, front and center," a strong voice ordered.

Erik proceeded to the center of the room and found Dr. Goebbels there waiting for him.

"Ladies and gentlemen," Goebbels continued, "you are wondering why we called you here. An act of unselfishness and heroism was carried out by an extraordinary individual. He overcame great odds and risked his life. He never questioned what was wrong or right; he just knew he had to save his Führer at all costs. His name is Major Erik Függer. Our Führer, as I do, believes he should be awarded for his acts of heroism."

Hitler approached Erik with the case in his hand. Goebbels helped Hitler and took the case, and Hitler stood before Erik. From the corner of Erik's eye, he saw the camera which faced his direction and was greatly relieved when a distant explosion rattled the foundation, causing the camera to drop and the lens to shatter on the floor.

Goebbels grinned and whispered, "Camera shy?"

"Yes, Dr. Goebbels."

Hitler spoke. "Major Függer's acts of heroism remind me of when I was a soldier during the First World War. I was awarded the Iron Cross First Class for my actions. We also have a medal for individuals who show outstanding achievements and heroism. They are known as war heroes of the Reich." Goebbels opened the case, and Erik couldn't believe what was inside. Hitler continued, "This is the highest medal of the Third Reich. I was planning for it to be awarded after the end of the war to Germany's twelve greatest heroes. But today, we have our first hero, Major Erik Függer."

Goebbels removed the medal—the Gold Knights Cross with

oak leaves, swords, and diamonds on it—and placed it around Erik's neck. Then he shook his hand and congratulated him. Erik clicked his heels and did the Nazi salute, and Hitler, with everyone else following behind, did the Nazi salute as well. Applause filled the room and everyone walked up to shake Erik's hand and thanked him. Kammler thanked Erik for saving his life and told him he could use someone like him in his outfit. Erik politely thanked him but turned down his offer. Before he left, Kammler turned to Erik. "Herr Major, by any chance did I leave some documentation on the plane?"

"Sorry, Herr Obergruppenführer I saw nothing."

Kammler studied Erik, nodded and left, and Zeuner walked and crossed the room. "You are brave just like your brother; thank you for saving our lives." Erik nodded in appreciation, and Zeuner leaned over and whispered in Erik's ear. "You actually turned down an offer with him."

"Yes, I did."

"He never offers anyone a position. It's an honor to work with him and do what we do at Peenemünde."

"Thanks, but no thanks."

"Why do you not want to work with us?"

"I have my reasons."

Zeuner nodded in understanding, shook Erik's hand, and excused himself. Then a short, skinny man, with hazel eyes, circular eyeglasses, and slick dark brown hair approached Erik. He wore a night-black SS officer's uniform showing the rank of Reichsführer. Erik quickly realized it was Heinrich Himmler and snapped to attention. Himmler extended his hand and said, "Congratulations, Herr Major." Suddenly his expression changed;

it appeared as if something had struck him. "By the way, have we met before?"

"Thank you," Erik replied, "and no, Herr Reichsführer, I am afraid not."

Hitler walked up to Erik and pulled him aside. "Thank you again, Herr Major. What can I do for you?"

"Two things, mein Führer." Hitler nodded and Erik continued, "I would like to go home to see my wife."

"Of course, and the second?"

"Always listen to Speer. And if he asks you to sign a document in the trying days to come, sign it."

"I will. Have a safe trip home."

"Thank you, mein Führer."

Erik made his way out, and Speer joined him. "Congratulations, Erik."

"Thank you, Albert. You deserve one of these, too."

"No, I do not." Speer pointed at Erik and shook his head. "You saved him, not I. Where are you going now?"

"Home to see my wife. I don't know how I'll get there, though."

"You can take my personal train."

"Personal train?"

"I have my own personal train, plane, car, and even petrol supply."

"As any Reich Minster should," Erik replied.

Speer nodded. "Erik, my friend, I hope to see you again. We've been through a lot in the short period we've known each other."

"I'd like that."

"I would as well. What do you plan to do after the war?"

"Spend time with my family. Maybe write a book."

"A book? What would you write about?"

"My experiences; I think you should write one, too."

"What kind of experiences?" Speer paused. "You are with Sicherheitsdienst." Erik glared at Speer as if asking how he knew. "Mrs. Kohl told me."

"Ah."

"I won't tell anyone you're a spy."

"I'm not a spy. I'm an analyst."

"Sure you are. Next, you're going to tell me you work undercover in a museum."

"Enough, Albert." Erik faced him. "You know what you should do?"

"Be quiet?"

"Yes, but besides that. You, Albert Speer, should write a book."

"You're not serious."

"I am. You have firsthand knowledge of what it's like to be a part of Hitler's inner circle."

"True, but do you think people would buy it?"

"I believe they would, Albert. Who knows, it might be a bestselling novel."

"What would I call my book?"

"I don't know … maybe … *Inside the Third Reich*."

Speer pondered for a moment, rubbing his chin. "That sounds like a good title. I would give you an autographed copy."

"Thanks, Albert. But I wouldn't mention today in your book."

"Why would you say that? I think it would make interesting reading."

"In my opinion, I don't think most people would want to hear that Hitler was rescued. Especially since the Allied powers and most of the world hate him."

Speer considered the matter. "I see your point."

"Thanks for your trust and help, Albert. You're a good Nazi."

"A good Nazi." Speer grinned. "I will have to remember that."

"Yes, do." *The world will never learn what I've done, and even if a few do, my name will never be known.* Erik thought.

But Erik knew that not only had he preserved history, but he also knew, as with any mission, the best moments come when the job ends, and the bullets stop. But first, he would have to race to the Kohl's residence and pick up the folder he had let Helmut hold. Now he had to make a long trip to Jamie, move, and get settled in Washington D.C. Then they could start a new life.

EPILOGUE: A NEW LIFE

*"Nobody can go back and start a new beginning, but anyone
can start today and make a new ending."*

—Maria Robinson

Kennedy Warren Apartments, Washington D.C., 1948

The Second World War was over, and the Cold War between the
United States and the Soviet Union was in its third year. A ceiling fan circulated the air in a brightly lit office, and a faint, musty
odor from old newspapers and books consumed the room. Bookcases were filled with historical and reference books covering the
European Theater of World War One and World War Two.

Erik was hunched over a desk covered with books and documents. His inquisitive eyes read and analyzed everything he
picked up. Every couple of seconds he wrote down detailed notes,
as the sound of graphite scratched the surface of the paper, breaking the silence. Occasionally he glanced at the typewriter and
typed a few sentences. A faint sound of a young child talking got
his attention. He lifted his head away from the typewriter and

glanced at the open door. His wife, Jamie, who was four months pregnant, stood there smiling. Their three year old son, Max, held her hand.

"Hi babe, how's the book coming?" Jamie asked as she walked around the desk to Erik.

He met her gaze and returned her smile, then stood and kissed her. "I'm done with the last chapter."

"That's great, babe. Do you have a title?"

He nodded. "*Project Pegasus: We Know Your Name.*"

"Sounds great. I love what I've read and can't believe some of the things you did with the CIA from the late nineties to 2008. You're really a hero."

"No, I'm not. I'm just an average guy doing what had to be done."

Jamie shook her head. "Don't ever criticize me for how I see you."

Erik sighed and looked at Max, who was fiddling with a key in the desk cabinet door. "What will I tell my son when he's older and he asks about me and the things I did?"

"Tell him the truth—that you were recruited by the CIA and were a paramilitary operations officer, and you made the world a better place." Erik nodded, and Jamie continued. "Erik, you're a fighter—you never gave up until the battle was over. No matter what you went through—the ups or the downs—you stood strong in the face of any issue while others ran. You're amazing."

He shook his head and replied, "No, I'm not."

"Yes, you are, Erik. And what makes you amazing is that you are the one who surprises everyone, including me, when the world comes crashing down. You hop right back up to fix it."

Max looked up and Erik stared into his son's eyes. Max's eyes were full of curiosity just like his father's. Erik picked up his son and hugged both Jamie and Max.

Knowing that his life as a CIA operative was behind him and that he, Jamie, and Max could start a new a life in 1948, Erik felt he had been given a measure of inner peace after changing his last name. He was now a free-lance writer under the name Erik Foge. Many of his articles had been published in historical or political journals, and Erik had invested the money Bonesteiner gave Jamie in secure investments that brought in a good return. He also used some of it to buy a Tucker Forty-eight and a place at the Kennedy-Warren. Like most women in the late forties, Jamie's job was taking care of their home and son. She was Erik's executive assistant when he did consulting work at the museums. Jamie loved her job as Erik's assistant, and she hadn't forgotten her duty to assist Erik in his needs, even if it was a small thing. However, they both kept a low profile.

Erik took a deep breath.

"Is there anything wrong?" Jamie asked as she pulled out of their embrace.

Erik placed Max down. "No. I'm just trying to get some things done for the Air and Space Museum."

"President Truman and the director of the museum were pleased with your work." Jamie opened Erik's appointment book which was full. "He wants to meet you next week."

"Yeah, I know." Erik pointed to the date he was to meet Truman. "I've been told that my work is excellent, but that's the kind of attention I don't want to draw to myself."

"Are you worried they'll come back for you?"

"No one can be too certain, but if they do, I'll be ready for them."

"Babe, if they were going to send someone, I'm sure they would have done it by now."

"Maybe you're right." Erik kissed Jamie on the lips.

"Good. You know we have a dinner invitation tonight."

"We do? With who?"

"Jack and Bobby. Remember? Jack called a few weeks ago and said he was going be in town and wanted to go out to dinner."

Erik grinned and nodded. "Let me grab my coat while you get the diaper bag. I'll meet you in the living room."

"How do you know Jack and Bobby?"

Erik shrugged. "I don't know. Maybe they saw me give a lecture."

"He said both you and he had served together."

"I was never in 1943…so I really don't know. I guess I will wing it."

They smiled at each other and Jamie left the room. Erik grabbed his coat off the coat rack and strolled to the window that overlooked Connecticut Avenue.

"Babe, are you coming?" Jamie yelled from the living room.

"Yes." Erik peered out the window. A man who wore a black suit and sunglasses and was loitering outside caught Erik's attention. The man nodded at Erik with a cold expression and then walked on down the sidewalk. A bald eagle landed in a nearby tree, and as he watched, Erik evaluated his situation:

With great knowledge of history comes great responsibility to preserve it. My gift is to know future historical events, both good and bad. But my gift is also a curse, the curse that I cannot interfere or change them.

Then without hesitation, Erik walked to his desk, opened a drawer, pulled out a Luger and loaded a magazine.

About the Author

Erik Foge holds a Bachelor's Degree in History, with an emphasis on Russian history and politics, from the University of Central Florida. His passion for history began at age thirteen when his parents sent him to Washington D.C. to learn about the United States and its governmental processes. The trip sparked Foge's interest in the federal government and the individuals within the Intelligence Community who are responsible for shaping the country's national policies. The characters in the Project Pegasus Series are drawn from Foge's friendships and interactions with people from within the Intelligence Community at-large, the NRO; the NSA; the CIA; an Admiral and the Master Chief of the Sixth Fleet; Navy Seals, Astronaut John Glenn, and others.